RAVE REVIEWS FOR
CAROLYN JEWEL AND *LORD RUIN*!

"Ms. Jewel's sensual, passionate and powerful love story keeps to the classic lines of the Regency historical and while adding a fresh new voice."

—*Romantic Times*

"Spectacular! Carolyn Jewel is a masterful storyteller who creates stories filled with magic."

—*Romance and Friends*

"Entertaining, satisfying and sensuous."

—*All About Romance*

Jewel keeps the pic fresh . . . fans will take

—*Harriet's Book Reviews*

ACCUSED!

Olivia's hand flew through the air. Sebastion caught her wrist, stopping her palm inches from his cheek. "You have no right," she said. "No right at all to level such an accusation."

"On the contrary. I have every right. Did you know, Miss Willow, that the very day before he died, my brother instructed his solicitor to begin an action for divorce?"

"I don't believe it." But something nagged at her. The harder she tried to think what, the more her head hurt. Something. Something important, and it refused to come to her. He lifted her chin, forcing her to look at him. His eyes burned into hers. Her scar felt like a white-hot knot.

"I do not countenance liars," he said. "And that includes old maids who pretend virtue they do not possess."

His fingers tightened around her chin. "Did you kill my brother?"

"No."

"How do you know?"

She opened her mouth to speak but all that came out was a sob. The light hurt her eyes. Too bright where the sun came in, too dark in the shadows shifting behind Sebastion. "I couldn't have," she managed. "I couldn't."

Other *Leisure* books by Carolyn Jewel:
LORD RUIN

CAROLYN JEWEL

THE SPARE

LEISURE BOOKS   NEW YORK CITY

*Many thanks to Jennifer Crump for her assistance;
to Pandy, for being a crabby old you-know-what;
and to my editor, Kate Seaver, for all her help and insights.*

A LEISURE BOOK®

February 2004

Published by

Dorchester Publishing Co., Inc.
200 Madison Avenue
New York, NY 10016

ISBN 0-8439-5309-8

The name "Leisure Books" and the stylized "L" with design are trademarks of Dorchester Publishing Co., Inc.

Printed in the United States of America.

THE SPARE

Chapter One

Captain Sebastian Alexander, late of His Majesty's Royal Navy, glared at his valet's reflection with eyes reputed to have frozen boiling water on the spot. To no avail. McNaught continued mixing another noxious remedy guaranteed to taste like poison. Sebastian turned on his chair and found the motion did not pain him as much as he expected. He ignored McNaught and his potion. "I am not mad, James," he said to the man beside him. A hound the color of a thunderhead raised its muzzle and sniffed the air. He stroked the dog's head.

"You are an Alexander." James did not look away from his collection of essays by Montaigne. "You are too practical for madness. Besides, you aren't old enough to fear your mind in danger of infirmity."

1

"I saw a sailor go mad once, and he was not yet twenty." At rest, Sebastian's face marked him as a young man, barely thirty, a handsome man with blue eyes and hair just shy of black. Certainly, unquestionably, his eyes were blue. As bitterly cold as ice at dawn. From across a room, his eyes pierced with a rapier's thrust to the heart.

James gave him a look. "I'll warrant his madness was not from age."

"The ocean broke his mind. We were becalmed seven weeks on water smooth as glass."

"Your mind is sound, of that I am convinced."

"I'm not to be back at sea for weeks yet. What am I to do with myself until then?" He shuddered. The hound at his side rose, and Sebastian rested a hand on its sleek shoulder. "If I don't get another ship right away, I might be here even longer."

"Stop complaining. Brave naval captains such as yourself are always at the head of the list for ships."

"Jesus." He rubbed his face with both hands, disliking the way his mind whirled all out of order. "I am ancient, James."

"Hardly."

"In my soul. Weary to the very core and adrift. Becalmed. I lack purpose." He drew a breath, felt pain blossom at the peak of inhalation, and then slowly exhaled. "I want occupation, and I am too exhausted to find one."

"You are in the very prime of life, Sebastian," James said in a very deliberate and annoyed manner. The idea of Sebastian Alexander succumbing to weakness was ludicrous.

Sebastian eased back against his chair. "Listen to me." He made a face of self-disgust. "Complaining like an old woman. A man makes of his life what he can. He doesn't sit about bemoaning his fate. I'll have my ship if I have to get down on my knees and beg for it."

James sat straighter. "You are Tiern-Cope. The world comes begging to you, not the other way 'round." He gestured, a wave that took in everything. "Forget the sea. Pennhyll is your purpose. Your position in life is now your occupation. You oughtn't go back at all. Your duty lies here."

Sebastian sighed. "I never wanted this."

"I daresay a gentleman doesn't want half the duties that fall to him, but that does not absolve him of responsibility."

"Of that, I am painfully aware."

"Sebastian, you are not old, and you are certainly not mad."

"Not mad." He laughed softly. "Last night, I saw—" He pressed his lips together, then continued because he feared silence would break his mind the way a glassy sea broke that young sailor. "I dreamed a man stood at the foot of my bed."

James closed his book on an index finger. "What an appalling lack of imagination."

"I thought it was Andrew."

"Was it?"

Andrew and his countess were both gone and their killer not brought to justice. By the time the black-bordered letter caught up with him, his brother was nine months dead, on the very heels, it seemed, of the death of their father. And then Sebastian'd been wounded and given leave to recuperate and put his affairs and estate in order. Six weeks of his leave had passed in a fog of pain. Nothing had been the same since he came to Pennhyll. Nothing. "Andrew is dead."

"Well, yes, of course he is. But this is Pennhyll, after all."

Sebastian almost let the subject drop right there. Except he couldn't. The mood of his dream clung to him like the scent of smoke on a man who went too near a fire. "Andrew never had eyes like that." He remembered the impact of staring into those eyes as if it had really happened. Blue eyes. Alexander eyes. Instead of the affable gleam so typical of his brother, eyes of keen appraisal. "Like ice in the morning."

"Is that all he did? Stand at the foot of your bed?"

Sebastian stared at the blanket on his lap. He did not like feeling ridiculous, and he was uncomfortably aware of the absurdity of implying a dream was more than a dream. Jesus, he must be mad. "He spoke."

"And?"

"As if my life depended upon what he said." The hound rested his head on Sebastian's lap. With an absent fondness, his fingers stroked the gray dome of the dog's head. Even wounded, Sebastian held the promise of action, as if he might at any moment leap to his feet.

"And?"

"I could not hear him."

"Actually," James said, lowering his voice and leaning with one hand at the side of his mouth. "It's normal to have dreams. Lots of people have them. I had one myself last night. About a lusty widow who—"

"I saw him as clear and solid as I see you right now, and then he disappeared. I don't want that." Sebastian pushed away the glass proffered by his valet.

"Pennhyll, my dear Captain Alexander, is haunted—"

"Damn potions addle my brains."

"—however—"

McNaught's round cheeks drooped. "A new tonic, my Lord. Prepared—"

"Jesus! That smells like—" James's book snapped closed as Sebastian continued. "Awful."

James shook his head. "I doubt you saw Andrew last night."

"Hell."

McNaught stared at the glass in his hands. "Wouldn't be proper medicine if it didn't, my Lord."

A smile flickered on James's face. "You did not see Andrew, but the fourth Lord Tiern-Cope."

"Sod off. Not you, McNaught."

"The Black Earl, dead for more than four hundred years, appears to the Lords Tiern-Cope to warn of impending doom."

"I mean it, James."

James's flint-gray eyes widened in mock horror. "It's plain why he appeared to you, Sebastian." He waved a hand and came perilously close to knocking over McNaught's potion. "A fate worse than death itself awaits you."

"Bugger yourself."

"Not what I had in mind." James pretended to dodge a blow and McNaught, seeing his potion once more in danger of being dashed to the floor, clutched the glass to his chest. "My dear Captain," James said in a drawl that sent Sebastian to the very brink of irritation, "you are not mad. You saw the Black Earl last night—"

"I didn't."

"—because your bride, the future countess of Tiern-Cope, is here. At Pennhyll. Or, more precisely, there." He pointed at the window before them.

"Where?" In the glass-paned conservatory wall Sebastian saw his own image, though faintly, as if this, too, had been depleted by injury. His reflection showed a leaner man than he used to be, with a pale face below dark hair. Next to him in the reflection he saw James seated and holding a book on his lap. A third figure appeared in the glass, looming just behind. McNaught, of course, though for an instant Sebastian's heart jumped unpleasantly. Some trick of optics made his servant appear quite tall. Nearly as tall as Sebastian himself. McNaught, however, stood no higher than Napoleon and a full foot short of his employer's height. Quite the trick of light for his rotund little servant to seem twice his height and half his weight.

Sebastian stared hard at the shadowed orbits of his eyes. Penetrating the reflected trio of invalid, friend and servant, he looked through himself. Outside himself. Thick hedges the height of a man's thighs marked the nearest garden limits and beyond that, lawns and more gardens. Instead of gray reflection, he saw filtered sunlight on a winter's palette. A freshly swept flagstone path led up-slope to a lawn twenty yards distant where, through the gap in the border, he could see people strolling or lounging on chairs. In the sizeable area of lawn cleared of snow, two women played tennis, watched by several men intent on the contestants.

James reopened his book. "You were sleeping when they got here." He shot a glance behind them. "McNaught, bless him, as much as told me it'd be my life if I disturbed your rest. Besides, I'm certain I mentioned she'd be here any day."

"Thirteen people." Sebastian shook his head dismally.

"Fourteen," James corrected. "Sixteen counting the two of us."

"You said a few." Sebastian didn't even try to keep the peevishness from his voice. "Only a few guests." What he wanted was the comfort of a ship under his feet and failing that, one night without dreams that felt more real than the stones of Pennhyll Castle.

"Sixteen is a very good number for a country outing."

"It's a damn crowd."

"You oughtn't complain, Sebastian. I've got you four ripe country lasses to choose from, any one of whom would be thrilled out of her stockings to be the next chatelaine of Pennhyll."

"I do not want any guests at all." He had never been the most social of men. Now, he was realizing how much he'd come to enjoy solitude during his years at sea. As for Pennhyll and his title; he didn't want either.

James shrugged.

"I don't want a wife."

"A problem, my dear Captain."

"I know I must wed." He snorted. "The earl must be married so he may start his nursery and ensure the succession."

"Special license at the ready, I trust."

He lifted a hand in a gesture of disinterest guaranteed to dash the hopes of feminine hearts. "All I need is a bride I don't want."

"Well, then."

"What I want is to go back to sea. If I cannot have that, I want to be left alone. And if I cannot have that, then I want to be married without the bother of country outings, or parties or wooing or of pretending emotion I do not feel. And never will feel."

"Sebastian, Sebastian, Sebastian."

"I want a wife happy to leave me my solitude, who makes no demands for love or affection. Will one of those young ladies do that?" He pointed, then stared out the window. "There are six young ladies, James. You said there were four."

"One of them is my sister. And though Diana is young, she's hardly a country lass."

"Which one is she?"

James looked out the window. "The one with the largest dowry."

Sebastian tried not to laugh but not hard enough to succeed. God save him, James did make him laugh, even when he didn't want to. The smile warmed his features and threatened to put life in his eyes.

"She's playing tennis. The brunette."

"Ah."

"Of the gentlemen, I've made sure you've no competition there. None are as rich as you are now, they haven't titles, and they're quite dull. I don't think even one of them has been to London in a decade or so at least. Good squires and yeomen all, I'm sure. And, aside from me, of course, none are as handsome as you, either. You ought to thank me."

"Why did you say there were four to choose from when there are six?"

"Why, indeed."

"If you were a sailor, I'd have you keelhauled for your insolence." His father echoed in his voice, full of

confidence and arrogance. He'd never once thought
he'd be the last of the Alexander men. Instead, the
youngest of three sons, he'd embraced a career at sea
and found that, like his father, he was born to command. He wanted that again, to return to the sea and
to command, because then his life would be his own
once more. Ever since he knew he would not die of
his wound, if he reached for the man he used to be,
he found nothing he recognized. The certainty of his
life and his place in it had forever sunk beneath the
waves, washed away in a tide of pain. He wanted his
old self, his real self, back.

James's eyebrows arched. "The gentlemen have
more polish than you. You're a bit rough about the
edges, Sebastian. But—" James sounded altogether
too cheerful "—that can't be helped."

Sebastian stared out the window. James's sister hit
the ball smartly. Her opponent, patently a novice at
the game, did not. A good many of the exchanges
involved her picking up the ball and attempting to
lob it over the net. She didn't make two in five shots,
though with practice she no doubt would soon make
a better account of herself. She moved with a vigor
out of proportion to her ability. Her bonnet, a useless
cap so far as he could see, flew off her head. Red hair.
Not auburn or Titian or strawberry blond, but hair
that was a deep and excessively blatant red.

Images from another of the wretched dreams that
plagued him flashed into his head. A woman swoon-
ing or perhaps falling. Red hair, red as a copper kettle
on fire. Sounds, too, he recalled with unpleasant clar-
ity. A deafening, roar. Fear. A shrill cry. Pain. A
woman's inconsolable sobs. Though quickly ban-
ished, the memories left an imprint, an echo of color

9

and emotion that once come to mind, like the contents of Pandora's box once opened, could never again be locked safely away.

Another volley cannoned over the net. The red-haired woman ran backward, arm extended. A difficult shot under any circumstance, and one she nearly made. The ball caromed off the edge of her racquet like a grouse startled from a bush and winged down the snow-covered slope.

To his astonishment, the redhead threw back her head and laughed. Though he could hear nothing, her body moved with laughter; without restraint, full of exuberance and joy. James's sister, Diana, laughed, too. Hands on her hips, she watched the redhead start after the ball. Several of the watching gentlemen closed in on Diana. No one followed the redhead even though she was, to his mind, the more appealing of the two.

Sebastian shifted on the chair, but nothing eased his discomfort. His ribs hurt like the devil. And yet he wanted desperately to be up and about. Inactivity suited him in neither body nor temperament. Outside, the light turned, and he could once again see through the window. The redhead walked toward the hedges, sliding now and then in the snow. Though she was not yet near enough to make out her features, he could see that she was a small woman.

"Your sister's grown quite tall." He'd met James's sister—half-sister, since they had only their mother in common—five years ago when he'd visited the Fitzalan estate in Middlesex. He'd been a third lieutenant then, newly promoted. Andrew was there, too. It was the last time he'd seen his brother.

James glanced at the window. "Yes."

Sebastian remembered fetching her a glass of lemonade. Strange how he remembered that detail but hardly any about her appearance. Youth. Blushes. A plump figure. Blue eyes, he thought, and, even at her age, an air of sophistication. He'd left the following morning for Falmouth and the Indian Ocean. If she was willing, why not? Marrying Diana would be an excellent solution to the problem of ending his single state.

By now, the redhead had come near enough that he could see she was older than he first thought, into her twenties, but with skin much suited to the winter skies of Cumbria. He'd been so long sailing the ocean—twelve years in all and the last five without port in England—the change in feminine fashions astonished him. Yet even he could see the redhead's clothes were not in style. No embroidered hems. No pelisse with puffy sleeves, no Brussels lace. Just white muslin and an encircling ribbon several inches above her natural waist. And the insistent red of her hair, bright against the snow. She crouched, angling toward the window as she searched for the ball in the dense foliage of a low hedge. Her mouth moved in a triumphant shout. She rose, ball clutched in one hand. A breeze riffled her hair, blowing curls across her cheek.

To his surprise, his heart did an awkward turn in his chest at about the same time his body registered significant interest to the south. She was pretty. Very pretty. With a smile that made him want another. He watched the sway of her bottom as she dashed uphill to James's sister. Significant interest.

"Who is the redhead?"

"One of your guests, of course." James coughed

11

into his hand. "Though," he said carefully, "not quite a country lass."

"The sixth," Sebastian said. "The one I am not to choose." The hound pushed its head forward beneath his fingers. Its eyes closed when Sebastian rubbed behind one ear.

"My Lord," said McNaught.

His valet's glass hovered inches from his face, floating like some ghostly apparition. Sebastian kicked the blanket off his lap in the hope McNaught would be distracted from his deuced potion. Pain licked up his side, a searing reminder that he was far from healed. Oh, he could hobble about well enough, but anything truly energetic—blanket-kicking or pointless games of tennis, or, for that matter, embracing one's wife-to-be—remained out of the question. But he'd begun to think it possible to one day walk in his newly acquired garden instead of admiring the prospect from an invalid's chair.

James waved one lace-cuffed wrist. "Diana was London's reigning debutante this season past. Absolutely without mercy. Broke at least a dozen hearts. Probably more."

"Why isn't she married?" He meant the redhead, but the moment the question left his mouth, he knew James would misunderstand, and so he did.

"Saving herself for you."

Sebastian glanced at his friend, taking in the golden hair and angelically male features of James, viscount Fitzalan. "Now, why should she do that?"

"All the young ladies want to be your wife. Including Diana. God's truth, Sebastian, old man. You've no notion how celebrated you are in Society. Hero of the

Indian Ocean. Pirates. Battles. Prize money. And that's without the title. With it, well . . ."

Sebastian rolled his eyes. "You exaggerate. As usual."

"No. I don't. Diana, like every other young lady of Society, spends hours imagining herself married to you. And probably dreams of you at night."

He tried again to fill in his faded and incomplete memory of Diana. He recalled brown hair, light eyes and very little more. He knew she was pretty. She must be if she'd broken the hearts of a dozen of London's most elite bachelors. Except, he needed a wife. Not a debutante. A sensible, capable woman. Not an orchid in need of fretting care. No, his wife must be content to live simply. If it came right down to it, he wanted a woman who wouldn't mind life on a ship and, at minimum, a woman who wouldn't resent long stretches alone while her husband sailed the seas. The familiar excitement for the waves and salty air failed to materialize. "I'm cold," he complained, staring at the discarded blanket on the marble tiles.

"You can marry anyone, Sebastian. No one is out of your reach. But I'd be pleased," James said, "if you married Diana."

"Arrange it, then." His indifference ought to worry him, but it didn't. How had such an attractive woman as the redhead stayed unmarried at her age? Some abiding fault perhaps. A distemper of manner or a horsey laugh. Or perhaps no sense of humor at all. Remembering her laughter, that seemed unlikely. Perhaps she was vain or haughty. He sighed. In fact, he would be quite satisfied if he were to wake up one morning and find a wife at his side, a ready-made helpmeet braced for a life in the country. He had no intention of living in London. Ever. "Get her to agree, and I'll marry her tomorrow."

"I've done what I can. She's at least amenable to the notion, for it seems that in addition to your reputation, you made quite an impression when you met her before. At the least, she already loves your naval record. Shouldn't be hard to convince her to marry you. Nothing could be easier, I expect."

"What about the redhead?" The sight of that flame-colored hair unsettled him, but he recalled with interest the nature of his response to first seeing her. Significant interest, and that was encouraging for the improving state of his health. He'd been coddling his injury too long and as a result, let his resolve to action grow soft. For years he'd solved his own damn problems, and here he was letting James take over his life. Was she as passionate as that hair of hers? "Is she a Scot?"

James turned his head to look at him, his smile gone. "That's her, Sebastian." He lifted his palms in a defensive gesture. "From everything I've heard, it's a miracle she didn't die with your brother and his wife."

Sebastian absorbed James's revelation with typical self-possession. "I'm surprised she came."

James's grin reappeared. "You are the leading citizen of Far Caister, Sebastian, in need of a spare for your dinner table. When Diana arrived without her companion, her most bosom friend whose name escapes me just now, I took it upon myself to importune the vicar for help. By merest chance, this woman's name came up, and she was soon convinced to remedy our predicament of numbers. She could not refuse. Your patronage might do her a world of good. Besides, by reputation at least, she is a lady of breeding, I assure you. Impoverished. But a lady."

"Not what I expected."

"No family to speak of. Next thing to an orphan. Her mother's an invalid, so I'm told." James waved a hand. "The proprieties are satisfied, the numbers once again even. Our spare is tolerably attractive, more than tolerably intelligent and quite enough on the shelf not to upset the other young ladies. Her reputation is nearly unassailable." His white-toothed grin reappeared. "And you are free to question her to your heart's content. For all the good it may do you."

Through the windowpane, Sebastian scowled. "The spare."

"Like you, in a manner of speaking."

"God-awful hair." But he saw himself with his hands buried in curls free from pins and cascading over her shoulders.

"There," James said, "you are much mistaken." His half-lidded glance swept the window. "Wonderful exuberance." Sebastian shot him a glance because he heard something in his friend's tone. "Wonderful." James's voice dropped a notch and turned into a whisper, a sound of endearments exchanged in a darkened room. "I do fancy her."

McNaught cleared his throat. "My Lord." The potion inched downward.

He could now see McNaught's fingertips, ending the illusion the glass had been floating in the air. "Oh, all right." He grasped the tumbler and tossed down the contents. Took it like a man, he did. Peppermint, he thought. Licorice. And a sharp aftertaste of some sort of patent remedy not quite strong enough to mask whatever ingredient gave off the faint smell of rotten eggs. Sulfur? Shuddering, he held out the empty glass. It vanished from sight. "The spare."

"Yes. The spare."

"Twenty-four years old." In all the times Sebastian had thought or read about his brother's death, the lone survivor of the tragedy had never been more than an abstraction to him. A name in the official records, without face or character, no existence outside her having been at Pennhyll. Now that he saw her, the reality jolted him. He remembered the pertinent details about her. "Never married. Daughter of Sir Roger Willow, deceased." Miss Olivia Willow, formerly a governess for Admiral Bunker, found near death at Pennhyll Castle with the bodies of Andrew, earl of Tiern-Cope, and his wife Guenevere. The earl and countess each dead of a bullet wound. In the coroner's opinion, they had died quickly. A crack shot, their murderer. Miss Willow, too, had been shot, but in her case, the bullet went a hair to the right and spared her the fate of Andrew and his wife. Unfortunately, she remembered nothing of the night in question. The conclusion of the inquiry was that Miss Willow had surprised the culprit during the commission of his crime and as a result sustained a nearly fatal injury. Only the alarm raised by household staff had saved her from death. No one doubted she would otherwise have been killed. The man responsible escaped into the night.

James glanced at McNaught. "A spinster, Sebastian, of advancing age with no male relatives looking out for her welfare and no dragon-eyed mama guarding her virtue. In short, a woman who will keep me entertained while we are here in the midst of all this frozen . . . vegetation. What is it? You look like someone's kicked your favorite hound." His face fell. "Don't tell me you fancy her, too. I saw her first, damn it all."

Sebastian stared at the windowed wall through which he could see the wild splash of red hair coming free of its pins. He didn't care how pretty she was or how lovely her smile. She was his best hope, likely his only hope, of discovering who killed his brother. He meant to have what was in her head, no matter the cost to him or to her. "As long as I get what I want from her, she's all yours, James."

Chapter Two

January 5

Olivia smiled because her role was to be pleasant at all times, to be at all times agreeable. She must pretend she did not feel the least bit awkward about being back at Pennhyll where three days had vanished from her life. A legion of emotions contributed to her disquiet, starting the moment she walked into the Great Hall; the fear of those lost days tangled up with the anticipation of meeting Captain Alexander. Whatever her anxieties about Pennhyll, she was done avoiding the past, done with living as if nothing terrible had happened to her. Something terrible had happened, and she was done with the pretense. She accepted the invitation because she wanted those days back. After a year without remembering, she'd come to believe Pennhyll was the only place she could recover those days.

For the moment at least, no one here took much

notice of her. They seemed content with her role as the spare. She was herself well-used to a house crowded with guests and even more used to near invisibility. Old enough now to be a chaperone and with the distinct advantage of being neither rich enough nor young enough to threaten the prospects of younger, better-situated ladies. She was the second-best umbrella, the one no one wants until the other can't be found. As befitted her status, she sat on a stool equidistant to fireplace and door; the very outskirts of the gathering but at the ready in case of need.

Snow had forced their luncheon indoors so that instead of a walk to the lake and a meal served in the crisp January air, they cowered inside, glad to be out of the sudden damp. Four of their number fell into the category of parent or guardian. The rest were younger. Five gentlemen and six young ladies, if she counted herself, all but Miss Diana Royce were from nearby, and thus well-known to Olivia. Since they knew her, they paid her little attention. Twice touched by tragedy, she occupied a peculiar position in society. By birth and long family history, she belonged to the gentry, no one denied that, but no one of her class wanted to befriend her. The taint of death and scandal clung too close.

To a man, the fathers held their Madeira and broke rank only if some feminine request demanded the semblance of attention. Mothers watched their charges with hawk-eyed stares that swept the room for signs of attachment, suitable or otherwise. Young ladies sat by each other with the bachelor gentlemen hovering near. One of the ladies played the harp well enough to be ignored. It would be another hour at least before she could excuse herself to wander the castle, hoping something would spark a memory.

All the setting lacked was their host. No one had met him, no one but Lord Fitzalan, who knew the earl before he was an earl, and his sister, who had met him once some years before. Lord Fitzalan, unmarried himself, numbered among the young gentlemen. For a nobleman, Fitzalan seemed sensible. High-spirited, a bit vain of his appearance, though not without cause, and not a dilettante. So far as she could tell, he was the only man here with more than an ounce of brain in his head.

"Do come sit, Fitzalan." Miss Royce, the viscount's half-sister, reclining goddesslike on a chaise, lifted herself on one elbow. "I miss your company here." How, Olivia wondered, did a nineteen-year-old girl acquire such ennui? The crowd around her shifted as Miss Royce patted the chaise. Her chestnut hair and dark, up-tilted eyes just slightly uneven made Olivia imagine her pining for an Italianate sun, one hand reaching lazily for another glass of wine or yet another sun-sweetened grape. What must London be like if girls Diana's age learned enough of men and their natures to find them so tediously dull?

Fitzalan sat on the edge of his sister's chaise. "I am here, Diana, your abject slave."

"If that were true, you would have bought me that phaeton I wanted. Mama said it would flatter me exceedingly."

"You cannot drive a phaeton in Far Caister."

"I can if I am in Town. I would be so fetching a figure in a phaeton drawn by horses to match my eyes. What do you think?" Diana touched her brother's arm while her gaze swept the admiring men,

19

all of whom rang in with enthusiastic agreement. Miss Royce must have a phaeton. And horses to match her eyes. Who could disagree? They'd none of them ever met a girl like Miss Royce, a natural flirt with the sort of brilliance one acquired only from a London Season and a Bond Street seamstress.

"Until I met Captain Alexander, now the earl," Diana said, "I thought my brother the handsomest man alive." She pointed to the portrait in pride of place above the mantel. Miss Royce did have fine eyes. "But, dear James, you're simply not."

"If I changed my mind about the phaeton?"

Her eyes sparkled. "Well, dearest James, since I know you are not sincere, I must say the same."

Fitzalan mimicked despair, and Diana giggled when he rolled off the chaise and pretended to lie dead at her feet. A few fathers or elder brothers looked over but, determining the cause of the commotion, returned to a heated discussion weighing the benefits of double lambing against risking the health of the ewes. The viscount turned onto his side and, propping his head up with one arm, peered past the crowd surrounding the chaise. "What think you, Miss Willow?"

Olivia, alarmed to find herself addressed, adopted her best flustered-by-his-attention expression. A woman's loss of aplomb upon a handsome man's notice rarely, if ever, caused offense. She liked to think she'd perfected an attitude of dizzy intensity. "My Lord, I've no experience of such matters."

"But your opinion means the world." Fitzalan laughed so that his teeth showed. "The very universe. Who is more handsome, me or the captain?"

Now here was a fine predicament. If she chose

Tiern-Cope, she'd insult Lord Fitzalan and vice versa. Drat the man. She wrung her hands. "Pray, my Lord, do not rely on my opinion in anything to do with fashion."

"Let us say this once that we shall."

"I am sure Miss Royce would look exceedingly well in a phaeton the color of her eyes." There existed a perilously fine line between the meekness she wanted to project and outright satire. From the tilt of Fitzalan's head, she'd just crossed it.

"My dear Miss Willow." Fitzalan grinned. "My dear, charming, lovely, exquisite Miss Willow. For all that our gentlemen's pride will be trampled like so much dirt beneath your feet, I hope you will not disagree with my sister. She would be utterly cast down to discover you do not share her opinion of our host."

Olivia let her eyes go still. Why did the only man here with any intelligence have to single her out? She did not want to be noticed. Second-best-umbrella status suited her just fine. The Far Caister girls might not have Diana's polish, but several, Miss Cage in particular, laid claim to some measure of beauty. Why didn't he banter with Miss Cage? "To be sure, I have yet to meet a gentleman who isn't handsome or a lady who isn't beautiful."

Fitzalan sat up. "What a useful opinion to have."

"But," said Miss Cage, the green-eyed brunette Olivia thought most likely to give Diana some competition, "what of Captain Alexander? The earl?" Miss Cage hadn't been five minutes in the company of Miss Royce before she, too, possessed the same air of boredom. The world bored her. The very breath in her lungs bored her. Julia Cage always had been a quick study, with an ear for music and language.

"Well," Olivia said, "it's my opinion all men look handsome in a uniform." She'd discovered during her stint as a governess that men liked to be admired. If they did not feel obliged to flirt, all the better. Disinterested interest suited a woman of her status. She'd never attracted much notice for any reason but her hair. Long ago, she'd realized the color put off most men. Red was simply not the fashion for a lady of any age. Men who weren't put off by her awful copper curls didn't want her—Miss Olivia Willow—they wanted what they imagined her hair signified. Thus, though she might seethe inside, impatient, annoyed or even on the edge of laughter, she'd learned to reflect a calm and dainty mendacity. Men soon met only the disappointment of their perceptions.

The viscount frowned, looking at her from under half-lowered lashes. "Yes, yes. But, Miss Willow, what of the good captain?"

She let out a breath and did her best to appear addlebrained by his notice of her. She supposed it was at least a little true. Lord Fitzalan was, indeed, well-favored, with exquisite manners and, despite his rank in life, not at all a terrifying man. "He's sure to be very handsome. The young ladies find him quite the beau, I'm sure. So dashing. A hero of the waves." She leaned forward, eyes wide and disingenuous. "I've followed his career, my Lord. He cannot help but be handsome, I am sure."

"The fashion, then, is for naval men."

"I'm sure I don't know, my Lord."

He jumped to his feet and strode, hands clasped behind his back, to the fireplace where he stared at the portrait for fully half a minute. The other men, seeing his attention no longer on his sister, closed in on Diana. With that, Olivia ceased to be the center of attention. Relieved, she left her stool and walked to a sidetable on which there sat a stack of drawing paper. Attract as little notice as possible, that was her motto. Second-best umbrella and all that.

She *was* nervous about meeting the captain. The earl. Lord Tiern-Cope. Would he appear tonight? She flipped through the sheets, the results of a morning the young ladies spent taking likenesses of each other, of the gentlemen or of a view from nature. Her head throbbed along the scar hidden by her hair, a point of blossoming pain, a familiar sensation but sharper now than usual, and constant since her arrival at Pennhyll. Andrew used to love reading his brother's letters, always with a titillating pause while he skipped over or rephrased some passage not suitable for a lady to hear without redaction. He was here. Captain Alexander at Pennhyll.

"Miss Willow."

The voice came soft and unexpectedly, and she nearly jumped out of her skin because she'd let her thoughts stray to the new earl and lost track of her surroundings. "Lord Fitzalan."

His eyes flashed the color of flint. "Forgive me if I startled you."

"I don't know what's got into me." The intensity of his regard unsettled her. Please, let him not be one of those men who thought a woman with red hair must be at the mercy of her passions. She put down the papers and let her eyes go blank. "Have you ever been absolutely convinced someone is about to leap at you from the shadows?" She felt she'd missed her mark, something she did not often do. To be convincingly vapid, a woman needed not just empty eyes, but a breathless voice.

He grinned. "Every time I walk a London street at night."

"For that you may have some excuse." Fitzalan studied her and, too late, she realized she'd spoken more frankly than prudence required. When dealing with the nobility, it paid never to forget one's place, however familiar they deigned to be. Never presume too much.

"And your excuse?" he asked.

"A nervous constitution." She fluttered her hand just above her chest so the viscount would imagine she felt her nerves just now. "A failure of my sex, I suppose."

Fitzalan gave her the sort of look a man expecting eggs for breakfast might give a bowl of cold porridge. Leaning against the table, he took up the sheaf of drawings, shuffling through them until he found hers, a sketch of a plate of grapes. In the conviction that no one would actually study her effort, she'd added a rather comical face in the shadow of one of the grapes. "These look good enough to eat."

"Ah, but just behind is your sister's most admirable portrait." Olivia brought out Diana's drawing and set it atop her own. "She took your likeness quite well." She tittered. "Miss Royce is an accomplished young lady. You must be so very proud of her."

"I do hope," he said softly, switching hers back to the top, "that around me you will not pretend you are an empty-headed twit."

She widened her eyes in hurt insult. "I've never thought of myself as a clever woman, but I'm sure I'm not empty headed. Most assuredly, I am not a blue-stocking. No, indeed, my Lord. I never read a thing, unless I am certain my soul will be improved." The lie came off her tongue with guilty ease. "I can't imagine what you mean to imply."

He touched the shadow with its lolling tongue and devil horns. "I think you can."

Blast. He smiled, slowly, and she could not help thinking it wasn't fair for an already handsome man to be twice as handsome just because he smiled.

"Can't you, Miss Willow?"

She sighed. "I am undone."

"Not yet," he murmured. Before she could make sense of the remark, he grinned at her. "Fear not, I promise to keep your secret." He examined Diana's sketch. "My nose isn't that long. Nor my eyes so small. And my chin is far more manly."

"Fishing for compliments, my Lord?"

"Shamelessly." He lifted his eyes. "Am I having any luck?"

"There are more than enough young ladies here who, I daresay, would be more than happy to tell you they find you exceedingly handsome."

"Do you agree with them?"

"As indeed you are."

"Oh, much better, Miss Willow. As to the likeness of our brave and doughty captain hanging there above the mantel, I want your opinion." He put down the sheaf of papers. "And mind you, nothing less than unadulterated truth. I've not my sister's scruples about opinions unshared."

"Accepting as true the brothers closely resemble each other, I find the subject rather harshly painted."

"But, of course," he said, eying Olivia while he once again studied the painting, "when this portrait was

25

done, he was still a lieutenant and understandably concerned with advancing his career."

"Which he did in exactly the manner suggested by his portrait."

A girlish voice called out. "Lord Fitzalan? You simply must come here and explain why your sister may not have a phaeton."

"A moment, Miss Cage." Fitzalan's attention returned to Olivia. "And that was?"

"With fierce determination."

"Can you tell his temperament from a portrait? Mere dashes of paint upon a canvas?"

She lifted a hand toward the portrait and found the gesture blocked all but her view of the painted eyes. "That is not the face of anyone much at home with a smile."

"You consider yourself adept at reading a gentleman's face?"

Olivia smiled. "I do."

"What do you read in mine?" Perhaps because he was aware their conversation was no longer private, he struck a pose. "Be brutally honest." He winked. "Lie if you must."

"Amiability, my Lord." She laughed because she could not help her amusement. "Nothing but amiability."

Fitzalan staggered. "Amiability?"

"Assuredly so." By habit, she fell into vapidity, but she did not like it as well now that Fitzalan knew the truth.

His eyes rolled toward the ceiling. "Damned by faint praise."

"My Lord," said Olivia, lowering her voice. "Don't be petulant. You know very well you are as handsome a man who ever walked this earth. I'm sure the young ladies are breathless when they are about you."

"But not you?"

"I'm not young, my Lord."

Briefly, his eyes darkened to a rain-cloud gray. "You've drawn my character accurately enough for, truly, I am amiability itself. You'll never know a man more amiable than I, as I mean for you to discover. Now, Miss Willow, what do you read in that face?" He pointed to the painting.

She approached the portrait. She, too, clasped her hands behind her back. Dark hair, the captain had, but not black. He wore a naval officer's uniform. Gold buttons sailed down one side of his coat and his shirt lace foamed over wide lapels. A cocked hat tucked under one arm showed black trim. His eyes gazed ferociously forward, a clear, pure blue, so clear she wondered at not seeing through to the wall behind. She turned sideways so as to see the viscount. "Oh, quite a lot, my Lord. Andrew loved to tell of his brother's adventures. Indeed, I feel I know him well, having heard so many tales of danger and bravery."

Miss Cage walked over and twined her arm around Fitzalan's, boldness she'd learned from Diana, who, when she deigned to rise, often made use of the gentlemen in such a manner. "What can you tell from the face?" she asked.

"Consider the strong cheeks."

"It's a very handsome face," said Miss Cage.

Fitzalan glanced at Olivia.

"Yes, I admit he is handsome."

"But?" said Fitzalan. He patted Miss Cage's arm.

"Notice how his cheeks angle toward his temples." Olivia spread her fingers, measuring the distance.

"The nose forming a fierce line between his eyes. The unyielding mouth and determined chin."

Miss Cage looked at Fitzalan. "Your sister told me she thinks his mouth gentle. I, however, to her replied that his is not so gentle as yours, my Lord."

Fitzalan's eyebrows lifted. "Thank you, Miss Cage."

Olivia faced the portrait again, absorbing the austere face. "Cold, those eyes," she said, thinking how different he seemed from Andrew. "As if he had no heart at all." A rather harsh opinion to hold of the man she used to imagine would fall helplessly in love with her. Not that she ever believed he would. Valorous sea captains might fall in love with redheaded spinsters, but, alas, noblemen did not.

"Miss Willow," said Julia Cage. "We find him dreadfully handsome. Even if he were not a hero, all we ladies would think him quite the gallant. If you were still in your youth, I'm sure you'd feel the same."

"Certainly," she said.

"You see, Miss Willow?" Fitzalan said. "Not cold. Just stern. Don't you agree? As an officer must be."

Olivia spoke softly. "Tell me, Lord Fitzalan, were you well acquainted with the previous earl?"

"He stopped coming to London two or three years ago, but before that we saw each other now and again."

"Since you have known them both, what is your opinion of him?" From the corner of her eye, she saw Miss Cage watching and listening intently. The subject of Tiern-Cope fascinated everyone.

"Captain Alexander, or, I should say, Lord Tiern-Cope, may not have his brother's charm, but do not discount him on that score. He is—" Fitzalan tipped his head to one side, searching for the correct word "—formidable."

Diana gasped. "He's been disfigured, hasn't he?"

The room fell silent.

"James?" Diana sat straight. One hand drifted to her bosom, and eyes big as sixpence fixed on her brother, pleading for a denial. "Maimed in the war," she said. "And ashamed to show his ruined face."

A collective gasp came from the ladies. Were all their hopes, then, to be pinned not on an earl by all accounts eager to take a wife, but on a viscount who'd so far proved immune to marriage-minded ladies?

Fitzalan's smile faded. "Surely, ladies, the allure of nobility and wealth will overcome the impact of any infirmities?"

"He *is* disfigured." Diana closed her eyes. When she opened them, they glistened with tears. "How badly has he been scarred? Tell me, James. Please, I must know."

"Nonsense, Miss Royce," Olivia said. "He was wounded in the chest. On the side, just here."

Fitzalan said, "Who told you that?"

The pile of coals in the fireplace tumbled down with a hiss and a flare of light. But that wasn't what made Olivia look away from the viscount. She looked away because the salon door swung open with a faint *whoosh* of air over the Chinese carpet, and the earl of Tiern-Cope walked in.

Chapter Three

Olivia's head flashed with a pain that left her momentarily blind. The air turned dense, too thick to breathe. In the middle of the maelstrom of sensation, just when she could see again and draw breath, there stood Andrew's brother, framed in the opening of the doorway. A mad impression dashed into her head: He wasn't real. Druid warriors must have magicked him into existence and let him loose to wreak havoc among dream-bound and waking mortals alike.

God knows he had the Alexander looks: blue eyes, dark hair and a narrow face. The resemblance to Andrew was remarkable, but something in the face set him apart from other handsome men, indeed, from any other man she'd known. The sharp cheekbones, the confident way he held himself, but most especially the eyes. Where the other gentlemen were open and gregarious, the earl's eyes gave nothing away and put a frost on his smile. Nothing of Andrew's gentleness, Olivia thought. Nothing at all. The sea had washed away whatever gentleness he'd possessed.

He stood perhaps an inch or two over six feet, but the impression of height came from his posture: rigidly upright. Tan breeches stretched taut over a flat belly and followed the shape of his thighs. His bottle-green coat, unbuttoned to show a gold-striped waistcoat beneath, did not fit as perfectly as Fitzalan's but his shoulders were no less broad for the imperfection. Above the waistcoat, the plain front of his shirt begged for less sober lace. His boots, though shined to brilliance below the turned-down tops, set no example of London fashion. No one who saw him walking down the street would think him an aristocrat.

Hair cropped unfashionably close to his head revealed a stubborn and determined physiognomy, a man who knew what he wanted and took it. Gauntness defined the ridge of his cheekbone more than nature intended. Every feature could be marked in the portrait. Except, to England the sea returned not the youthful lieutenant of near-legend, but a man fully grown and in command of himself. There was no denying his striking looks, but it was his air of assurance, Olivia decided at last, that set him apart.

Tiern-Cope stared at them as if they were furniture in his way, a look devoid of welcome or interest. He was thirty, which for a man was still young. Though in truth younger than Andrew, he seemed a thousand years older and where Andrew wore his emotions on his sleeve, the captain was about as easy to read as a block of granite.

Diana leaned forward, hiding her face behind her spread-out fan. "James, you're such an awful liar."

Olivia didn't see how anyone could have heard that soft exclamation over such a distance, but she felt a ripple of awareness come from the earl. He swept the room and each of its occupants in ruthless assessment. Olivia fancied his gaze lingered when it reached her. Her hair, of course, which she knew from long experience was coming free of its pins. Everyone who saw her for the first time stared at the shocking copper curls. His glance, and that was all it was, ended almost before it began, which was to be expected. If there was anything good to be said about her position in life, it was that her lack of rank afforded ample opportunity to study people. Olivia considered herself a student of knowledge gained through observation.

"James." A slow curve of his mouth brought no warmth to his eyes. He bowed, rather stiff and more to the left than the right. Diana smoothed her skirt. Miss Cage fluttered her fan and turned pink. Feminine hands went to curls or lace, adjusting and readjusting. The gentlemen stirred. One or two tugged on their waistcoats. Despite the flurry of activity on his behalf, the earl's expression did not soften.

Olivia frowned, disappointed, which she realized was unfair of her. The good people of Far Caister, herself included, knew more about the naval career of Captain Sebastian Alexander than they did about Admiral Nelson. Andrew had been so full of life, a cheerful man who rarely lost the opportunity to relate his brother's exploits in the highest of terms that she hadn't expected a joyless man whose mouth refused to move beyond the facsimile of a smile he wore right now. Olivia wondered if he'd ever truly smiled in all his life. Probably not. How sad that Andrew's brother should have no joy in him. How disappointing. After all those tales of courage at the line of battle Olivia had constructed a very different picture of the man. A girlish, romanticized ideal that, of course, had no relation at all to reality.

"Good afternoon," the earl said.

"Lord Tiern-Cope," said Fitzalan, bowing. Any trace of his usual good humor vanished with the serious business of introducing the earl. "You remember my sister. Miss Diana Royce."

The captain—no, Olivia reminded herself, the earl—walked to Diana with a stride that put her in mind of an animal; the vicious sort with sharp teeth, relentless energy and boundless hunger, which was an odd impression to have of a man so recently and sorely wounded. Heavens, what must he be like at full health?

"Miss Royce," said the earl, taking Diana's hand and pressing it between his. His voice flowed over the room like silk over stone. Here stood a man used to giving orders and having them followed. And everyone in the room, from oldest to youngest, responded to that air of authority.

"My Lord." Diana, dazzled like the others, swept into a low curtsey, completely abandoning her boredom. Olivia liked her better for the uncertainty, though doubtless that was her own lack of polish showing.

Lord Fitzalan cleared his throat.

"Miss Royce, do not stand on my account." The earl caught Fitzalan's eye and added, "Treat Pennhyll as if it were your home. Please." With another stiff bow, he extended his elbow to her, and Diana put her hand on his arm. He led her to the chaise, seeing her seated before he faced the room in general. Olivia could not help but recall the rumor that Tiern-Cope had a special license, and that he intended to be married and return to the Navy forthwith.

Fitzalan managed the remaining introductions. The earl acknowledged everyone with a bow and a murmur. Not impolite, just not warm. In order of precedence, Olivia came dead last and so, eventually, only she remained to be introduced. Fitzalan remained silent long enough to give Olivia the unpleasant thought that he did not mean to present her at all. Tiern-Cope's arctic eyes landed on Fitzalan.

"James." Inflection made the word a query, but no one doubted he'd uttered a command for introduction.

"Ah, yes, do forgive me." Fitzalan guided Olivia's gloved hand to the earl. "Miss Olivia Willow. May I have the pleasure of presenting the Right Honorable Sebastian, earl of Tiern-Cope and master of Pennhyll Castle?"

He must know something of the night his brother died, that she'd been there, too, and nearly died herself. Perhaps he blamed her, certainly she doubted he pitied her. He didn't strike her as a man likely to pity anyone. Whatever he thought, she ought not expect anything beyond polite reserve. She got less. Tiern-Cope took her hand without even an approximation of a smile. Rather the opposite in fact. Well. So be it.

"Tiern-Cope, I present Miss Olivia Willow of Far Caister." That might have sounded grand if only Far Caister weren't a village not a mile from the castle walls.

While she curtseyed she felt him taking in everything about her, from her satin slippers scuffed at the toe and much down at the heel to the lack of ribbons and lace on her gown. This meeting wasn't anything like what she'd imagined, nor was the man, for that matter. Without doubt, any interest he showed was due to that awful day, and still the intensity of his regard made her wish for finer jewelry than her coral beads or for gloves better able to withstand such scrutiny. Most especially, she wished for a grander place to call home than Far Caister. The vanity of her regret struck her as so absurd that when she raised her eyes, she was smiling. Not at him, of course, that was accidental, but he might be excused if he thought so.

She met a pair of cold, blue eyes. "My Lord."

"You have red hair." The remark most definitely accused.

"Red, indeed," she said. For heaven's sake, did he think she had red hair just to irritate him? "Hopelessly red, my Lord. And violently unfashionable." She grinned and made sure her eyes emptied of emotion. "The bane of my existence, I'll be the first to tell you." She cocked one eyebrow, still smiling. "I am content with my hair, for I know I shall never be mistaken for anyone else." A titter guaranteed he'd take her for just another gormless female. She despised herself for it.

"You and I have much to discuss." He watched her with something between a glare and a glower. That, too, was unfair of her, she decided. For all she knew, this was his usual expression of good cheer.

"Sir," she said. Of course he wanted to know about that night, only there was precious little she could tell him. In her head, she saw him pacing the deck of a ship, a cat-o'-nine tails clenched in a fist while sailors cowered at his feet. The image, perversely, since it seemed so apt, made her smile again.

Silence reared up, a vast, icy wall. Oh, Miss Cage was right, the man was handsome, handsomer even than Fitzalan. Handsome, she thought, without actually being handsome, at least not in the manner of Fitzalan's faultless looks. Once, long ago, that mouth might have been gentle, but now the stern, cheerless face chilled to the very bone. With some effort Olivia kept her smile, though her cheeks ached with the effort.

"The earls of Tiern-Cope," he said in voice about as blithe as basalt, "once owned nearly every soul in Far Caister. So I'm told."

Olivia called on a hard-won ability to speak in modulated tones whatever the cost. No one, absolutely no one, could take offense at her reply. No groveling toady could be more obsequious in the face of insult. "I've heard the same."

"Only nearly?" Fitzalan said. "My dear Sebastian, why on earth didn't you own them all?"

His head moved enough to take in Diana and her brother without losing sight of her. The plane of his cheek caught the light and cast the rest of his face in stark shadow. Olivia shivered at the sight. What a terrifying man. "A failing on the part of my ancestors."

If Fitzalan had made the retort, she was sure they would all have laughed merrily, but the captain sounded as though he'd like to reach through the years and show the earls Tiern-Cope what it meant to be noble. No one moved. Like people increasingly horrified that a pebble dropped down a chasm had yet to hit bottom, no one spoke. No one dared.

Olivia hurried to fill the silence. "The earls of Tiern-Cope have been the pride and lifeblood of Far Caister for so long no one hereabouts thinks anything but that they could be master of us all."

"Including you, Miss Willow?" His eyes landed on her like the sharp edge of a knife. Her headache pulsed, a slash of pain along her scar that made her long to lie down in a darkened room.

"Certainly, my Lord." She felt sorry for Miss Royce. A husband with no joy in him would be worse than remaining a spinster at twenty-four.

The blue eyes stayed on her with relentless chill. "Why aren't you married?"

"I beg your pardon?"

He stared until she felt the size of a walnut about

to be cracked beneath his heel. "You heard me."

Fitzalan groaned. "Sebastian."

By the merest of margins she kept a light tone. "Never loved and never in love, I suppose." A bald-faced lie, but the truth was not his affair, no matter how horrible his aspect.

"What of your relations?" A smile slid over his face, then vanished like seawater into sand. "Did my ancestors once own yours?"

"Sebastian. Not now."

She pasted on another vapid smile, but the wall of cheerful nonchalance crumbled under that deepening gaze. "Happily for the Willows, the relation was more testamentary than proprietary."

"Indeed." Though his expression didn't change, his voice sneered.

"Sebastian!"

With a quelling look at Fitzalan, he bowed. "How fortunate for you, Miss Willow." When he left her to claim the seat nearest the fireplace, an excruciating silence filled the room. It was, Olivia thought, like having a wild animal to visit. Everyone watched him warily, uncertain of his tameness except for Fitzalan, who apparently knew he wasn't to be trusted. The viscount went to the sideboard and grabbed a bottle and a glass. "Drink?"

The blue eyes fixed on Fitzalan. "Help yourself, James."

"Don't mind if I do. Sherry anyone? Diana? Miss Cage?" He shrugged when his sister shook her head. "Miss Willow?"

"Oh my, no, thank you. I never touch spirits in the afternoon." Olivia gave a mental roll of her eyes. For pity's sake, she sounded like somebody's aged aunt, the one nobody much liked.

"Well, I do." Fitzalan filled his glass. "Cheers."

"You should follow Miss Willow's example, James."

"No, Sebastian." Fitzalan settled his weight on one hip. "I don't think I ought."

"Suit yourself."

"You're enough to drive any man to drink."

"I did warn you, James." Another smile appeared and then vanished, incongruously young in that age-less face. "I have all the manners of a sailor."

She'd never seen anyone so thoroughly terrorize a room. Everything about the earl suggested experience of a life lived close to the edge and in full acceptance of any and all consequences. No telling what he might do.

Fitzalan cleared his throat. "Fine weather we're having, don't you agree? I'm sure in London it's nothing but ice and snow the color of ash."

The others stole surreptitious glances at Tiern-Cope. They probably didn't speak for fear they would suffer Olivia's fate and be smartly slapped down. Still, Olivia could not, in good faith, leave the viscount dangling. She cleared her throat and plunged into the fray. "For the time of year, the weather is fine indeed, my Lord."

"I wonder, Miss Willow, if we will have new snow." Fitzalan drank the rest of his sherry. "Do you think we shall have snow, Miss Cage?"

"I'm sure I don't know." Most brave of Miss Cage, Olivia thought, to speak at all.

The earl left his chair for the fireplace where he stood with his hands tucked into the small of his back. He studied Diana with what Olivia found an unsettling gleam of possession. Like a wolf stalking its prey, Olivia thought. Now there was another apt comparison. The man was a wolf playing at domesticity. He'd come into this room decided on Miss Royce for his bride. That he wasn't capable of self-doubt was plain. She wondered why he hadn't brought the vicar and married Diana on the spot. The notion of Mr. Verney hiding behind the door, ready to spring out Bible in hand brought a smile to her lips. The earl's attention shot to her. Just in time, she hoped, she smoothed her expression and let the smile drain of all but the pretense of emotion. His look left a wake of shivering anticipation that did not quickly dissipate. He was, after all, *the* Captain Alexander. Andrew's brave and daring younger brother.

"Miss Diana Royce," the earl said. "I trust you had a pleasant journey to Pennhyll."

Diana's fan waved a hurricane beneath her chin, and she giggled, which gave a measure of the earl's effect on everyone. Olivia watched him, gauging his reaction to the girlish sound, but she could divine nothing from his expression. "I must say, my Lord, that I despise nothing more than traveling, and, I daresay, the roads could do with some improvement."

"No doubt," he said.

"The country," she said, "is not at all like Town."

"Which do you prefer?"

"Oh, Town, of course. All the best people are in Town. There's ever so much to do there."

Tiern-Cope refused to smile, and poor Diana, breaker of countless hearts, wilted under that basilisk stare. None of the young ladies were in any way prepared for a man like he. The earl might have begun life as privileged as any nobleman, but he'd been a dozen years at sea, commanding the elements, not catering to feminine sensibilities.

This time Fitzalan leapt to fill the breach. "Now that Tiern-Cope is with us, we must think how we will entertain him."

"What else but a ball?" said Miss Cage. She brushed a hand over her curls and fluttered her eyelashes. A waste, a sad, sad waste, for the earl took no notice whatsoever of her effort. Nor Fitzalan either. A few of the young gentlemen added their approval of the idea. Brave souls. And what a pity they faded into the background, spaniel puppies in the presence of a full-grown wolf.

"A ball," Fitzalan said. "In celebration of your recovery, Sebastian."

"I am not in a condition for dancing. Not yet. Nor," he added, "would I be able to organize such an affair. Unless, of course, you wish to dance upon a ship. With a ship under my feet, nothing is impossible." He swept the room with that cold and barren gaze and settled on Diana with the same passion a man might have for assessing the state of a fence. "Until I have a suitable hostess to guide me, social niceties must continue to escape me."

"Miss Willow," said Fitzalan, desperate appeal in the loft of his eyebrows. "What is your opinion? Shall we have dancing?"

"Oh," Olivia said with a jaunty wave of her gloved hand that belied her twisting anxiety. "I think our young ladies and gentlemen here should be much amused by a dance. On ship or off. A winter ball would be just the thing."

"One thing I dislike more than a stupid woman,"

the earl said, "is an intelligent one pretending she is not."

No one quite knew what to make of the remark because he'd spoken to no one in particular, and was now a masthead of wooden silence.

"Come now," Fitzalan said. "We must have a dance."

"I do so adore dancing," said Diana.

With a flash of insight that shocked her, so deep and sure was her understanding, Olivia realized Tiern-Cope meant what he'd said when he deferred the suggestion of a ball. She knew herself how recovery from serious injury sapped one's strength and will. He was in no condition for dancing and ought not be downstairs at all. His wound pained him considerably. That he gave no overt sign of discomfort was proof of iron control, not intractable nature.

"Perhaps not right away," she said. "When Lord Tiern-Cope's had a chance to learn the country and, I am sure, love it as all Far Caisterians do."

"Splendid advice." Fitzalan clapped his hands. "Splendid. What would we do without your wise counsel, Miss Willow?"

"Muddle along, I'm quite sure," said Olivia.

"Well, Sebastian? What do you say? Will you make a liar of me? And disappoint all the lovely young ladies?"

"Very well," the earl said at last. But he did not look pleased. "When I am able."

"Give us a date, Sebastian."

"Six weeks." This brought a round of groans from the young ladies for whom a ball six weeks distant seemed a lifetime away.

"Why not St. Agnes' Eve?" said Miss Cage. "We

41

young ladies can fast in the hopes of dreaming of the gentleman we're to marry."

Diana sat straight. "What a marvelous idea."

"That is too soon," said the earl.

"Come, come, Sebastian," Fitzalan said. "That's nearly three weeks from now. Plenty of time for you to recover your strength." He glanced at the ladies. "Miss Cage has hit upon the very thing." His grin spread. "We unmarried gentlemen will fast as well. So as to dream of our future brides."

"Oh, we must," Diana said. "James, we must."

"There, you see, Sebastian?"

"I have another idea," said Diana. "Oh, James, it's a simply brilliant idea."

"Do tell."

"Is not Pennhyll reputedly haunted?"

"Yes." James's eyes sparkled. "By the Black Earl."

"Ghosts are a particular passion of mine. Tell me what you think." Diana clasped her hands. "A seance to call upon the spirit of the Black Earl."

Tiern-Cope whirled, eyes flashing with exasperation. "Miss Royce—"

Diana fluttered her brown eyes at the earl and then at, of all people, Olivia. "What do you say, Miss Willow? Isn't it the most magnificent idea you've ever heard?"

"An idea among ideas, Miss Royce."

"Splendid." The earl didn't smile, and his eyes stayed cold as January ice. "Have your ball, Miss Royce, but as to a seance—I will not participate in anything so rank with superstition." He walked toward Diana, then turned on his heel and returned to the fireplace. He didn't move like a man still recovering from a wound. His coattails hung about six inches above his knees in the back and each stride forward displayed a length of inner thigh and a flash of firm roundness above, long legs shaped by muscle. Nature had carved him inside and out, Olivia decided, honing him to one purpose: survival. Indeed, in watching him walk, her original and fanciful notion that he resembled a wolf seemed fitter than ever.

"We'll summon the Black Earl. I'm sure of it." Diana's eyes flashed.

"Bilgewater."

"My Lord," Olivia said. "It's all in fun."

He turned on her. "And just what do you know about the Black Earl?"

"According to legend," she said, "the Black Earl met his death sometime during the night between the twentieth and twenty-first of January. Quite possibly on St. Agnes' Eve. It's said that from dawn to dawn on the anniversary of his death, he meddles in the affairs of the living."

He fixed her with another of his implacable stares. "Do you believe that?"

"I'm sure I do. Why, half the people of Far Caister claim to have seen the Black Earl right before some misfortune befell them."

Diana sat up. "Have you seen him, Miss Willow? Oh, do tell us what he was like. Were you unbearably frightened?"

"I'm told that when an earl of Tiern-Cope sees the Black Earl, it means he is soon to be married."

Lord Fitzalan clapped the earl on the shoulder. "There you have it, Sebastian. Your doom awaits."

Diana leaned forward. "What did he do that was so awful anyway?"

"Yes," Fitzalan said. "Do tell us, Sebastian."

"I refuse to repeat such a monumentally thick-headed fabrication."

"Miss Willow," said Diana. "You will tell us, won't you? I simply must know."

"According to the story, he treated his wife abominably." Olivia did not look at Tiern-Cope, but she could feel his eyes on her. "Before they were married, he spread lies about her honor and prevented her from marrying a man who loved her deeply. He's also said to have locked her in the dungeon, but so few survived imprisonment at Pennhyll, I'm sure it's not so. At some point, so goes the tale, he saved her life, and then he forced her to marry him."

"Since you have nothing to say that is not ridiculous, Miss Willow, say nothing at all."

"A high price to pay, even for one's life, don't you think?" Olivia couldn't help this last comment as she suppressed a smug grin. Poor Miss Royce, she thought, poor, poor Miss Royce. She sent a prayer of thanks to whatever guardian angel had seen to it she was the spare instead of a candidate for countess.

Chapter Four

January 10

Sebastian's carriage drew up before the Crown's Ease, which, so he'd been told, was Far Caister's only inn. A sign hung over the street: a jester leaping through the center of a crown. The innkeeper, standing with one hand on his substantial waist, filled the doorway, watching with quiet eyes as Sebastian descended with McNaught behind him.

"Good afternoon, sir," Sebastian said. He took a breath and waited for the pain to recede. "How's your ale?"

The innkeeper moved out of the doorway, inviting them in with a sweep of his hand. "Good as any in Britain, my Lord."

"A pint then, of your best." Sebastian went inside, McNaught following.

A clean establishment, he noted. The better part of the ground floor was a tavern with, at this hour of the day, only a few patrons, some plainly travelers stopping for a bite to eat before continuing their journey, waited on by a young barmaid. He picked out the locals easily enough. Old men, mostly, enjoying drinks near the fire. There would, of course, be a cellar room for men who made their livings with their hands and backs. For them, rough benches and long tables and a wench who didn't object to supplementing her income in the horizontal. He sat by the window, hat on the table. McNaught made his way farther inside with express orders from Sebastian to find out exactly what the people of Far Caister thought of his brother and of Miss Olivia Willow.

Sebastian looked out the window. The inn, situated on a rise, overlooked part of Far Caister. Streets took the path of least resistance to geography, following no logical plan but convenience of construction. Buildings of dappled stone and neatly maintained roofs of thatch or slate sported doors painted in bright colors, blues and reds or greens. Charming and rustic, but hardly appealing to a man like Andrew.

"Be snowing soon," the innkeeper said, placing a mug before him.

"I haven't seen snow since I joined the Navy." He lifted his ale. "To His Majesty King George III."

"His Majesty. And to your health, my Lord."

"And yours, Mr. . . . ?"

"Twilling. Titus Twilling, my Lord."

"Your health, Mr. Twilling."

"What do they do for winter if there's no snow?"

"Hurricanes, monsoons and rain." Sebastian sipped his pint again because he knew Twilling wanted his opinion. "Excellent." And it was. Warm and rich, with just a hint of bite at the end. "Local brew?" A boy, fifteen or sixteen, strode into the inn, arms swinging. He stopped short and snatched a cap from a head of jet hair.

"Far Caister's best." The innkeeper caught sight of the boy. "Mickey. Come here, son." He put an arm around the boy's shoulder. "My eldest, my Lord. Michael F. Twilling."

Sebastian nodded. "Pleased to make your acquaintance, Master Twilling."

The boy clutched his cap to his chest and bowed. "My Lord." His feet looked too big for his body, his legs too long, arms and elbows awkward. He wouldn't want to be that age again for all the gold in Christendom.

Twilling chucked his son under the chin and got a narrow-eyed look in return. "He's a right smart, boy. Our own Miss Willow told me so herself."

"Did she?"

"Been teaching Mickey his letters and numbers." Plainly, Twilling was proud of the boy and in high awe of Miss Willow. "And the other children of Far

Caister, too. He's a head for figures, Mickey does. Miss Willow borrowed books from Pennhyll for him, she thought he had that much promise. Now he helps me with the accounts. Able, lad. Right able. High spirits, he has, but a good boy."

Mickey squeezed his cap. "Is that your hound outside, my Lord?" He was well-spoken, without much of the local accent.

"Yes."

"He's fine, my Lord. Fine."

"Thank you."

"Do you hunt with him?"

"Not yet." Sebastian considered the boy and tried to remember if he'd ever been so raw in his life. "Do you mind, Mr. Twilling, if I have a word with young Master Twilling? A moment only, and then he may go about his duties."

The innkeeper nodded. "Mind your manners, Mickey F."

"Aye, sir." He turned to Sebastian. "My Lord?"

"Sit down, if you like." The boy shook his head. "Miss Willow taught you your letters and numbers."

"She did, my Lord." Mickey pressed his cap to his heart, his cheeks flushed from something more than cold. Adoration, Sebastian thought. Well, he was at that age, after all, when women fascinated and enthralled and utterly awed. He did remember that. The shaky, thrilling, bumbling first encounter. A pretty woman like Miss Willow, with her grace and manner would seem a goddess to a boy like Mickey, the subject of fevered male fantasy. "And others of us from Far Caister, too."

"I hope you study diligently."

"Aye, my Lord."

"Did you often see her with my brother?"

"No, sir."

"He never visited during your lessons?"

"Once, sir."

"Then you did see her with him."

"But he came with the vicar, Mr. Verney. And left alone, my Lord."

He made an effort to soften his voice. "Do you think Miss Willow was fond of him?"

"We all thought she would marry him, my Lord." His eyes flashed. "And that he wanted to marry her."

"How could that be when he was already married?"

Mickey squeezed the life out of his cap. "He wasn't then. It was after Miss Willow was hurt he up and married Miss Alice. Mrs. Verney, now, of course."

He hoped he gave no sign of his momentary confusion. "Miss Willow and Mr. Verney courted?" He curled his palms around his mug. *Never loved and never in love*, she had said. And here a broken romance. Broken why? On account of Andrew? Or something else? "They did not marry, though. What happened?"

Mickey shrugged.

"Had Mrs. Verney a better fortune?"

"Miss Alice? Not much, sir."

"Then why do you suppose? You may be frank with me."

The boy's eyes narrowed. He squeezed his cap, chewing on his lower lip. "He was afraid she'd be crippled like her mother, that's what I think."

"Ah." He wondered if Mickey was right. Had the good vicar of Far Caister thrown her over when it seemed she might not fully recover her health? Craven if true.

The boy returned Sebastian's solemn gaze. "When I heard what happened at Pennhyll that night, that she might die, I prayed for her." He straightened. "I prayed for her, my Lord, and she didn't die. And she wasn't crippled like her mother, either."

"What do people say about that night?"

Mickey shook his head. " 'Twas a terrible thing, my Lord. Some say the Black Earl did it."

"What do you think?"

He shrugged. "No one from Far Caister could have done it, that's sure."

"Does Miss Willow still teach you?"

"We're on holiday while she's at Pennhyll. Did you really capture twenty pirate ships?"

"Twenty at once?"

"Aye, sir. And sail them all against the Spanish."

"There were five. We sank one and lost another to fire. I got men on the others once we had them in hand and sailed to Tortuga where we settled a disagreement with a few Spaniards."

"But they were pirate ships?"

"They were."

"I wish I'd been there to see it."

"How often does Miss Willow hire a horse from you?"

The boy lifted one shoulder, wary now, seeing danger before him, which piqued Sebastian's interest. Twilling was right. Mickey was a bright boy. "Once in a while."

"Regularly?"

"No, sir. Just sometimes."

"Where does she go?"

"I don't know, my Lord."

"How long is she gone?"

"She always comes back the same day." He clutched his hat by the rim, turning it in a circle.

"When did she last hire a horse?"

"T'other day."

"When, exactly?"

"Wednesday, my Lord."

"And you've no idea what she does nor whom she visits?"

"No, sir. It's her own business when she rides out, sir."

"Indeed, that is so." Sebastian took a crown from his pocket and gave it to him. "Thank you. Good day to you, Master Twilling."

"Miss Willow is a good teacher. She's kind. And a lady." The boy placed the coin on the table. "I'll never say otherwise."

"Nevertheless, thank you for your candor." Miss Willow, it seemed, possessed a talent for inspiring strong emotion in men of all ages. "May I trouble you to fetch my valet for me? You'll find him downstairs, I believe." He pushed the coin toward the edge of the table. "For your trouble."

Mickey bowed. "My Lord." He left the coin on the table.

The innkeeper reappeared after his son left. Sebastian, with a contented sigh, for the ale was excellent, pushed his empty pint across the table. "I thank you, Mr. Twilling. You have a fine establishment."

"Honored to serve you, my Lord."

When McNaught appeared from the back of the tavern, Sebastian rose. Inside the carriage, with the curtains drawn, McNaught patted his belly and said, "A charming village."

"What did you learn?"

"Your brother was well-liked."

"Mm."

"They're in high awe of you. Fighting off pirates at every turn, making men tell all their secrets with nothing but one look from eyes like daggers."

Sebastian snorted. "What of Miss Olivia Willow?"

"She is much admired." McNaught ticked off his findings, listing little Sebastian had not himself learned or surmised.

"Yes," he said when McNaught concluded with the story of Miss Willow's broken engagement. "The good vicar of Far Caister who could have married Miss Willow and did not." He frowned. "See that Mr. Verney and his wife are invited to Pennhyll this afternoon."

"My Lord."

With a sigh, he tried to ease his position, but there was no comfortable way to sit. "I cannot imagine Andrew giving up London for Far Caister." His ribs ached with a fierce heat. "Unless, of course, there was a woman involved."

"You need rest, my Lord."

"No, I don't."

"I'll prepare a tonic as soon as we're home."

"Splendid." But he didn't smile when he said it.

Later that afternoon, Sebastian waved off another offer of bread and butter from Diana. The taste of McNaught's potion lingered. The vicar and his very young wife made an interesting pair. Mr. Verney must have been nearing forty, a bit round about the middle, his hair thinning. But he had a ready smile and intelligent eyes. Clearly, he held his wife in great affection. And why not, when Mrs. Verney was a pretty woman with blond ringlets and brown eyes who adored her husband? She was not, however, Miss Willow's equal in manner or deportment, that he must allow. Mrs. Verney lacked something when compared to Olivia Willow. Grace, he thought. Intelligence. Wit. Quality, and all that one meant by the word.

"Shall we walk in the gallery?" Sebastian asked. James could be counted on to entertain Miss Willow while he cornered the vicar, and Diana and Mrs. Verney seemed to have hit well together. At first opportunity, Sebastian stepped next to Mr. Verney and said, "May I ask you about my brother?"

"A fine man," Verney said. "I was proud to know him." The clergyman's spirit might be in the heavens, but the rest of him stood on terra firma. A match between Miss Willow and the vicar was not as far-fetched as he'd originally thought. Verney had to know Miss Willow was superior in every way that mattered. So why had he settled for less? Perhaps Mickey was wrong and the choice had not been his. He slowed, Verney alongside him, until the others were several feet ahead. "Andrew and I wrote each other, of course, but I've been at sea all these years. It was a shock to learn of his death, coming so soon after our father. To say nothing of the manner in which he died."

"Of course, of course."

"I feel I didn't know him at all."

"How may I help you, my Lord?" He smiled in an encouraging manner. "Spiritual guidance? Or something else? Surely not guilt over his passing?"

He paused before a gold-framed saint. He knew enough about art to recognize a Giotto when he saw one. Why would any man lucky enough to engage Miss Willow's affections not do whatever it took to keep them? She would have been an admirable wife for a man of Verney's station in life. In fact, he strongly suspected she would have been a far better match than Verney would otherwise have hoped to make. Mrs. Verney was proof of that. Why her when he might have had Miss Willow? He wondered which of them broke it off. With a glance at Verney, he said, "What was he like? What sort of man had he become?"

"One we all admired."

"I understand he took an interest your school."

Verney's eyebrows lifted. "He did. I approached him about subscribing the school, helping us find a location other than Miss Willow's parlor, contributing to expenses and the like, and engaging Miss Willow as our permanent instructress. He not only agreed, he condescended to observe a class. I can tell you, the children and Miss Willow made us proud that day."

"You worked closely with her on the endeavor." Hands clasped behind his back, he strolled, the clergyman at his side. Had Verney ever kissed Miss Willow? Had he known the feel of her mouth or the texture of her skin? Bastard if he had and then jilted her. Fool if he had.

"Once the subscription committee agreed on the particulars, indeed, I did." He sighed. "Our grand plans came to naught after your brother passed on. But Miss Willow continues to teach the children when she can." Sebastian could see what was coming a mile off. He waited while Verney, with a grin, said, "With your help, we might revive the idea of a permanent school. And do a good turn by Miss Willow, who surely deserves a steadier income than she now has for her efforts."

"Yes." Sebastian remembered to smile. "A school

seems a worthy cause. I'm sure whatever my brother approved is more than satisfactory."

"You won't regret your generosity." His eyes twinkled. "I'll inform the committee straight away. What a celebration we shall have. A happy day for us all. Ah, but you asked to speak about your brother, not be dunned for every charity in the parish. What else may I tell you?"

"To be honest, what you've told me so far, sir, does not sound like the brother I knew. He was a man of many parts, but I cannot imagine him taking an interest in your school." He slowed because his body protested the distance of their walk. "My father despaired of him."

Verney stared down the gallery. "When he came to Pennhyll, he was quite a different man from what he became later on. There was a deal of talk about his wild ways. Heavens, yes, that's quite so."

"You will not offend me with the truth." Jesus, he hated this weakness of his. He stopped, letting his throbbing muscles rest and his heartbeat slow.

"A good many women."

"That's familiar." Sebastian pulled himself straighter yet in the hopes of easing the pain in his side, but everything cramped or throbbed or just plain hurt. Ahead of him, James put an arm around Miss Willow's waist.

"He changed. Completely. Why, he even started coming to Sunday services, and the women— That stopped entirely. Not so much as a whisper. Your brother stayed at Pennhyll, and if he gave parties, it wasn't for his friends from London. He invited the local gentry."

"If that's so, then Andrew indeed changed."

"Yes."

"What of his countess, Mr. Verney?"

He drew a breath. "Lady Tiern-Cope was not suited to life in the country."

"Meaning?"

"After a time, your brother—" Verney grimaced. "How shall I say this? He became suspicious of his wife."

"With reason?" Sebastian sat on an upholstered bench nestled between a Fra Angelico and a pietà by an artist he did not recognize.

The clergyman pressed his lips together. "There was some unpleasantness." He lifted his hands. "Gossip, my Lord."

"When did the gossip begin?"

"I can't give a precise date, really."

Sebastian raised one eyebrow.

"I'd say a year and a half before the tragedy of their death. Yes, I'd say that's so."

He kept his face still and cast out a lure just to see what might come back on the hook. "I have reason to believe, Mr. Verney, that at the time of his death Andrew had a liaison." From the corner of his eye, he saw James with his arm still around Miss Willow's waist, leaning to whisper something to her.

"My heavens." Verney sank onto the bench next to Sebastian. "This is a surprise. I cannot imagine who, my Lord. Indeed, I cannot."

He studied Verney. "Two years ago Miss Willow returned to Far Caister."

Verney flashed the color of a beet. "Oh, that is quite impossible. Absolutely not." He threw an arm into the air to punctuate his words. "Your brother may once have earned a certain reputation, but I repeat, he reformed. To suggest that Miss Willow could be enticed to— It doesn't bear thinking. You mistake her, my Lord." His voice shook with passion. "Oh, gravely, indeed. That poor girl nearly died."

Verney collapsed forward, elbows on his knees, covering his face with his hands. His shoulders heaved once, and then stilled. When he lifted his head, his expression was utter misery. "Nearly two days without waking and then fever. We expected she would die any moment. Thank the heavens, she did not. Dr. Richards said even if she lived she might not regain her full faculties. And for a time, so it seemed. My God, but I never saw a woman so altered. Miss Willow was full of life and spirit and to see her like that—at death's door. My heart broke. Praise God she recovered."

The others were far enough ahead they hadn't heard the outburst. He didn't sound like a man with reason to jilt his intended bride. He sounded more like a man still in love. "If I am forced to ask unpleasant questions, sir, it is because the inquest was a whitewash. Whoever killed my brother and his wife walks free because the woman who could answer my questions recalls nothing. Nothing at all."

"For which one may say God is indeed merciful."

He leaned against the wall, stretching out one leg. "Mr. Verney, what do you know of that night?"

Verney opened his mouth, then closed it. "The earl and countess gave a party, as I am sure you know. Miss Willow came. Keep in mind, I was not a witness. I did not attend as I was feeling poorly. Would I had not stayed home."

"Had you already broken with Miss Willow?"

Verney turned white. "You are well informed, my

Lord. However, I must answer that before that day, the thought never entered my mind. Indeed, I had decided to marry her. We'd worked closely on the school, and I had every reason to admire and respect her character and her spirit. My affection for her was firm and resolute. If I'd gone to the party, perhaps what happened might have been prevented." His voice went low. "We might now be married."

"What prevented you?"

Verney touched his head, scrubbing his hands through the wisps of his hair. "She insisted upon releasing me from my promise." He let out a breath. "A vicar's wife must be untouched by stain of scandal. So she told me."

"You married almost immediately."

"In my shock, I turned to Alice, my wife, for comfort and found my life's companion."

"How fortunate."

"God works in mysterious ways."

He studied the vicar and rose. "I'm told there is another Giotto farther down the gallery." He gestured. "Shall we?" His dissatisfaction never settled, never assumed any comfort among the other bits and pieces whirling about in his head. He did not feel he'd had the full truth from Verney. He wondered if, when the time came, he would have even half as much of the truth from Miss Willow.

Some time after the Verneys departed, Sebastian retreated to his room where he swallowed another sulfurous potion without complaint and endured McNaught's lecture on the dangers of overexertion. "I'm sending for Dr. Fansher," McNaught said while he rerolled the fabric for his bandages. "You need someone to put the fear of death into you."

Sebastian flexed his arm and paid for the movement in a blossom of pain along his ribs. "Very well." His wound felt hot. "Call Fansher."

"Rest, my Lord. You must not tax yourself."

He lay on his bed, legs sprawled while he stared at the canopy overhead. Though he appeared to be doing nothing, his first lieutenant would have known just how deceiving was that appearance. Sebastian focused his thoughts, separating what he knew from what he suspected and both of those things from what he hoped was true.

Andrew's wife, flighty and self-centered, unhappy in the country and, it seemed, in the marriage. Enough to seek comfort in another man's arms? Andrew would never tolerate such a situation. As for Andrew himself, did a womanizer ever reform? Quite likely, Andrew did have a lover. And he must at least consider the possibility that his mistress had been the desirable Miss Willow. She had James dancing on a short leash. Why not Andrew as well? God knows she had a mortifying ability to remind him how much he enjoyed sexual relations and, worse, put him in a way of wondering whether Andrew had enjoyed her in that same fashion. On the heels of that improper thought, he wondered for himself what she would be like as a lover. Eyes like molten honey, luscious copper hair and a smile that made a man happy just for seeing it. Jesus, what a pleasure that would be. That his brother might have been enthralled by Miss Willow wasn't at all farfetched.

He drew a long breath and let the world settle around him. Any tendency to overlook or excuse the truth must be ruthlessly suppressed or he might find himself dancing at the end of Miss Willow's leash, too.

And, he might never know who killed his brother. Nothing had been stolen, not jewelry from the two women nor Andrew's sapphire ring, which Sebastian now wore on his own finger. Why would a robber find his way to a salon when he could have gone to the butler's pantry for the silver? To his mind, the killings had all the hallmarks of passionate motive. He thought it quite likely the murderer had been a lover of one of the three. The delicate Miss Olivia Willow, with her additional injuries, was surely the likeliest candidate.

If he proved the worst, he *would* see her brought to account. He would.

Chapter Five

January 15

"My Lord." Price cleared his throat. "Mr. McNaught wishes to know if you require a change of raiment for your excursion to Far Caister."

Sebastian looked at Price from over the top of one of the letters from the morning's post. "Who is Mrs. Edward Leveret?" he asked.

"I believe, among other things, Mrs. Leveret heads the committee for the establishment of a school for Far Caister's less fortunate children, my Lord."

He scanned the page again. His brother's papers tilted in a precarious stack before him, threatening to fall at any moment. "What do you know about Miss Olivia Willow being a teacher?"

"Miss Willow's name has been put forward for the post of instructress, as it is a task she has previously performed with some success, my Lord."

"And?" He watched Price's face for signs of an opinion contrary to what he'd already heard but saw only his usual doleful expression.

"Most consider her a worthy candidate, my Lord."

"Do you agree I should approve of her in such a capacity?"

"I would not presume, my Lord."

"She wants money, of course, Mrs. Leveret, but as well she wants the right to tell families that Tiern-Cope has personally recommended their teacher."

"Most assuredly, my Lord."

His position gave him some responsibility to families like that and to women like Mrs. Leveret. James all but had Miss Willow in his bed. Like as not, she'd be his mistress before the week was out. If it weren't for James's priority of interest, more than likely he'd be considering much the same arrangement himself. She was a thoroughly bedable woman. His duty in the matter seemed clear enough. He reached for his pen and scrawled a reply at the bottom of Mrs. Leveret's note.

Madam:
    I cannot recommend her to you.
Captain Sebastian Alexander

As an afterthought, he added, "Tiern-Cope" beneath his signature. He refolded the note and handed it to Price. "Deliver this."

Price took the letter. "Your excursion, my Lord?"

He put away his pen. "I'll be there directly."

"My Lord."

Half an hour later, Sebastian stood with one foot on the bottom edge of the open carriage doorway, his forearm crossed over his thigh. Mrs. Leveret's letter and his reply to it were absent from his thoughts. One of the drays stamped, iron-shod hooves ringing on the cobbles of the inner courtyard. Both animals were the color of flax. In the whole of the stables there wasn't an inferior animal to be found. He tugged at his cravat and gave James a sideways glance. "I do not play the lover well."

"Best learn." James's head whipped toward the door, but it was a false alarm. A footman hurried toward them carrying an armload of blankets. Miss Royce wished to shop, and, as Sebastian had already seen, what Miss Royce wanted, Miss Royce got, generally with little more than a smile in payment, but with a frown across that pretty brow if necessary.

If one believed appearances, Miss Willow had, during her time at Pennhyll, become Diana's dearest friend. Sebastian, cynic that he was, could not help the unworthy thought that Diana's friendship with the spinster had more to do with the advantage she gained by comparison than on account of any similarity in their characters. Certainly, their looks could not have been more dissimilar and as for their characters, well, he could not imagine that Miss Willow had anything in common with a spoiled beauty like Diana Royce. Olivia Willow possessed a fine mind, however she pretended otherwise.

James stooped to pick up a handful of pebbles. "God knows Diana's vain enough for a dozen women, Sebastian, but she needs some encouragement." He tossed a pebble. It skipped over the cobblestone courtyard and hit the rampart wall.

"I intend to marry her, which she well knows if you've done your part. Isn't that enough?"

"For me, yes. But she finds you neglectful. Compliment her. Really, Sebastian. You must play the game."

"Has it gotten you anywhere with Miss Willow?" Considering what he'd seen already, perhaps it had. She liked to withdraw when people called at Pennhyll, but James never let her alone for long. Beside him, James frowned and threw another pebble. So. "No success yet."

"Since I do not intend to marry her, the dance is more intricate. Besides, the woman insists on her principles."

"Perhaps she believes in them." Then again, the harder a man worked for his prize, the higher the perceived value, and he did not doubt Miss Willow knew that quite well. Every girl who'd been to her first ball knew that much about men.

"Fear not, Sebastian. I aim to bury those principles."

"Mm."

"See if I don't. As for Diana, you have no principles to overcome. You're going to marry her, for Christ's sake." He tossed another pebble. "Tell her you adore her eyes and that her lips remind you of—" The door opened again. Diana appeared, wrapped in an ermine cloak and muff. Miss Willow descended the stairs just behind her. James's gaze was riveted. "My God, just look at her."

"Your sister is beautiful. And she's well aware of it."

"Not her. Miss Willow. I'm randy every time I see

that hair. I want my hands full of those curls and her full of me." He made a low noise, and Sebastian added his silent agreement to the sentiment. "I do fancy her maidenhead, Sebastian, I truly do."

The idea that Miss Willow retained her virtue startled him. "What makes you think she has one?"

"Of course she has. A young lady can't lose her handkerchief without all of Far Caister hearing of it. Believe me, if she'd lost her virginity, everyone would know." Sebastian frowned, for there was a deal of sense in that. James waved at the door. "Diana, at last. And Miss Willow." To Sebastian, he said, "I've the luck of the devil today, old man. That cloak is hardly thick enough to keep an infant warm on a day such as this. I'll soon gallantly have my arm around her to keep her warm." Grinning like a boy in possession of a new top, he turned to Sebastian. "Out, damn principles."

Like Fitzalan, now the waiting was over, Sebastian stood at attention as the two women came down the last stairs. "No doubt her Cumbrian nativity enures her to the cold."

"If I should manage to contrive, my dear Captain, to separate from you whilst we tour the village, pray do not wait for us. No matter how badly we are missed. Diana will survive an hour or two or three without Miss Willow's charming company. And you, Sebastian, might use the time to practice your charms on my sister. Why, you might even try proposing. She won't say no."

"If you have your way, James, Miss Willow will find her life and reputation irretrievably altered after you are gone from Pennhyll."

"I want her," he said in a low voice. "I will have

63

her. No matter what." Sebastian raised his eyebrows at that, and James made a face. "Don't even think it." He gave a mock shudder. "I'm not that far gone."

"Are you certain?"

"Sebastian. I can't marry her. She's been a governess. She has nothing. Has been nothing since her father died."

"Then leave her be."

"I'll be discreet, if that's what you're worried about. And, I'll find us another chaperone once I've got her tucked away someplace convenient."

"I'd prefer the parish not be burdened with Fitzalan by-blows."

James shrugged. "I'll support it. Hell, if I have a dozen on her, I'll support them all. Does that ease your mind?"

"Jesus."

He held up a hand. "Peace, Sebastian. Peace. I'm a gentleman, and one way or another, a gentleman pays for his pleasures. With Miss Willow, I find myself inclined to more than my usual generosity. I promise you, if she finds her life altered, it can only be for the better."

"Without a husband?" Why, in the name of God, was he so concerned about her fate? If Miss Willow let James talk her onto a mattress, what concern was that of his?

James adjusted his waistcoat. "Attend, Sebastian. I'll show you how to properly woo a female."

The women reached the carriage. Fitzalan kissed Diana's cheek and gave his hand to Miss Willow. "Miracle worker, Miss Willow."

"How so?" Only polite interest, Sebastian noted, frowning again because, damn it all, the pieces did not fit together. Olivia Willow was not what James hoped; the sort of woman who could be seduced out of her good sense. She was as far from being a flirt as Diana was near to being one. In fact, if not for her unfortunate history, he'd have put her in a class with the other young ladies of Far Caister.

James continued to hold Miss Willow's hand. "I expected another hour's wait at least before Diana presented herself, and here she is, a vision in white."

"Thank you, James."

Diana smiled at Sebastian, and all he could think while he looked at her was she was hardly out of the schoolroom and couldn't possibly understand anything about a man who'd sailed to hell and back. A bride to be pampered and cherished. A treasure to display. All a gentleman desired in his wife. Trouble was, he could not imagine making love to Diana. The thought left him cold.

James cleared his throat. Loudly.

"Fur becomes you, Miss Royce," he said. That earned him a grin from James, a tutor proud of his pupil. What nonsense this was. Diana knew very well how she looked. Why did he need to tell her? Since Miss Willow showed no sign of expecting a compliment from him, and, indeed, could not think he would make her one, he said nothing to her, which appeared to suit them both just fine.

In the carriage, Diana settled against the seat, her hair shining dark against a field of ermine. James eyed his sister, then turned to Sebastian and mouthed the words *compliment her*. But at just that moment, the groom lifted the stairs and closed the door and the delicate combination of opportunity

65

and motivation vanished. Sebastian heard the snap of reins. "Walk on."

Diana touched her curls then turned so her back was to Miss Willow. "Do fix this for me. My hair shall be wretched in five minutes, I'm sure." Miss Willow obligingly did something with hairpins with the result that, at the conclusion of the procedure, Miss Royce looked no different than she had before.

Light flashed over Miss Willow's hair. There must be fifty colors of red, all of them some variation of copper fire. When she finished examining Diana's hairpins, she put a hand to her mouth to hide a yawn.

"I hardly slept a wink myself last night." James surveyed the women. "I wonder if the same thing kept us awake, Miss Willow."

She smiled pleasantly enough, but managed to convey displeasure. "I doubt that, sir."

"I fell asleep the moment my eyes closed," Diana said. "What kept you awake, James?"

"A ghost, dear sister."

"Oh," she breathed. "Never say so. Truly?"

Sebastian looked away since derision was liable to be fatal to an offer of marriage. Ghosts, indeed. Diana, he was coming to realize, was not about to give up her ridiculous idea of a seance to summon the Black Earl.

Diana buried her hands deeper in her muff and leaned toward her brother and him. "In London, Mama and I attended a seance. Don't laugh, James. We did, and it was most astonishing. The spirits predicted I would be married before the new year is out, and that I should come to the country to find my husband. They did. They moaned and pounded on the walls, and Lady Fields swooned when they said her late husband wanted her to invest in the three percents. Is that what kept you awake, James? Miss Willow? Oh, do tell."

Miss Willow shook her head. "Much to my regret, I've never seen a ghost. Nor heard one either."

James's eyes twinkled. "Oh, now don't spoil the fun, Miss Willow. As for me, 'twas the Black Earl himself I heard. Who else could it have been rattling his chains and moaning outside my door half the night?"

"Angry, perhaps, for not investing in the five percents before he died," Miss Willow said.

"Pish." Diana made a face and sank against the seat. "You're such a liar, James. I don't know why I listen to anything you say."

"Diana, I am wounded to the quick."

"If you really saw the Black Earl, what was he like?"

"Quite the hair-raising experience, I confess. I can hardly bring myself to describe the horror."

"The truth, James, have you really? Miss Willow, make him tell the truth. Besides, I thought the Black Earl only appeared on the anniversary of his death. Did you not say so, Miss Willow?"

James grinned. "I didn't say I saw him. I said I heard him. Though an Alexander might see him at any time. Tell us, Sebastian, when you saw the Black Earl did he rattle chains and howl at his fate?"

"You saw the Black Earl?" Diana put a hand to her heart.

"Your brother, Miss Royce," Sebastian said, "heard nothing but the wind and the timbers settling." What kind of mother would she be, filling her children's heads with superstitious nonsense? Hell. He might end up with a nursery full of vain, idiot offspring. Miss Willow yawned again, but he suspected she hid amusement behind that forgery of a yawn.

James sighed. "What a pity you have so little imagination, Tiern-Cope."

The carriage stopped, signaling the end of the drive to Far Caister and, more specifically, their arrival at the Crown's Ease. Villagers stopped to gape, and shopkeepers appeared in doorways to watch. The coachman's chest swelled to bursting and the grooms, too, made a show of their duties, snapping down the steps, holding harnesses, shouting instructions to the ostler.

James took in the hubbub with an amused and more tolerant smile than Sebastian. A murmur rose. Diana, wrapped in ermine, flashed an ankle as she stepped down, reaching for Sebastian's hand. Her gown, peeking from the cloud of ermine surrounding her, proved a confection of green-and-yellow silk gauze that made a striking contrast with her glossy hair. Diana took the adoration in stride, indeed, as her due. She was a beauty, no doubt of that. So, why did she leave him without the slightest stirring of passion? What if he couldn't bring himself to kiss her? Certainly, he could. Of course he could. Whether he wanted to was another matter entirely.

Miss Willow came down next. She, Sebastian noted, made nothing like the impression Diana had. Her shopworn gown of white muslin was so precisely like the one she'd worn yesterday as to be, in fact, the very same. With the exception of that copper-on-fire hair, she was quite ordinary. Well, in all honesty, not ordinary. No one with hair that color could be called ordinary, and he had to allow she was pretty, and without the aid of fashion. Several in the crowd tipped a hat or bent a quick knee, not the least in awe of her.

Though respectful, they gave gap-toothed, gnarled grins. A few lifted a hand in greeting. The manner in which the villagers greeted her bothered him. Miss Willow would not command this sort of affectionate respect if her name had been inappropriately linked to Andrew or to any other man.

The thought gave him pause. If James was right about anything, it was that privacy did not exist in Far Caister. An illicit relationship between her and his brother could not have been kept quiet. She was an old maid, nearing twenty-five, for God's sake, who lived with her ailing mother. Andrew could not possibly have called on her without remark. The servants would know if he'd entertained her at Pennhyll, and it seemed the height of unlikelihood they had managed to conduct an affair at some other location. While he didn't doubt Andrew's expertise in trysting, he did doubt his brother possessed the discipline for a prolonged and secret affair with the village spinster. He had a sudden and rather unpleasant recollection of his reply to Mrs. Leveret's inquiry. Sebastian's belly hollowed out. Had he been hasty and done Miss Willow an unpardonable disservice? He caught a glimpse of James staring at her with frank and open lust and decided he'd only anticipated the event.

"How fortunate you are, my Lord," Diana said, "to live near so quaint a town as this." Onlookers nodded, finding favor in the remark. Sebastian felt an undeniable shock to hear evidence that the villagers took as much or even more interest in his future wife than did he. Whatever he did for himself, he owed Far Caister a wise choice. If beauty and position were the criteria then Diana must be his countess.

James offered Miss Willow his elbow, which she

accepted with the sort of smile an elderly aunt saved for a favored nephew. If she had any chastity to keep, it would be despite James's best efforts. The man was beside himself with longing and prepared for extravagance. No woman in her position could remain proof against James's determination.

Miss Willow acted as their guide to Far Caister, stopping, of course, at every shop that caught Diana's eye. Sebastian found himself toting up receipts for her purchases, beginning with a chapeau Diana swore was naval in its inspiration. He was obliged to suppress the opinion that he'd never allow such a contraption aboard any ship of his. Besides the hat, he doled out money for ribbons, lace, gloves and chocolate. James failed to coax Miss Willow into making any selection for herself or accepting what he purchased, with the sole exception of a single praline. Which she promptly gave to one of the children drooling at the window. Boys in fustian and homespun woolens followed as they walked past a cobbler's. Fitzalan dug into a pocket and threw out a handful of coins. One boy caught a shilling and displayed it triumphantly. His eyes sparkled as he cupped his hands around his mouth.

"Oi! Miss Olivia. Seen the Black Earl, yet?"

She stopped, standing with hands folded and face quite serious. "Oh, indeed I have." Sebastian ended up standing behind her, tall enough to see over her head, and close enough to smell her hair and see the bare nape of her neck. Copper tendrils wound over her ears and trailed down the side of her throat. If he wanted to, he could touch her waist or caress that pale nape.

"Aye, Miss? For true?"

"Just last night he breathed upon the very sheets where I lay trying to sleep." The boys went wide-eyed, riveted by her encounter with the infamous spirit of Pennhyll Castle. "He waved a great sword in his hands, sharp enough to take my head in one fell strike. The blood froze in my veins, I was that sure he would murder me in my bed."

"But he didn't, Miss Olivia," said another boy, who must have been all of six or seven.

"My hair frightened him away."

The boys hooted with laughter, and Sebastian heard a snort of amusement from James. He wanted to smile himself, for that matter.

"No," said the first boy, frowning like he'd eaten a green apple. "The Black Earl wouldn't be afraid of you, Miss."

"I don't see why not." She touched her head. "I assure you, with this hair, I'm frightful, indeed."

"He's a ghost, Miss. He'd not be frightened by the color of your hair." He crossed his arms over his chest. "I reckon a ghost don't see color."

"We know what it means, don't we?" asked another. "When a woman sees the Black Earl." The boys nodded to each other.

"What does it mean?" Diana asked.

Jesus. Diana was as bad as those ragamuffin boys, worse because she ought to know better.

"Nonsense," said Miss Willow.

The eldest boy's eyes glazed with admiration when he looked at Diana. "Why, my Lady, when a woman sees the Black Earl, it means she's to marry the master, that's what."

James dissolved into laughter.

"You are bold as brass." A laughing Miss Willow

71

shook a finger at the lad. "As brass. Go on, all of you. Lord Fitzalan hasn't any more coins for you today."

"Did you really see the Black Earl?" Diana studied Olivia, waiting, it seemed, with baited breath. Sebastian, doing the same, saw James watching as well.

Miss Willow sighed, sounding for all the world like a governess whose patience has just been stretched past its limit. "Miss Royce, there's no such thing as ghosts." She put her hands on her hips, which brought the fabric of her cloak in tight. Small woman, she was, but curved where a man liked to hold on. Another salacious thought entered his head, which was what a damn shame it was for any woman to have a figure like hers and no man to enjoy it.

Diana's mouth turned down. "Then why did you say you'd seen the Black Earl?"

"Because they wanted me to," she said, rolling her eyes. "Boys live for such terror."

James laughed. "I'm sure they're disappointed the ghost didn't lop off your head."

"Undoubtedly, my Lord." She smiled, an enchanting, uninhibited grin. "Shall we visit the churchyard?" With a glance at the sky, she said, "We've time, I think, before it snows."

The church stood at the eastern edge of the village, built of the same dappled stone as the rest of Far Caister. A pointed arch over the door and a round stained-glass window above pronounced its ancient lineage. "Our church was built in 1072. It's a matter of some local pride that William the Conqueror attended services. Others insist King Arthur himself heard mass here. The earls of Tiern-Cope have a pew, and there's a lovely statue of the sixth earl and his wife. In the Black Earl's day, however, the family attended services in the chapel at Pennhyll."

She walked toward the churchyard and unlocked the gate. "Behind is the graveyard and though 'tis a sad place, the view is worth admiring, for beyond that one sees nothing but snow-covered fields and in the distance, Pennhyll. In the spring there's green that breaks your heart." She walked through the gate. "The church, as it happens, stands on the only ground not owned by the earls." A smile played around her mouth. "Just as we Far Caisterians cannot forget Who made us, neither can we forget to whom we must pay the rents."

"Don't be impertinent," Sebastian said as he passed her.

"Was I?" she murmured. "My apologies. My Lord."

Diana had her arm wrapped around his as they walked, too near his wound so that he must breathe quietly against the ache in his side. They'd kept a moderate pace so far, but he wasn't used to so much activity. He disengaged enough that Diana's hand didn't constantly brush his tender ribs. James and Miss Willow pulled ahead. With Diana clinging to him and waiting, he was sure, for conversation in the form of compliments leading to a declaration, he could think of little except he would be glad when he was married, if only to be done with this nonsense of romance and courting. He would marry, do his duty by his title and return to the sea, and Diana would adjust to his neglect. But whenever he tried to imagine his wedding night he couldn't think of anything to do with pleasure.

He faced her. "You have lovely eyes, Miss Royce." He despised himself for saying so and came close to despising Diana for her pleasure when every woman on earth had eyes in her head. One pair of eyes was much like any other. What a ridiculous business this was. He looked at Diana. A lovely girl, and that was the trouble. Diana was still a girl. "Miss Royce?"

"My Lord?" She seemed to be waiting for him to continue in a similar vein, but he could not utter even one more insipid word. Let the woman earn her compliments, by God. He thought about going down on one knee, but the snow made him think the better of that.

"Miss Royce." *Will you marry me?* Four simple words, stuck in his throat. She tilted her head. "Miss Royce. You are a lovely girl."

"Thank you." Her lips parted, and she smiled so that he almost thought he wasn't making a mistake.

"I think we'll get on. Don't you?"

"Oh, yes. You aren't half as strict as James is with me. He's constantly scolding me. You never do."

"Splendid."

She smiled. He ought to kiss her. What if he couldn't kiss her? Damned if he could do it. While the silence continued, the first flakes of snow fell to the ground. "Come, Miss Royce." He took her arm, using care to arrange her against his uninjured side. "Shall we return?"

"Yes, do let's." She glanced to where her brother and Miss Willow stood about fifty paces north of the churchyard gate, near a row of headstones darkening in the melting snowfall. Surprisingly, James had backed away, leaving the object of his lust alone. "James, do come along. Miss Willow." She waved to catch Olivia's attention. James left off staring at Miss Willow and walked to Diana. Miss Willow, however, remained before a gravestone less gray than most. After the serene brunette of Diana, that flame hair was a jarring sight.

"Miss Willow," Sebastian said. When she did not move, he took several steps toward her and called again with more than a flash of irritation. "Come along."

"Leave her be," James said.

"I don't mean to stand here in the snow whilst she dawdles and your sister catches her death."

She brushed the gathering snow from the top of the marker, and that was the last straw. He left James with his sister and closed the distance to her. Instead of feeling relieved that he and Diana had arrived at an understanding, he felt tense. "All the reflection in the world cannot bring back the occupant, no matter how poignant the epitaph or deeply felt your sympathy."

She traced the engraved letters on the stone. His eye followed. ROGER CATHCART WILLOW and TOBIAS KINGSLEY WILLOW. Her father and brother. "I miss them," she said, twisting a bit to look at him. Her eyes were an unusual color, pale brown, like honey raised to the sunlight. He had never, ever, seen a woman look like that, as if she'd lost everything that mattered. He understood the desolation far too well. "Sometimes," she said, "I wish I had died, too."

"That," he said, "is foolish."

"Who would have taken care of Mama?"

He held out a hand to help her back to the walk. His fingers tightened around her hand as she stepped over the now icy ground. He pulled too hard, because she ended up just inches from him, stumbling and then losing her balance. He caught her around the waist. Their eyes met.

His insides reacted like a ship teetering on an ocean

swell, poised for the wrenching drop to the trough. When she didn't look away, the thrill of descent ripped through him, pure and primal. Even if he could have, he didn't want to look anywhere but at her. Her eyes went right through him, grabbed his soul in both hands and shook it hard. Straight nose quite narrow at the bridge, a chin just short of pointed, round cheeks curved like satin over a woman's hips. Red hair thick with curls framed her face. A corkscrew tendril fell over her forehead. Extravagant hair. Unseemly in color and appearance. Jesus, but a man wanted to bury his fingers in that hair just to see if it would burn.

Whether she understood the reaction behind his scrutiny or for some other reason, her cheeks flushed pink. She looked away. "All these years, and I miss them still."

"Come," he said. "We'll be frozen if you don't come out of the weather." He turned and walked toward the gate without waiting to see if she followed. Diana drew her hood over her head when he reached her. She pointed to the walkway and waved.

"There are Miss Cage and her father. Miss Cage and I are planning the seance. You can't imagine how much we have to do before St. Agnes' Eve. Do let's go, my Lord. My coat and muff will be ruined, and James will refuse to buy me another one. He never lets me buy anything."

Miss Willow walked past, and James tried to take her arm, but she had her hands deep in the pockets of her cloak and appeared not to notice his attempted gallantry. She stopped at the gate, waiting for them. Sebastian wanted to laugh at James's disgruntlement. He had the look of a fellow turned down flat, he did.

Diana held out her arm to her brother. "Come along, James. Miss Cage and I are in the most dire need of your expertise. Planning a party is ever so much work." Her eyes sparkled. "I simply adore parties. Dear James, please. My boots will be ruined. Absolutely ruined, I'm sure."

James gave him a look and shrugged. Diana waved to Miss Cage again. "Miss Cage. Miss Cage. Have you got . . ."

He hoped Diana was enjoying herself, because his wife-to-be wasn't going to have many opportunities to plan parties after they were married. Diana and James, unaware for the moment that he and Miss Willow weren't right behind them, turned the corner for the safety of the walkway, and Sebastian found himself alone with Olivia Willow.

Chapter Six

He was alone with Olivia Willow exactly as James had hoped to find himself. Her eyes, fixed on him like pools of warm honey, lent an already pretty face deeper interest. When she didn't pretend to be unintelligent, her eyes fascinated. He wondered how she'd look with her hair spilling over a pillow and him staring into her face from just a few inches above. The image had a predictable result that made him glad for the length of his greatcoat as much as for the fact that he'd buttoned it against the cold.

Despite his private thoughts, at this precise moment, the mood was decidedly different from what

James had intended, and he meant to make well sure it stayed that way. Miss Willow's intentions were similar because she nodded before heading past him. She made a surprised sound when he grabbed her arm and halted her midstep. Though he was mainly in control of himself, he felt a spark of arousal the moment he touched her. With an irritating poise, she faced him.

Red hair tumbled down her forehead and along one side of her cheek. Curls twisted in the breeze and sparkled with flakes of snow. Her chin was level with his chest. She made him feel brutish, clumsy and outsized. Though a large man, he was none of those things and certainly able to make love to a small woman without injuring her.

"You are far too self-possessed," he told her. He forced his voice flat and dry as dust so there could be no question of his complete dispassion toward her.

She stared to one side, hiding her eyes from him. "A great fault, I am sure."

"It is." Damn her for agreeing with him. Damn her for having herself so firmly in hand that he wanted to shake her out of her control.

"My former employer," she said, staring now at his cravat, "Admiral Bunker, often said that the man who commands a ship of the line must be straightforward and brook no nonsense. That he must be quick to think and to say what is on his mind." She looked into his eyes. "You, sir, have all those qualities and more. I have nothing but admiration for your record of success. The *Achilles*, the *Resplendent*, the *Courageous*. You've served your country ably and made all who know you and know of you proud to be English." A light flickered behind her eyes and he, who had never cared to hear his praises sung, wanted more. He wanted to hear more of that admiration in her voice. "But I hope you will permit me to tell you that when a man finds himself in gentle society, among young ladies such as Miss Royce who have been brought up with immense delicacy and consideration, he must temper his words and his manner, however sorely it goes against his nature."

"If you mean to criticize, say it outright."

"You will not win Miss Royce's heart if you persist in such brutal honesty as you have just shown to me."

"I cannot afford to make a mistake about you."

"And you can about your future wife?"

"My future wife is no concern of yours." He used the dry voice again because she'd scored a hit with that last remark.

"You are correct, my Lord."

He let go of her, but he did not change the distance between them. Despite his desires and James's belief that Miss Willow would prove no better than she ought to be, Sebastian failed to see in her anything but what she appeared to be: a spinster of irreproachable reputation and declining fortune. She stood before him, gloved hands clasped as prim and proper as any gentlewoman of unremarkable past. There was not now any attempt to pretend less intelligence than she in truth possessed.

"Why did you come back to Far Caister?" he said.

"My mother is not well." He liked the sound of her voice. A deliberate tone, an alto that settled on the ears like velvet over a bed.

"Tell me what you recall of my brother's death." All that he needed was in her head: how and why his brother had died and the identity of the man responsible.

She swallowed, drawing her cloak tighter about her. "You understand, my Lord, that I have no recollection of that night or of the days immediately before and after?"

He nodded.

"Andrew and Guenevere were giving a fete, and I was invited. I know that's so because I found the invitation which I gave in evidence at the inquest, though I have no recollection of going to Pennhyll that day. My first memory afterward is of waking up there." She inclined her head toward the mountain, meaning, so Sebastian understood, Pennhyll.

"The last you recall?"

"Teaching. The day before. I teach the children of Far Caister. That day, I drilled the students on irregular verbs."

"After you woke up at Pennhyll, what then?"

"I asked what happened, but no one would tell me." Her eyes flickered with the recollection, turning a darker shade of honey. "I didn't understand why until Dr. Richards told me. That Andrew and Guenevere were dead."

Snowflakes glittered on one of her curls, and he brushed them away. "Dr. Richards gave evidence at the inquest. According to him, you were severely injured that night."

She nodded, the color draining from her cheeks.

"I understand the subject must be painful for you."

"You want to know." She leaned forward, an earnest note in her voice. "You deserve to know. My shoulder was broken. A cut, here." She touched the back of her head.

"And the gunshot." What sort of villain beat and shot a woman and left her for dead? A desperate man, a man under no restraint from conscience.

"Yes." Tipping her head to one side, she parted curls of copper hair just above her temple to display an indented, jagged scar about the length of his first finger. He'd seen enough wounds to know she'd been fortunate, indeed. She let her hair fall back into place.

"You recovered. But for your memory, of course."

"I have headaches, and my shoulder sometimes hurts." She astonished him by giving a brilliant smile. Full of light, like the one he'd admired when he first saw her. "Perhaps we might trade stories of injury and recovery. My scar itched terribly."

"What about your dreams?"

For a moment, she froze. Then, without, Sebastian thought, awareness of what she was doing, she rocked, clutching herself around the waist, a slight flex at the hips and then back. "I used to wake in the night."

"Used to."

"Yes."

"Why?"

"I can't remember why. I can never remember."

"Try, Miss Willow." He brushed more snowflakes from her hair.

"I want to. I truly do. I came to Pennhyll again because I thought being there might help me remember."

"Has it?"

"No. Not yet." She continued to sway. Her face was composed, but the air felt full and heavy, as if it would vaporize if compressed even one more inch.

"You're afraid, aren't you? Afraid of remembering."

Her eyes shot to his. "Mama complained I woke her." He tipped his head, silent encouragement. "I screamed. That's what Mama told me. That I woke her with my screaming. But I don't think I ever did."

"You remember the feeling." If he continued to press her, would she fall from the thin edge of her control?

"Yes."

"Tell me that, then." They stood close, and if he occasionally touched her shoulder or caressed her cheek, she took no notice.

"I wake up crying. My heart is pounding, my head hurts and sometimes—sometimes I cannot breathe. I feel I am being smothered and that if I do not get away, I will die." She lapsed into a silence he chose not to break. Eventually, she lifted her hands an inch or so apart.

"Did you do anything unusual in the days preceding?"

"Oh, no. My life is quite dull."

"Tell me about Andrew and his wife." Jesus, she was a pretty woman. Damn James for telling him of his designs on her, for now he could not help thinking of her in a passionate embrace. His passionate embrace. He did not think of Diana or of any other young lady in such a prurient fashion, but her, hell, yes. He wanted her so badly, it hurt. In his head, he removed her gown and unlaced her corset. The images came to him with such intensity he wondered she didn't see them herself. "Did anything seem out of the ordinary with them?"

Her eyebrows drew together. "No."

"But?"

She flushed. Not deeply, a pale pink. Naked. Twining her body around his, straining up to meet him.

"Miss Willow. Please. However difficult this must be for you, you must tell me all that you know or surmise."

Today, she was not wearing her coral necklace. No other piece of jewelry took its place. How easily he could imagine her bare neck exposed to his searching mouth. Indecent, really, that naked throat.

"Guenevere, though she possessed many fine qualities and in many ways I considered her my friend, in truth, she rarely saw the world except through her own eyes."

"You thought them unhappy."

"I admired your brother for his spirit and his joy in life, for his intellect and his unswerving love and admiration for you and your accomplishments."

"But?"

"Guenevere was very unhappy." She shivered and drew her cloak closer. Then she surprised the hell out of him. "You could help me. Help me remember."

"Miss Willow."

"You could." Her voice fell low and urgent. "Andrew never said so, but I guessed some of what you did in the war. You made people tell you things they did not wish to reveal."

"They were sailors and soldiers, men of war, not women of gentle birth."

"I want to know what happened to me. Sometimes I feel so close to knowing—to remembering everything." She put a hand just over her head, as if pushing against a barrier. "Here. It's all here. Only I can't see. I can't make myself remember."

Lord, she was pretty. And while the color of her hair was outrageous, he could not stop imagining his hands entangled in her curls. Or her body against his. Her breath hot against his skin. "You don't know what you're asking."

"I know I cannot bear not knowing. You could help me remember. I know you could."

"Jesus, you're serious, aren't you?"

"Yes."

"No matter what I've done in the name of my country, I've never, ever subjected a woman to that sort of questioning." Questioning that broke down barriers and made a man talk whether he wanted to or not. He glanced at the tops of his boots. "Astonishingly, I have some scruples left."

"My Lord." She startled him by grasping his hands. They felt small in his. Cold, too. "Please."

He refused absolutely to return her tremulous smile.

"You don't know what it's like," she said. "Living with a hole in your life. You want to know, too. Don't deny it. Whoever killed Andrew and Guenevere is free because his identity is trapped in my head."

His body coiled with anticipation. Only a fool would turn down the very thing he most wanted: her memories and, he had no doubt, should he stoop so low, her sex. They'd be alone. They had to be. He couldn't question her like that with anyone present. Not even McNaught. What would she be like? That body, her body, soft and sweet in surrender to him, under him, moving with him. He did mean to discover who killed his brother and up to now he would have sworn to the high heavens he'd do anything, anything at all, to know what had happened to Andrew. Here she was, offering everything he wanted, and a good deal more besides, if only she knew.

"Please," she whispered.

He drew himself up, trying to stop the images in his head, the pounding of his heart, the conviction that he must and would possess her. He put his hands on either side of her head. "Are you sure?" She nodded. He knew he ought to say no, but what came out of his mouth was, "Very well."

She swallowed. "Thank you."

"You may not say so later."

"Nothing could be worse than not knowing."

James hailed them from the street, waving so his hat tumbled off his head. "Come along you two. Sebastian."

"When?" she asked.

He stroked her cheek with the side of his thumb. "I'll send for you."

Miss Willow nodded, lifted her chin and walked past him, a wisp of red hair trailing in the breeze. He followed. When she reached the causeway that wound around the side of the church and back to the street, she joined James, his sister and Miss Cage. The ladies linked arms and walked ahead, heads together.

James stuck out a hand and stopped Sebastian from passing. "Are you poaching?"

He pushed away James's hand, shooting a glance at Mr. Cage, who had let the ladies walk ahead. "As if you didn't intend to ruin her for a decent husband."

"God in heaven. Am I to find myself with the dilemma of protecting her from you, of all people?"

"That is not necessary, I assure you." Snow fell in increasing thickness, staying on the ground now. Sebastian ignored the cold and wet. His mood was peevish, and he made no effort to hide it.

˜James gave him a look. "You do intend to marry Diana?"

"Consider the matter all but settled."

"Well, well."

"I expect you'll be making an announcement on St. Agnes' Eve."

James grinned. "Excellent."

"In the meantime, what do you intend to do about Miss Willow?"

"Have her in my bed, of course."

"She'll not fall in without a ring on her finger."

"Then let her think she'll have one." James smiled. "She's leading me a chase, I won't deny that, but Sebastian, for pity's sake, I'll take care of her. On my honor I will. And—" He kept his hand on Sebastian's chest. "I'll thank you not to interfere."

Chapter Seven

January 17

Olivia glanced up from her notebook to see Price, Pennhyll's butler, in the doorway of the tower parlor she already thought of as her unofficial office. She closed the cover in case his eyesight was better than she thought. The pewter-haired butler watched with what she fancied was a gaze of sorrowful concern. He always seemed on the verge of a solemn delivery of terrible news or just leaving to attend a dear friend's funeral. *Good morning, Miss. I regret to report the world has come to an end.*

"Yes, Price?" she asked.

"My Lord Tiern-Cope requests a moment of your time this morning, Miss."

Her heart slammed against her ribs, but she lifted her pen and squinted a little so Price would think she was consumed by thought instead of caught completely off guard by the summons. She wasn't ready. She'd let herself believe he didn't mean to follow through, and was relieved to think so, too.

Price gestured toward the door. "He is most anxious to speak with you." She put away her pen, blotted her journal page and slid the book into the desk drawer. She had a sudden recollection of Tiern-Cope staring at her before they left the churchyard in Far Caister. Eyes like blue ice. A ruthless man. No mercy in him. None whatever.

The butler waited while she draped her shawl around her shoulders, which she fussed over more than necessary. "This way, Miss."

She followed him from the salon. She felt like a criminal on her way to the gallows. They turned a corner to a wood-carved hallway. A hard left took them through a closet lined with shelves of jars and dried plants and then into a salon of ivory and blue accented in yellow the shade of new butter. Olivia frowned at his back while he opened a double set of doors leading to a parlor of crimson and gray. She did not think herself far wrong in supposing Price was taking her to the earl's private quarters. Where they were unlikely to be interrupted. No wonder Price disapproved. From the parlor, they passed through a withdrawing room with gilt doors.

"Mind your step here, Miss Willow." He stopped at the next set of doors but instead of opening them tapped on one of the gilt panels. "Miss Willow, my Lord."

"Permission to enter." That voice gave no hint of anything save that the speaker possessed a soul of granite, which did nothing to quell the racing of her pulse.

Price opened the door and nodded as she passed him. Although not large, the room imposed on her senses. To her right, three high, arching windows let in early light of day and offered a sweeping view of the hill falling away from the rear of the castle. Portraits lined the opposite wall from above the wainscoting to the ceiling. She noticed little else after that, for Lord Tiern-Cope stood from the desk. Hands clasped behind his back, he made the very slightest of motions with his head, conveying at once both an acknowledgment of her and, so she imagined, his approval at seeing her. He must have expected her to refuse. She ought to. She wanted to.

"Thank you, Price," he said. "Dismissed."

"My Lord." Price bowed and on his way out, very pointedly left the door open.

Tiern-Cope glanced at the desktop and set aside a stack of papers. A tray with a teapot, one cup, a saucer and a half-eaten scone took up the space to his right. To his left sat a wooden chest about a foot square. She supposed he locked the household cash and his most important papers in the chest. He gestured to a tufted armchair, inviting her to sit. "At ease, Miss Willow." All business. Not a drop of warmth. She had no idea what to expect. Except that she would at last know what she'd come to Pennhyll to remember, for she had no doubt as to the reason for his summons.

"My Lord." She perched on the edge of the chair,

fighting the urge to put a hand to her aching head. Lack of sleep, she decided. Since coming to Pennhyll, she'd begun having nightmares again, horrible dreams of someone threatening her, of running and running and however fast she ran, never escaping. She'd not slept well since. "I'm ready."

Still standing, he moved another sheet of paper to the pile on his right, ignoring the chest, the tea and her. He wore fawn breeches, a brown waistcoat and a camel-hair jacket. Despite the informality of his dress, he seemed more formal than ever. No level of informality disguised his Alexander looks. What, she wondered, would happen if the present Tiern-Cope ever learned to smile? Half the women in Far Caister swooned over him without his mouth so much as twitching. If ever he did crack a smile, she suspected the rest would swoon, too, while the other half fainted dead away. He looked up, and the question seemed irrelevant. This man surely never smiled in all his life and never would. "I have not been myself since I came to Pennhyll, Miss Willow. I do not sleep well."

"An epidemic, it seems."

His icy gaze fell colder yet. "I am well aware of my social shortcomings, Miss Willow, and I hope you will make an allowance for them, as well as forgive me for bringing you here in order that we may be private."

Her heart flew to her throat. "I imagine it's necessary. Privacy."

He gave her a stare that made her wish she'd chosen a chair farther from his desk. Lord, that icy-blue gaze could peel paint from the walls. "Are you absolutely certain," he said, "that you agree to this?"

"Yes."

"Then I may expect your full cooperation."

"Yes."

He looked at her. "*My Lord*." After a long moment, he said, "I will have you know your place, Miss Willow, and have you stay in it. Is that understood?"

"Yes, my Lord."

"What is your income per annum?"

"It varies, sir."

"Let me ask the question another way. May I presume that your father left you and your mother adequately provisioned for his absence?"

"No. He did not."

"Your father owned property. A fairly considerable estate."

"Yes, sir."

"And he took no steps to provide for his family?"

"It seems not."

"You will not be disrespectful." He spoke in an uninflected tone, but the effect was worse than a shout.

"I cannot believe he left us nothing." She met his gaze and found no comfort in the chilly blue depths. "I engaged an attorney to look into Papa's estate."

"And?"

"Nothing came of it but his bills."

He moved from behind his desk until he stood before her, hands clasped behind his back. "Had you no guardian?"

"My uncle, I suppose."

"You don't know?"

"I was ten when my father died. No one told me what was going on. My uncle looked after us. For a while."

"What does your uncle say about your fortune?"

"He passed on seven or eight years ago. My cousin Mr. Hew Willow has the estate now."

"Why doesn't he look after you?"

"I do not know."

"Where is he?"

"I don't know. He's been away. We don't correspond."

"Miss Willow."

"There was talk of a duel, sir. I heard, and I believe, that he fled England because he killed a man. Or nearly so. I do not know the particulars."

"A swordsman, I take it."

"I've no idea. My cousin is considered an excellent huntsman, though. He lives for shooting. He would surely have used a pistol though, for all I know, they fought with cudgels."

"You have no guardian and the man who ought to be responsible for you is not. How, then, do you support yourself? Are you a charity case? A burden upon the parish?"

"I have a small stipend from teaching in Far Caister." She stared at his neck cloth in a vain attempt to avoid the chill blue eyes.

"And yet," he said in words sharp enough to cut paper, "you are compelled to carry away food from my kitchens."

Her eyes snapped to his, and she felt her face go hot. "My Lord?"

"Do not play the fool with me. I well know you are not."

"What does this have to do with your brother?"

"A great deal, since it speaks to your character. Or lack thereof. The fact is, I have been asking after you, and I am no longer at ease with my previous opinion of you. You're not at all what you seem. What you pretend to be. I will call you to account for that."

"I hope, my Lord, that you will not blame your staff for their generosity."

"Do not concern yourself with my staff. They understand their duties."

"If you will send me your bill, I will repay you. My Lord."

"Have you ever been robbed, Miss Willow? Of possessions. You or your mother, perhaps."

"No."

His eyebrows rose. "Proper respect, Miss Willow," he said softly.

"No, my Lord."

"Perhaps you aren't aware of the loss. Perhaps you believe certain valuables of yours were merely mislaid."

"No."

"Are you certain?"

"My Lord." She took a trembling breath. "I regret my recent actions exceedingly. You have made me understand I should not have done so. I assure you, I will not in the future."

"Why aren't you married? What was it you said? 'Never loved and never in love'?"

"Yes. My Lord."

"Is that why you jilted Mr. Verney?"

"I beg your pardon?"

"Don't waste my time, Miss Willow. Why did you jilt Mr. Verney?"

"I did no such thing." She watched him walk to the door and close it. The lock engaged.

"He tells me you broke off the engagement. One of you is lying."

Her voice fell just short of a whisper. "He made his reluctance more than plain, and so I released him from his promise. A clergyman cannot have a wife connected with scandal."

"And your heart?" Tiern-Cope returned to her and stopped six inches from her knees. "Was it irreparably crushed?"

The words lodged in the back of her throat. She swallowed hard. "I thought he loved me. I was wrong."

"Did you jilt him because someone better came along?"

"No one did, my Lord. Isn't that plain enough? I have red hair," she said.

Something flickered across his expression, consternation perhaps, or surprise. "Believe me, your hair is not the impediment you think." He gave a short laugh. "I dare say some men find your hair quite compelling."

"Red hair or not, I am nearly twenty-five." The familiar pain of loss hit hard. "I am too old and too poor."

"Not the first blush of youth, I agree, but not so decrepit that you might not find a protector should you set your mind to the matter. Why, I do believe there's at least one man here who would happily put himself forward in just such a capacity." He crossed his arms over his chest. "Not so long ago, my brother, perhaps?"

The room went quiet as the grave. Instead of making an imprudent retort, which she was quite certain he would have been pleased to crush beneath his metaphorical boot heel, she folded her hands on her lap and regarded him thoughtfully. "I think, my Lord, I deserve to know what you mean by that."

"How long did Andrew support you?"

"He didn't. Why would he?"

Tiern-Cope curled the edge of his mouth at her denial. "He was generous."

"Yes, of course. But what on earth does that have to do—" Then, she understood. Two spots of color flamed in her cheeks, she felt them hot as embers. "What a vile thing to suggest." She spoke softly because everything in the world depended upon her remaining calm. "That I would deceive Lady Tiern-Cope, who was my friend, in such a despicable manner."

"Miss Willow, let me make myself quite plain."

"I think you have."

"You were Andrew's lover."

"No."

"He was a handsome man, Miss Willow, who deserved his reputation as a rake. He collected mistresses the way other men collect snuff boxes. You would not be the first young lady to fall prey to a charming rogue."

"I never did." Her head pounded, and she put her hands to her temples, wishing she could rub away the throbbing pain.

"Don't hide your face from me. I said I'd call you to account, and I will. I wonder what is your true character. Innocent spinster or desperate female who steals from her host? Neither James nor his sister, thank God, have any idea of what went on between you and my brother."

"Nothing did."

His lip curled. "Well, perhaps James does know, and that's why he's after you like a dog after a—"

She shot to her feet. "How dare you? You— You— You—rascal."

"That's the worst you can think of? Rascal?"

"If I were a man, I'd—I'd—"

One eyebrow lifted. "What?"

"I don't know. I'd—"

"Shoot me dead?"

"Your brother was my friend."

"Your *particular* friend?"

"He was kind to me and nothing, nothing ever happened between us. Andrew was good and kind, and never, ever anything else. You're just like all the others. Men who think my hair means I cannot control my passions. That I haven't a good character. Well, I do have. I defy you to prove otherwise."

"Miss Willow," he said crisply, striding to his desk. He swept a hand above the box. "Do you recognize this?"

"No."

"Look closer."

"Why?"

"Because I told you to." He pushed the chest across the desk. It skidded, but stopped just before the far edge. Metal straps curved over the rounded top of dark wood. "Well?"

"If it's full of money, yes, it's mine."

"Answer me."

"I've never seen it before."

He flicked up the metal tongue. "Are you quite certain?"

"Of course."

The top opened with a chirp of stiff hinges. More quickly than her eye could follow, he turned the chest toward her. "Look inside, Miss Willow, and tell me that again."

His mouth thin with anger made her heart hammer, but she felt nothing. No emotion whatever. In his view whatever was inside damned her. She walked to the desk and looked into the chest with no idea what she would see but certain whatever it was would be easily explained. And then let him grovel with his apology.

On the very top of the jumble of items inside lay her father's watch, engraved with his name and the outline of the tree that represented their family name. Her heart swelled. Tangled in one of the fobs was a slender gold chain with a willow-engraved medallion, a gift from her father just a few months before he died. His signet ring, two bracelets and several dozen buttons. Her brother's pocket knife. Beneath those, a pair of kidskin gloves, an ivory fan, tortoiseshell haircombs, embroidered handkerchiefs, a set of silver brushes and combs. The trappings of a life long lost to her.

"My dear Miss Willow," he drawled, shaking his head in mock disappointment. "How could you have been so careless with your things?"

She touched the watch and the pocket knife. "I thought I'd never see these again. How did you— Where did you get them?"

"Andrew."

Their eyes met over the chest. Anger and suspicion filled his, not that his reaction mattered anymore. "How is that possible?" Oh, her heart was going to break. Surely, it would.

He pointed at the open chest. "You're a clever girl. Let's see how fast you think on your feet. Explain how your belongings came to be here. In my brother's effects."

"I don't know."

"He was a married man, Miss Willow."

Her hand flew through the air. He caught her wrist, stopping her palm inches from his cheek. "You have no right," she said. "No right at all to level such an accusation."

"On the contrary. I have every right. Did you know, Miss Willow, that the very day before he died, he instructed his solicitor to begin an action for divorce?"

"I don't believe it." But something nagged at her. The harder she tried to think what, the more her head hurt. Something. Something important, and it refused to come to her. He lifted her chin, forcing her to look at him. His eyes burned into hers. Her scar felt like a white-hot knot.

"I do not countenance liars," he said. "And that includes old maids who pretend virtue they do not possess."

The world pressed in on her, eager to crush her.

His fingers tightened around her chin. "Did you kill my brother?"

"No."

"How do you know?"

She opened her mouth to speak but all that came out was a sob. The light hurt her eyes. Too bright where the sun came in, too dark in the shadows shifting behind Tiern-Cope. "I couldn't have," she managed. "I couldn't."

He leaned close. "How do you know?"

She closed her eyes and trembled. She was dissolving inside. The side of her head, exactly along her scar, felt like fire. A familiar, choking unreality wrapped her in silence.

"What is it?"

She could see a face, a leering, grinning face that

97

refused to come into focus. Her stomach pitched. Panic rose like a wave, drowning her. She heard Tiern-Cope's voice, but she could not see him or understand what he was saying to her. Her lungs refused to work. A moan echoed in her head, a man's guttural, drawn-out cry. Someone screamed, a high drawn-out keen of anguish and despair, deafening her, drowning out all sound. She was suffocating. Fingers gripped her, imprisoned her, stopped her breath. The side of her head exploded with pain. The world went white and then, suddenly, black. Silence, blessed silence. And then, nothing. Not even silence.

Her eyes fluttered open and for the space of a heartbeat, she had no idea where she was or even who she was. Someone behind her had an arm around her, just beneath her breasts and a hand over her mouth, pulling her head hard against his shoulder. He held her so tightly she could not get a full breath. She struggled, but his hand over her mouth did not ease. His arm tightened. Panic threatened.

"Are you going to scream again?"

Relief flooded her because she knew the voice. Tiern-Cope. She shook her head, and his fingers loosened. His arm eased around her torso, sliding around her when she breathed deep, filling her lungs. His fingers splayed, brushing the side of her breast, lingering. His other hand slid off her mouth, over her throat.

"Sit down," he said in her ear. He released her, guiding her toward a chair. She sat, a bit unsteadily and found herself looking into Tiern-Cope's blue eyes. Blue eyes. She stared at his eyes, trying to remember why she was relieved when every cold, hard line of his face seemed focused on her. "What happened?" he said.

He moved closer, and Olivia found she had to look a long way up in order to meet his eyes. She shook her head.

"What happened? What did you remember?"

"I don't know."

"A frequent lament from you." He reached for her, tipping her head upward, thumb brushing the crest of her cheek. She felt his finger sliding in the damp of tears. "What scent is that?"

She hesitated. "Mine, do you mean?"

"Yes. It's familiar." He smiled, and her stomach dropped straight to the floor. If he wasn't so hellishly fierce, he'd be a threat to innocence the county over.

"Verbena, my Lord."

"Pleasant."

"Thank you."

He leaned down and put a hand on either arm of her chair. "Miss Willow," he murmured. "You are a most lovely cipher." He smiled in exactly the way he did in her imagination, a slow, intimate smile that made her heart fly and her stomach flutter. His eyes drifted closed. His lashes, though not long, were absurdly thick. Despite that, she could not but think that he was a *man*. A grown man, tried and proved, and she was in woefully over her head.

He drew in a breath and leaned closer, hands gripping either arm of her chair. The idea that he meant to kiss her sent her to giddy heights. She wasn't the least bit prepared for the way her skin burned with heat or the way she melted inside. Beneath the unfamiliar warmth, she felt panic gathering. Her head throbbed. She felt short of breath, a familiar sense of suffocation. He leaned closer yet. His breath stirred the hair at her temples. She could smell soap and wool and linen and beneath it all, him. How many times had she imagined him leaning this close to her? Heroic Captain Alexander, desperately in love with her and ready to lay his heart at her feet.

"Verbena," he murmured.

She hadn't ever been kissed, or at least nothing more than a brush across the cheek or forehead, and she wanted to know the sensation. Just before she succumbed to a very great stupidity, she brought her hand between them and give him a push. "No."

His lips moved, forming the silent word, "Hell." He gripped the arms of her chair, his eyes squeezed closed, mouth white with tension. She watched him take a breath that quite deliberately did not move his rib cage.

Too late, she realized she'd hurt him. "Oh, my goodness. Are you all right?" She wanted to disappear in a puff of smoke, to vanish from the face of the earth. "I'm sorry. So sorry." She'd have stood up but he still clutched the arms of her chair. "Shall I call someone? Price?"

He shook his head.

"Your manservant?"

"No." He spoke through clenched teeth and did not move. Then he focused on her, with no sign of pain in his face. "Do not even try to deceive me." The man's voice possessed the mercy of forged steel. He reached for her, cupping her face with his hand. "What happened the night my brother died?"

"I don't know." Her breath caught in her throat because his fingers traced the curve of her cheek. "I've told you, I can't recall."

"It happens I am the magistrate." He released her, spreading his fingers wide. "I just found that out. If you try to leave Pennhyll, Miss Willow, I'll have you arrested and bound over."

"For what?"

"Theft, of course." He returned to his desk and sat. Ice could not have been cooler than his expression. She knew he meant every word. "Something of mine is sure to come up missing. Another Stilton, perhaps. Once it gets out you're a thief, I doubt you'll find honest employment hereabouts."

"I am not—" Her voice trembled, and to her horror, she felt tears burning her eyes. "My Lord. I am not— I will not—"

"I don't know what happened the night my brother died, but you, Miss Willow, are indisputably in the center of it. If you'll not tell me the truth, I have no further use for you this afternoon or any other." He picked up a pen as if he meant to bend to some task of great importance. "You have wasted enough of my time. Take the box with you. With my compliments." He opened one of the account books on the desk and began to do sums on a sheet of blank paper. Without glancing up, he said, "Good day." She did not stir. He ignored her for half a minute. "I said, good day."

"I sold them."

His pen stilled, and after a bit he looked up. "Why?"

"Because we needed to eat and pay the rent, that's why."

"All at once?"

"No. A few things at a time. I don't know how they ended up here."

"Where did you sell them?"

"A pawnbroker."

"In Far Caister?"

"No."

"You have the regrettable habit of refusing to answer the simplest of questions." He leaned against his chair. "Where did you sell your things?"

"Carlisle."

"Miss Willow."

"Acton Street. Off Bellby Road." He looked at her with one eye and she could not imagine what had ever possessed her to think he had the smallest amount of mercy. "You said you'd help me."

His lip curled. "Your mistake, if that's what you thought I said."

"You said you'd help me remember."

He tapped one finger on the desktop. After a moment, he looked at her from beneath his lashes. "Not at the risk of a noose around my neck."

"What does that mean?"

He leaned back, elbow on the top rail of his chair. "Exactly what you imagine."

To her horror, she wiped at her cheek and found her hand came away damp. She fumbled for a handkerchief.

"I told you that you would not thank me." His eyes turned a sharper blue than ever. "And now I find myself in the novel position of admitting an error in judgment." He gazed at her. "Either you know what happened and have succeeded in keeping it from me, in which case, I congratulate you, or else there is some true impediment to your recollection. If the latter, the usual procedure will fail me. If the former, some level of coercion would gain me my object. Eventually."

"I cannot live like this. Not knowing."

"There is a thin line, Miss Willow, between what I

want from you and what I am prepared to do to get it." His eyes glittered. "I cannot thank you for making me consider using a woman in such a fashion."

"My Lord—"

He slashed a hand through the air with such force she heard the movement of air. "Your permission does not absolve me of the guilt." He rose, planting his hands on the desk. She felt scalded by the heat of his gaze. "Make no mistake, Miss Willow. What's in your head belongs to me, and in due course, I will have it. But not—" His voice fell. "Not at the cost of what little decency is left me." He drew in a breath and sat down. "Now, when I said *good day*, Miss Willow, I was not remarking on the weather. You will kindly oblige me and leave."

Chapter Eight

January 18

McNaught braced himself as the carriage navigated the sharp curve away from Pennhyll. Wheezing with effort, he spread a blanket over his employer's lap. Sebastian swept it aside. "Stop your infernal fussing."

"That's a bitter wind outside, my Lord. Your constitution cannot withstand the strain."

"Bugger my constitution."

McNaught withstood the profanity with his usual affectation of deafness. "Where are we going?"

"Carlisle."

The valet blanched at the thought of four hours in

a carriage. "I've sent for Dr. Fansher." As if that would shorten their errand.

He gave McNaught an even look. "I never told you not to."

McNaught lifted the curtain and peered out the window, letting in the pale light of dawn. He settled back on the seat. "At least there's decent inns in Carlisle." Frowning, he said, "I wish you'd told me, my Lord. I'd have packed a change of clothes."

"We're not staying the night."

"But we'll be the entire day on the road. Dr. Fansher would never approve of this."

"With Andrew's horses, I expect we'll make good time."

McNaught shook his head. "Worse than a cat after a mouse when you've got an idea in your head, you are."

"My one virtue."

"Small consolation when both man and mouse are dead."

"So long as you bury us both at sea, I don't give a damn." Two hours and a change of horses later, Sebastian washed down a last bite of roast chicken with a glass of surprisingly good Madeira the very color of Miss Olivia Willow's eyes. He didn't know what to think of her anymore. He could not separate his desire for her from the woman herself. His usual methods were out of the question, so he must find another way to jar her memory. He handed the basket to his valet. "You must keep up your strength," he said.

"Thank you, my Lord." McNaught fell to. A trencherman, he was. A piss poor traveler, but a trencherman. The man snored, too, and when he wasn't snoring, he fidgeted and talked. Incessantly.

In another hour and a half, they reached the outskirts of Carlisle. Sebastian tapped on the hatch when the buildings changed from residences to shops. "Slowly," he told the driver. They were in a good district, not the best, but one that would have looked safe to a young woman after riding twenty miles on a nag hired from the Crown's Ease. If she'd not lied about where she went. Trouble was, he didn't think she was a liar.

The coachman directed them off the main street, navigated to Bellby Road, made another turn and came full stop. "Acton Street, my Lord."

Sebastian opened the door, ignoring the waiting groom. Though he stepped onto the walkway without assistance, he winced when he shook out the aches of traveling. To his right an assortment of shops of the nicer sort stretched along both sides of the street. Tea parlor, a lending library, a milliner. To his left, the street narrowed. The shops were less cheerful, the paint not so bright, the bricks not so clean. With McNaught at his heels, he walked left, the way increasingly narrow and dreary. Passers-by gave him wide berth, tradesmen mostly, men with pinched faces and nervous eyes. A few bowed.

Candlemaker, solicitor's office, printer and a glovemaker, but no pawnbroker. Three more shops, and he'd be at the end of Acton Street. He'd have to try the other side. He stopped without being certain why. The hair on the back of his arms prickled. Slowly, he looked up and down the street, eying the doorways and shadows. Nothing. No cutpurse lurking. The window display of the second-to-last shop came into his field of vision. Amid an arrangement of other items including a gentleman's watch, a silver knife and a meerschaum pipe, lay coiled a string of coral beads.

"Wait outside, McNaught."

The proprietor bowed when Sebastian walked in. Smallpox had left his face heavily scarred, but he would not have been a handsome man in any event. He looked Sebastian up and down. "Have I the honor of addressing the earl of Tiern-Cope?"

"Yes." Outside, McNaught paced, an apple with legs, ready to dash to the rescue should Sebastian show signs of incipient collapse.

"My Lord."

"May I ask how you know who I am?" Sebastian surveyed the interior. In the detritus of old clothing, utensils, pots, a flute, battered walking sticks, chipped plates, pens, bowls, shoes, boots and dusty bottles of indeterminate contents, he caught here and there the sheen of silver candlesticks, the glitter of gold leaf on an empty picture frame, an alabaster vase and a porcelain box painted with dainty roses. Set apart from the jumble of clothes, three gowns shone out. All of them of such fine quality any lady might wear them. Draped over a dressmaker's stand was a cashmere shawl and on the floor a pair of dusty satin slippers. Whatever lady had once worn those gowns, she had been of a delicate size. The colors would suit a red-head.

"My Lord." He nearly swept the floor with his nose, he bowed so deeply. "Pardon my saying, but you are the living image of your brother."

"You've seen my brother?"

"A most amiable gentleman, your brother, my Lord," said the shopkeeper, rubbing his hands together. "Most amiable, indeed." He shifted his feet and

Sebastian thought if he bowed again, he'd slap the back of the man's head. By God, he would. "An honor, your Lordship, to have you in my little shop. What may I do for you? How may I be of assistance?"

"The coral beads."

"Ah." The shopkeeper hurried to the window, eyes bright. McNaught stared through the window. "Just arrived, my Lord." His head bobbed on his thin neck, still bowing as he reached. "The very finest coral, as you can see." He turned, the beads draped over his hand. "Excellent color. Gold clasp. Suitable for any young lady of quality."

"Who brought them in?" There couldn't be two such necklaces in Cumbria. He could see them even now, around her neck on the very day he first laid eyes on her.

"Ah." The tip of his nose quivered. He hefted the beads, holding them toward the light. "A very pretty gift, my Lord, and a bargain at, ten pounds, shall we say? Shall I wrap them up for you? Discreetly, of course."

"Who?"

"They need restringing. You've a keen eye, your Lordship. Eight pounds? If not these, I have pearls." He reached into another cabinet and took out a pink velvet case that he opened with a flourish. "Perfectly matched. Name your price. Fifteen pounds for both."

Sebastian stared. "If you wish my custom, you will tell me who brought them to you."

His eyes shifted, landing first on the beads, then the pearls, on anything but Sebastian. "A lady of distressed circumstances."

Sebastian recognized the loyalty Miss Willow seemed to engender in so many who knew her. "Red hair?" Copper on fire, curls a man longed to see loose and flowing.

He shrugged.

Sebastian took a crown from his pocket and toyed with it, passing the coin from fingertip to fingertip. The man's eyes followed the movement.

"Perhaps she did have red hair."

"What else did she bring you?"

"Hair combs, earbobs, gloves and such." He wiggled his fingers as if to demonstrate the inconsequential nature of the list.

"Gowns?"

"A frock or two."

"A gold watch, perhaps?" He could see the man considering his answer, and he held out the coin. The shop smelled of dust and overcooked beef.

"Engraved." The coin disappeared into his pocket. "Fine workmanship."

Sebastian held out another coin.

"A medallion, as well. On a gold chain. That was engraved, too." He put a hand perpendicular to his lips so that his index finger rested just beneath the tip of his nose. "Such things, your lordship, as a lady of quality might have and wish to sell if her circumstances were reduced."

"Of course." He brought out a guinea, not speaking until the man's eyes lit with the passion of gold. "What arrangement," he said, "did you have with my brother?" The shopkeeper reached for the coin but with a flick of his wrist, Sebastian palmed it.

"Ah." The man licked his lips.

"Well?"

"I wasn't to let anyone know. Sworn to the utmost secrecy, your worship."

His belly shrank. Jesus. Had they met here, his brother and Miss Willow? Sebastian made the coin reappear and let it rest on his palm.

He snatched the coin. "To purchase, at a favorable price, anything a certain young lady brought in." His tongue darted out, wetting his lips. "And to reserve them for him alone. After that, I sent him whatever she brought me. He always settled his accounts, my Lord. Prompt as you may."

"Indeed."

The man's face lapsed into stillness. "It's not what you might think. I may have misapprehended myself at first. She never brought the sort of things a man gives. She's proud, my Lord, a real lady, but never any airs with her. Always a kind word."

Relief swept through him, surprising him with its intensity. She hadn't lied about selling her things nor, it would seem, her reasons for doing so. "How much did you give her for the beads?"

The shopkeeper's eyes narrowed. "A fair price."

"How much?"

"I'm a man of business." He rubbed his palms together. "I've myself to watch out for. There's not been much call for fine things lately. With the war on, more want to sell these days than buy."

Sebastian held out the last coin he intended to give the fellow.

A grin distorted the pockmarks around the man's mouth and cheeks. "Two pound, my Lord. Two pound."

He took the beads, twining them around his fingers, seeing them looped around Miss Willow's slender throat. "And a fine business it must be."

"My Lord."

"Your arrangement with my brother continues with me. She's not to know."

"Of course not, my Lord." He bowed low.

"Send me everything she's brought you since my brother died. With your bill, of course."

"My Lord."

"Good day, sir."

"My Lord?" he said before Sebastian had quite reached the door.

"Yes?"

"I don't know what he did with what he bought of me." He shrugged. "Like as not she would have sold them again if he'd given them back to her."

"Thank you for your assistance." Sebastian left the shop with McNaught at his heels. He nearly knocked him down when he whirled and strode back. He stopped short of the pawnbroker's and instead threw open the door to the office of Mr. Simon Melchior, solicitor.

A clerk on a high stool slipped off his perch. He kept a hand on the papers piled on his desk. "Good day, sir. How may I be of service?"

He was not recognized here. Andrew was not recognized. "Mr. Melchior, if you please."

"Have you an appointment?"

"No."

The clerk looked him up and down and Sebastian supposed that even serviceable clothes marked him as a higher class of client than usually came to call. "I'll see if he's in. May I tell him who's inquiring?"

If ever his title was to be more than a nuisance and a bother, now was the time. He handed over one of the cards McNaught took care to put in all his coats.

His eyes widened when he read the engraved card. "My Lord. A moment only, I am sure."

A thin, hawk-nosed man with steel-gray hair rose from his desk when Sebastian strolled in.

The man bowed. "My Lord."

Sebastian turned. "Outside, McNaught." He waited for his valet to retreat, then closed the door to the inner office and turned his attention to Melchior. "How much did Miss Olivia Willow's uncle steal from her?"

"May I know the reason for your interest?"

"Can you not imagine?" Sebastian flicked out his coattails and sat. "Surely, Mr. Melchior, there can be no harm in telling me what I will inevitably discover on my own. I would prefer not being put to the bother, of course."

The solicitor returned to his desk but remained on his feet with his fingertips resting on the desktop. "A most interesting case. Not my usual sort."

"I am happy to pay you a retainer for your services in the matter, if that will help you recall the details."

"I recall the details sufficiently well, my Lord. Though, perhaps a suitable retainer would not be out of order." He tapped a finger on his desk. "Say, a hundred pounds?"

Sebastian nodded and let the silence ripen.

"A widow's jointure of seven thousand pounds. As for the young lady, thirty thousand hers directly and twenty-five that would have been her brother's, all withdrawn from the funds within months of her father's death and invested in a series of ill-advised and miserably failed ventures, I am sorry to say. In addition, there's a small, unentailed estate on the border of Pennhyll left to her by her paternal grandmother.

That estate I might mention, was mortgaged a month after Roger Willow's death for thirty thousand pounds sterling. About twice what it was worth, I'd say. And lost to the lender thereafter."

"Fifty-five thousand. A fortune."

"Yes."

"Yet, nothing came of all your work on her behalf."

"I do not make it a habit to work for free, my Lord, or upon a hopeless speculation. She has no money now, and any number of powerful interests against her." Melchior snorted. "She ought to have hired me thirteen years ago when she might have afforded the cost of a decent barrister. We could have done something then, though I suspect the outcome would not have been much different. Still, we might have gotten her something."

"The whole of her fortune is gone?"

Melchior looked down his nose. "Her guardian did nothing to protect her interests. Considering he allowed the mortgage at so inflated a price, one wonders if he did not have a hand in the robbery."

"Who is he?"

Melchior stared down his nose then glanced up. "You do not know?"

"No."

"None other than your father, my Lord. A relationship, of course, that terminated upon his death." Melchior's hawk nose twitched. "She has since been quite without the protection of the earls of Tiern-Cope."

Sebastian rose. "Have your clerk send me whatever papers are in your files, Mr. Melchior."

"My Lord."

"If she comes to you again, inform me immediately. A full accounting of any request she may make."

"Naturally," Melchior said.

"She, however, must be satisfied with some appropriate delay of the law."

"My Lord."

"Good day." On his way out, Sebastian paused to address the clerk. "By how much is Miss Willow's account outstanding?"

"Thirty-seven pounds, eleven shillings, eight pence."

"Be so good as to present the bill to me at Pennhyll Castle."

"My Lord."

During the return to Pennhyll, Sebastian let silence cover him, feeling all the while the weight of the beads in his pocket.

"What amuses you?" McNaught asked.

"Nothing."

"You laughed."

"Did I?"

"Yes."

He slipped his fingers into his pocket, touching the smooth surface of the coral. Once, these very beads had nestled against Miss Willow's skin, warm from the heat of her body. Was this how Andrew felt when he found out how she lived, and who was responsible for it? Had his benighted brother fallen in love with Miss Willow and against all his years of rakehell living, actually acted nobly? Buying up whatever she sold in order to keep a roof over her head and food on the table. And here he was, her beads in his pocket, and him paying off what must be to Miss Willow, a crushing debt to Melchior. Jesus.

Oh, he was in a fine fix. Like his brother with the rest of Miss Willow's possessions, he couldn't return the beads. Besides, the pawnbroker was right. She'd only sell them again as soon as she had some new expense to meet.

"Ah," said McNaught, delving into the basket again. "Here we are."

Sebastian eyed the potion his valet was mixing. The stench was worse than the last. "I don't want that. Besides, we have one last call to make."

McNaught handed him the glass. "To your health, my Lord."

"Splendid." He drank it down. "Just sodding splendid."

Chapter Nine

A servant admitted Sebastian to a parlor that even in full dark possessed a stirring view of Pennhyll rising into the night sky. Dr. Richards had been his father's personal physician, and for Andrew as well, when he came to live at Pennhyll. Judging by the house, the occupation had served him well. Dr. Richards came in almost immediately. A man of some sixty years, he had white hair covering his head in a distinguished crown. Though his skin hung slack around his chin and eyes, he bore signs of having been handsome well into his late maturity.

"My Lord." He bowed. "My deepest sympathies for your loss."

"Thank you."

"Please sit." Richards gestured to a chair.

"I'll stand by the fire, doctor. You, of course, must sit if you wish."

"I've already dined, but I am happy to give you something. I had a most excellent pork loin tonight."

"Nothing, thank you."

"Something to drink? I had a fine Bordeaux with my dinner."

"Thank you."

Richards called for the wine. When it came, he poured two glasses and offered the first to Sebastian. "To what do I owe the honor of your visit?"

"A matter of some sensitivity." Exhaustion seeped into his bones. He'd be glad to see the inside of his room.

"My Lord." Richards nodded. "I was in the service of your most illustrious family for over thirty years. Believe me, you may rely on my discretion even today. Whatever you say to me now stays between these walls."

"I have come about Miss Olivia Willow."

"Ah." He lowered himself onto a chair. Richards' massaged his misshapen knuckles. "Perhaps I might relieve your curiosity about a few matters."

"Such as?" He finished his wine and placed the glass on the mantel.

"More?"

He shook his head. Richards poured himself another glass. "Miss Willow is her mother's sole source of support, and I would hazard the guess that the cost of hiring a woman to look after her mother whilst she is at Pennhyll means she will go without necessities for some time to come."

"What of her mother?"

Richards's hand, resting by the bottle, curled into a fist. "Her brain is irredeemably compromised. The centers of speech and reason—damaged. She cannot walk and has difficulty moving her arms. She sits for short periods and can feed herself with assistance. In the last two years, she's become markedly worse, which brought Miss Willow home from Land's End. You were a boy when she was injured. Perhaps you don't know the full story." Sebastian tightened his hands behind his back. "You know your brother Andrew was married at Pennhyll."

"I was at the wedding." He kept his impatience at bay. Just.

"And your brother Crispin came to his untimely end two days later."

"An accident. He fell from his horse." Jesus, he was tired.

The doctor drank more wine. "I'd have done the same myself, I suppose, sending you back to school after the accident. Your father did the right thing."

"Explain."

Richards sighed and rubbed his hands. His dark eyes lifted to Sebastian. "My Lord, your brother Crispin died as a result of the same accident that crippled Miss Willow's mother and took the lives of her father and brother."

He could have sworn the air thickened, but Richards seemed unaffected. "And what of Miss Willow?"

"Essentially unscathed."

Sebastian drew a breath. "An accident nevertheless."

"In a manner of speaking."

"Either it was an accident or it was not."

"The Willows were on their way to church, Crispin on his way home. One family beginning its day, another man ending his evening. For good or ill, the road was deserted that morning. Your brother was elated, shall we say, and, no doubt, driving too fast for the conditions. Your father was a proud man, my Lord. Rightly so. He would not have a word breathed against his heir, and he had the money and influence to see that any who knew kept their knowledge to themselves."

"Well done."

Richards shook a finger at him. "The morale, young man, the very fiber of our nation depends upon the infallibility of those who rule. You've been in command. Once your authority comes into question, there's no hope of men following you and that way lies peril. Your father understood that."

"Did Andrew know?"

"That, I cannot say. I never told him about Crispin, if that's what you're asking. Perhaps I ought to have." He crossed one thin leg over the other. "Your father did what was required of him, never doubt that, my Lord."

"Does Miss Willow know?"

He pulled his chin closer to his neck, shaking his head. "I hardly think so. She was a child at the time. Nine or ten years old. And your brother, though injured, did not linger at the scene. He might have survived his injuries if not for infection."

"You're certain?"

"Quite. I attended his last hours."

"Certain the road was deserted."

"Of all but the Willows and your brother."

Sebastian stared at the tops of his boots. "To your knowledge, was Miss Willow ever my brother's mistress?"

Richards breathed deeply, a long nasal inhalation. Sebastian's pulse skipped. "If I must, I'll find a midwife whose discretion may not be as trustworthy as your own and have the matter proved beyond doubt."

The doctor slumped on his chair, leaning his forearm on the table. "The lives of the Willows and the Alexanders seem destined to intersect in the most unhappy of ways."

"Speak plainly, doctor."

"My Lord, it has already been my unfortunate task to perform just such an examination of Miss Willow as you have mentioned."

"And your findings?" Sebastian felt his heart sink when Richards said nothing for the time it took for ten deep breaths. The disappointment surprised him. "Well, then."

"My Lord." His lifted his hands. "Her injuries were severe."

"The night my brother and his wife were killed, you mean."

"Yes, of course. Coma resulting from a bullet wound across her left temple. Broken clavicle, compound, which I set. Her other contusions, though many, were not life threatening." His mouth twisted. "Fever set in. The wound in her head suppurated. You're a fighting man, so you must know she is lucky to have survived. I did not believe she would. Loss of memory from the blow to the head, but I've seen it before after this sort of insult. I'd be surprised if she ever regains full memory of the night."

"In your opinion, would she be in any danger if she were to recall?"

Richards looked out the window. "Perhaps it's best she does not."

"Why?"

"I cannot predict what would happen. She might well suffer a complete breakdown."

"She does not strike me as a weak-minded woman. Quite the opposite. Furthermore, I fail to see how the loss of her memory has anything to do with the loss of her virtue."

"This is most difficult. Most difficult."

Sebastian felt a hand squeezing his heart. "You examined her the night Andrew was killed."

"My Lord."

He tilted his head, puzzling out the reason for Richard's reluctance to speak. "You said she received a blow to the head. Separate from the bullet wound?"

"Ah." Richards drummed his fingers on the tabletop. "A deep and copiously bleeding wound to the left of the occipital bulge, which I stitched."

"There was no mention of this at the inquest."

Richards blanched. "The coroner accepted my findings."

"A full and complete disclosure will go a long way toward ensuring I make no mention of perjury. Between us, at least, I should like to have the facts of the case as they are in truth."

"I performed a thorough physical examination of Miss Willow earlier in the day at which time I stitched her head." Richards lifted a hand, but let it fall to the tabletop. "The back of her head, my Lord."

Sebastian stilled himself, kept his face free of emotion, but his belly tightened with a premonition of what he would hear. "What else?"

"Hysteria brought on by a traumatic assault." The doctor met his eyes without flinching. "I was worried she might be a risk to herself."

"Do you mean a suicide?"

"She was badly, badly used." Richards grimaced. "Indecently, my Lord."

"That opinion is nowhere in the records."

Richards gestured.

"You gave false evidence under oath."

"Discreet."

"A nice distinction, I should say." He locked his fists behind his back and stared at Richards. "Upon what ground did you withhold this evidence at the inquiry?"

"Upon my longstanding obligations to your family, sir. Upon my duty to see the Alexander name continue in its high regard. I knew her father and considered him my friend." He stared at his fingers, stretching them out. "I did not see what was to be gained by revealing the girl's shame."

Jesus. He squeezed his fisted hands, tucking them tight against the small of his back.

"By the time of the inquest, I was certain there had been no additional consequences. And, to be quite honest, given her fragile mental state at the time I first examined her, I feared for her sanity if she were to recover the extent of what had happened to her." His voice rose. "It's a mercy, my Lord, a mercy, she does not recall. Had I revealed all that I knew, the damage to her reputation and to the reputation of your family would have been irreparable. There was no one to charge with the assault. No witnesses to corroborate my physical findings and testify to the necessary elements of her ordeal. And whoever killed your brother and his wife would still be at large." He lifted his hands and let them drop to the table. "I didn't see the point."

descent to Far Caister. As always, she paused to look at the castle. Pennhyll never failed to stir her. Mist shrouded the hilltop, and snow lay soft on the vales, smoothing the landscape of its definition. She felt she was the only person left in a world so intensely alive she wondered that any heart could hold the beauty. On her right, a few snow-covered oaks deepened to native wood. To her left the gray towers of Pennhyll pierced the sky. From this point on the path, the castle, she fancied, looked as it must have in the Black Earl's day. None of the additions showed, only ancient walls and crenellated towers, with snow clinging to ledges, chimneys and roof tiles. Indeed, she half expected to see the Black Earl pacing the ramparts, a notion no doubt brought on by the approach of the St. Agnes' Eve ball, and Diana's foolish plans to summon the Black Earl.

A hundred yards to her right, white mist eddied with a rising breeze. She watched with an uneasy amazement as the flurry thickened and coalesced. She heard the faint sound of metal sliding along metal. At first indistinct, the shape moved toward her, a density of snow and wind from which a decidedly human figure took form. His head was bent as if distraught or perhaps deep in thought. The shirring sound of metal, of chain mail or a sword drawn from its scabbard continued. The precise sound from her dreams.

Heart in her throat and frozen in disbelief, she watched the form take on substance, a hint of color. A man, without doubt a man. Gray breeches, a charcoal greatcoat and no hat. His boots broke through the snow. A greyhound trotted at his side, metal collar jingling. The snow settled groundward, but the wake of his stride flared out his coat. He continued toward her, so rapidly he'd be upon her in seconds. The realization that he was no figment of her imagination leapt into her head, a whip to movement. Tiern-Cope. The last person she wanted to meet. The very last.

She darted off the path and veered onto a rock-strewn incline that, if she didn't break her neck, and he kept his present course, which she assumed would be toward one of the newer entrances to the castle, would put her safely away from his notice. She lost her footing on the outcropping of frozen slate and scraped her shin. Cold air burned her lungs, but from the top she surveyed the plain of stark white that surrounded Pennhyll. A moment or two to let him come to the crest of the path where he would turn toward the castle and leave her free to continue to Far Caister.

But no. Never was a man born more contrary to her wishes. Of course, he didn't stay his course. He headed away from Pennhyll, toward Far Caister. How could he have moved so quickly? Unnerving, to say the least. The dog gave a low bark, and she abandoned the idea of a mad sprint back to the path in the hope of staying ahead of him. She had just time to scramble back to the path before he rounded the corner.

Pulling her cloak closed, she feigned surprise. She thought he meant to sweep past her, which would have been at once mortifying and welcome, but at the last he stopped, and with an eerie silence. He nodded, an arrogant nod, full of itself and reeking of pomp and importance. Despite the distance separating them, she saw purple smudges beneath his eyes and above, a blueness that froze.

"I wondered what the devil sort of beast could be that color and prowling so early in the morning. I ought to have known it was you. Bareheaded, which

makes you a brazen chit. And if not brazen, then unwise, for the morning sun has yet to melt the ice from
the road."

Occasionally, ignoring rudeness cured it. "Good
morning, my Lord," she said. All perfectly pleasant.
He had but to step aside, and she could show him
her back. He stared. Without moving. "I did not mean
to intrude."

"On Pennhyll?" He did not make room for her,
which left her standing on the very edge of the road,
uncertain footing, indeed.

"Your solitude."

"Walk wherever you like."

"Thank you." The dog stretched its muzzle to her.
Without thinking, she crouched to scratch behind its
ears.

"Ask permission before you touch my hound."

She tilted her head toward him. "I beg your pardon.
May I?"

"What else can I say but yes, when the hound, who
snarls at every man and beast but me, lays its muzzle
on your knee?"

"Try not to blame the dog," she said. "He's lovely.
Has he a name?"

"Pandelion."

She could see his boots, muddy and wet from his
walk. She crooked her fingers around the back of Pandelion's ears and crooned, "Pandy. My love." In the
same breath, she said, "Are you walking to Far Caister,
too?"

"Do you address me or the dog?"

"Since Pandy does not answer me, you, my Lord."

"I dislike people who pretend they're something
they aren't."

"Pray you never meet one here in Cumbria." Perfectly pleasant. If it killed her, she'd be perfectly pleasant.

"And I despise those who believe I won't notice the deception."

With a sigh, she stood. Pandelion kept her head by Olivia's knee, and she let her fingers dangle to stroke between the gray ears. "I imagine you would."

His eyes met hers, cold as midwinter. "I have been to Carlisle."

"Oh."

"The pawnbroker confirmed what you told me." He clasped his hands behind his back and stared at her with an expression she absolutely could not fathom. "I absolve you, for the moment, of any wrongdoing in respect of your belongings."

"How did they come to be at Pennhyll?" She edged toward the path, but Tiern-Cope refused to yield. "Do excuse me."

"I have discharged your debt to Mr. Simon Melchior." His eyes flicked over her.

"That was presumptuous." And none of his affair, either.

"Nevertheless, it is done."

"I paid Mr. Melchior six shillings a month on account." She did not like being beholden to him, not in the least. "I trust you will accept the same from me."

"Pride is an abiding sin, Miss Willow. It does not flatter you. I did not buy up your vowels to Mr. Melchior in order to dun you for the amount. I told you I have discharged your obligation to him, and so I have done."

"So you can arrest me for the debt?"

His face registered exactly nothing. "Because it suited me to do so."

"Why?"

"Don't be impertinent." Satisfied with Olivia's attentions, the dog retreated to lean its head against Tiern-Cope's thigh. With an absent motion that bespoke fond habit, he stroked the sleek head. "It's early to be walking out."

"I'm making away with your silver."

He moved nearer, the dog coming along. She stood her ground, though the distance between them felt uncomfortably close. "James said you liked morning walks."

"That's true."

"Indeed." He stared at her, but she refused to let him intimidate her. She was sure he made it a habit to intimidate people whenever possible. But she did back off the path to even less certain footing.

"If you opened up my heart," she said, "if you looked inside, you would find Cumbria." She spread her arms, gathering the snow-covered meadow to her in one expansive gesture. "Right now, I am writing this view on my heart." She could not help a grin. "I am stealing it from you, my Lord, and you shall never have it back." His reaction was impossible to gauge—he might as easily have been amused as angry for all she could tell. "In Land's End I lived near the sea, which I never did before. On my half days, I used to watch the water for hours."

"Did you write the sea on your heart?"

She shook her head. "I never felt anything but lonely when I looked at the sea. So cold and bitter, never a moment's ease or forgiveness."

"Precisely why I like it."

"Here the colors are so intense it hurts my heart. In winter, pure white, and come spring, a green so deep it takes your breath. There's nothing like it anywhere in the world."

"Land's End and Cumbria. Is that the extent of your experience of the world?"

"Not much compared to your adventures, I admit." Nothing in his face changed. Quite likely he didn't find his life interesting. "But it's Cumbria that's inside me, somehow. Not Land's End. I think if I knew I would never see the mountains of Cumbria I would die inside."

"God save me from women of overwrought emotion."

"Overwrought?" She kicked the slush covering the rocks. Her toes were going numb. What did he mean by standing here chatting as if they sat to tea?

"I prefer sensible women."

"Such as Miss Royce. Yes, I understand."

"A woman who feels nothing in excess of what is proper."

"No one really lives without strong emotion, my Lord."

"Twaddle."

"You're wrong."

One dark eyebrow soared toward the sky.

"There's no sweetness in life without sorrow behind. Such beauty as this—the hills and sharp, clean air in your lungs, the earth beneath your feet— mustn't be squandered. To see and feel and embrace life you must save moments like these."

"In the end, your savings avail you nothing. Rich or poor, life is a battle we are all fated to lose, Miss Willow."

She settled her weight on one hip. "After my father died, I learned that one minute might be happy and the next full of grief." She took a deep breath. "Right now, for instance. This very moment. All is well and right. I am in good health. I have shoes on my feet and clothes to wear. My meals of late have been certain and regular, and so I am not hungry. There are even a few coins in my pocket. This moment, this very moment and none other, is perfect, and I adore it utterly. To complete excess."

"The tide will turn, Miss Willow." A smile lurked around his mouth, but no, that was not possible, that the earl of Tiern-Cope should smile, and at her.

"It hasn't yet."

"You may find the sea casts you onto the shores of paradise." His voice was low and soft, and Olivia felt her heart stir at the sound. "Or through the very gates of hell."

"So it might." She gave herself a mental shake. Lord Tiern-Cope could not possibly be flirting with her. Impossible. "But that won't stop me from embracing this moment in all its beautiful perfection."

"With but one flaw, Miss Willow."

"Whatever could that be?"

"Don't even try to tell me I don't spoil the present perfection of your moment." The corner of his lip twitched and then gave up. He smiled, and she, perverse creature that she was, felt like she'd been tossed off a cliff with him standing at the bottom to catch her. "Pennhyll is beautiful, I'll give you that."

"A miracle."

"I am not without sensibility, Miss Willow."

"I meant a miracle that we agree."

He made a small movement of his head. "Do you

love Pennhyll as well as you do the mountain upon which it sits?"

"I find it much like you."

His mouth quirked, and then, curved in another smile. She stared, transfixed by the sight. "Unpleasant and forlorn?"

She tipped her head to one side, considering him. She felt an odd sensation of understanding this harsh man who was, in fact, a stranger to her. "Not entirely unpleasant, that I will admit. Nor forlorn, either."

"Do not tell me you find me amiable."

"Certainly not. Like Pennhyll, you are strong and fierce." She felt, ridiculous as it was, that she knew him better than she knew herself. "To make a life here is to have courage and heart, and those you surely have."

Their eyes met and locked. If Cumbria were to take the form of a man, here he stood. Half-tamed, and that half much in doubt, forbiddingly beautiful and dangerous to the unwary. A voice in the back of her head warned that she ought to keep her silence, but she plowed on.

"You belong here." Without thought, she stepped toward him and touched his cheek, following the line back to his temple. His skin felt warm, the heat of him filled her. Inside her, in her heart and in her soul, she knew him. She knew everything about him that mattered. All of him was inside her right now, complete and right and heartbreaking because he was lost. He turned his head and for a moment, she felt the warmth of his breath against her gloved palm.

"My poor, dear Captain Alexander. You are too young to feel such desolation. You think you've lost your heart, but you haven't. It's here at Pennhyll. It's

129

in the ground and the air, the trees and the stone, everywhere you look. You have only to take it. Take what is yours."

He closed his eyes, and she felt or heard or imagined that something snapped. Without warning, he grabbed both her arms and pulled her toward him. His eyes burned into hers and for a deathless moment her head swam with the heat and nearness of him. She stared at his mouth, the fullness of his lower lip. His greatcoat caught another gust of wind and flared out enough for her to see his narrow hips, plain breeches and battered but sturdy leather boots supple with age rather than fineness of material. "I am so sorry," he said.

A tide of emotion pulled her inexorably to sea. Worse, whatever his intention, she wanted him to act, would give up all modesty in return for feeling this way even a moment longer. If he tried to kiss her, she'd let him. Ruin came of moments such as this. Disgrace and whispers and babies out of wedlock. And for the first time in her life, she understood why such things happened.

"I am sorry." Abruptly, he released her. The air seemed lighter, the world larger. She reeled back, disoriented from the loss of contact. Her heel landed on a loose rock, and she stumbled. He grabbed her a split second before she would have pitched onto her backside.

Her hands landed on his shoulders, and her cheek hit smack against his chest. He smelled of morning-damp wool. Soap and linen warm from his body and something else she didn't recognize but that felt close and intimate. Her lower parts were immediately in a knot of heat and everything, everything in the world, felt right. His arms tightened around her. She looked up, into eyes bluer than blue. The pull began again. Her heart tripped.

"Take care," he said.

"Thank you."

He said, "Why are you walking so early in the morning, Miss Willow?" Pandelion whined, then stood at attention, facing the direction of the castle.

"Why are you?" Suddenly, it struck her that his arms remained around her waist. He realized it, too, and let her go.

His eyes flared with chill light. "By reason of a stubborn refusal to any longer accept my weakened state."

"You're not weak." She wasn't at all sure what had just happened, she only knew the mood had changed. Everything had changed.

"I will conquer this."

"That, I believe."

"Even a dull and pulsing pain in my ribs is a damn sight better than being flat on my back and drugged to the gills to keep me from howling at the pain of breathing."

"I well recall that."

"You, however, should not be walking out at this hour." He looked at the hand in which she clutched her parcel. "Without any hat a'tall."

"You're walking out," she said, holding her breath in case he demanded to know what she had.

"I am a man, Miss Willow, who may do as he pleases while you are a young lady who may not."

"I am hardly young, my Lord." She used the no-nonsense voice she'd discovered worked well on misbehaving children. With him, the tone failed utterly.

"Not even my first Luff dares speak to me with such insolence."

"I am not one of your lieutenants."

"But you most certainly are a lady. And should comport yourself as one."

"You're the only one ever to question my character."

He crossed his arms over his chest. "I had good reason."

"You were wrong."

"It seems I was. But my brother is dead, Miss Willow. Will you blame me for caution in so serious a cause as finding his killer?"

"No." Her anger collapsed because he was right. "I cannot. If it were my brother, and I had the power to do so, I'd do the same."

"I am relieved."

She put one ankle behind her and curtseyed. "I won't detain you any longer. Good morning to you. My Lord." She slid past him, but felt immediate resistance, as if someone were tugging on her cloak. She looked behind her, but Tiern-Cope was two steps away and her cloak free of restraint. He fell in with her, and the air settled. "Are you following me?" she said.

"No."

He kept pace. After a bit, she said, "You are following me."

"That I must escort you on your errand is glaringly apparent." His mouth curved in a smile that made his eyes flicker with warmth. "Even to a woman as brainless as you pretend to be."

"I beg your pardon?"

"I am escorting you. Not following you."

"Don't make it sound so dreadful. Besides, I assure you, it's not necessary."

He reached for her parcel, brushing her hand in the process of hooking his fingers in the ribbon that bound the package. "And I assure you it is."

Chapter Eleven

"Give me that," Sebastian said when Miss Willow thrust her bundle behind her.

She opened her mouth to object, but thought better of it, or so he hoped. The top of her head came no higher than the second button of his greatcoat, which meant he stared down into her golden eyes. Her fiery hair, that age-old hallmark of a mischievous and passionate nature, curled willy-nilly above her ears and around her forehead. Were she five years younger she might have been styled gamine. Maturity suited her features.

"Your parcel, Miss Willow." He extended a hand.

She sighed but gave him the cloth-wrapped package.

He gestured. "Shall we?"

Without a word, she set off. She had a pert step. Every so often, the hem of her cloak and skirt flicked out and showed her ankles. He thought of the package in his room, just arrived from Carlisle. The gowns and slippers. A pair of stockings that when he saw them, he'd held in his hands and imagined sliding off her legs and then his fingers slipping between her thighs. The parcel's contents were bulky, soft on one side and rather than tuck it under an arm, he let it dangle by the ribbons as she had done. "We'll discuss the weather," he said.

"It's cold, and it often snows this time of year."

"All right, Miss Willow, something else, then. What is your errand in Far Caister?"

"Did you ever hear," she said, "the tale of your brother testing the portcullis at the castle?"

"Your errand?"

She looked at him sideways. "Lord Fitzalan is right. You have been out of society too long."

He drew a breath. He did not, in fact, have a right to every thought in her head. He wanted them all, every last one, but must content himself with only a few. "Miss Willow, I no longer believe you were my brother's lover."

"Why, when he had my things?"

"He did. But I regret the conclusion I made as a result."

"Thank you."

"I have a further confession." He caught her shoulder, stopping her. The sun edged higher in the sky, almost directly in her eyes. He moved so as to block the light. "Your uncle was not your guardian. My father was. And he stood by while you and your mother were robbed of all that should have been yours."

Her forehead creased. "How much?"

"Fifty-five thousand pounds. Or thereabouts."

After a moment, she said, "I ought to have hired a better lawyer."

"I did not think I would hear such news as I have just now given you with such calmness."

She shrugged. "Would you feel better if I swooned?"

"I would certainly endeavor to catch you if you did."

"It's a great deal to take in, my Lord. It doesn't seem real. I've never had fifty-five pounds at once, let alone fifty-five thousand of them."

"A fortune."

"Is there any left?"

"By the time you retained the services of Mr. Melchior, Miss Willow, the money was gone."

"Then I can do nothing."

"That seems so." He clasped his hands behind his back. "Tell me, on the day of the accident, when your family met with such tragedy, who else was with you?"

"What difference does it make?" She started walking again.

"Perhaps none," he said. "But I should like to know the answer."

"My uncle."

"But not in the carriage."

"No. He rode. How did you know?"

"Because no other answer makes sense."

"Why not?"

"Mind where you're walking, Miss Willow."

She stopped at a cow path that angled across the road. Hoofprints made craters in frozen manure. She hopped over. He could not help himself, his attention flicked to her backside as she landed with hardly a sound. Even with the dratted cloak he could make out the curves. She faced him—he got his eyes up just in time—hands lifted to proclaim the ease of the task.

Olivia Willow was the kind of woman a man wanted to have without restraint or worry for her distaste of anything he might wish to do. In fact, he hoped she would enjoy the act as she enjoyed everything else in life. Making love to her would be interesting to say the least, and in no way ordinary. Everything she did, she did with enthusiasm, including hopping over muddy cow paths. Sebastian didn't want to imagine she would make love any differently. She couldn't be the sort of woman who would lie there waiting for her pleasure or worse, for his. She would take her pleasure, or learn to, by God. Demand it, shake it from him like ripe fruit from a tree. And with what he was telling her now, he would never have it from her. She looked at him. He needed considerably less than a hop to cross.

"Very nimble, Captain. Well on the road to recovery, I should say."

"Miss Willow." He took her by the shoulders again. "I have not told you all."

"What more could there be?"

"My brother Crispin drove the carriage that killed your father and brother."

She stepped free of his hands.

"I am very sorry."

"How long have you known?" she asked.

"Since yesterday.

"An accident."

"Crispin was drunk. What's more, your uncle knew the truth," he said. "My father bought his silence with your inheritance."

She started walking again. "Did Andrew know?"

"I expect that is what compelled him to collect what you sold."

"I understand."

"As I knew you would. You're a clever woman."

"He felt sorry for me."

"Yes."

"Do you?" She peeked at him.

"Yes."

"Well, don't. I don't want your pity."

"I do not pity you."

She looked away. "Good."

They walked another while in silence. He matched his step to hers because he was damned if a woman, and most especially a woman who could barely lay claim to five feet and seven stones, was going to walk him into the ground. His side began a slow burn, and he ground his teeth against the cramping in thighs and calves unused to prolonged and vigorous use. Fortunately, the path soon leveled out, and he caught his breath.

She went ahead a few feet—him with his eyes again darting to her hips—then stopped. "Here we are." She faced him. The breeze ruffled her hair, and curls dangled like copper corkscrews about her face. She held out her hands in expectation of his returning her parcel.

He'd hardly been aware of the change in scenery, from snow-covered hills and open slopes to stone buildings and cobbled streets. But, indeed, they stood on the threshold of a doorway squeezed between a tobacconist's and a stationer's. "If you're in need of cigars, Miss Willow, you had only to ask. The supply at Pennhyll is extensive."

Her mouth curved, and he wanted her to keep smiling. "I'll remember that in future." From a pocket, she withdrew a key. "Good day, my Lord."

"What is this place?" Now that they'd stopped, his body registered violent objection to the abuse of a mile's walk down the mountain. Hell. To pay. Pandelion whined.

"Home," replied Miss Willow.

He held out his hand for the key.

She sighed. "You're a very managing sort."

"I am a man, Miss Willow."

"I dislike being managed."

"Alas," said Sebastian.

Darkness enveloped them when the door to the street came closed, and with the draft of air he caught a whiff of scent, not flowery but with undertones of something that made him think of the outdoors. *Verbena,* he remembered. He kept a hand pressed to the wall while they climbed the stairs, an effort that sapped his strength. Four damn flights. At her soft instruction, he stopped at the top of the stairs and fit her key to the lock, by feel since the stairwell was dark as the inside of a storage hold. He heard the rattle of metal parts and then the click of tumblers. His hand gripped her elbow. The air rasped in his throat. With every beat of his heart, his body thrummed with hurt. The muscles of his thighs and calves tightened into slivers of pain. His ears buzzed, and his head felt stuffed full.

"My Lord?"

Her voice sounded far away. Damnation. His stomach rolled as if he sailed in rough seas. "Bloody sodding bugger," he said. His knees buckled.

"Ouf."

He had no breath to protest when she propelled him inside. He reeled against the door jamb, taking her with him because of her arm curled around his waist and because his legs refused to hold him. The simple physics of their position, her supporting him and him with his arm clinging to her like a barnacle to a ship's hull, brought them to a heap on the floor. By virtue of the wall behind him, he managed to end in a sitting position. He threw back his head, willing the pain to vanish or else just have done with him and swallow him whole. His world narrowed to the effort of breathing, of surviving the cramped muscles and white-hot pain in his ribs.

Miss Willow remained by him, tucked under his armpit. For another moment, he was glad she hadn't moved. Just when he had the presence of mind to comprehend how inappropriate their position, and how much he wished to continue it, she slipped free of him and faced him, kneeling to his left. The package rolled away.

"I told the servants not to give you food."

She reared back, not in avoidance of him, but in preparation for standing. "I'll send for the doctor."

He grabbed her wrist. "No."

"To Pennhyll, then. For a servant."

"No." His hand tightened around her wrist when he felt her try to rise.

"My Lord."

"That's an order, Miss Willow." Hell. His thighs felt permanently cramped, and his chest streaked with agony.

She pulled away, but he did not release her. "My Lord." Her voice came to his ears like the softness of new snow. He imagined the warmth of her naked wrist seeped into him, worked its way into his being; that the longer he touched her, the more some part of her melded with him, and that as they spoke that warmth worked an alchemical transformation on his soul until not even God himself could say what was him or her. "You're hurting me."

He eased his grip. He imagined her naked, her curls loose and bright as a fire. His imagination gave her larger breasts than he knew she possessed. Quite likely her waist would be small, and from watching her walk, he believed his surmise of proportionally long legs was accurate enough. Her wrists suggested ankles similarly small, besides which he'd seen enough to know that was so. As for a well-turned calf or slender thighs, she hadn't the size or build for anything but a thoroughbred's legs. The thought of her backside made his groin tighten. Soft under his hands, firm against his belly he hoped. Her mouth required no supposition, he saw its shape well enough, a kissable shape. Her eyes, that peculiar shade of brown, flashed like honey held to firelight.

With her free hand, she touched his brow, flitted over his cheek and last, and most surprising, the back of his neck. "No fever."

"I'm fine."

She turned away, but he caught her and brought her back, holding tight to her upper arms despite the pain. He imagined her hands touching him, her mouth and tongue on him, her voice soft and full with need while she kissed and stroked him everywhere a man could desire. He saw himself catching her breasts, one for each palm, and he felt her arching into his hands with her mouth parted on a groan of pleasure. He imagined taking her in this very room, laying her on the floor and mastering her insolence with long, hard thrusts deep inside her. He imagined her crying out with need of him. Now, that, he would enjoy.

She reached for the buttons of his coat. His hands flew out, grasping both her wrists.

"The devil." He was damned if he was going to make love to her on the floor.

Chapter Twelve

"If you won't let me send for the doctor," Olivia said, bending close, "at least let me have a look."

Sebastian bit the inside of his cheek and brought himself back to something like his normal self. He managed a nod. What a fool he was. Miss Willow had no reason in the world to consider him in anything like the light in which he'd just been thinking of her. She didn't even like him, for pity's sake. Couldn't possibly like him. Not now.

Nearly as competent as McNaught, she was, with quick, sure hands. He must have been favoring his wounded side, for she softened her touch there when she slid the garment off his shoulder. She dispatched the buttons of his waistcoat just as quickly. Her fingers brushed his shirt front and then separated the halves, reaching a hand to his injured side. "I need more light. Can you make it to that chair or will you stay here?"

Aware she had pointed, he shook his head. "Not yet." She rose, and he listened to the step of her boots across the floor. He heard her strike a flame, then smelled a mutton-fat candle. Through his closed eyes, the darkness lifted. She knelt at his side again. "Do you think your wound has broken open?"

He opened his eyes and lifted one shoulder, the one that didn't hurt him.

She pushed aside his waistcoat again, holding it away from his body. "I don't see blood."

"There's still a bandage."

"Oh. Then it's not soaked through, thank God."

"I'd rather not, if it's all the same to you."

She hesitated and then said, "That's wicked of you, my Lord."

"I'm a wicked man, Miss Willow." He was pleased to hear her laugh. Like her smile, the sound of her laughter lifted his spirits.

"I shan't remove the bandage. I might never get it back on if I do. Would you mind much staying without your coat? I don't want to cover you if your wound has begun to bleed."

He nodded assent.

Her fingers probed the spot where the bandage made a thickness beneath his shirt. He smelled verbena now instead of the candle, saw the curve of her cheek, the twists of copper falling away from her forehead. Arousal crept back. The floor might be just the place to find out how well she kissed and whether her mouth was as soft as it looked. She sat back presently, and their eyes met: collided, more like. Thick, russet lashes framed eyes the color of fine sherry. "No blood," she said, and then pressed her palm over his left chest.

"Waste of time, Miss Willow. I haven't a heart."

She snorted.

"Tired, nothing more." Aware of the impropriety of her seeing him with his torso next to bare, with his body undergoing an urgent reaction, he grabbed the edges of his waistcoat and fastened a few of the buttons. "If you'll help me stand, I think I can make it to that chair."

With a nod, she did as he asked. Once he was seated, she moved to the fireplace and quite capably started a fire. "You'll catch your death in here."

"I don't think Diana could start a fire to save her life."

"She'd have a dozen admirers to do it for her."

He buttoned his coat, too, because she was right: The air felt damned cold. "You taught school here? In this room?"

"Yes." Her head swivelled to him, attention landing on his buttoned coat. "You'll not leave until I say you may. And that, my Lord, is an order."

"You have no business amusing me."

She smiled. "My apologies. But I did tell you not to cover yourself." He arched one eyebrow in response. "On your head be it." She brushed off her hands and rose. "I'll not cry at your funeral."

"You sound like McNaught. Mother hens, the both of you. It's irritating."

"Tea. You need tea, that's what you need." She fetched her parcel from the floor. "If I go see if the kettle's on in—in the other room, you'll not expire on me, will you?"

"No."

Her departure left Sebastian in sole possession of the tiny parlor. He stood out of pure spite for her concern and the sake of his pride. Miss Willow made her life here, and he wanted to absorb the setting down to the smallest nuance of his family's crimes against her. A man could walk from one side of the parlor to the other in two steps. Not even a dozen candles would pierce the dreariness or erase the shadows. The Turkish rug looked as if it might have been cut down to fit the floor, the colors a vibrant echo of a once suitable setting.

He moved closer to the fire. Between the carpet's edge and the hearth the floor planks were black with age around spots worn white by years of use. Half a dozen coals lined the bottom of the battered scuttle. The fire was the size of a saucer, a few coals heaped in the center of a fireplace that didn't see many fires. The walls were whitewashed brick, the ceiling low with dark planks transversed by heavy beams. There were two doors, the one through which they'd come and the one through which Miss Willow had disappeared. One window looked onto the building next door, so close he could touch the sooty stone. The other had a view of Pennhyll.

There were two chairs, the table at his elbow and a wooden bench built into the window. One chair was a crude thing, bulky unseasoned pine. The other possessed a lightness of form that told of skilled woodwork and superior design. The table, delicate cherry, would not have been out of place at Pennhyll. On the mantel, propped against the wall, leaned a small, unframed portrait of a smiling older man whose red hair was too like Miss Willow's to mistake for anyone but her father. He carried the candle near. At the father's side stood a boy of perhaps nine or ten with sandy hair and a smile as joyful as his sister's. A collie pranced at his feet. In the distance behind them, a grand house and farther in the distance, the towers of Pennhyll. Quite a contrast, the life depicted in the painting and the one embodied in a room bare of comfort.

The second door opened. Miss Willow used a hip

to keep the door open and then balanced her tray on one hand while she gently closed it. "Sorry to have taken so long. I had to check on Mama and Mrs. Goody."

"I trust all is well."

She smiled, lifting one hand to brush a curl from her forehead.

Jesus. How could Andrew have laid a hand on her in violence? What possible excuse was there for such an offense? She'd told Andrew no. She'd refused his advances, as she would refuse any James made toward her, and his brother could not let her be because the privilege of his position gave him a life where a man came to believe nothing ought to be denied him.

"Yes, thank you. They're fast asleep, bless them, and they'll swear the both of them they slept not a wink all night and up with the sunrise." She put the tray on the table and then lit another candle brought with her from the other room. Just as capably as she'd started the fire, she filled a cup with tea and poured in a dollop of milk. She presented the saucer with a flourish. "My Lord. There's bread and fresh butter here. Help yourself."

"Miss Willow—"

"Please." Her eyes skittered away from his. "Not now."

He sipped and found it exactly to his taste. "Where do you sleep?" Damnation. He'd not been at sea so long that he'd forgotten the impropriety of asking a lady such a question as that. Well, when had he ever observed propriety with her? Besides, he wanted to know, and like his brother, her desires meant nothing in light of his own.

"Bread, my Lord?"

"Yes, thank you. Won't you have some?"

With a steady gaze, she said, "I'm not hungry." She'd stripped off her gloves somewhere between leaving him and making tea so that her hands were naked.

Sebastian watched the graceful arch of her wrist as she filled a cup for herself. A motion as gracious as anyone might see in the best drawing rooms. Her long fingers ended in nails serviceably blunt. She took no milk or sugar, and he wondered if it was preference or because he'd had the last of the milk, and she wanted to save the sugar for another day. She turned the cup, but not before he saw the chipped rim now hidden against her palm.

"It's your good fortune we have the flat with the kitchen."

"Indeed." Each moment felt more intimate, more comfortable and easy. He enjoyed the sound of her voice, the light in her eyes, the way she smiled, and how he felt when he looked at her.

Her mouth twitched, and she leaned forward in a confidential manner. "Well, perhaps kitchen overstates the case just a bit, but we can have tea when we like, and that's saved our lives on more than one occasion, I'm convinced of it. I've always sworn by the restorative powers of a cup of hot tea. That's what this country needs." She smiled fully this time, and his heart did another awkward turn in his chest. "More tea for everyone." She sipped and shuddered. Her clear eyes met his over the raised rim of her cup. "Goodness, it's hot. Caught me quite by surprise. I hope yours is not too hot."

"Perfect." Desire rose in him because she was so pretty and so sincere in her enjoyment of a cup of tea and because he was a man alone with a woman he admired.

"A Willow never accords a guest anything less than perfection."

"It took my valet a month to remember how much milk I like." Images from his dreams filled his head. Her skin beneath his palm, his thighs brushing hers.

She set down her tea. "Do you miss the Navy?"

"Yes."

"Every minute I spent away from here, I missed Mama, and Far Caister and seeing Pennhyll rising above the mist. And yet, ever since my return, I find myself remembering the day the children picked me the loveliest bouquet of flowers because someone had told them it was my birthday, and I nearly cry from missing them. They could be dreadful brats. Conceited and spoiled. You can't imagine what they were like at the beginning."

"Was it your birthday?"

"No."

"Were they disappointed?"

"It was such a lovely, thoughtful gesture. I wouldn't have spoiled it with the truth for all the flowers in the world. You see, and I suppose I ought not to admit it, but in all my years, no one has ever given me flowers. I've always thought that quite sad." She picked up her cup. "You ought to give Miss Royce flowers."

"Thank you for your advice."

"Andrew spoke of you often, you know. He was proud of you. Whenever you had an adventure, he was sure to read the account to anyone who would listen."

"Adventure?"

"Well, so it seemed to us. I suppose to you it was

all perfectly dull. For us, however, every moment a thrill." She tilted her head. "Still, I think you miss the Navy because you were very good at commanding a ship, not because of the adventures. It must have been difficult to leave."

"I haven't left."

She cocked her head in a way that invited silence or confidence, whichever he preferred. His choice surprised him.

"If ever a man wants to feel sure he's alive, he should sail into the line of battle." His chest tightened, but not from his injury. Why couldn't he remember what it was like? The very things that had once filled him with pride and anticipation now felt distant, as if he'd made them up or had happened to another man, and all he had was the broad detail of someone else's life. "Fighting the French. Confounding them and outsailing them and outgunning them. Using sea, wind and sail to make a ship do what I want." Every word was a bald-faced lie. Once, he'd felt those things, but he didn't anymore. He didn't feel anything. Nothing. Except where Miss Willow was concerned, he felt nothing at all. The realization shook him. It was true. He never felt alive except when he was with her.

Her mouth quirked. "Where you might die at any moment." Her legs crossed at the ankles. One foot tapped a silent beat against the other. Her boots were damp from the snow, and the sole of one was separating from the leather upper.

"When you command a ship there's no time to think about dying."

"You make me want to join up." She gave another of those grins that made her eyes dance. "What a shame they don't press the ladies as they do the men."

He assessed his physical state. Still an edge of desire, less sharp than before but there, distracting him. The pain in his side felt as it had at Pennhyll; present but not debilitating. His thighs no longer trembled. "I was born for the sea." What he wanted now was a taste of her mouth. He wanted to take her in his arms, hold her. Kiss her and make everything right.

"How fortunate for you, then, that your character suited your predicament. Not everyone is so lucky."

"It's in me, here." He tapped his chest where he knew there was nothing. "Not a drop of blood. Just salt water."

"So I've come to suspect."

He let that bit of impertinence pass. "I wanted to join the Army. But an Alexander spare who isn't a clergymen is always a sailor, and my father refused to let me break with tradition. No one defied my father for very long. Not even Crispin."

The name landed between them like a boulder.

"Forgive me," he said.

She nodded. "It's all right." Her tongue touched her lower lip. "It doesn't seem real. None of what you've told me feels real."

"Did Andrew ever mention him?"

Her eyebrows drew together. "No. Not that I recall."

A man in the grip of passion either acted on that passion or removed himself from the temptation. He could not act. However much he wanted her, to act would be unconscionable. He was going to marry Diana. He had no business settling his affections elsewhere. None whatsoever. He placed his cup on the table. What crime, he wondered, would the last of the Alexander men commit against her? Jesus. He was alone with her. Her reputation and future rested in his hands now. And he wanted her so intensely he did not trust himself to continue as a gentleman. "You were correct about the tea. I'm restored now."

He rose, found his overcoat and pulled it on. She followed him to the door. She straightened the lay of his lapel and then brushed off a bit of lint. "I'll speak to the staff about the dusty floors."

He clutched his side. "Do not make me laugh." Nor think another moment about having her in his arms. Sliding one hand high on the doorjamb, he leaned toward her. "What do you want most in life, Miss Willow?"

"For my mother to be well."

"Imagine you had that." His fingers rested on the nape of her neck. "What do you want for yourself?"

"Peace on earth?"

"Come, Miss Willow. I want a serious answer from you. Better yet, a selfish one." Though she stood inches from him, she seemed not to notice their proximity. As a grown man, he could control his base urges. He'd done so for years. He would do better by her than his father and brothers. Slowly, he lifted his fingers from the back of her neck. His palm took their place.

Head tilted, she considered him. "You'll laugh."

"Try me."

"A family. Children."

"What? Not thousands of pounds at your disposal? A mansion? Jewels to dazzle you? Servants at your beck and call?"

She rested the side of her head against the doorway and looked at him from beneath her thick red lashes. "I always thought I'd be married one day with half a dozen children at my knees." Her eyes danced again, and for a moment, the space of a breath, he was caught like a fly in a web. "I was right about the children at least, though I was sure they'd be mine."

"Are you sorry?" What soft skin she had, such a tender nape.

"That I'm not a wife and mother?"

"Mm." He imagined her with a husband, with children. His children. He saw her gravid by his doing, and him cradling an infant in his arms, the one he'd made in her. He could give her what she wanted, and, of course, he could imagine the act of making her so.

"I am. Yes." She smiled, a little sadly, he fancied. "But not inconsolably, my Lord. I expect, indeed, I hope, I'll soon be teaching again, with another passel of children to care for."

A deep breath caught the scent of her, a faint impression of outdoors, herbs, verbena and something light. Her nape under his palm made him feel his strength, and how easily he could overpower her. She was his, if he wanted her. She could not stop him doing just as he liked. The earl's ancient rights over Cumbrian serfs paled in comparison to what he might have by brute strength. Just as his brother had done. "Jesus, no."

"My Lord?"

Unthinkable. What he wanted was her willing and compliant. Never force. "You are too thin," he said. For all the ways in which she ought not to appeal to him, she did that and more. Desire surged in him. "Ladies ought not to have hollow cheeks. Damn me if you weigh seven stone. You're not even as tall as McNaught."

"I've hopes of growing five inches by Michaelmas."

He wondered if she felt the same pulse of arousal. If so, she had better control of herself than he. He pushed away from the door, astounded and dismayed by his thoughts. "Put on your cloak, Miss Willow. It's time we went back."

"Let me send to Pennhyll. Someone will fetch you."

"No."

"You are a stubborn man, my Lord."

He shrugged and wished he hadn't. His side throbbed. "It's only a mile, for pity's sake, I'm no weakling."

"Pride is an abiding sin, my Lord," she said evenly. "It does not flatter you."

"Devil take you, Miss Willow," he replied just as evenly. And then he couldn't stop himself. He smiled.

She smiled back. "We'll ask for a dog cart at the Crown's Ease."

"Very well."

"Let me check on Mama before we go."

After she'd made her good-byes, she returned with her gloves and her cloak. She pinched out the candles and broke up the fire. "Shall we?"

They walked to the inn, taking their time. Twilling came to the door, and Sebastian lifted a hand in summons. "A good morning to you, my Lord," Twilling said. "And to you, Miss Olivia."

"Good morning," Miss Willow said. "I've overdone myself, I'm afraid, and Lord Tiern-Cope has kindly offered to send for a carriage to bring us back to the castle. I thought instead you might lend us a dog cart to take us up the hill."

He gave no sign he saw through the excuse, just shouted for the ostler and gave the instructions when the man appeared. While they waited, Sebastian leaned against the wall by the door. He didn't dare take her inside, for he'd be forced to ask for a private room, and that would cause talk that would do her no good. He owed her better than that. Miss Willow stood to one side of him, close in case of disaster but far enough to satisfy propriety.

"Far Caister is a busy village," he said.

"Now the earl is back, there is much to do. And with the dancing day after tomorrow, there's even more than usual."

"Ah, yes. The dancing. And the seance. What nonsense."

"She's very young."

"Too young."

"That is not a permanent condition, my Lord."

He looked at her. "Do you believe in ghosts?"

To her credit, she did not laugh. "If you mean ghosts like the Black Earl of Pennhyll, no, I do not."

"Do you mean to say, Miss Willow, that you don't believe he's going to haunt us from dawn to dawn on the anniversary of his death?"

"Don't be ridiculous."

"But?" He could see himself reaching for her, folding her in his arms, molding his mouth over hers.

"The dead do haunt us. I believe that. In our minds. Not in body."

Across from the Crown's Ease, a man on horseback surveyed the street. By his clothes a gentleman, and with an eye for horseflesh, judging from the thoroughbred on which he sat. A traveler, Sebastian supposed, since to his knowledge, he'd met all the gentry of Far Caister. He must be deciding whether to go inside the inn. After a while, he realized the man was staring at Miss Willow. Curious. For a full minute and more, he'd sat his horse, taking his eyes off Miss Willow long enough to study him. "Who's that?" With his head, he indicated the man on horseback. "He's been watching you since we stopped here."

"Really?" She looked. "Where?"

"On the bay there. Across the street."

Whoever he was, he knew he'd been noticed, for he nodded at Sebastian and urged his horse toward the Crown's Ease. The gentleman, there was no doubting that much, lifted his hat in greeting. He had an open, friendly smile. "Good morning."

"Sir," Sebastian said, sliding his arm underneath Olivia's. He was under thirty, with a mouth primed to grin that made an otherwise unremarkable face interesting. His boots gleamed like jet, the cut of his coat showed off a suspiciously narrow waist and his cravat was starched to a razor's edge. His riding breeches looked as if he'd have a devil of a time peeling them off. He hadn't quite the legs for it.

The gentleman stared at them. "Olivia," he said, lifting his hat again. He glanced at Sebastian. "It is *Miss* Olivia Willow still?"

"Yes," Sebastian said. And if he knew her name, why was she silent? He drew her closer to his side. The ostler brought around the dog cart. The stranger had to back away, but he nudged his animal forward once Sebastian helped Olivia in the cart and climbed in himself. Pandelion jumped in the back while Sebastian arranged a blanket over Olivia's lap, tucking it around her legs. The paleness of her eyes struck him once again as more lush in effect than her hair. Damn her fantastic eyes. And now he had this absurd idea of being her husband stuck in his head. Bouncing their son on his knee.

"Ah. But not Miss Willow for long, I take it."

"And you are?" Sebastian said.

"My cousin," said Olivia. "Mr. Hew Willow."

Sebastian nodded, but just barely. "Mr. Willow."

"How long have you been back, Hew?"

"Arrived just yesterday." He looked at Sebastian. "Who is your companion, Olivia?"

Sebastian met the young man's gaze. He felt a wave of dislike. "I am Tiern-Cope."

"Tiern-Cope?" Hew Willow's eyes widened. His horse danced, hooves ringing on the street. "But Andrew— You must be the younger brother. Captain Alexander. Good heavens." He got his horse under control and inclined his head. He shot a glance at Olivia. "Lord Tiern-Cope. My deepest sympathies for your loss."

"Thank you."

"I'll call on you, Olivia. Are you still in Far Caister?"

"Yes, but I am staying at Pennhyll."

"Are you now?"

"Yes." She gripped the side of the cart. "Good day, Hew. Welcome back."

Sebastian drove slowly, aware of Olivia next to him. Occasionally, her shoulder touched him or his arm bumped her. He spread his thighs wide, crowding her because he was a perverse son-of-a-bitch, it seemed. Within sight of Pennhyll he stopped the cart and set the brake. "Are you in love with your cousin?"

"What?"

"I saw how you looked at each other."

She shook her head.

155

"Is he married?"

"I don't know. He wasn't a year ago."

He touched her temple. "Remember, what's here is mine, Olivia." Her intake of breath at the contact did not escape his notice. "And I don't share what's mine."

Chapter Thirteen

By eleven o'clock a dozen of Sebastian's neighbors crowded the salon off the Great Hall. Mrs. Leveret and her husband, Mr. Cage and his daughter, among others, gathered for the experience of eating the earl out of house and home. Footmen and parlor maids brought in food and drink and carried out the empty plates. One of the Leveret daughters sat at the pianoforte, butchering Haydn. Price appeared in the doorway. After a pause to sweep the room with doleful eyes, he made his way to Sebastian. "Mr. Hew Willow is calling, my Lord."

The announcement caused a sudden hush. He looked away from Price because Olivia Willow's unspeakably red head lifted from her game of Patience. Their eyes locked. His heart thudded, just the once before he mastered himself, but the arousal nearly flattened him. She sat at the edge of the gathering, near a corner where shifting light cast shadows behind her. He reached for the card on Price's salver.

Bone-chilling cold shot up his arm the moment he touched the card, as if he'd plunged his hand into a river of ice. Clouds passing over the sun made the light and dark behind Olivia shift and interchange, taking on the shape of a man. Not Andrew, but another man with familiar blue eyes. The hilt of a sword rose above his back, held in place by leather strap that crossed his torso. The rectangle of paper slipped from Sebastian's fingers and fluttered to the ground. Price bent to retrieve the card, and over the top of his stooped-over butler's back, Sebastian saw Olivia's eyes fix on the tray. Behind her, the figure advanced until it stood beside her. Indeed a man, dressed like someone who'd just stepped from the court of Edward II. Black hair fell to his shoulders. He wore a tunic with the Tiern-Cope crest on his chest. Cobalt and red.

Card in hand, Price stood, blocking Sebastian's view of Olivia. "My Lord?"

He stood up, but when he looked at Olivia, he saw—only Olivia. He searched the shadows behind her. Nothing. No movement, not even the suggestion of a man. "What shall I tell him, Miss Willow?" Sebastian said.

"I've no idea." With one of the empty smiles she was so expert at giving, and which he despised, she returned to her card game. The bend of her head exposed the nape of her neck and one copper curl fell free of her pins.

"Mr. Hew Willow, you say?" Diana asked.

The butler inclined his head. "Yes, Miss Royce." The man sounded as if he'd just confirmed that, indeed, his entire family had perished by shipwreck.

"Is he young and handsome?"

"I cannot say, Miss Royce."

Miss Cage clapped her hands. "Oh, yes, Miss Royce. Indeed, he is handsome. I'd heard he was home."

"Miss Willow," Diana asked, "is Mr. Hew Willow your relative?"

"He is."

James came to attention, none too pleased, from his expression. "My Lord Tiern-Cope," said Diana, "if Miss Willow won't tell you so, I shall. Invite him up. Do, please."

Olivia's glance inevitably lit on him, since he controlled at least the immediate future. She wasn't expecting to find him watching her, for when their eyes met a faint color crept into her cheeks. Jealousy twisted in him when he remembered the heat of Hew Willow's stare, how worried he'd seemed that Miss Willow might be spoken for and under another man's authority. Why the devil was he back and interested in the cousin he'd neglected for so long?

Sebastian nodded at Price, and his gray-headed butler gave a sorrowful bow. Not much later, the sound of bootsteps in the hallway floated through the open door. Olivia hesitated in laying down a card, and then her neck bent lower, hiding her face. Odd, he thought. One wouldn't think a woman with hair like that could hide from anyone, but she managed to make herself nearly invisible. Outside the door, a man laughed. The young ladies turned, a few patted their hair or smoothed a wrinkle from a skirt.

"This way, Mr. Willow."

Sebastian straightened. The hair on the back of his neck stood straight. He rose, his hand dropping to his hip. Every fiber of his being, every nerve in his body screamed of approaching danger. If he'd had a weapon, he'd have drawn it. And been prepared to use it. James, too, faced the door. The anticipation could have been served up like a goose on a platter.

"Thank you," someone said from the hallway.

The infamous duelist, Mr. Hew Willow, walked in. The heir so bloody relieved to know that Miss Willow remained *Miss* Willow, who must know she ought to have been an heiress and was not.

Hew went directly to Sebastian and bowed, heels clicking. He wore a different set of riding clothes, tight fitting, held a hat under one arm and his riding whip in the other. A lock of snuff-colored hair fell over his forehead. "My Lord. Good afternoon."

"Mr. Willow." Sebastian kept his hands clasped behind him and forced himself to smile. He did not like Hew Willow any better now than when they met in Far Caister.

"Thank you, my Lord, for seeing me." Hew surveyed the room with eyes the color of day-old coffee, stopped on Diana and registered a male appreciation of her and Miss Cage. Quite natural for the man to admire a pretty woman when he saw one. Eventually, though, Hew's attention settled on his cousin. "I've intruded." He spoke to Sebastian, but he meant the words for Olivia. While Hew stared, James examined him head to toe, assessing his rival.

"Allow me to present my guests, Mr. Willow."

Willow's expression went from grave to delighted. When he was introduced to Diana, he took her hand in both of his. "An exquisitely lovely girl." He gazed into Diana's tilted eyes. "Charmed, Miss Royce, charmed indeed to make your acquaintance."

Diana gazed at Hew from beneath her thick lashes. "How wonderful to meet you, Mr. Willow." Those tilted eyes did their work; Hew held her eyes a moment too long. "Did we meet in London?"

"I had not that pleasure." He swept the floor with

his hat. "I look forward to our acquaintance." A grin leapt to his mouth. "With your permission, that is, my Lord Fitzalan."

"I believe you know Miss Willow," Sebastian said when he came to presenting Olivia. He acknowledged his treacherous state and took care to keep any hint of it from his voice. "Of Far Caister."

"Yes. Of course." He put his hat on the mantel before going to her. "Dear cousin Olivia." His voice softened. "I am so very pleased to see you again."

"Hew." She stood, clutching a book in her hands as if it were a shield.

He took it from her. "I have been away too long." He looked first at James, then Sebastian. "Do not tell me I am too late."

Chapter Fourteen

Sebastian watched Olivia. Though she appeared composed, he felt the slightest pressure would break her apart like porcelain stressed to the point of shattering. The turmoil beneath the surface was a living thing. Another cloud moved over the sun. Shadows skittered behind Olivia again, taking shape. From across the room, a man's eyes glittered like blue ice. While Sebastian watched, the apparition reached both hands behind him and drew the sword from its scabbard. He heard the ring of metal vibrating. The light changed, and he vanished.

"Dearest cousin," Hew Willow said. "I am glad to find you in such good health and excellent looks." He scanned the room again and, once again, paused when he got to Sebastian, long enough for an up-and-down glance.

He knew he didn't imagine the challenge in Hew's eyes. He itched to throw the fellow out on his breeches-clad arse. Hew dropped Olivia's book onto the table and grasped her hands. She stiffened. Her face was blank. No blush, no smile, not a hint of welcome. And not that ridiculous vapid stupidity she sometimes affected either. She seemed paralyzed. James, frowning at Hew's hands enfolding Olivia's, stepped forward.

With a twist of his upper body to take in Sebastian and the others, Hew said, "I've known her since she was a girl."

She tugged on her hands, but he did not let go. Emotion flashed over her face. Distaste? Fear?

"I used to watch her running through the fields, all arms and legs and braids bright as a new penny." He shook his head, smiling still. This time, Hew directed himself to Sebastian. "Your father, my Lord, warned me she'd grow into a beauty one day." He spread his arms wide, taking Olivia's with him. "And she has. Look at you, Olivia."

Olivia tugged on her hands. "Hew."

Though his smile remained, something moved in his dark eyes, disquieting. "You want your book." He reached for the volume but rather than return it, he examined the spine. "Southey. Not only a beauty, but an intellect. Certainly, one cannot quarrel with your reading." He handed it to her. "Lord Fitzalan," Hew said, turning. "I believe I met your aunt, Mrs. Carmody, in Naples last June. Delightful lady. Just delightful. I was pleased to make her acquaintance. I hope she continues well."

"As well as can be expected." James brushed a speck of lint from his sleeve.

Olivia let the book slide from her fingers and onto the table. She sat down, back stiff as a dressed hide. With trembling fingers, she took her cards and squared them in preparation for shuffling. Instead, she let go the deck and pressed her palms onto her lap.

"Do give your aunt my regards," Hew said to James.

"Staying long?" James looked less and less pleased by Hew's polish. That he could claim some acquaintance with his family must rankle almost as badly as his close one with Miss Willow. Olivia bowed her neck, pressing her fingers to her temples. Her head must be hurting again. Lord, but he could feel her tension. More and more of it every minute. He thought about how she'd taken care of him in Far Caister. She spent her life looking after other people, and no one looked after her. Least of all her prodigal cousin.

"That, my Lord," Hew said to James, "is not entirely certain." He craned his neck to look at Olivia who stared at her lap. "That depends upon—matters I must attend to whilst I am here."

"And what does bring you to Far Caister?" James's smile was spring, but his voice was pure winter.

"I've neglected the estate, and my duties at it, for too long. It's time I came home. To stay."

"You live near here?" Diana languidly waved her fan.

"Just over the hill, as a matter of fact."

"Perhaps we've seen your home while we've been

taking advantage of Lord Tiern-Cope's fine stables."

"Likely so, Miss Royce. The Grange abuts Pennhyll on the east."

"The Grange?" Diana said. "Yes, I recall. A very pretty estate."

"Are we to meet your wife, Mr. Willow?" Just a hint of vinegar lurked behind James's inquiry.

"That, my Lord, is yet another obligation I have neglected to satisfy." His gaze flickered over the room but at last landed on Olivia. "And one I hope soon to remedy."

Under other circumstances, Sebastian would have been hard pressed not to laugh. Two weeks ago, he would have, and heartily. Hew's reappearance in Cumbria was doubly fatal for James. Not just a male relative to look out for Miss Willow, but one who all but announced himself her suitor. Hew Willow sounded exactly like a man prepared to offer the world in order to be forgiven some transgression. God knows, Olivia deserved someone to care for her, someone willing to look after her and see that she was protected, as a wife, not a mistress.

"You've come just in time," said Diana.

"So it seems," Hew said with a look at James.

"We're to have dancing on St. Agnes' Eve, Mr. Willow." Diana's eyes sparkled. "If you are looking for a wife, you must come. We'll have any number of eligible young ladies."

He made a leg, and Sebastian would have bet a fleet of ships he'd perfected it at Almack's. "I hope, Miss Royce, you will reserve a dance for me." He turned to Olivia. "Save me one, too, cousin Olivia. You will be there, won't you?"

"Of course." She reached for her cards. No one but

Sebastian noticed her hands tremble while she laid out a game of Patience. He leaned against the mantel, removing himself from the ebb and flow of the gathering in order to watch and let matters settle. This was unexpected, his dislike of Hew Willow, and more, his dislike of Olivia's reaction to her cousin.

"I'm keen on seeing the Black Earl," Hew said when Diana told him of her plans. "When I was a schoolboy home on holiday, I used to sneak into Pennhyll and look for the Black Earl. All the other boys in Far Caister bragged of at least one dread encounter with the Black Earl. Your brother, my Lord Tiern-Cope, had not yet come here, you were sailing the oceans and your father off to London."

"Did you ever see him?" Diana asked, eyes round with excitement. "I should adore hearing about your encounter. The more I know, the more likely I shall succeed in summoning the Black Earl."

"Never got past the caretakers, more's the pity. They were well prepared for young boys looking for thrills. Price, as I recall, was particularly fierce. He caught me in the library once and threatened to tan my hide. I believe he meant it." A smile lit his face. "What an ogre. I worried he might follow through when I called just now."

One gained nothing by denying the truth, however unpleasant, and the unpleasant truth here was that if Hew Willow were married he would not care one whit how much attention the fellow paid to Olivia. Hew represented not just a rival for James but for him. The truth, once acknowledged, could be dealt with. He would deal with this revelation about the depth of his attraction to Olivia Willow. He must, since he had told James he would marry Diana. He pushed off from the mantel, checking the shadows. Nothing. He wasn't going mad.

Hands clasped behind his back, he started a circuit of the room. Hew kept pace with Sebastian's progress around the room, turning so as to keep him in sight. From the corner of his eye, Sebastian occasionally caught a flicker of shadow, a flash of blue eyes. But whenever he looked, he saw nothing. Hew Willow was free to marry where he liked, while Sebastian was not. If Olivia's cousin indeed wanted to marry her, then he, Sebastian, ought to do all he could to encourage the union. He wondered if Hew knew about the money kept from the Willow women. He must know. Melchior would have made it his business to contact the successor-in-interest. He stopped at the sidetable and put a selection of food on a plate. Two petit-fours, ham, bread, some cheese. He carried it to Olivia and set the plate by her elbow. "Miss Willow."

She stared at the offering and then him.

"There's no harm in accepting a kindness. Even from me." No men lurking in the shadows.

"Thank you."

"Shall I ask your cousin to stay to dinner?"

She placed a queen atop the king of spades. "You are master of your own table."

"The jack there." Sebastian pointed at the queen. "I am very much master here. But, as you well know, sadly lacking in the social graces. Advise me."

"Very well." Again, she turned to look at him. "Do not ask him to stay."

"Why not?"

"If you do, the numbers will be uneven."

"I believe he declared himself your suitor."

Her eyebrows drew together. "You are mistaken."

"He acts as if he is." His finger brushed the curls from her neck. The sensation rocked him. Her skin felt warm. Rose-petal soft. "When a man stares at a woman like that, the way your cousin looks at you, what else can he mean? I would not want to deprive you of a suitor who might bring you flowers."

"He is not my suitor." She looked behind them, to where her cousin sat next to Diana, and in so doing left Sebastian staring at the way her torso twisted, the line of her waist and bosom and her throat. Small she was, but her figure was in no way insubstantial.

"Liar, Miss Willow." He wanted her. Pure and simple. Lust. Nothing deeper. Nothing more complicated. A man could always control his lusts, however urgent.

"As you say."

"He seems quite the jovial young man, yet you went the color of chalk when he came in."

"Did I?" She turned her head, and the connection between them, at the very spot where his palm touched her nape, flared with heat. He'd settled on Diana. He would marry Diana, not a copper-haired spinster far too used to managing for herself. A woman so tied up with the Alexanders he might never make sense of the past or her role in it. He was not Crispin or Andrew or his father. He knew the meaning of restraint.

"I wonder why?" he said.

She shook her head. He felt the pull of attraction when he looked into her eyes. More dangerous than sailing unarmed into a sea of enemy ships. His head filled with thoughts of her in his bed, of claiming her as his and none other's. He could not. He was not free to attach himself to anyone other than Diana.

"Mr. Willow." He faced Hew. "Take a turn about the room with your cousin. You must have a great deal to talk about."

Hew stood. "Indeed, my Lord. We do."

He never felt so helpless in all his life as when Olivia took Hew's hand. He stood there, feeling ridiculous and jealous both, and over a woman he was supposed not to like. He returned to the mantelpiece, one foot propped on the grate while he pretended not to watch Hew and Olivia, though he followed them with his eyes every step. It seemed to him that as Hew walked with her, Olivia's mouth thinned with tension. Her smile never once appeared.

Mr. Cage approached him for an opinion on the war, and for some minutes he lost track of Olivia. When he was free again Hew and Olivia stood by an arched doorway partially concealed by a fern on a high stand. Shadows in the doorway shifted. He blinked. Shook his head. Olivia faced the room, listening to her cousin with fists clasped at her sides. A man stood in the arched passage behind them. The same blue eyes. Sodding shadows. He strode to the doorway, eyes fixed on the figure. Any minute he expected the figure to vanish. He wasn't mad. He wasn't.

Hew threw a hand in the air. ". . . Olivia. Why not?"

A footman walked through the door, balancing a tray. He had blue eyes and wore the Tiern-Cope livery. Hew looked over his shoulder. "Oh, it's you, Lord Tiern-Cope." He turned to Olivia. "Do you mind awfully, Olivia, if I have a moment with Lord Tiern-Cope?"

Sebastian glanced at the doorway. A mirror hung on the corridor wall, just opposite the door. He must have seen reflections in the mirror, not the ghost of his long-dead ancestor.

"Not at all." She reached for Hew's arms and gently pushed so she could pass. "Do excuse me. My Lord."

Sebastian bowed and, like Hew, watched her walk to the center of the room. James intercepted her, drawing her into conversation. "She is my relation," Hew said when Sebastian and he faced one another. "I have some responsibility to her."

"I'd say that's so, Mr. Willow."

"I am quite aware, my Lord," Hew said, "that I have neglected certain obligations."

"You have."

"I am here," he said, "to remedy my neglect."

"Full amends?"

"If possible."

"Then I would say your first order of business is a frank talk with Lord Fitzalan about his intentions."

Hew's eyebrows shot up. "You were cozy with her when I saw you in Far Caister, and you've been watching her like a hawk from the moment I came in. Perhaps the first act of my reformed relations with my dear cousin should be a frank conversation with you about your intentions, my Lord."

"Mine are simple enough. While she is my guest at Pennhyll, she is under my protection."

Hew cocked his head. "Really?"

"A responsibility I take quite seriously." Sebastian clasped his hands behind him, tucking a fist into the small of his back. "Let's you and I talk about your intentions first. Past, present and future."

Chapter Fifteen

January 20

"Price told me I'd find you here, Miss Willow."

Startled, Olivia turned on her chair. Tiern-Cope stood just inside the parlor, tapping one hand against the side of his leg. His eyes were two shades lighter than his blue coat. Surely, it was unnatural for anyone to have eyes so piercing. From the mud on his boots and his mussed hair, she supposed he was just done walking as opposed to on his way to it. She closed her journal. "My head aches, and I wanted a moment's quiet, that's all."

His eyes swept the room, pausing behind her where there wasn't anything but shadows. Then, his attention fixed on her journal. She slid the book into a drawer. "I should like a word with you."

"Certainly." She indicated a chair.

He glanced at his boots and shook his head. "Might we walk in the garden? I won't detain you long. You'll have plenty of time to change for tea."

"Yes, of course." She scanned his face for some clue to his mood but, as ever, saw nothing but cold reflection. He helped her arrange her shawl around her shoulders and then held the door for her, waiting for her to precede him.

"This way." He gestured when they reached an outside door. She went through, and he followed. Late afternoon sun cast long shadows on the terraced garden where despite the snow, it wasn't cold, and the sky was clear. Olivia walked beside him. He kept his hands behind his back. They passed under an arch covered by a leafless climbing rose.

"A pretty garden," she said to break the silence.

He shrugged. "I expect you have more reason than I to know the truth of that." He lifted a hand, palm out. "Only because you have surely been here in the spring."

"It is lovely then."

"Are you warm enough?"

"Yes."

"My good friend Dr. Fansher is here at last. I've taken a liberty, Miss Willow, and told him of your headaches. He's most anxious to examine you."

She thought of her dwindling supply of coins, and her present lack of employment. "I've been to the apothecary in Far Caister."

"Never mind the cost, Olivia. I insist, and so does he."

"That is kind of you both."

"My first Luff writes me there are three ships due at Falmouth, and he expects I shall have my pick of the command of them."

"What, all three?"

"Those three plus another score."

"A fleet." Her heart sank even as she felt a surge of pride on his behalf. "That's splendid news indeed, sir."

"I have only to be married and quickly."

"I've no doubt you're up to the task, my Lord."

"Forgive me, I did not ask you to walk with me in order to tell you of my wedding plans."

"No."

"I've asked to speak with you at the request of your cousin. He is of the opinion, and I concur, that some advice is best heard from a disinterested party."

"What sort of advice, my Lord?"

"Allow me, for the moment, to act in the place of a guardian, an office more necessary than otherwise because your mother's condition means you have not, I believe, the benefit of a parent's wise advice." They left the garden for the lawn, the way marked by lumps of snow-covered stones. Wide enough for them to walk side by side. Snow crunched under their feet.

"Go on."

"It is a common trick among rogues to promise an innocent woman a future marriage in return for a present liberty. And she, flattered by the notice of a handsome and well-formed man of some fortune and consequence, grants that liberty. Once the liberty is gained, the impetus for a permanent union vanishes. The price is inevitably greater for the woman than for the man. She pays with her honor and reputation, and once those are spent, she cannot regain them, however naive or sincere her belief in the promise made to her."

She took a deep breath. "You believe my conduct leaves me open to such a charge?"

"Your behavior, so far, has been irreproachable."

"Then what prompts you to be so free with your advice?"

"Don't be impertinent."

She glanced down, saw the battered tips of her boots hitting the hem of her gown. "My apologies."

"I believe, and your cousin concurs, that you are in danger from a rogue just such as I have described."

"May I know of whom you speak?"

"Who else but James—Lord Fitzalan?"

"He's done nothing dishonorable. I assure you."

Tiern-Cope matched her stride on the path. "May I ask if he has engaged your affections?"

"I find him amiable in the extreme. I cannot complain of his character, my Lord."

"And if I told you he plans to let you believe he'll marry you, if that false impression will gain him his designs upon your person?"

"I would not believe it."

"Your faith in him is admirable."

She tipped her head toward him and found him watching her. "And that faith will not falter until I have evidence to make me believe I should have so poor an opinion of him."

"If it is then too late?"

"He flirts with all the young ladies, my Lord. That doesn't mean he proposes to them all or means to seduce them all. I appreciate your warning, but Lord Fitzalan has done nothing to make me think he has inappropriate intentions." She laughed. "Why would he? I have red hair."

"So you do, Miss Willow."

"There you have it."

"I confess myself mystified by your conviction that your hair renders you unattractive."

"You don't like my hair."

"I cannot imagine how you got that impression. That, however, is not the issue at hand. James has admitted to me he means your reputation no good."

She slowed, hearing the ring of conviction in his voice. "Is that true?"

"You are a very pretty woman, Miss Willow, and men notice you. James admires you. He admires your person, red hair and all. Rest assured, if I may be bolder than I ought, he desires more than is proper. I have warned him from this path, but I cannot guarantee he will take another. I regret my friend would deal with you so coarsely. He is charming, Miss Willow. And he intends to convince you of a very great untruth, which means he is more charming than usual."

They came to a fork in the path. Left to the lake and the boathouse, straight on to the oak. She liked James. He amused her. The truth was she was flattered by his attentions, and she took some pride in thinking she'd earned the respect and admiration of a man like Lord Fitzalan. And Tiern-Cope was right. She had begun to think Fitzalan meant more than friendship. She felt the corner of her mouth twitch downward.

Tiern-Cope nodded in the direction of the oak at the end of the path. "Let us walk just there and back." When they reached the tree, he grabbed a branch and dislodged a waterfall of snow from the leaves. "Better, now?"

She pointed to Pennhyll. "There's my window." They faced the north tower, the oldest wing. "Three floors up. Do you suppose if we wait long enough we'll see the Black Earl pacing the ramparts?"

"No, I do not."

"Of course not." She gave him a look surprised they were getting on so easily. "It's just that sometimes—"

"What?"

"Nothing." She turned. Staring into the oak leaves over her head, she wished her head did not pound.

She felt like someone was pounding a nail into her skull. "Look. Mistletoe."

"So there is." He faced her, a smile on his lips. "I am not going to kiss you."

Despite the ache in her brain, her stomach did a flip. "I didn't ask you to."

His eyes darkened. "You're in pain, aren't you?" He touched her temple, and she leaned her head against his hand.

"Yes." The inside of her head felt stuffed full like an iron band slowly tightened around her brain.

"Still having bad dreams?"

"Nightmares." She put her palms flat to his chest and spoke to the buttons on his coat. "Always the same. A face looming over me. I can't breathe. I feel helpless. And frightened."

"Hush, my heart." His fingertips nudged her chin up so that she looked into his face. "Hush."

She leaned against him. "Why can't I remember?"

"It isn't time, yet." His hands landed on her shoulders.

"When, then? When will it be time?" She pushed away, leaving his embrace. "I'm cold."

Tiern-Cope faced her. "I am at your command, Olivia." He slipped a hand under her elbow. They walked toward the castle in comfortable silence until he released her. Then, she found herself taking two steps for every one of his. Perhaps ten yards from the house, he whirled, and she collided with him. He steadied her, and they backed apart. "There is one other matter I wish to discuss."

"Yes?"

"I've spoken at length with your cousin. He, too, is concerned by the way in which James singles you out, and upon less knowledge of the circumstances than I. In the main, I should say, he has convinced me he has your interests at heart." He plucked the edge of her shawl, twitching it over her shoulders. "Given the circumstances, your cousin is prepared to make amends in the only way left him. With all that my family has done, I cannot help but feel responsible for you."

"I told you before, I don't want your pity."

"You do not have it." He clasped his hands behind his back. "Let there be no mistake. Marriage, Miss Willow, is what your cousin intends and what James does not. Your cousin's offer you will have in earnest."

A sick feeling uncurled in the pit of her stomach. Her head throbbed. "He doesn't love me. Nor do I love him."

"What does that signify?" His eyes snapped with frost. "You do not know him well, for all that you are such near relations. But he has much to recommend him. He's possessed of a substantial estate, as well you know, and can certainly support a wife in comfort. Your antecedents are impeccable. Though by marrying you he would raise you from your present difficulties, he, on the other hand, cannot be said to be marrying down. It is a remedy he ought to have seen sooner than this."

"Was it your idea?"

"Not entirely. Come along."

When they reached the door from which they'd exited, Tiern-Cope held it open. "Come now, Miss Willow, you must admit your future is not a bright one. Marriage to your cousin is an excellent solution. Nothing could be more logical."

"I am sure that's so."

He followed her through to the salon. At the doorway to the interior hall, he stopped her with a hand to her elbow. "He will be here for the ball and that bloody ridiculous seance of Diana's. When he proposes, Miss Willow, you will accept him."

"I don't want to marry him. He makes me— Oh, I can't describe it." His eyebrows lifted in amusement, and she knew what he was thinking. "You are a wicked man. Not that."

"Not what?"

"Uneasy. He makes me uneasy." Lord, his eyes were blue.

"You're not used to being courted."

"It's not as if I've never had a beau."

"Very well, then. Courted by someone you do not know well. Doubtless you would be—uneasy—if I were courting you."

"That's unkind, my Lord."

"How so?" He waved a hand, towering over her. "Marriage is the only solution to your predicament." She couldn't back up because he continued to hold her elbow. He put his back to the door. His eyes moved around the room, paused on something and then focused on her. "Have you another candidate in mind? You have only to tell me his name, and I will do what I can for you."

"Women such as I don't have their pick of suitors."

"What do you mean, women such as you?" He leaned against the wall by the door, arms over his chest.

"Like me. Like this."

"Like what?" He captured her wrist. "Women like what, Miss Willow?"

"My Lord." She released a world of frustration in the honorific. Did he not understand the problem? "I have red hair."

"By God, you do." And then he kissed her.

Chapter Sixteen

Sebastian started in full possession of his faculties, aware of what he was doing but enjoying it too much to question the wisdom of kissing her. He wanted to kiss her, so he did. He was. He had no difficulty clearly and precisely carrying out the process, no matter what he thought he saw in the shadows. At first he had just a taste of her mouth, for she barely parted her lips. A kiss charmingly unschooled, which meant, besides surprising her, she hadn't done much kissing before. He pulled back. She looked bemused.

"Your eyes aren't a proper color," he said. "Women with red hair ought to have green eyes. Yours are brown and not even a proper brown at that."

"I'll remedy that. Just as soon as I can."

"You've only one or two gowns, and I daresay that pitiful thing is your only shawl. Look at this," he said in a low voice, reaching for a fraying edge. "How many times have you mended this? A dozen? Several dozen?" His fingertips hovered above the rise of her chest.

"There is no help for it, my Lord."

He trapped her chin between his thumb and fingers, forcing her to look at him, staring into her face and at her mouth. "I never make love to women as small as you." He sounded raw, and he really didn't care. "My tastes, such as they are, run more to Diana's sort. Prettier than you. Taller. More substantial. I need a woman I'm not afraid to break in the depths of passion. I need a woman who gives back in full measure." He ached. He positively ached. "And yet, Miss Willow, I find myself constantly thinking you are a very pretty woman."

She frowned, and he tightened his hands on her.

"Your eyes— A man could sail into them fathoms deep." He studied her as if he could deconstruct her by force of will. "A man might decide your figure is your best feature, or perhaps your mouth. But I find myself inclined to believe your eyes hold first rank among your many charms. No wonder James wants you."

The wall against his back made a convenient prop. Leaning against it, he caught at her lips with his. She gasped into his mouth. Whether the cause was outrage or shock or passion, he took advantage. He was a scrupulous man when it came to women in whom some other man had an interest. He wasn't so far gone over her that he didn't consider the priority of James's claim or Hew Willow's intentions; he just let the thoughts flit through his head and off to freedom from morals.

He put his hands on either side of her waist, pulling her against him, thumbs just at her hips. His tongue bridged the gap between her lips. Tightness took hold in his belly because she didn't deny his mouth. Indeed, no. Her chin angled toward him so he did not have to bend quite so far, and her fingertips balanced on his biceps. He remained in control, bringing her along to the deeper embrace he craved.

The unfamiliarity and newness of her, her inexperience, seduced him as thoroughly as the most intimate and accomplished of kisses. The perfume she wore, just a whisper of scent, filled his next breath. Her lips felt full and soft beneath his and tasted as sweet as any woman he'd known in his life. Hell, as sweet as anything he'd felt in his life. This feeling of completion was what he'd been looking for since he came to Pennhyll, for his entire life since he became a man. He'd wanted to kiss her for a very long time, and now that he was doing it, he wished he'd not waited so long.

When he pushed aside her arms so he could bring her tight against him, cup the back of her head with his palm, she offered no resistance. They came as close as two dressed people could get. She softened against him. His brain, which had been leading the way quite nicely while providing such information as she felt nice, she smelled good, her mouth was responding under his and that everything so far suggested she would let him kiss her a deal longer, ceased functioning.

The tightness in him uncoiled like a spring. He had no more control of himself than he did of an ocean tide. The currents swept him away. His arms encircled her, grounding him when the room disappeared in a wave of emotion. The world condensed to just the space occupied by their bodies. Oh, Jesus. She was exactly what he needed: soft and warm and passionate. When her mouth yielded to his, quite suddenly he was the one kissing with all the eagerness of a tyro desperate to understand his craft.

Instinct and greed took over. He swept his tongue into her mouth, his hands shifting up and down her back, molding her to him, and he actually trembled with the desire raging through him. What he wanted was to be inside her. No, he needed it. Required it. He would die unless he was. They could have been standing on the quarterdeck in the middle of a pitched battle, and he would have wanted to be inside her. The sooner the better. He stopped kissing her just long enough to say, "Olivia."

He peeked over her shoulder, and sure enough, there in the corner, not quite free of the shadows, he saw a man. The pattern of his tunic flashed with color. Gold. Crimson. Well, he'd vanish again in a moment, and he had better things to do than watch shadows. "That was much too fast," he said. "I'm not usually a clod." Easing her back, he smiled. "It's been a long time for me, and I—"

"Why did you do that?" Her breath came rapid and uneven. Her eyes were pools of honey.

He touched one of her curls. "Because it's you." He scrubbed his fingers through his hair, then let them drop again to her shoulders. "Because I haven't—" He stopped short of the earthy phrase that came to mind. "Not since Maçao and that was— God, months and months ago. Because I want to make love to you. I have since the moment I saw you." He stroked the side of her face, unable to believe the extent of his need or even begin to fathom the impulse that had him begging like some downy-cheeked boy. He stared at her mouth and wondered why it drove him mad with desire. A pleasant mouth and not more. Not lush or plump or winsome. An ordinary mouth he wanted with extraordinary heat to kiss again. So, he did.

Everything in the world was right with kissing her. His body settled right into hers. He brought her head toward his, his mouth over hers and the whole thing started over. He spread his thighs and brought her between his legs, hard against him. She was better at it this time. Miles better. The damn shadows flickered again. He turned so that her back pressed against the wall, his palms just above her shoulders. Slowly, her eyes closed, as if her lashes were unexpectedly heavy. He was hers, he thought. She owned his heart and his life. He put a finger beneath her chin and brought her face back to his. Through a veil of deep red lashes he saw the honey-gold of her eyes. "You have the most beautiful eyes of any woman I've ever known."

Her arms lifted and went around his shoulders. "That's very sweet."

He bent his head and brushed his lips over hers. Her eyelashes fluttered against his cheeks, then stopped. With a bit more display of finesse this time, he explored the surfaces of her teeth, her tongue, the inside of her cheeks. His lips sought and took, firing a need that drew him closer and closer to conflagration. In the back of his head, he heard someone in the hallway, distant, and not headed in their direction but the sounds reminded him they were far from private. With his mouth hovering over hers, he said, "Olivia. My love. My own. If we're to continue this, I want you on your back." He breathed deep. "If you cannot agree to that, then we stop now."

She opened her eyes, a sleepy look. The look of a woman thoroughly kissed. His body wound itself even tighter.

Chapter Seventeen

January 21, 12:00 A.M.—St. Agnes' Eve

The clock in Olivia's room tolled midnight. Uneasiness carved a hollow in the pit of her stomach as she readied herself for bed, and not just because the closed curtains of her window covered a space large enough to hide a man. She hadn't gone downstairs for supper, instead, pleading headache, she cowered in her room. She hadn't the courage to face Tiern-Cope after what had happened this afternoon. Nearly happened. This time, he really and truly had kissed her. She hadn't imagined his mouth covering hers, the sensation of his arms holding her close, or how she'd leaned against him, and she had most certainly not imagined the way her body wanted more. Except she'd panicked, and she really didn't understand why when even now she wished she was still in his embrace.

She shivered. With the covers up to her chin, she watched the shifting light from the fireplace. One thick wall sloped outward and another boasted a window ledge six feet deep and tall enough to sit in. The ledge narrowed in a squared-off V shape and ended in a slender window facing an adjacent tower. The opposite wall had another window with three large steps cut into the ledge. That window overlooked the back of the castle where the moat had been before some Tiern-Cope ancestor decided to enlarge the rear of the castle. Carved stone outlined the fireplace in the third wall, and in the fourth was the door to the hallway. In that same wall, another door near the corner—so short even she had to dip her head to get through—led to a small room for the necessary. As for furniture, there wasn't much: the wardrobe, a desk, a chair, a dressing table and a four-poster bed with blue hangings. Quite the grand bed. Her favorite thing about the room. In the Black Earl's day, no doubt, tapestries had covered the now bare walls. She suspected if the hour were right and she were to lie just so in the larger window, she might see the moon. Right now, however, the walls chilled to the very bone. Another draft rippled through the room.

The terror that had overwhelmed her when Tiern-Cope kissed her wasn't really gone. She probed the edges of that moment. The panic hadn't come because of anything he did. She'd felt safe in his arms. She remembered the longing, an ache of wanting, the feeling that at long last her life had come right. And then, suddenly, a wave of unreasoning fear swept everything away and left her cowering, trembling and empty. He hadn't made fun or been angry or insistent. He just stopped.

The fireplace flared, coals hissed and popped. Olivia listened to the sound die down, shivering despite the fire. Where on earth was that infernal draft coming from? She distinctly recalled fastening the window locks, but one must have worked loose because night air stirred the curtains. A slow, deliberate motion that for one heart-stopping, breath-stealing moment convinced her someone crouched behind the fabric. The air swirled, chilling straight through the covers.

She slipped out of bed. Arms clutched around her for warmth, she went to the draped window ledge. Dread crept up her back like frost on glass, but she forced herself to reach for the curtain. Perhaps a barbarian Scotsman from one of her less tormented dreams lurked behind the fabric, deadly claymore drawn for attack. Her heart slammed in her chest. She held her breath, let it out and told herself she was being silly. She drew aside the curtain.

Cold air surged past, but no sword streaked down to chop off her head, no Highland warrior attacked from inside. Indeed, the latch was loose. She hiked up her nightdress and climbed into the ledge. The stone beneath her feet felt like ice. Outside, a pale crescent of moon shone on the snow-covered ground below, a layer of white covered the sill. She secured the lock in the fitting and, backing out, drew the curtain closed.

In bed once more, she curled into a ball with the covers tight around her for whatever warmth she could find. The opposite curtains moved, a ripple of motion, and it did seem as if there was someone behind them. It did. She pulled the covers to her nose, ignoring the curtains and the shadows, thinking she'd rather dream about the Black Earl separating her head from her neck than find herself awake in the night, shaking with fear and unable to see the face that so terrified her. She remembered Tiern-Cope's arms around her, the protection and comfort of his presence. He'd held her, just that, until her panic passed. He never complained or insisted on an explanation. He just held her until she felt safe. How strange, her drowsy mind thought, that the only place she felt safe was in the arms of man who didn't like her. Came of his being a hero, she supposed.

She was halfway to deep sleep when the door creaked, a noise loud enough to rouse her, yet soft enough to doubt her having heard anything. She lay motionless, listening but hearing only the wind outside, the clock, the sounds of an ancient building. Normal sounds, but still her skin prickled. Pressure built in her head. Her pulse beat in her ears. The feeling of pressure thickened, stealing over her, a sense of envelopment, a shift in perception. Not her pulse, but footsteps. Someone pacing. Ten steps toward the fireplace. Ten back to the foot of her bed. The sussuration of fabric against fabric. Metal sliding along metal, a low ringing sound, and mixed with that a murmuring. She peered into the darkness but saw nothing. No moving shadows, no figure approaching her bed, just the inert shapes of furniture and the resulting shadows. The resonance in her head grew, half convincing her she heard footsteps and the low, regular sound of breathing. The murmuring began again, a breath, then a whisper.

My love.

Steps paced near, and she swore she could feel the air thicken. Pain lanced along her temple.

My heart.

Unendurable pressure. She tried to move, but couldn't. Her limbs were frozen, trapped in her nightmare. More footsteps. A breath on her cheek. Cold air wafted through the room.

My own.

A face flashed before her eyes. She tried to breathe and couldn't get air into her lungs. She screwed her eyes shut, but the face didn't go away. The features blurred, looming, threatening, laughing. She knew that face, but the recollection refused to come. Terror like she'd known only once before in her life consumed her. Her lungs refused to expand. Or couldn't. She was going to die. She knew it. A scream bubbled in her throat.

The fullness in her head vanished, leaving deafening silence in its wake. In one motion, she shot to her knees, throwing back the covers, gasping as if she'd run from Far Caister to Pennhyll. No matter how hard she stared, there was no one. Her door remained shut tight. Not even a difference in light around the frame. The only sound was the wind rattling the glass in the windows. There wasn't anyone in the room. She trembled, heart tripping like a sparrow tangled in a net. There was nothing. There was nothing and no one here. She sat with her arms wrapped around her drawn-up knees, taking slow breaths. This time the dream had changed. The footsteps and voices were new. The endearments, those were new, too. She didn't remember that from any previous nightmare.

Why couldn't she remember?

She stared at the dark folds of the hangings as if they were to be her last sight in the world of the living. Another coal popped. No barefoot, tartan-covered Scotsman hid in the widow ledge. No foully murdered earl walked the halls of Pennhyll. The curtains stirred again, languidly, as if an elbow or perhaps the blade of a sword disturbed the fabric.

This time she refused to acknowledge the prickles of fear running up her spine. She got out of bed. Even though her belly felt empty and her knees shook so she barely trusted them to hold her up, she checked the windows. Both of them. Again. Both were open.

She secured the last and climbed down. As she closed the curtain, the wind outside rose. A draft came down the flue and made the fire flare. Startled, she whirled and this time there was someone there. She couldn't help it. She let out a yelp.

A young woman stood at the side of her bed, very young, practically a girl. She wore plain clothes in thick woolen given shape only by the apron around her waist. A white cap on her head gleamed like bone in the dimness. "Good evening, miss," she said, dipping into a curtsey.

"Good heavens, you frightened me nearly to death. I didn't hear you come in."

"I knocked, miss. Several times, so I was sure you were asleep. I've come to look after the fire." She held up a bucket of coal before crossing from the hearth to the door. "There's a chill on tonight."

What a relief to discover such a mundane explanation of her dream; she'd translated the sound of the servant tapping on her door into footsteps, and the sounds of her tending to the fire into the Black Earl himself pacing her room. "It's always chilly in here."

"I reckon," the girl said, "it's usually cold on St. Agnes' Eve."

"Why, so it is. I hadn't realized. St. Agnes' Eve, I mean. You're new here. At least, I've not see you before. What shall I call you?"

"Edith, Miss." She finished with the fire and rose.

"Have you been here long, Edith, or were you hired for the party tomorrow?" She laughed, a thin, nervous sound. "Well, I suppose I ought to have said today."

"A while." She went to the bed and plumped the pillows. "I'm sorry I frightened you. I was certain you heard me knock."

"I didn't. I was thinking of the Black Earl and . . . and St. Agnes' Eve."

Edith untangled the covers and then faced her. "You'll dream of your future husband tomorrow night, that's sure."

"What if I forget to fast?"

"Who knows? Perhaps you'll dream of him to-night."

"It's more likely I'll dream of the Black Earl wandering the halls of Pennhyll angry with Miss Royce for summoning him."

"The Black Earl can't be summoned," Edith said, smiling.

"Why not?"

She put a finger to the side of her nose. "If he wants you to see him, you will. Otherwise . . ." She shrugged. "Come to bed, Miss. You'll catch your death if you don't."

"Have you seen him?"

Edith adjusted the covers when Olivia was back in bed. "That I have."

"Well?"

"I could feel in my bones he repents his wicked ways and wishes he could put things right."

"Really, Edith." Before the present earl's father had decamped, leaving the castle empty and Far Caister without the considerable monies derived from the family's employment and custom, the last six or seven earls of Tiern-Cope enjoyed good relations with the locals, and perhaps a more benign Black Earl. It was a fact of faith and legend that the fourth earl preferred a bloody melee with the Scots over attending to his wife and children or to his duties as lord over his people. No one ever spoke of the Black Earl with anything but fearsome awe.

"What time will you be needing me in the morning?"

"I'm to Far Caister early to see Mama. I'll be up before you, I expect."

Edith curtseyed. "I'm happy to come whenever you call." At the door, she hesitated. "The Black Earl won't hurt you. He'd never do that. My word on it."

"Thank you, Edith." Olivia hid her smile. She wouldn't offend Edith's dignity for all the world. Besides, the assurance felt strangely comforting. She was not, herself, even half as superstitious as most people who grew up in the shadow of Pennhyll Castle. But, considering the history of the earls Tiern-Cope, and the fact that she was in a room of the original castle— for all she knew perhaps the very room where the Black Earl had met his death—she could not shake off the dread of something not of this world.

"Good night, my Lady."

"I'm not 'my Lady.' "

"You are to me."

"Good night, Edith." She blinked, and Edith was gone as quickly and as quietly as she'd appeared.

Five minutes later, she did fall asleep and leave behind the unfamiliar shadows of the present.

Olivia stood in a room easily fifty paces across. In her sleep, she smiled because she felt as if she'd been lost for years and had only now come home. Tourmaline silk shot with narrow lines of cream covered the walls. On the floor an exquisite rug of Chinese design. Bronze curtains hung floor to ceiling, tied back with tasseled ropes of silk. Twin pier mirrors hung on opposite walls, framed with gilt so bright it must be newly laid on. On the mantel candlesticks in the shape of dragons poised to breathe fire and smoke. The furniture shone with the gold of walnut and ash and fittings glittered whenever the shifting afternoon light hit them. The Tiern-Cope crest was carved in the marble above the mantel. A maid polishing the table looked up from her work. "My Lady."

"Edith?" But Olivia saw her mistake in the next instant. Not Edith, though the resemblance was haunting.

The servant curtseyed and swept up her rags. From a connected room, a man called to someone. Olivia turned her head in that direction, and when she looked back, the girl was gone. Memories whirled in the back of her head. Not frightening this time. The owner of that voice made her smile. He protected her, and he loved her. When she was with him, the world felt right. As long as she was with him, she was safe.

He entered the room, crossing at an angle to her so that she saw just his shoulders and a glimpse of flat stomach. Not a stitch of clothing covered him. Not one. She could see the backs of his thighs and his bare behind. Round and strong and firm. Dark hair cut short gave his profile greater sternness. She knew beyond certainty she had every right to be here, with him perfectly naked. Her heart swelled with joy, a feeling so intense she wanted to cry out to the world.

He stopped at the window and stood there, one arm resting atop the sash, staring at the hills rising toward Scotland. His arm came forward on the sash, and he shifted so that he faced her. "Well," he said in a soft voice that made her breath catch. His voice was velvet, liquid velvet, and she was drowning in it, filled all the way to her soul. That voice, a woman could love. "Good afternoon."

Bluer eyes she'd never seen. Nor more piercing ones. She drowned in eyes of an incredible, piercing blue. The light shimmered as a cloud crossed the sun. But this man, this man with eyes like frost on a window, whose eyes made battle-hardened men quail and who seemed so foreign to tenderness, made her complete. Memories simmered beneath the surface of her thoughts. Any moment she would remember something important, and the world would come right. But the harder she tried, the more stubbornly recollection eluded her. She did not want to remember unpleasant things, things that frightened her. She much preferred remembering she loved the man in front of her. No one could long forget that kind of emotion.

"Come here into the warmth," he said easily. He reached for her, taking her hand and pulling her toward him. "I've been waiting for you." He stroked her hair, shifting a bit to let the light fall on her. "For a very long time."

She, too, reached for him, following a line in the air along the length of the forming scar that marred his chest. A corona flared around him until she moved past the point where the sunlight hit her eyes. She stared at his chest, at the gashed and ill-healed flesh, and he, seeing her attention, took her hand and brought her fingers to his mouth. She felt the warmth of his breath, the pressure of his lips, soft and warm. "I wish you had never been wounded," she said. "Even though it brought you home to me."

He took one of her curls between two fingers and lifted it to his lips. "Dearest." He breathed in, a long, slow intake of air. At the moment of exhalation, he released her hair. He was very large, Olivia thought. But he never made her feel insubstantial or weak. His mouth curved without haste. She wasn't even certain at first that he meant to smile but, slight as it was, her stomach dropped straight to the floor. She would do anything, anything at all, to continue being the recipient of a smile like that. He glanced over his shoulder. "McNaught. There you are."

A short, round man came in carrying a silk dressing gown over the crook of an arm. "My Lord," he said, holding out the silver robe.

He drew on the dressing gown with an uneven shrug of his broad shoulders that protected his wounded side. "Were you looking for me, my own dear heart?" He spoke easily, but something lurked beneath the surface, a dark sort of purr, like a cat, inscrutably satisfied. "That will be all, McNaught."

The valet nodded and withdrew.

Her head ached a little, a sense of fullness, and she felt memory tugging at her, clamoring to be known. But she didn't want to know. She belonged here. Nowhere else. She pushed away every thought except him.

His mouth curved ever so slightly. She could have touched his chest if she'd not been paralyzed by his fiendish beauty and that slow, rare smile. He'd not fastened his dressing gown. Part of his wound showed, violent pink, an angry weal where something had pierced his skin. She lifted a hand in a warding, as if she could heal him with the gesture. A man might die from a wound like that. Her open palm touched his chest just below his heart. With no fabric between her hand and his chest she felt the smoothness of his torso, the hardness of muscle, the beat of his heart beneath warm skin. "You were wrong," she said. "You do so have a heart."

"It belongs to you."

With deliberate care he covered her hand with one of his and glanced at the bed. His smile sent a shiver from her head to her toes. Sebastian. The name flashed into her head, touching the world in which Lord Tiern-Cope was going to marry someone else. Something pulled at her, but she couldn't leave him. His hand over hers flattened her palm on his chest. He put his mouth near her ear. "You're a beautiful woman. Must I tell you that constantly? Ah well, I don't mind if I must."

"I'm dreaming," she said.

"Let me make your dream more pleasant still."

"Oh, do, please," she said.

"Happy to oblige you, madam." He bent close. Her hand was on his naked chest, and it felt wonderful. She felt more than a little dizzy. He touched the outside of her thigh. "Are your legs bare?"

She laughed in reply. He threw his arms around her, sweeping her up to carry her to a chair. When he sat, she ended up straddling him, her palms on the back of the chair. "Oh, my."

His hands slid beneath her skirts, finding her garters and moving past while he kissed her throat. She felt him pressing her down, but she resisted. "Must you torment me?" He growled deep in his throat. One hand left her waist to delve again beneath her skirts. "My little witch. Are you going to refuse me again?"

"Refuse you? Perish the thought. I can never tell you no."

She felt his fingers brush her inner thigh. His hips

shifted, and then in one swift movement, he was inside her. Both his hands held her waist, guiding her, filling her. He reached up and unfastened the front of her gown. Her breath caught when one of his hands slid around to her most intimate part. He moved with her, his mouth finding her breast and then, without warning, she felt as if every nerve in her body concentrated just there, around him. "Yes," he said, right before his mouth closed on the skin of her neck.

She threw back her head and felt his lips slide down. She let the convulsion of pleasure take her, concentrated infinity in her body. When she could think again, she raised her head from his chest and looked into eyes of chilling blue. He remained inside her, and she felt suddenly uncertain of herself and of him. Memories rose up, crowding out the satisfaction, fear lurked at the edges. She did not want to know. "Hold me," she said.

His smile spread. "My heart," he said. He wrapped his arms around her.

"Sweetheart," he whispered. "My own. My life." The endearments made her shiver inside, pulling her inexorably nearer him. "My love." He cradled her in his arms.

"I love you," she said.

"I know." He slid his hands under her skirts again and before long, the world shattered like glass.

She awoke with a start, sitting upright in the bed with both hands clutched over her galloping heart. The curtain swelled and billowed with a draft that chilled, and darkness leapt from moonlit corners whenever the fabric lifted with the waft of air. She *had* closed the window. And locked it.

Chapter Eighteen

Sebastian woke with his side throbbing like the devil. He'd slept away too many weeks of his life not to find himself perversely glad of his wakefulness. Awake he did not dream of his dying brother or tearful redheads nor hear the inconsolable cry of an orphaned child. Nor did he dream of Olivia Willow compliant in his embrace, of coming into her again and again. Jesus. The woman obsessed him even when he was sleeping. He felt a tightening of his belly when he thought about kissing her. Unwise of him ever to have kissed her, but Lord, they were good together.

The damned building made eerie noises. Groaning squeaks from floorboards settling. Creaks and thunks of centuries-old timbers swelling with the humidity of an unusually cold and wet winter. Through some acoustical whimsy the wind rushing over the battlements and past the windows howled with a sorrowful basso undertone before rising to a shriek. A man in agony. Sebastian had heard enough of that sound to last him a lifetime. To make matters worse, every so often there arose from the kennels such a keening and furor you'd think Satan himself rattled the bars. And perhaps he did.

The house was haunted all right, Sebastian thought as the wind rose to another chilling screech. But not by an earl murdered and dead these four hundred

195

and seventy-five years. No. A far more recent soul haunted Pennhyll. Even the walls breathed Andrew's essence. His brother, who was not at all what he ought to have been. And now, here he lay in Andrew's bed thinking there must be some way to reach into the emptiness and retrieve the brother who should never have died, to make him explain what in God's name he'd done to Olivia, and why.

With a sigh, Sebastian threw back the covers and swung his legs off the bed. His side blazed, retribution for his recent overexertions. Slowly he moved and avoided prostrating pain. A month ago, the effort would have left him sweating on the sheets, afraid to stir without someone there to catch him if he fell. He grabbed his robe and, keeping his left arm below the level of his heart, pulled it onto his shoulders and fastened the belt about his waist. Lamp in hand, he left his room and the bed that had been his brother's and his father's and so on back through the ages even, one supposed, to the bloody dead Black Earl.

His bedroom lay at the end of a series of connecting rooms, each opening into another. Bedchamber, antechamber, withdrawing room, parlor and salon, after which the pattern repeated itself in more or less a mirror image. From the second parlor, however, rather than proceed straight, he left by another door to the right. There, he found what fifty years ago would have been called a closet and been used for the receiving of visitors. Another door led out of the closet to a corridor. Wood just short of inky black surrounded him, ceiling to floor carved with rosettes and vines so real he expected them to wave in the unseen breeze.

Thick walls muffled the keening wind. The hush

struck him as unnatural. Once, just off Curaçao, in the moments before battle, he'd felt that sort of silence. A ghastly quiet that lifted the hair on his arms and shrunk his belly and balls to nothing. By habit, his right hand dropped, ready to defend himself. He swore he heard the sound of steel slipping from a scabbard, but of course he hadn't, for he had no weapon, and the carved-wood hall was empty. Feeling foolish, he tightened the sash of his dressing gown.

He went left just to prove he wasn't unnerved. A maze could not have been more confusing than the right and left turnings, stairways appearing from nowhere to lead up or down and sometimes sideways into the depths of the house. Every architect ever to put his stamp on Pennhyll ought to have been sentenced to a lifetime traversing these Byzantine halls. He missed the orderly arrangement of a ship, where everything had its predictable place. He opened the occasional door but found empty salons or chambers filled with sheet-covered furniture. Nothing alive, nothing lived in. Nothing but room after empty room. A man could house an armada here and have space to spare.

The floor sloped down half a step. The architectural indicator, he decided, of where the Tudor wing met the medieval. He seemed to have circled back to the original castle. In at least one case, he remembered hearing, they'd built right over the ramparts. He stepped into a damp, misty cold and was painfully reminded he wore only felt slippers on his feet.

Overhead, stone ribs arched to a central point, the interstices filled with cavorting stone animals. He ascended a narrow, twisting staircase and came out in an even more ancient hall. The walls, white-limed after long-gone practice, felt solid and watchful. But not lonely. And not deserted. Five yards ahead, a thin line of light illuminated a slice of the adjacent wall. A weak yellow glow, but steady as from a lamp.

Not a sound did he hear as he approached, just a graveyard's silence. Using the tip of his finger, he pushed the door until he could see in. Thick beams in the arched ceiling betrayed the medieval origin of the room while shelves of books filled a recess in the opposite wall as high as a tall man might reach. To the left, royal blue curtains draped walls tinted a once popular shade of orange. Columns of gray-veined white rose from floor to ceiling and flanked the marble fireplace. An oil painting hung above the mantel: pink and red peonies in an ivory vase.

The scent of tobacco hung in the air, stale and musty. More a recollection of tobacco than anything else. He moved inside, and his feet sank into silk carpet. Such heaven to his freezing soles he walked in farther. The wind howled again, rattling the window glass behind the curtains. Though fainter than from his bedroom, he heard the answering din from the kennels. The very hounds of Hell could not sound more fearsome. The perfect setting for a ghost. This thought came at the exact moment he looked to his right.

At the far end of the room a figure in white bent over a mahogany desk, writing by the light of a single lamp. Blood covered its head and dripped onto the desktop. Though he did not believe in ghosts and knew to his marrow that in the next moment he would make sense of what he was seeing, fear rippled up his spine. For a moment, a mere instant, he regretted his disbelief in God and in the next remembered the war and why he'd lost his faith. He blinked. And blinked again when the vision remained unchanged. Red from crown of head to table top, a thick and sinuous trail of blood flowed to the desk. The dogs howled louder still, and the wind wailing past the dawn-lightened window could have been a man's dying breath. Behind him, and through no action of his, the door slammed shut.

The apparition gave a very un-ghostlike shriek and jumped from the chair, sending it to the floor with a muffled thud. A quite real-and-in-the-flesh woman. His grasp for religion irritated him, and he focused that irritation on her, as if she'd intended to frighten him back to the Anglican Church.

"Miss Olivia Willow. What the devil are you doing here?" Jesus, this was just what he needed. Miss Willow in the flesh when he was feeling so disinclined to the sort of self-discipline that would keep her safe from him. She bent to right the chair. Whatever it was she wore, nightdress, chemise, the fabric pulled tight along her back and lower to display pleasant curves.

"Good heavens, you frightened me nearly to death." Straightening, she put a hand to her upper chest. Behind her, the lamp hissed and flared. Sebastian had the absurd image of Venus stepping from flame. "I didn't hear you come in."

He walked in far enough to place his own lamp on a table. A draft swept the room, and he moved away from the whisper of cold air, ending up closer to her than he intended, though still a fair distance away. "You haven't answered my question."

"I couldn't sleep." She smiled freely, cheerfully, one of those smiles that made him want to smile in return.

He stood his ground and refused to return her smile. A man who made war for his living had little use for smiles and less for spinster redheads hopelessly tangled with his family history. "I often come here to write. It's warmer here than in my room."

Sebastian started toward the desk. When he stood but two feet distant, he said softly, "My brother used this room."

"It still feels like him."

That was true. Everything about the room felt like Andrew. He half expected to see his brother on a chair before the fire, ready to light his pipe and waiting for his mistress to attend him. "Why are you here? Besides making me think you're a ghost."

She laughed softly and touched a bound volume of paper open to a place nearer the end than the middle. Ink glistened on one side of the pages. Her long, bare fingers matched the script on the page. He couldn't make out individual words, more's the pity. He wanted intensely to know what she'd written. He felt quite certain this was her diary. Her most secret thoughts laid out on the pages. "Passing strange you'd be writing at this hour."

"I'm an early riser, my Lord, and off to Far Caister, soon. To see Mama. You didn't think I was a ghost, did you?" Her skin gleamed as if lit by the dawn yet to come. Shadows rendered her face in fey beauty, a fairy trapped in the world of men. Another smile, very small, appeared. A smile to enchant a man's soul. "For, you know, I thought for a moment that *you* were a ghost. I heard a noise earlier, but when I looked, no one was there. Until just now when you came in."

"Your hair looked like blood." He reached for a lock, turning a ringlet around his finger. She had the sort of curls that would never lie flat, small coils from top to bottom and surprisingly soft considering the determination to twist.

"Oh, dear." She laughed, sunlight and silk wrapped in one soft sound. "I'm so sorry."

"Did you take me for the Black Earl?" He hoped that would make her laugh again.

"Oh." Her smile drained away. "No. No," she said. "I took you for Andrew." She spoke with wistful innocence. "I saw you, and—"

He raised one eyebrow.

Her smile drained away. "For a moment, the resemblance was remarkable. Uncanny, really."

Silence gathered while he waited for her to master herself. Not an uncomfortable quiet, but pregnant.

"Now," he said, "it's I who am sorry." He reached around her, leaning close enough to smell earthy verbena and beneath that something secret and wholly feminine, and to feel her flinch when his arm brushed hers. Strange how the desk had looked like mahogany before. Now he would swear the thing was the dark honey of oak. Pretending he hadn't noticed the contact or her reaction to it, he picked up her diary.

With a cry of outrage, she tried to snatch it from him, but he lifted it out of her reach, which wasn't hard because he was bigger, at least a foot taller, and despite his injury, quite a bit stronger.

"Give it back. You've no right."

He scanned the page. Once again, he was set on his heels. "And what, pray tell, is this monster of which you've written? The wolf that will take your life?"

She shrugged, backing away to put a lamentable distance between them. A fine display of unconcern

201

in no way convincing. He wondered if she knew how much her eyes gave away. The callowest lieutenant could hide more from him. She stretched for the diary, but he raised it nearer his head. If she wanted the book, she'd have to lean against him to reach it. She didn't. Instead, she eyed his hand like a gunner's mate peering along a cannon sight. "My private thoughts are *not* your affair. Most certainly not."

He laughed. Really, he knew her too well and read her too easily for her to think she could fool him. "It's about me, isn't it?"

"No."

"Liar." Her shoulders stiffened, and he knew his guess had hit home.

"I'm not."

"I'm your wolf."

"No."

"Yes, I am, and you know it." He brought her journal to his eye level—which remained out of her reach if she meant not to touch him. He fanned a few pages then stopped and pretended to examine the page but, really, he watched her. Panic filled her remarkable eyes. "True enough, I am nothing like Andrew."

"You're not."

"Neither am I a monster."

"I wrote that before I knew you."

He grinned. Both lamps flared and wavered with the draft that plagued the room. The air here was no warmer than in the hall. She looked him square in the eye, judging, he suspected, the likelihood she could retrieve the book without touching him. He leaned in to place the journal on the plain oaken desktop. "I'm flattered you spend your private hours thinking of me."

She snatched up the journal and faced him. Carefully, she thumbed the side of the pages. Her middle finger, he saw, was stained black where her pen had rested against it. The corner of her mouth lifted, trembled a little. Her chest lifted with a breath that caught when he moved so close there was but an inch between his chest and her bosom.

He felt awash in her, full of a rutting lust for the deep scent of verbena and for red hair twined around his fingers. The light continued to flicker so that the shadows danced with shapes unnervingly like a man peering at them from the darkened corner of the room. But whenever he stared at the shapes, the darkness broke apart and became again formless shadow. Briefly, he wondered if he could be dreaming. But dreams were not as real as this. He was awake. Alone with Olivia Willow. Consumed by her. He wasn't to be trusted.

She backed up, and he walked forward until he stood smack against her, pinning her against the desk. Satan's own smile appeared on his mouth, had he but seen it. More than worthy of the Black Earl at his most horrific. He put his hands on the desk, one on either side of her, thinking how her hair was flame bright against that sea-blue background. He felt her thighs, her hips, along his body, the side of her slipper against his foot. She pretended nothing untoward was happening but with such poor success he threw back his head and laughed. The laughter felt good. Joy and triumph came together in him, gathering her in and joining them as tenon joined the mortise. The moment felt right. God, it felt good to feel again.

"I won't take anything you don't offer me, Olivia," he said, imagining her body against him, moving, shifting, yielding to his every pleasure. The image filled his mind, a thousand times more intense than any dream. "I swear it. In return, you will have passion. And love. I swear that, too."

She fumbled behind her for something and produced the book in which she'd been writing. She held it tightly. Hard use bent the corners of the uneven green cover. "What do you want from me?"

"You," he said in a low voice. "I want you." He heard the faint ring of metal moving against metal, a sword sliding in its scabbard. Next, that damn wind would have him hearing an army at the gates. "I promise you," he said in a voice so thick with lust he didn't recognize it for his own, "I have more than enough passion for us both. I'll love you right out of your mind."

The shadows in the corner formed into definite shape. A man. Not just shape, but color, too. A flash of blue and red. "I am not mad. Therefore, this is a dream, and a hellishly real one at that. And so, lovely Olivia, what's the harm if we indulge in each other now? We'll be married soon."

She stirred, and for a moment, he would have sworn she wasn't in his arms. He shook his head, and she came back into focus, warm and supple and soft in his embrace. He stroked her back near her shoulder blades. He would not let her go. Not when she was at last where she belonged. Damn that lamp for flaring so. The shadows behind her moved and swirled into impossibly human shape. His skin prickled despite knowing the impression for a trick of uncertain light.

"Sebastian," she whispered. She touched his arm. The effect of his whispered name shocked him. His gaze settled on her fingers resting atop his sleeve. A shiver of heat and arousal shot through him. Would she touch his naked skin as daintily as this? He'd been months without a woman, and at the moment he felt the abstinence like the edge of a blade to his throat. He felt pressure built in his head, behind his eyes and between his ears. Cold chilled the room. The lamp flared, then settled into a steady flame that stopped the shadows from moving.

She was gone. Vanished. He didn't know what the hell had just happened, except that he had not held her in his arms. She had not let him kiss her six ways from Sunday nor melted in his arms nor whispered his name. A sense of loss ripped through him, ruthlessly deep. "Olivia." He shouted. "Olivia!"

He awoke with a gasp and a heart pounding like hurricane winds on a hapless ship. First light through the window bathed the room in pearl light. Bloody, sodding St. Agnes' Eve.

Chapter Nineteen

January 21, 8:11 A.M., sunrise

On his way out of the castle Sebastian met whispers cut short at every turn. Some fool of a footman claimed he'd seen the Black Earl pacing the ramparts. Ridiculous. Even McNaught, whom he would have thought immune to such superstition did not belittle the gossip as he usually did. He helped Sebastian into his coat and cautioned him against walking out so early. Superstitious fools the lot.

Indignation spurred him to walk from Pennhyll at a rapid pace. Pandelion trotted at his side. Snow had fallen during the night, and he could see a set of footprints in the formerly pristine snow. Small feet. Olivia, he was certain. Every now and then the hem of her gown or cloak had skimmed her tracks, blurring the shape. He cursed under his breath. No matter what sort of dreams he had about her, Olivia Willow was not his concern. Not after tonight. She could live her own life, damn her to hell, with Hew or James or no one at all. He was not responsible for her present status in life, nor her future one.

He reached Far Caister in record time. Fifty-six seconds ahead of his usual pace. And, despite having pushed himself, his legs didn't wobble, and his lungs didn't burn. In short, he didn't feel like he'd been thrown overboard and left to drown. Mightily pleased to feel as if he could cover the return journey at the same clip, he hardly slowed as he entered the village. At the Crown's Ease, the innkeeper stepped out just as Sebastian reached the door. Broom in hand, Twilling touched his forelock in a now ritual greeting. "Best of the morning to you, my Lord."

"Mr. Twilling."

He leaned on his broom. "Right bit of business up at Pennhyll since last I saw you, my Lord."

Sebastian gave him a look.

"Preparing for your night of dancing and carousing. A merry success, I hope."

"Thank you."

"The young lads and lasses here are prepared to dream of their future wives and husbands."

"Codswallop."

"Oh, aye." He took a bit of bacon from his apron

and when Sebastian gave the nod, offered it to Pandelion. "I'm predicting a good business at the Crown's Ease, my Lord."

"Indeed?"

"Geoffrey Peterman's cows broke through his fence last night. Still chasing after them, I expect. Seven of Calvin Barfield's ewes dropped twins yesterday, and six of 'em sickly things." He tugged on the end of his nose. "Nyllie Williams near cut off his foot when his best axe slipped and then broke." The innkeeper nodded slowly, but his twinkling eyes gave him away.

"Don't tell me."

"Not five minutes ago I saw Harry Leroy, and he swore he saw the Black Earl pacing the ramparts of Pennhyll."

"You can't believe that nonsense."

"I reckon I do. I'll sell twice the amount of ale what with all the tale-telling there'll be tonight. May the good ghost send me as brisk a business every night."

Sebastian laughed. "And a good morning to you, Mr. Twilling."

He moved out of the doorway. "Kettle's on, my Lord."

"Later, thank you. I'm feeling fine, and I think I'll walk to the end of town and back."

Twilling took up his broom. "Watch your step, my Lord. Trouble's afoot whenever the Black Earl's about." He put a finger alongside his nose. "I can feel it when the old man steps out."

Sebastian set off, pulling up his coat collar against the chill. The Black Earl, indeed. Overhead, the sky turned from pearl to pale blue. A wagon blocked the street he meant to take, so he veered left down a street of gray shadows. He came up short when he recognized the tobacconist's and then the stationer's shop. Between them was the door to Miss Willow's flat. Was she inside? He stood while the sky shifted between palest blue and orange. More color emerged. He felt like he'd forgotten something and that any moment he would remember what. But he had no reason for being here save coincidence. A rope of mist curled from the upper window of the Willows' flat. Strange, considering the lack of wind. The acrid scent of smoke floated on the air. An orange glow flickered at the window and then, with a *thump* that rang in his ears, the glass shattered. He threw an arm over his head, twisting away from the shards and splinters raining down.

The wagon driver dropped the sack he was loading and rushed down the street. "Fire!"

Smoke billowed from the upper windows of the building. Someone started ringing a bell. While the other man pounded on doors, rousing people from their homes and beds, Sebastian tried the entry door and found it shut fast. What if Olivia were inside? She'd walked to Far Caister this morning. He knew it. Where else would she have gone but home? The door flew open just as he raised his leg to kick it. A wide-eyed woman hugging an infant to her chest stumbled out, followed by a man carrying a trunk. A window opened to the street and someone started tossing out furniture. People streamed out, laden with belongings. Children sobbed. Men called to each other. Women cried out for loved ones.

An obese woman clutching a ragged blanket staggered into him, nearly bowling him over. She gripped his arms, eyes red-rimmed. He thought his heart would stop, because he knew. He went hot and cold all at the same time. His skin prickled with certainty. He just knew. Olivia was trapped inside.

"There! Up there!" she wailed. "Save them. Dear Lord, save them. The poor woman cannot walk and that little thing cannot carry her."

He thrust the woman into a pair of waiting arms and raced up the stairwell. The higher he went, the thicker the air and the harder it was to breathe. Smoke curled from under the door to Olivia's flat. He stripped off his cravat and wrapped the fabric around his nose and mouth. Two kicks shattered the door. Fire consumed most of the far wall and threatened the ceiling. Smoke cut off his breath. He stooped for better air lower down. The mantel was on fire, but the painting of Olivia's father and brother hadn't yet caught. He lunged across the room, grabbed it and shoved it in his pocket.

He found Olivia in the second room, dragging another woman toward the door, sobbing, pleading, praying as she inched them closer. A roaring, crashing boom shook the structure. The roof caving in. Timbers big enough to crush a man. Ashes stung his eyes, embers skittered in the hot air. Beneath his feet, the floor bucked like a living thing, hot and treacherous.

He scooped the older woman into his arms and grabbed Olivia's wrist. He mouthed the words, "Follow me." Smoke tore at his throat, and he could only pray that Olivia understood what to do. He made for the inner doorway. From across the parlor, he saw the wagon driver balanced at the top of the stairwell, motioning with one frantic hand, the other arm flung over his mouth and nose.

Heat pulsed, the sound of the flames deafening. With Olivia's mother cradled against his chest, Sebastian headed for the stairs, Olivia behind him, clinging to his coat. A shout rose when they came out. Someone held out his arms to take Olivia's mother. Thank God. Jesus, thank God. He swallowed great gulps of air and staggered from the building. He turned, expecting to see Olivia and to pull her into his arms. Someone pounded on his back, striking his wounded side such a ringing blow he doubled over.

"Your coat, my Lord!"

The garment was on fire. He stripped off his great-coat and flung it smoldering into the snow. Ignoring the pain in his chest, he scanned the crowd for red hair. She wasn't here. "Olivia!" He grabbed a man lugging a blanket loaded with his possessions. "Olivia Willow. Have you seen her?"

"No, my Lord."

Sebastian lunged toward the building. Someone blocked his way, but with a roar of despair he shoved the man aside and sprinted up the stairs. Air thick with ash and smoke and heat dropped him to his knees. One of the massive ceiling beams creaked, a long, slow sound that vibrated between his ears. The floor quivered, and the air danced before his face. He looked, trying to see through the smoke. There. A flash of red near the inner door.

He crawled toward the color. Flames licked through the floor behind her, a line of spreading or-ange surrounding Olivia's inert figure. He stretched an arm and got hold of her hair. He pulled with every ounce of strength he possessed. She slid forward. His fingers curled around her arm, then her torso. He hauled her toward him. The ceiling beam dissolved in flame and crashed with a whoosh of scalding air. The floor where she'd lain collapsed into flame.

Sweeping her into his arms, he lurched to his feet. He wheeled toward the stairs, sliding and skidding down.

Another roar rose up when he burst into fresh air. Olivia slid free of his arms, collapsing in a fit of coughing, sinking to the street with her arms tight around her chest. "Where's Mama?" she said, when she got a breath.

"Safe," he said. Soot streaked her face, and her eyes were red. The fire had singed her curls. Another cheer pulsed on the air. He was mystified until he realized it was snowing. Huge flakes drifted onto the street. Several landed on Olivia's head. He wrapped an arm around her shoulders, pulling until she gave in and leaned against him. "My heart," he said. "You're safe."

He held her close and while he waited for his heart to stop thudding, he heard snatches of conversation. The fire, most seemed to agree, originated in the building next door. A chimney fire from a flue that hadn't been cleaned in years. With one arm still around Olivia, Sebastian signaled to someone. There were benefits to his new station in life. Before five minutes passed, he procured a driver and a cart and had the three of them, himself, Olivia and her mother, on their way to Pennhyll.

Pandelion appeared, and at a sign from him, jumped into the cart.

Upon their arrival at the castle, he avoided discussion of anything but the barest outlines of the fire upon the need of seeing to Olivia and her mother and then a claim of wanting a bath and a change of clothes, which, in point of fact, he did. He'd bathed and was dressing when Fansher came in, satchel in one hand. "Ned."

"I heard the news," he said. "Are you all right?"

In answer, Sebastian spread his hands.

"Sit down. I want a look at you, young lad."

"Have you seen to Miss Willow and her mother?" He stripped off his shirt.

"In good time."

James poked his head into the dressing room while Ned removed the bandage. "A moment?"

Sebastian lifted a hand, beckoning to him. Hands thrust in his pockets, James sauntered in and threw himself onto a chair. "That scar of yours looks a sight better."

"Will I live, Ned?"

"Mm." He probed Sebastian's ribs.

"Ouch."

"Serves you right." Dr. Fansher straightened. "I want a longer look later. No excuses."

"Fine."

McNaught came in with fresh clothes. James frowned. "Not that waistcoat. Something bright. Where's that one with the gold stripes?"

McNaught's mouth drooped. "If only he would wear it."

"What's wrong with gold stripes, Sebastian?"

"See to Miss Willow and her mother, Ned."

Fansher put away his watch. "You need to rest, Captain."

Sebastian glared at him. "For God's sake, Ned, will you go to them?"

"Anxious, are you?" Fansher gave him a look that Sebastian returned with measure. "On my way."

"Stroke of luck you were in Far Caister when the fire broke out, Sebastian," James said when the doctor had gone and McNaught had disappeared to fetch the new waistcoat. Sebastian busied himself with fastening his shirt.

"I walk there every morning, James."

"To Miss Willow's apartments?"

He turned, put a hand to James's midsection and pushed him enough to make him take a step back. "If I didn't know better, I'd think you were implying something distasteful."

James laughed. "I must have forgotten whom I was talking to. You're not that sort, are you?"

"No, James. I'm not. If ever I take Miss Willow to my bed, it will be as my legal wife, not some fraud to satisfy an itch."

McNaught returned and Sebastian put his arms into the sleeves of a new waistcoat.

"Not likely since you can't stand the woman. Can you?"

"Leave it be."

"I want to marry her."

Sebastian made a face.

"I'm serious." James raised his hands. "But you've warned her off me, interfered at every turn."

"What if I have? She deserves a husband, James, not a dissolute nobleman who'll cast her aside as soon as he's bored. You told me, quite pleased with yourself, I might add, that you meant to deceive her."

"I know what I said." James paced. "But I don't mean it anymore."

"You'd do anything, you said. Except marry her."

"All that's changed. You were right about her all along. I've known for days now that I've fallen in love with her. Head over heels, Sebastian."

"You're too late. She's going to marry her cousin."

James stopped pacing. "I'm a better catch by any measure."

"Her cousin never once mentioned his ability to support bastards as if that counted in his favor."

"She cannot abide her cousin." He drew a breath. "I've written to my mother. Told her I've met my future wife."

"That's your affair, of course."

"Tell her you were wrong about me."

"I wasn't."

"But you are now."

"She's a grown woman, James, and I am not her father. It's her cousin who's responsible for her. Settle things with him."

"She doesn't care a fig for him, that's plain as day. But she'll listen to you. Tell her I'll agree to any marriage settlement she proposes."

Sebastian pushed aside McNaught's hands and buttoned his own coat. "Fifty-five thousand pounds should do it."

"Done. I'll have my solicitor send you a copy of the contracts."

"Splendid."

Chapter Twenty

Dr. Fansher stood at the bedside with Olivia. He'd administered a draught of laudanum to her mother, and after drawing the covers to her chin, he nodded, an invitation to follow him from the room Tiern-Cope had given her mother. "Is there somewhere we can talk, lass?"

"Down just a floor." Since her mother's room was in the same tower as Olivia's, she led Dr. Fansher to the parlor below her own quarters. A draft as frigid as the earl's stare whispered through the room and raised gooseflesh on her arms. She sat and gestured for Dr. Fansher to do the same, though he declined in favor of standing by the fire. "Is she all right?"

"As ever she can be, Miss Willow. Rest is the best thing for her right now."

"Thank you for seeing her."

Fansher crossed his arms over his chest. "It's you I'm concerned about."

"I'm fine." She liked the doctor, with his Edinburgh burr and head bald as the moon. He wasn't all that much taller than she was, either.

"Ah, now, lass, you sound just like Captain Alexander, insisting all's well when it's not."

"Is he all right?"

"You show a touching concern for him."

"He saved my life."

"Nothing wrong with him a good long rest won't cure."

"He'll never do it." She smiled. "Nature never made a man more stubborn."

"That's the truth of it. Now, let's see to you, shall we?"

"I'm fine. Honestly."

"Begging your pardon, but you do not look it. Captain Alexander—" He smiled. "Lord Tiern-Cope tells me you suffer from headaches."

She nodded.

"Have you not been sleeping well?"

"I sleep just fine."

He gave her a look.

"No. I haven't been."

He held out his hand. "May I?" He pressed his fingers to her wrist, counting. When he released her, he said, "Eighty-five beats per minute. Elevated." Next he listened to her chest. "Breathe. Again. Once more." He straightened and looked into her eyes and mouth. "Lovely teeth."

"Thank you."

"Now, let me see your head." He clucked in dismay when she showed him the scar. "You were fair in the eyes of God when you got that." His fingers probed. "Worse megrims since you came to this wee cottage of the Captain's?"

She nodded.

"And you cannot recall how you got this scratch of yours?"

"No," she said.

"You are too thin, Miss Willow. Your complexion is pale. Your eyes shadowed by your cares."

She shook her head.

"Let the Captain's staff look after your mother for a bit." He put a hand on her shoulder. "You've been through enough, Miss Willow, to make even a Scotsman think of his bed with longing. Promise me you'll rest today." He tilted his head. "I've a feeling Captain Alexander—Lord Tiern-Cope—would never forgive me if something happened to you."

"He's been kind to me."

"Which I dare say is proof enough."

"Of what?"

"I've known him ten years now, Miss." He grinned, eyes twinkling. "Has the Captain told you how we met?"

"No," Olivia said.

"May I?" He indicated a chair.

"Please."

"We made our acquaintance at sea, as you might expect. In the middle of a pitched battle. Smoke so a body could not breathe 'twas so thick. I was ship's surgeon on the *Courageous*. Eighty-four pounder, she was. We met the French and engaged them. We'd fired all cannons on the *Deluge* and thought she was done for. Mast shot clean through and the sails like nets there were that many tears. I was on the gun deck, tending to the wounded there, to get them firing if they could be roused and patched. I could see topside through a great gaping hole in the deck above. They struck their colors and gave permission to board. When we came near enough the French started firing. Cowards all of them, for they killed good men who never expected such a trick. Captain Farral took a bullet to the heart and three more officers besides. We thought we were done for. We didn't have a man fit to take over.

"But your young man, Miss Willow, Lieutenant Alexander in those days, was on the frigate *Achilles*, well behind us we thought. But no, suddenly there she was, off our port bow and tacking. For an instant, an instant mind you, we heard nothing but waves and wind and dying men and timbers creaking, for the Frogs were waiting to get close enough to board us, and then came a sight I'll never forget 'til I'm cold in the ground. A man jumped from the *Achilles* clean across twenty feet of ocean right before a hundred French and one of them, thinks I, fires, for there's a crack like a shot." He slapped his palms together in imitation of the sound.

"Deaf as I was from the cannons, lass, I heard that clear as anything, and I'm thinking the poor fellow's dead and consigned to the deep. Then, like the very Angel of Death himself, here he comes. A cat couldn't have walked any lighter than he. He scoots right down through the hole in the deck, through smoke thick as soup, and he looks at the gunner's mate with eyes like blue fire, and he says calm as ever you like, 'Sir, will you fire that cannon or shall I?' And there the mate was, bleeding from his leg—he was naught but a boy, he was—and thinking he'd soon be as dead as the gunner, but he says, 'Aye, sir, I will.'

"That crack I heard wasn't any gun but Lieutenant Alexander hitting the deck after he jumped. By then, the *Achilles* engaged the French and never mind us. We were done for, so they thought. Blasted a hole clean through her side, we did. I never saw the like before and never after."

"He jumped twenty feet?"

"That he did," Fansher said. He stood, looking around the room. "We routed the French and Lieutenant Alexander saw us repaired and sailed to Bermuda along with the ship, which, it turned out, carried gold, and made us richer than ever we dreamed. I asked to be assigned to his ship. As it happened, they'd lost their surgeon. I sailed with him until just before he got that hole in his side."

"I never heard any of that."

"Oh, the lad would never tell it himself. I knew him at sea, but this place suits him as I never thought dry land would. Aye, lass, it does."

"He is Tiern-Cope. He belongs here."

"That he does. But he needs a woman at his side. The right woman." He fixed Olivia with a stare. "And I'm thinking it isn't Miss Royce." He smiled. "Well. I'll check on you and your mother later today, Miss Willow. And be taking you to task if you've not gotten some rest. Mind you, eat every bite of food sent to you. I expect you fit enough to dance a fling with me tonight."

Olivia laughed. "Thank you for your kindness."

"So long as you are kind to him."

"You'll send me your bill, won't you?"

He took her hand between both of his. "I see how it is between you. He's gone off course, and it's up to you to set him back on it. Don't let him get away. Dig in your heels, lass and keep him. It's the best thing for him." He released her. "Now, Miss Willow, you go to sleep yourself. Doctor's orders."

"Thank you again."

Taking Fansher's advice wasn't hard. She was exhausted. Back in her room, she crawled into bed, letting her head sink deep into the pillows. Did Tiern-Cope ever feel his body was too small to contain his emotions? No, she decided. That man took life by the throat, stared eternity in the eye and accepted what came. His life was as wide as the ocean while hers seemed as constricted as the pages bound between the covers of her journal. She lay on her back, staring at the shadows. Her thoughts drifted to Tiern-Cope and in her head she saw him leaping onto the deck of a doomed ship. Such a stern countenance, and, she suspected—no, she knew—an unyielding character, but not for ill. Fansher was right. He'd lost his way, that's all. Handsome as the very devil himself, too. Handsomer than Andrew. Handsomer than Fitzalan, if only he would smile.

She slipped toward the oblivion of sleep. Warmth stole over her, a warmth edged with—well, what was it, exactly? Eagerness. Anticipation. A strange certainty that *something* would happen to change her life utterly. She would not spend the rest of her life in the terrible solitude of these last years with nothing to look forward to but loneliness and poverty.

Outside, the spit and caterwauling of a tomcat snarled through the air. A dog howled, a mournful bay expressing, no doubt, frustration at his inability to chase the tom. For some time after her return from Land's End, and before she and her mother had moved to Far Caister, she'd not been able to sleep. She'd gotten used to her bed at Land's End. But she soon came to feel at home. With her mother's health in increasing decline, they moved to far cheaper lodgings in Far Caister. Soon enough, she couldn't imagine not being comfortable with old ticking and a duvet that had been on her parents' bed at the Grange or minding that her pillow was little more than a square of rag-stuffed linen. Now, she didn't have even that.

The patterns overhead shifted so that, had she an imagination prone to hysteria, she could easily convince herself something hid in the curtains above her head. She imagined a face in the shadows and folds of fabric, a face with sad, hollow eyes. The sliver of light shining through a crack in the window curtains disappeared. Shadows deepened and swirled and the face became even more uncannily real.

Unnerved, she listened to the wind. The creaking hinges of a loose shutter somewhere on the tower sounded oddly smooth, a sort of ringing sound of metal sliding along metal, which meant the sound wasn't hinges at all, but someone sharpening a knife. The air had a bite to it, a promise of colder weather to come that made her pull the blanket higher and more snugly about her. Sunlight reappeared, winked out again then returned. Her eyes drifted shut. With each breath she tasted the damp tang of sea air, felt the rocking of waves, the cry of an ern. The earl's mouth on hers, so warm and gentle and eager, yes, eager, for her. And she for him. One last time, she heard the cat spit and yowl, and then she was fast asleep.

She stood in a hallway, cold and shivering. In one direction, the library at Pennhyll, in the other, eventually, and after a series of twisting hallways and narrow stairs, her tower room. The wood-covered walls were not so dark as she remembered, but she recognized the vines and flowers carved into the squares. Masterwork, the carving. The wooden flowers appeared to wave in a gentle breeze. She made her way to her room. But at the floor below she saw a light from the parlor. Strange that someone would use it.

She pushed open the door—it wasn't completely shut—and found another world.

Instead of plastered walls painted orange, panels of fabric covered the walls, and instead of lamp oil and coal, she breathed in the scent of beeswax candles. Fireplace and mantel dominated the center portion of the wall opposite her but the marble columns were gone. Her desk was gone. Where there ought to have been bookshelves, there rested a canopied bed bedecked with silk curtains embroidered with a lion rampant. The bed sat on a dais with gold railing around the perimeter. Next to the bed a broadsword for a warrior's hand rested in a wooden frame. Arranged at an angle to the fireplace was a chair of sunburnt brown with metal rivets sunk deep into the stuffing. One cobalt pillow lay on the rush-covered floor.

A man sat on a chair turned toward the fire so that she saw mostly his hair and a portion of his face. She blinked, and like that, the room changed, became recognizable as the salon she used for her office. The man was still there, not upright nor dressed, she saw upon coming nearer. Clothing lay in a heap on the floor, a coat and some heavier garment. His dark head rested on the chair back. His eyes were closed, his mouth curved in a secret, inwardly intense smile. Sprawled atop him, head bent so that she'd not initially been visible, a woman slipped her hands down his chest. His arms circled the woman, but did not hold her. Instead he worked at his cuff, fumbling with a square of gleaming gold. One had already come free, for the cuff dangled open, but the second proved more difficult.

"Sod it."

One violent jerk sent the cufflink arcing into the air. It hit the wall with a metallic *plink* and tumbled into a corner. The two of them worked at his shirt until it was over his head and drifting downward to join the other jumbled clothes. The woman stroked his naked chest, fingers gliding over muscled ridges from chest to belly, the other hand braced on the chair back next to his head, holding most of her weight.

Now his hands held the woman's waist, slipping lower to clutch her to him. Her chest was bare, and while Olivia stood rooted to the spot, he leaned forward to press his face to her bosom. His mouth opened, and he kissed her breast, slowly and with lavish attention. Outside, wind whipped past the stone walls and set the hounds baying in their kennels so that the woman's moans were lost in the sound.

The dark-haired man freed her hair, running his fingers through her curls, lifting them high and letting the mass of copper fall down her back. Red hair, as coppery as her own. Surely, there wasn't another female in all Cumbria so cursed with hair that color. The woman's head fell back and gave Olivia a view of her partner's face. As if her thoughts had flown to him, his eyes opened, and he looked at Olivia. For a moment, it was like seeing someone else's eyes in a familiar face, and then she realized he wasn't a stranger at all. The face flickered and shifted, not one face but a dozen men with eyes like blue ice, until at last the man's features settled into the familiar.

Pleasure eased the edges of Tiern-Cope's face, and with his mouth curved in a smile he resembled his brother more than ever. But the eyes gave him away. They were cold, a lifeless, icy blue. He grasped the woman's hips, and this woman who had Olivia's copper hair and even her features, cried out in a low, guttural moan of pleasure incapable of containment. "I am coming," he said. He opened his eyes again, looking at her, and she wanted to weep from the heartbreak.

His hips came up, and he gasped and said, "My heart. My love. I'm coming."

She slid away, down and away, and into the safety of Sebastian's embrace. His arms enfolded her, warm and tight. *Hurry*, she thought.

Chapter Twenty-one

12:16 P.M.

Sebastian took refuge in a parlor in the medieval wing of the castle. Refuge from the uproar of preparations but not from the thought of Olivia marrying her cousin or of James's plea to intercede on his behalf. An overstuffed leather chair brought up to a fire that glowed with the promise of warmth invited him to sit. Jesus, he was tired. His chest ached, and his throat hurt from the heat and smoke he'd breathed in. Light through the window slanted across the floor and illuminated a table on which there sat a bottle of brandy. French brandy. Some portion of the prizes awarded him over the years. He'd shipped everything to Andrew, who converted what he sent to cash. But, it seemed, not everything. Delicate stuff, French brandy. He walked to the table, found a glass near the bottle and poured himself two fingers. He ought to be upstairs resting before the evening's madness, but he didn't fancy McNaught and his potions just now. Not when he could have brandy and a moment's rare and welcome solitude.

Glass in hand, he made a circuit of the room and found it disturbingly familiar. A charming room he was certain he'd never been in before. Marble columns rose to the ceiling at either side of the mantel. Over the fireplace a painting of peonies looked so lifelike he expected any moment to catch their scent. Open curtains of cobalt blue contrasted with the orange plaster walls. Near the oriel the surface of a walnut desk was cluttered with all the implements of a letter-writer: pen, ink, seals, wax, blotter and several sheets of paper bearing the Tiern-Cope crest. Obviously, someone used this room. He extended a fingertip from the hand holding the brandy and moved the papers. Underneath lay a clothbound book such as anyone might purchase in the lower sort of shops. A green cover, much battered with corners bent and frayed. He opened it, saw two thirds of the pages filled with a neat feminine script, and closed it against further invasion. His head ached, or put better, felt stuffed full. The coals shifted with a hiss of flaring ember. He shivered. Pennhyll could be damned cold sometimes.

Intending to sit out of the draft, he turned—and stopped in his tracks at the sight of a man lounging on the sofa, legs stretched in a disrespectful sprawl. He wore dark leggings and a blue tunic worked with red and gold. A baldric crossed from right shoulder to left, but his scabbarded sword rested against the sofa, well within reach. Spurs at his heels clinked when he shifted his legs. His eyes burned like blue coals. Alexander eyes.

"Et voilà," the man said, lifting one hand.

The door opened, and Sebastian watched Olivia Willow walk in with a confidence that told of her conviction she was the only person to use the parlor. Curls tumbled unchecked around her face, her hairpins not up to the task of holding her hair in place. What the woman needed was combs, he thought, something substantial to keep that mass of hair in check. She went to the desk, moved the stack of papers, then rifled through the books piled near one corner.

"Blast," she whispered, shifting her weight from one foot to the other. One at a time, she opened the drawers and searched without finding what she was after.

He thought the man on the sofa spoke in a chilling drawl, but, in fact, Sebastian discovered, it was he himself who said, "Looking for this?"

She whirled, scattering some of the papers on the desktop. She looked right through the man on the sofa. Past him as if he weren't there. Jesus.

"Oh. It's you," she said.

Sebastian put down his brandy. "Miss Willow."

"I haven't thanked you for saving my life."

Sebastian lifted a dismissive hand.

"I can't ever repay you." She took a step toward him. "If there's anything I can do . . ."

"In good time." He lifted the clothbound book Sebastian had found on the desk. Without even opening it, he knew what she'd written inside.

"May I have it please?" She held out her hand.

Sebastian ignored the Black Earl, but goose pimples

raced down his back and arms when he reached for the bottle of brandy on the nearby table and poured himself another nearly full glass.

"Are you drunk?" Olivia asked.

"Not in the slightest."

The Black Earl glanced at him, but Sebastian refused to meet the look.

"My Lord," she said. "That's mine. Give it to me. Please."

The Black Earl's attention returned to Olivia, and Sebastian said, "A woman with eyes like yours oughtn't pretend to be anything but what she is."

"I'm sure I don't understand what you mean."

"And I'm bloody well certain you do." Sebastian heard his voice as if it came from outside him. Did he always sound that forbidding? No wonder she disliked him. He took a long pull from his brandy. "Tell me, Olivia, has Fitzalan confessed that he loves you?"

"You told me he does not."

"He'll soon come around. He does love you. Perhaps you should accept him when he offers."

"If he offers." She laughed. "If he does, I'll know he doesn't mean it."

"Oh, he will mean it."

"Make up your mind. Who am I to marry? Lord Fitzalan or Hew?" Her smile cracked for just a moment.

Sebastian gave her a sidelong glance.

"What I need," she said, "is a rich aunt with no living relative but me."

Glass lifted, he smiled. "A very old and infirm aunt. Have you got one of those?"

"Why, my Lord Tiern-Cope. I do believe you've made a joke."

"I am not without humor, Olivia." Sebastian saw Olivia's breath catch. "If you want your journal, come get it. I wonder if you have written as stingingly of Mr. Hew Willow as you do of me. I don't deserve it, you know."

"You're in a quite strange mood, my Lord."

"Yes." His eyes roved up and down, devouring her.

She tipped her head, considering. "You are drunk."

His mouth quirked. "Tell me, has it been difficult for you, caring for your mother all on your own? No father or elder brother looking after you? No husband to whom you may cleave?"

She shrugged.

"This morning, everything but the clothes on your back burned. You have no place to live. No money to replace your losses. What will you do now?"

She shrugged again. "Make do."

He held out the journal. "Come get the damned thing."

But she stood by the desk and, watching her, Sebastian knew her pulse leapt, that her blood heated, and that someplace low in her belly seemed empty and in need of filling.

"No? Well, then. Perhaps I'll keep it." He tossed it on the sofa and sprawled beside it, ignoring the Black Earl who sat on the sofa arranged across from him. Sebastian looked her over, shaking his head. "What will you do?"

"We've managed, Mama and I."

"How often do you tell her you've already eaten and then go without? Never any new clothes, wearing your shoes through to your stockings. I'll wager you've taken in lodgers. Your Mrs. Goody. Is that her name? Struggling to pay some fool of a lawyer holding out hope of a miracle recovery."

Hope and denial and despair flickered over her face, one after the other, and in place of that, last of all, resignation. The collapse of all hope.

"Your fortune is gone. You will never have it back." He sat forward, one hand over a knee.

"I'll have the teaching post soon, I'm sure. I'll be able to put away something for the future."

"And if the post goes to someone else?"

She swallowed. "Since I haven't a rich aunt, I suppose a husband will have to do."

"But which husband?" He made a gesture that prevented her reply. "I've seen too much death, too many men reach the end of their hopes and dreams, and I am tired of it. Sick with it. Just once, just once in the whole of my eternally damned life I want to know something turned out right."

"I'm sure it will, my Lord."

"Olivia Willow, my heart, you are a decent woman who doesn't deserve her lot in life."

She went still, eyes large and full of emotion locked away tight.

The Black Earl glanced at Sebastian, but he steadfastly ignored him. He leaned forward. "I'd give my life for you," he said to Olivia. "You know that."

"That's the sort of man you are," she said. "Brave."

Sebastian tried to breathe normally but couldn't.

"Come get your damned journal. You're safe with me, if that's what's got you worried. As you are not safe with Fitzalan. And most certainly not safe with Hew Willow."

"Very well." She walked toward him, extending a hand.

The moment she was near enough, he grasped her wrist and tugged her toward him. "Sit, Olivia."

She twisted, trying to land so they wouldn't be close. Despite her efforts, she ended next to him anyway. Not touching, but quite close. Laughter rang out. His, not hers.

"Now, answer a few questions for me, if you please."

"What questions?"

"About your family. Your father and brother. God's teeth. Never mind them. Tell me about you. What do you feel when you are with me?"

"You *are* drunk."

"Hm. A little, I think." He returned his glass to the table. Sebastian started when the Black Earl looked directly at him. A knot of pain flared behind his eyes, and he squeezed them closed, hands to his temples.

"Are you all right?" she asked.

He grasped her arm, curling his fingers around her wrist. With his free hand, he lifted a hand to her hair. First, just his fingertips touched, then he slid his fingers into her curls, skimming the curve of her skull. "Like silk when it ought to burn." He breathed in and caught a trace of verbena in the air. "You're right. I am drunk."

"My Lord."

"We're good together, you and I."

He could not take his eyes off her mouth. "Your mouth is luscious." The words weren't his, but he spoke them. The feeling was his though. He straddled her, one knee on either side of her thighs, his hands on the back of the sofa to either side of her face, the better to glare at her, to accuse her of creating this great gout of lust that threatened his control. She gasped. Her hands came up and pushed against his chest, though he noted she was careful to avoid his wounded side. "I told you, you are safe with me."

"Yes, always."

He let his weight swing forward so that the only thing keeping them apart was her hands braced against his chest. He ignored the trickle of pain along his side. The heat of brandy and verbena flared into desire. "I'm going up in flames. Olivia."

"My Lord—" Her eyes widened.

"You have the same dreams I do, don't you? Is this what you're dreaming right now? My hands on your body, my mouth on you." He cupped her face. "We should make love and have done with it. He'll be happy then. I'll wager you're snug in that room of yours having this very same dream."

"Please."

He held her gaze and put a finger on one of the fastenings at the front of her gown. He did hope they weren't decorative. "Please, what?" He slipped the button free of the loop of fabric. "Stop?" Methodically, he continued with another and another. "I will if you say so. All you have to do is say yes."

He heard her breath leaving her lungs while he pushed aside the two halves of her bodice. She wore a chemise of ivory linen, round at the neck with shoulders no more than two fingers in width. No lace, ribbon or tucks. Plain linen. Her corset pushed her bosom upward, but made a further exploration a matter of some struggle and disappointment.

"My Lord." The whisper trembled in the air.

"What?"

"Is this real?"

"I don't know, and what's more I don't give a damn

231

if it is or not. You feel so good." He put a hand on her throat, the palm of his hand just above the swell of her bosom, curling his fingers around and sliding them upward until her chin tipped toward him. Her hands fell to her sides and because of his position, landed on his thighs. "Olivia."

He leaned forward and kissed her mouth, trapping her against him while he fought to loosen his cuffs. She sighed against his lips, and he kissed her. Her fingers tightened over the large muscles of his thigh. He got one cufflink through his sleeve and with the dangling cuff, slid his hands down to just beneath her shoulder blades.

"Sod it," he said, tugging on the other shirtcuff until he felt it give. He curled one arm around her, holding her close so that when he pulled away and rolled to put his back against the sofa, he brought her with him, reversing their position. She straddled him. Her eyes went wide. She braced her palms against his shoulders to keep herself from falling onto him. His thighs parted, further separating her legs. He slipped a hand to the back of her head and brought her mouth to within inches of his own. He needed her. He angled his other hand, which lay at the small of her back, around to her waist.

"I want you to call my name," he said. His fingers pressed against her waist and came around to her rib cage. He swept a thumb over her breast, pressing upward, stroking, moving, until her eyes dazed. "Say my name, Olivia."

"My Lord." She gasped, and he heard confusion and wonder and passion in the sound.

"Not that," he murmured. He struggled with fastenings of his upper clothes, pulling at his shirt. "Captain Alexander. Say, 'Yes, Captain Alexander, I will do whatever you ask.'" The other cufflink refused to come apart. A tug and the bit of metal flew through the air to land God knew where.

"Captain Alexander."

"That's it," he said, at last letting his mouth brush over hers. She let out a cry when he stood up with her in his arms. Slowly, he slid her down and stood with his hands on her shoulders.

"Let me go," she said, eyes wide and staring past his shoulder. Her fingers trembled while she tried to rearrange the front of her gown. "Fix your shirt, my Lord."

"I'll never let you go," he said. "Never in a thousand years."

"My Lord," she whispered. Her shaking hands plucked at his shirt, trying to put him to rights, too. "Price is at the door."

Sebastian cursed.

"My Lord." Hell. Indeed his butler's voice.

He took a long, deep breath before he turned his head toward the door. "Yes, Price?"

"Captain Clinton Egremont has arrived."

Chapter Twenty-two

Price, Sebastian thought when Olivia had left, and with her clothes looking not nearly as rumpled as he thought they ought, was in his element, what with the fire having ruined one coat of middling quality and landed two newly destitute woman at Pennhyll. One of the ladies was not at all well, and the other, well, actually Sebastian wasn't at all certain what Price thought of whatever he'd seen. And now an unexpected guest bearing God only knew what sort of horrible news. "*Captain* Egremont?" he said, facing the desk as if fascinated by its contents and not the least interested in his visitor.

"Will you see him?" Price asked.

"Show him in." By time Price returned, Sebastian had managed to make himself decent. He wondered if he'd imagined Olivia. He didn't think so.

The sight of a naval uniform jolted him when Egremont walked in behind Price. Then the memory of sea air, of tar and caulk, of sails snapping in the wind, men shouting or singing, all of it came so clear in his head he could taste the salt. He walked to Egremont, hand out to clap him on the shoulder. Lieutenants together and fast friends during Sebastian's rise through the ranks until, at last, Sebastian had his first command, and they were separated. "So, it's Captain Egremont, now."

Egremont stood, an uncertain smile on his rugged face. With Sebastian's hand still on his shoulder, he bowed, hand sweeping the top of a boot still damp from the snow. "I have that honor, yes. My Lord."

"How are you, Captain?" Sebastian said.

"Fine, thank you. My Lord."

"Not 'my Lord.' Sebastian," he said. "And sit down, for God's sake."

"Yes, sir." When that brought a scowl, Egremont managed a thin smile. "You've recovered from your wound." He sat on the sofa where just moments ago Sebastian may or may nor have embraced Olivia.

"Yes." Sebastian clasped his hands behind him and walked to the fireplace.

Egremont laughed softly. "Earl of Tiern-Cope, but still Captain Alexander. I'd recognize your walk anywhere. I can see you still; hands behind your back pacing the quarterdeck while you sail us into battle." He crossed his arms over his chest then uncrossed them. He tilted his head, studying the fireplace. "I'm on my way to Falmouth."

"By way of Pennhyll Castle?" Sebastian said.

"Falmouth by way of London and Pennhyll Castle, if you can believe that."

"What ship have you got?" God, he could feel it all, the snap of canvas in a freshening wind, wood creaking, a ship splitting the water.

"The *Adventure*."

"Thirty-four gun frigate," Sebastian said.

"Captain at last."

"You deserve the post, Egremont."

"Thank you."

"Now, I hope you're staying for a good long visit." He shook his head, smiling. "Not long, I'm afraid.

We're on blockade in French waters. My Lord."

Sebastian wished he could smash the reserve between them. "Nothing's changed, Egremont. I'm still the same man who thrashed you at cards every night."

Egremont looked around him. "You live in a castle. The butler calls you 'my Lord Tiern-Cope.'"

"I'm still a sailor." He shrugged. "A sailor."

"How is your wound, sir? I heard at least once that you'd died of it."

"Fansher's looking after me."

His grin widened, looked more natural. "Must be nice to have the old man about."

"It is. Will you stay the night at least? There's a damned fancy party here tonight. And a severe shortage of dashing gentlemen."

"I left my things down the hill and walked up here." He grinned. "I wondered if I'd be allowed through the front door. Thought I might be sent 'round the back."

"I'll send for your things and for tea, too, if you'd like something to drink and a bite to eat."

"A meal would do me well just now. I've been traveling for days, it seems. And, if it's not terribly bold, I wouldn't mind a room straight away. I feel like I've not slept in a month. My Lord."

"Egremont," he said, "if you call me anything but Sebastian, I'll knock you flat."

He laughed. "You've done well for yourself, and I don't mean the title or the castle." He sat again, crossing one booted foot over a knee. "This suits you, you know."

"What?"

"Pennhyll. Living here."

"Tell me about the war."

"The *Glory*, I was first lieutenant there as I hope

you recall, was on blockade most of the last year. Near Toulon. Not like you, sailing to hell and back."

"Much action?" He glanced at the corner. The Black Earl stood there, silent as the grave.

"Some." He grinned. "Enough prize money to ask Kate to marry me."

"Bring her here after you are married." He wondered at the invitation, for like as not he'd be thousands of miles from Pennhyll when Egremont got married. "I'd be pleased if you did."

"A kind offer, and one to which I shall hold you, Cap—Sebastian—when the war is over. Kate would much like it." They fell silent while tea was brought in. It was done with silent efficiency. All Sebastian had to do was lift a hand to signal his satisfaction.

Egremont stirred milk into his tea. Leaning back on his chair, he said, "You'll think I'm ripe for Bedlam, but I dreamed of you last night. We Welsh set great store by our dreams. Did I ever tell you my grandmother was a witch?" Egremont's mouth twitched, but his eyes stayed serious. "It's said my mother inherited the self-same talent. They had the second sight. Both."

"You, too?"

Egremont shrugged.

"Might have told me that before now. Could have come in useful."

"Kate's the one who told me certain dreams are sure to come true. Now let me tell you about the dream I've just had and be done with it."

"Go on."

"Three times I dreamed of you. Each time I knew you by your eyes. That uncanny blue.

"I dreamed of you in the chapel. At your side was

a woman with red hair. The priest read the vows, and you were married and happy, Captain. Happy at long last." He threw up his hands. "There you have it."

"And you believe dreams are a portent of the future?"

"Kate would say I must tell you. You wore a tunic down to your knees, in brilliant blue and gold, as one of your fine ancestors might have worn."

"I take no stock in dreams."

Egremont refused to laugh. "She was so real. Red hair and curls like my Kate would kill to have."

Behind him, the fire popped, and Sebastian shivered.

"Red as a new penny, Captain. And very pretty, if I may say so."

"I've had my bloody fill of dreams."

Egremont reached into a pocket and drew out a thick envelope. "From the Admiralty, my Lord Captain." He held it out. "Command of a fleet, I'm sure." He grinned, looking much more like the man who'd been his friend and trusted lieutenant. "If Fansher's been looking after you, then no doubt you're hale and hearty. There's talk of an offensive, smashing what's left of Boney's Navy. If ever a nobleman were fit for command of a fleet, it's you. Perhaps I'll be sailing under your command again.

Sebastian took Egremont's packet, thick enough to be several commissions. *The Right Honorable Sebastian Alexander, Earl of Tiern-Cope.* His orders had come at last.

Chapter Twenty-three

Olivia slept until half past twelve. By the time she'd been to visit her mother, her stomach reminded her she'd missed both breakfast and luncheon. Wearing the only gown that remained to her, she left her sleeping mother in search of the others and something to eat. Twenty feet from the hallway that lead to the more modern wing of Pennhyll, Olivia's garter fell to the floor. Her stocking drooped around her ankle. "Oh, bother." She snatched up her garter and checked the hall behind her. Empty and silent as the grave. She ducked into the nearest room, a darkened salon with windows closed up so tight she had to leave the door ajar for light. Throwing the garter on a nearby table, she leaned against the wall and hiked up her skirt. From toe to two inches above her ankle, the stocking was silk sprigged with dainty pink flowers, the rest thick cotton.

Cool air whooshed over her, and she heard one of those strange noises to which Pennhyll was so often subject. Feet softly stepping, or someone sighing or metal parts moving. Her shoulder blades itched as if someone behind her stood poised to touch her shoulder. No one was ever there. Except, of course, in her imagination.

She smoothed her stocking and fastened her garter before going into the corridor. Dead center in her back, her skin pimpled. A finger reaching, touching her . . . right . . . there. A draft swept the hall, carrying a breath that sounded for all the world like a low reverberation of her name. *Olivia*. She checked the hallway. Nothing. No one lurking in a corner, no shapes half glimpsed in the shadows and still the footsteps echoed in her ears, the rhythm of conversation, murmuring. Cloth sliding against cloth.

My heart.

She clapped her hands to her ears, but the voice echoed as if it were inside her head.

My love.

"No."

Olivia.

Brilliant blue flashed at the periphery of her vision. Not behind her but in the salon where she'd been standing so that anyone passing by would see her with her skirts up to her thighs. The Tiern-Cope livery was green, not blue, so she hadn't seen a servant. No servant would wear a color that bright. No servant could afford the sort of fabric that held a dye of such a rich hue.

With a steadying breath, she peered left down the hall, then right. "Miss Royce?" The jingle of metal parts moving made a bell-like sound, receding with the source. "Lord Fitzalan?" The air stirred, carrying the scent of old leather and musty cloth and beneath that a tinge of something acrid. The itch between her shoulder blades flared into dread. She wasn't mad. She wasn't. "Hullo?"

Farther down the hall something shimmered, a trick of the light perhaps because the hallway remained empty. The sparkle of silver didn't fade. She squinted and for a heart-stopping instant she saw a man watching her from the shadows. The hilt of a sword rose above his shoulders. His hand rested on the belt around his waist. The bell-like jingle came from the scabbard moving against his chainmail shirt. She blinked, and the man wasn't there. "I am not mad," she whispered.

Someone touched her shoulder, and she let out a yelp.

"Olivia?"

She whirled. Her cousin watched her with those dark, dark eyes that always made her think of nightmares. When her heart started beating again, she said, "Leave me alone."

He took a step back, hands raised. "You called out. Besides, I'd like a word with you. More than a word, actually." Olivia shook her head, but he took no notice. "I know Tiern-Cope's spoken to you." He moved closer. "Dear cousin. Let's not beat about the bush. I've been to Far Caister, seen where you live. Used to live. You were never comfortably settled, but your situation is more dire than ever."

"I'll manage somehow."

"But you needn't manage at all. Olivia, marry me and put to rest the cares I see in your face. If you're worried about your mother, don't be. She'll have the best care I can provide."

"How kind you are, Hew." She swallowed the lump in her throat. What sort of daughter turned her back on an end to the disaster her life had become? Light flashed behind her eyes, momentarily blinding her.

"You belong at the Grange." He took her hands. "Cousin. Olivia. Do not worry. Let me take care of you. Even if you tell me no, I'll take care of you." His fingers curled around her wrists. With her vision only partially cleared, she struggled to keep her balance. "Dearest Olivia. Tell me your answer is yes."

She opened her mouth to speak, but nothing came out. God in heaven, this was a momentous decision, life changing. Permanent. "I want Lord Tiern-Cope to negotiate the terms."

"Terms?"

"Yes."

She willed herself not to react to the tightening of his fingers around her wrists. His eyes flashed. "What terms could you possibly have?"

"A jointure." Her throat felt thick. Her scar ached, pinpricks of pain. "Set aside for me now." She swallowed hard. "And clear provisions for any children."

Hew's eyes narrowed. She rotated her hands, trying to loosen his grip. He was going to leave bruises. His mouth curled. "Do you imagine," he said, biting off his words, "that I will not take care of my wife and children?"

One last time, she twisted her wrists. "Hew."

He let go of her. "You insult me."

"What if something should happen to you, Hew?"

"I said I would take care of you."

"My father did not take care of my mother. Or me."

He opened his mouth to say something but stopped. He gave a curt nod. "I'll speak to Tiern-Cope." He reached for her again. "In the meantime, Olivia, let me assure you I am well pleased. We'll do well together." He took a step toward her. "May I kiss you?"

The man with the sword flickered into her vision. His hand went up, grasping the pommel of the weapon strapped across his back. The sound of steel coming free of the scabbard vibrated in her ears.

Hew touched her shoulder, bending toward her and then turning to look. "What are you staring at?"

"Nothing." The face from her nightmares filled her head. Fear and pain built in her so that she thought her body would shatter from the effort of trying to hold it in. His head dipped again, and she stumbled back.

"We're to be married." His eyes glinted. "I have acceded to your demands. Why shouldn't I kiss you?"

Her head swam.

"Olivia?"

She did not know which way was up. Her head threatened to burst open.

"Have you a vinaigrette? My God, Olivia."

She heard an echo of sound, a deafening clap that brought a scream boiling up. She tried to take a breath and could not. She could not feel the floor beneath her feet.

"Olivia? My God, what's the matter?" He clutched her shoulders. Some atom of memory transformed him into the face from her nightmare. Fear welled up as if it were happening all over again. She thrust out her hands and connected with his chest, rocking him onto his heels.

"Don't touch me." Her stomach threatened to turn inside out. Her head hammered so she could barely speak from the pain. "Don't touch me." The man in the shadows moved toward Hew, his sword out if its scabbard. He roared. She clapped her hands over her ears to block out the sound. The swordsman advanced, weapon raised.

"There's nothing there," Hew said.

The man brought down the sword in a deadly arc. She screamed, scrambling back.

"Olivia."

She ran and didn't slow until she came to a hallway that terminated in a multipaned window of thick, old-fashioned glass. Her breath rasped in her throat, but the dizziness and nausea eased enough that she stood steadier on her feet. She heard again the gentle ringing of metal sliding against metal. Musty air rose up with the same smell of leather and dust, an acrid undertone beneath. She whipped her head toward the end of the hall. At first she didn't see anything. The light shifted and swirled, and the swordsman materialized from the shadows. Gold and red emblazoned his tunic in a chevron against a cobalt background. The sword was back in its scabbard, strapped across his back. He was tall, with broad shoulders and dark hair, and he looked like Sebastian. Timed to the wind stirring the ivy outside, he vanished through the wall.

She blinked and walked toward the end of the hall. The stonework came to a point above the window, indicating she'd ended up in the medieval portion of Pennhyll. Ivy on the outside walls partially covered the window and filtered the waning light. Nearly all the window panes had some flaw or bubble that made the passage of sunlight a matter of unpredictability. What's more, clouds scudded past the sun and that same wind moved the leaves and threw irregular, flickering shadows on the carpet. To her right was a doorway, with a stone arch over the top.

"Olivia?" A distant voice. "Where the devil did you go?" Hew. Coming nearer. She bit her tongue, heart thudding like a hammer on an anvil at the thought of her cousin coming after her. Her stomach cramped, and her skull threatened to split. "Where are you, Olivia?"

A flight of circular stairs led downward, but no one had been here in ages. Even the air smelled musty and old. Cobwebs hung in one corner of the doorway; dust coated the stairwell. The light shifted behind her and cast a shimmering shadow on the stairs. Outlined in the dust on the stone floor was the perfect imprint of a pointed-toe boot.

"Olivia?"

She plunged down the stairs, descending a spiral no wider than her shoulders. The blackness went unrelieved even by the usual arrow slits. Despite the lack of ventilation, the air felt less musty than it had farther up. Her shoes echoed on the ancient stone. In the back of her mind she thought if Hew were to follow her, she would hear him. The twisting descent into blackness dizzied her until she was certain her foot would miss the next stair. Another turn and light appeared on the walls and stairs, a spreading gray against black. She reached a landing where light outlined a door. The stairs continued down. The door opened easily, and she exited into a large and empty room.

The door closed, disappearing into the pattern of the wallpaper. If she hadn't come through it, she'd never have known it was there. She felt a shiver of unease. The room felt familiar, the surroundings comfortable, though she knew she'd never been here before. Green silk covered the walls and curtains the color of new bronze hung at the windows. The furniture was beautiful, if one liked exquisite veneers, gold fittings and round-bellied chests-of-drawers. Smuggled from the Continent, she thought, or, more likely, prizes won by a ship's captain. Portraits lined one wall as high as the ceiling. The largest hung in the center. An armored knight sat a wild-eyed destrier. He clutched a plumed helm under one arm in a pose reminiscent of Tiern-Cope's portrait in the salon. The knight smiled with Andrew's mouth, but the cold blue eyes could have been the earl's. Behind him another man held a pike in one hand, atop which a banner rippled with the wind, bars of crimson and gold against a cobalt background. The bannerman rode a bay horse and though the shadows made it difficult to be sure, his hair looked red.

The sensation of familiarity persisted. She turned from the portraits. An empty room, but not uninhabited. A newspaper lay on a table. The folded pages no longer retained sharp creases. Beside the paper a crystal goblet held a few drops of bloodred liquid. In the very center of the table was the painting of her father and brother. She picked it up. The canvas smelled of smoke. The fire had damaged one corner, but it hadn't been burned with everything else. Her mouth trembled. Tiern-Cope must have saved it, and if so, then this must be his room.

No sooner had that horrifying thought occurred than a low, pained moan lifted the hair on the back of her neck. She looked around her, but there was no way to tell where the sound came from. A second moan, briefer, a little softer, but just as agonized had her turning toward another door, open more than wide enough for her to have been spotted by anyone inside.

She heard the sound again. Definitely coming from the other side of the open door. Not imagined. Someone was hurt. A now familiar prickle of gooseflesh moved along her arms and spine. The spot between her shoulder blades itched with the expectation of a dagger's icy chill. Had she not been distracted by the painting on the table, she'd have seen into the other room just by turning, which she did now.

Tiern-Cope stood near a window so the sun fell on his head and shoulders. In the strong light, his hair, a rich brown just shy of black, looked disturbingly short, cropped as it was close to his neck. He was coatless. And shirtless. Oh, Lord, he was naked. Or very nearly so. His broad and very naked back was not smooth or soft as she had imagined of men. Muscle flowed over bone and sinew and gave his torso shape the way a sculptor gave shape to marble. Nor was his skin pale. His back had a golden tone. He'd sailed the Indian Ocean. Andrew had read her his descriptions of Maçao and Barbados, of long weeks on blockade in the brilliant sun on the other side of the world.

One white-knuckled hand clenched the top of the window casement. On his smallest finger, a cabochon of pale, silky blue caught the light. His chin pointed toward the ceiling. Dr. Fansher examined his rib cage, probing until he elicited another exclamation from his patient. Tiern-Cope shifted toward her. His closed eyes were the only reason he did not see her. His skin was faintly brown everywhere she could see, a lovely, warm color that reminded her of summer. How much had the tropical sun seen of Tiern-Cope, she wondered, that he could be so brown?

"The devil." The earl sucked in a hissing breath. "Damn you to hell, Ned. Do you mean to break my ribs again?"

Unperturbed, the man continued his examination. A red gash surrounded by very pink and puckered scar tissue ran from about four inches below the earl's armpit forward and upward to nearly his nipple. "You should have had this looked at sooner."

"I did."

"By whom?" He sounded offended.

"A doctor in Far Caister. Fitzalan sent for him."

"It's not healing as quickly as it should."

"That's why you're here, Ned."

"Move so. A bit more, Captain." He stopped short and bobbed his head. "I beg your humble pardon. My Lord."

"Hell, Ned. Not you, too. Don't you 'my Lord' me. I cannot abide that from you."

"I need a better look. I must be certain they've not left behind a bit of the bullet."

"You'll not cut me open, you cursed sawbones."

With a start, she understood this wasn't like seeing the swordsman. This was no dream or hallucination. She really was here. The moment could not be more improper. She'd blundered into Tiern-Cope's private quarters, and he wasn't dressed. She shouldn't be here, let alone be spying on him. She had to leave, but she just couldn't. The sight of Tiern-Cope in his naked skin paralyzed her. The muscles of his chest were every bit as defined from the front as from the back and they disappeared right down into the band of his breeches along with a narrow trail of dark hair. He was, simply, magnificent.

"Enough, Ned." He sighed and gingerly moved his arm. "I've had enough for now." He reached for the shirt dangling from the back of a chair. Turning away, he drew it on but left the front gaping open. "Besides, I'm better than I was. I've been walking to Far Caister and back every morning for the last week."

"Probably what set you off."

"Bollocks. I've had a belly full of laying about like an overcooked potato."

"Saving lovely ladies and their crippled mothers from fires. Aye, lad, you've been a worthless nit, you have." Dr. Fansher turned, a grin on a weathered face browner than Tiern-Cope's. "Later then, Captain." He moved out of sight. "My Lord."

"Don't go. Not yet. I want to talk to someone with some sense. If I must converse about the weather or the color of Diana's bloody eyes even one more time, I'll puke."

Olivia didn't dare move now, not when as much as a twitch from her might attract their attention. "When you're a married man, I'll pour us both a nice warm ale, and we'll talk about the old days when we were young and foolish."

"Sod off, Ned. I'm still young."

"That you are, my Lord." Dr. Fansher reappeared with a bag in one hand. He retrieved his coat from a table. "I'll set aside the lager."

"Stay. Ned." His eagerness made him sound like the young man he was.

"Are you really to be married? To Miss Royce?"

"I don't want to talk about that."

"Ah, now, what about Miss Willow?"

"Now there's a woman worth a man's time. She's the only one here worth talking to."

"Just your sort, I thought. Intelligent. Attractive, too."

"Jesus, yes."

"Why all this talk about you and Miss Royce if it's bonnie Miss Willow who interests you? Do the headaches worry you?"

"Can you help her?"

"The lass was lucky to survive her injury. As for her memory—"

"Never mind that." He made a sharp gesture. "I don't want her reliving what happened."

"You care for her that much, then?"

"She suffered an unspeakable ordeal, Ned."

Dr. Fansher put his bag on the table and rested his hands on it. "Do you want my advice?"

"Yes."

"Waste no more of your time with Miss Royce when it's Miss Willow you want."

"Get out, Ned. You know the way."

With a laugh, the doctor bowed and left by another door.

Once he was gone, Tiern-Cope reached for the gaping fabric of his shirt, pulling it together the merest bit. Olivia followed the disappearing expanse of muscle. She saw herself caressing his chest, running her hands over skin and muscle. Her palms tingled as if she'd touched him. He sighed and threw himself on the chair, legs sprawled. The upper halves of his shirt fell open and Olivia saw nothing but golden leanness and the livid scar. Dream and reality bled one into the other. She didn't know if she'd seen his bare chest before now or dreamed it. Did she recall the shape and feel of a man's muscles moving under sun-touched skin, or was that something else she'd dreamed? Tiern-Cope stood, careless of his open shirt, as any man would in the privacy of his own quarters. Horrified, Olivia realized he was heading for the room in which she hid, and only his preoccupation with the fastenings of his shirt kept him from seeing her.

The stairwell down which she'd come was too far.

She'd never make it in time and besides, she wasn't sure if she knew how to open the door from this side. She dashed to the only other exit. Thankfully, it wasn't locked. She closed it as gently as she could.

She leaned against the wall and prayed for a miracle to transport her safely to her room. No such luck. She was in another hallway. Across from her, a niche contained a marble bust of Socrates. To her right, the hall showed only darkness. To her left, another hall extended perpendicularly. Which way led out, she had no idea. Left then. Away from the darkness. She came to six stairs terminating in an alcove where pink roses decorated a walnut table. Cut from the greenhouse just this morning, by the look of them. Behind the flowers hung a gilt mirror. Her cheeks glowed as pink as the flowers, and her eyes were far too bright. Sinking onto a wooden settee nestled along the wall, she bowed her head to her knees and groaned. It hit her, then, what a wicked thing she'd just done, spying on the earl. Seeing him practically naked. Listening to his private conversation.

"Sebastian," came a masculine voice from the opposite end of the alcove. "We're off." Lord Fitzalan came up a flight of stairs, heading toward the earl's quarters, which, apparently, one reached by the stairs where she now sat. Trapped.

A shadow darkened the alcove. She snapped to attention. Tiern-Cope stood over her, one eyebrow arched. "What are you doing here?"

Buff breeches hugged lean, muscled thighs. A clean white shirt, cravat, embroidered navy waistcoat and navy coat completed the picture of male beauty. The way he gazed at her so intently, she felt as if he were trying to read her mind. God help her if he could. Her pulse raced triple-time.

"Well?" he said, tapping his fingers on his thigh.

"I took a wrong turn."

His mouth quirked, but he did not smile. "Quite a wrong turn. Are you well enough to be out of your bed?"

"You saved my painting." Oh Lord, where had that come from?

He studied her, eyes moving over her from head to toe and back. "How did you get into my rooms without anyone noticing?"

"I was lost."

"Is that so?"

"Yes."

"What *do* you see, Olivia?"

The moment went deep with silence as his voice rippled up her spine. "Nothing."

"Liar." His eyes pinned her. "I think you see exactly what I do."

"Where are you, Sebastian? Diana is waiting." Fitzalan came up the last stair and stopped dead when he saw them. He smiled, and it was cool water to a parched throat after the burning look the earl gave her. His eyes shifted from Tiern-Cope to her. "Good afternoon, Miss Willow."

"My Lord."

"I hope you are well, Miss Willow."

"I am, now that I don't smell like smoke."

"Your cousin is here," Fitzalan said. "He's been asking after you."

"Thank you."

"Come along, Miss Willow," said Tiern-Cope as if it were natural for them to be chatting here, so close to his quarters. "No doubt the others are waiting for us."

Fitzalan inserted himself between her and Tiern-Cope. He extended his elbow to her. "Yes, Miss Willow. Do come. We're done with tea and Price is about to give us a tour of the castle."

Chapter Twenty-four

2:13 *P.M.*

"The library at Pennhyll houses one of the greatest collections of books and manuscripts assembled in all of Britain." Price's voice resonated as he opened double doors that ran the considerable height of floor to ceiling. Olivia sighed with the envy that the sight of all those volumes always inspired. Miss Cage and her father, Mr. and Mrs. Leveret and Mr. Verney and his wife added to the number of guests arriving for the St. Agnes' Eve festivities. Alice, now Mrs. Verney, strolled arm-in-arm with Olivia. Mr. Verney walked with Fitzalan, Hew and the Leverets while Tiern-Cope escorted Diana, one hand fisted in the curve of his lower spine. Captain Egremont walked just behind with Dr. Fansher. The arrival of Captain Egremont had Pennhyll in an uproar. Lord Tiern-Cope was going back to sea, and he could no longer afford patience in offering for his bride. Everyone expected Fitzalan would make an announcement about his sister and Tiern-Cope tonight.

"Oh now, this is lovely," Verney said, looking over

his shoulder. "What do you think, Mrs. Verney? Shall we redo our library?"

"How you do go on, Mr. Verney." Alice glanced at Diana walking on the arm of Lord Tiern-Cope and bent her head to Olivia. "He ought to order himself new boots, don't you agree? Tasseled Hessians would suit him. Like Lord Fitzalan's. Or your cousin's."

Olivia couldn't help a smile in return. "Perhaps a striped waistcoat, too, in gold and blue, I should think."

"Surely two more handsome men than Lords Tiern-Cope and Fitzalan there have never been. Both so tall and broad-shouldered. Ah, here is Mrs. Leveret. Dear Madam, how do you do? By the by," Alice said, leaning toward Olivia. "I'm sure Mrs. Leveret does not mind if I share her wonderful news." Alice tucked her arm under the older woman's.

"Indeed, not," said Mrs. Leveret.

"The school committee has taken a three-year lease on the Lodge."

"That's excellent news," Olivia said. "Far Caister will have a grand school." Relief flooded her. The school could not be opened a moment too soon.

"Renovations begin Tuesday next."

"There's better news yet," said Alice.

Olivia felt the weight of the world lift from her shoulders. At last. At long last. Surely, the school committee would agree to advance her enough of her salary to find new lodgings. "I should like to hear it."

Mrs. Leveret lifted her chin. "We have engaged our professor."

Her heart stuttered, but she smiled. "Have you?"

"Shall I tell her, Mrs. Leveret, or will you?" Alice patted Olivia's arm. "Such a thrill for us. I'm sure you'll be as excited as I was when I heard."

For a moment, hope soared. But Mrs. Leveret aimed her smile at Alice, not her.

Alice clasped her hands. "Mrs. Leveret's nephew just down from Cambridge. Mr. George Marshall. We are most ecstatic to have his services, I can tell you. An exceptional man. Quite exceptional."

"I'm sure you're right." Olivia nodded. "I look forward to meeting him and helping in any capacity that I may."

"I think, Miss Willow," said Mrs. Leveret, "that though we must thank you for your past efforts, my nephew, Mr. Marshall, has the school well in hand and no doubt has his own notions about its proper conduct."

"I am more than willing to assist, Mrs. Leveret."

"How kind. But with your mama so ill, I would not dream of imposing further. Mrs. Verney, will you come with me? I'd like a word with you."

"Of course." Alice turned to Olivia. "I'm sure you're as thrilled as I am about the school. Official at last. And a headmaster from Cambridge. What a condescension for us. How very fortunate we are, said I to Mr. Verney."

While Price pointed out the gothic arches above their heads and demonstrated the working of the ladder that reached to a height of twelve feet, Olivia walked to a set of mullioned windows overlooking the gardens. The extent of her latest reversal sank in. The earnings on which she had counted to meet her expenses had just vanished. She had no employment, and now, no prospect of employment at anything like the salary she needed. No way to pay Mrs. Goody, no money for lodgings and everything she owned burned in the fire, every pot or pan, every stick of furniture.

She stared out the window. Panic welled up, a tightness in her chest, a prickle of anxiety that grew and swelled until she thought she could not bear it. Snow drifted past the diamond-paned glass. White-covered lawns extended for yards and yards in every direction. Farther away, mist shrouded the treetops. Clouds gathered at the horizon, promising a storm. How marvelous to live such a life, where one might look out a window and know that as far as the eye could see and farther one still did not reach the limits of one's possessions.

Olivia left the window for a glass case containing a manuscript open to an illumination of the letter *T*. Next to that was a sheet of vellum on which gleamed the Tiern-Cope crest. The colors, cobalt and gold with reliefs of red and silver seemed as bright as the day they'd been inked. Above the shield arched the words *Chomh Crua Leis An Iarann*. Everyone in Far Caister knew the translation of the Gaelic phrase: "As Hard As Iron."

She looked over her shoulder and saw Tiern-Cope had separated from Diana, and that Fitzalan, Diana and Miss Cage, with Hew as her support, were at the moment unaware that he'd left them. Like any good parent in the presence of three such eligible men, Mr. Cage was absorbed in a book. Light from the windows between shelves of books shadowed Tiern-Cope's face in grave profile. The look of cold reflection much suited his temperament, she thought.

He half sat, half leaned on a corner of a table, imagining, she supposed, Diana in the role of his bride. He shifted, taking no notice of her, or of Diana, for that matter. Today, though, he would announce his engagement to Miss Royce. He must, for unless everyone was much mistaken, Captain Egremont had brought his orders. Light flared around him so that all she saw for the instant he moved through the light was his outline against a snow-filtered glow.

In the next glass case a banner, tattered at the edges, rested on a background of black silk. Woven of gold cloth it, too, depicted the Tiern-Cope crest. Below it lay a shaft of dark wood three or four feet in length, broken at one end, as if it had snapped under some terrible strain. Despite the centuries since the banner was sewn, the needlework retained an otherworldly brightness. The lion prepared to leap off the fabric; the unicorn just now reared up.

A breath of cold air swept through the room and, with the shifting of light from the windows, stirred the hair on the back of her neck. She shivered. Her head ached worse than ever, the familiar pain along with a sense of fullness, a pressure behind her ears.

"Still lovely, isn't it?" a low voice asked. She turned and saw Tiern-Cope.

"Yes."

"Did I startle you?"

"No. . . . All right. Yes, you did."

He smiled his slow, cold smile. With a nod toward where Price demonstrated a secret passage that led to the upper floor of the library, he said, "I've had the tour before." Fitzalan, Captain Egremont, Hew, Miss Cage and Diana were being allowed, one by one, to walk up the hidden staircase. "I'm told the Black Earl himself saved the banner you are admiring."

"Perhaps a Willow fought in whatever battle broke that pike," she said.

"Do you suppose he had red hair?"

She smiled. "A Willow might have held the banner. But he would not have allowed it to break."

"Surely not," he said. He stepped closer. "According to legend, had not the fourth earl been murdered, we might have been kings."

"I believe that." She traced on the glass the outline of the ragged banner. "Imagine the stories it could tell."

The earl smiled again, and his resemblance to his brother struck her. The man at rest might be his brother's twin. Except she found him far more compelling than Andrew. He bent closer. The air crackled with invisible energy. He, too, touched the glass, and his fingers brushed hers. A glancing touch, inadvertent. The contact made her heart thud. He wasn't wearing gloves, and his fingers resting on the case were proportionally long for his hand. He'd held a cutlass in that hand. Those fingers had pulled the trigger of a pistol with mortal intent. "Do not romanticize war, Miss Willow. If that banner could speak, be assured it would tell horrible tales."

She moved her hand off the case because his hand was too close, but clipped the side of her finger on the wooden edge. A sliver jabbed into her finger, right through her glove. She yelped and pulled on the wood. It broke off. "Ouch."

"Allow me."

"It's nothing. A splinter. I'll soon have it out."

With a tilt of his head, he took her hand. "I said, allow me."

"I do not like managing men."

"If I were to manage you as I ought to do, you'd understand what it means to be managed. And appreciate my present restraint. Now hold still." He drew off her glove and turned over her palm, angling it toward the light to see the sliver lodged under the skin of her smallest finger. "Fitzalan will not stop staring at you when he thinks no one is watching." He pinched the bit of wood between thumb and forefinger and pulled it out. "There. Hardly worth the name splinter."

"Thank you."

Still holding her bare wrist, his other hand touched her cheek so softly it was more a whisper of air than a caress. Olivia discovered she was standing right up against him. The entire time they'd been talking, he'd drawn her nearer or else she'd moved closer. She wasn't sure which. The snow brought with it cold that swept through the windows. Dark clouds swirled in the sky so that the shadows constantly changed. The tip of his finger touched just below her palm. His fingers cradled the back of her wrist and a portion of her hand. She wasn't the least bit afraid, because she knew she was safe with him. "A grand passion, Olivia. Settle for nothing less."

"As if that matters."

"He's not a bad sort."

"Hew?"

"James. If matters do not fall out as I hope, you might do worse than James."

She frowned. "Then why did you warn me about him?"

"Why do you think?" He traced a feather-light line along the pulse point of her wrist. Feeling as warm as his voice, she shook her head, then watched in disbelief as he brought her arm toward him.

"Don't do something you don't mean. Please don't."

He drew her closer. She lifted her free hand to push

259

him back. "No mistake. My love. I mean a great deal with you."

"You mean to break my heart, don't you?"

"Could I?"

Her hand drifted to his shoulder. It wasn't a lack of response on her part that had her standing as if benumbed, but too much. "I couldn't bear it if you didn't mean it," she said.

"Come to me, Olivia."

And she did. Because Sebastian would never harm her. Sebastian made everything right. The softness of his lips on her throat just above her collarbone, the scent of him, the size and power of him, but most of all, the sensation that inside she was melting, dissolving, kept her motionless. His lips parted and moved to the point where throat became shoulder. She discovered he still held her wrist because he brought her arm sideways away from their bodies, interlacing his fingers with hers.

Like that, nothing separated them. But he wasn't the one pressing her against him. He didn't need to. She leaned forward, her chest to his but bending her head back. One hand clutched his shoulder, hanging on for dear life. The other tightened around his hand. She felt his fingers skim through her hair, molding the back of her skull, moving her head just enough to expose more of her throat or neck. Then, he stopped.

"No," she moaned. "Please."

He smiled with an easy, fluid grin, a glint of triumph in his blue eyes. He touched her cheek. The caress left a chill in its wake. Her eyes fluttered open. His arms were around her. "I mean every moment. Every heart beat."

the north courtyard, "on the exact location of the original motte built by the first earl's ancestors." He indicated an incline at the top of which one could see a crumbling foundation. In the middle of the ruins, a tall figure stood with one foot propped on a stone. The sword strapped across his back rose over his shoulder, and the sigil of the earls of Tiern-Cope shimmered across his chest. Olivia closed her eyes, but when she opened them again, the figure was still there, so real and true to life she could see the brilliant blue eyes, the folds of his tunic, and the buckle on his belt. She looked around, but no one else noticed him. She glanced at Tiern-Cope, standing with Diana. He stared, too, at the spot where the swordsman stood. As if he'd sensed her attention, Tiern-Cope turned his head. Their eyes met.

Fitzalan glanced at the gathering clouds, and then at her. "Cold?"

"Not at all."

He slipped off his coat and draped it over her shoulders. She stiffened at the contact. "Are you going to marry your cousin?"

"Yes."

Fitzalan searched her face. "Why, if you do not love him?"

" 'Twas here," Price said, "the barons *Iarann* fought off many a highland barbarian. The barons were never defeated in battle. Nor were any of the earls Tiern-Cope." He turned and led them to a doorway in the north tower, a massive rectangle of stone that housed Olivia's rooms. He rattled a set of keys. While he unlocked the door, he continued to speak. "*Iarann*, as some of you may know, is Gaelic for iron. The man who sired the original baron was Irish. He came to

England to be civilized by an English bride whom he married, so the story goes, because her red hair reminded him of Ireland." He pointed upward. "Indeed, the motto of those Irish ancestors is carved over the lintel of what was once the original entrance to Pennhyll. *Chomh Crua Leis An Iarann.* 'As Hard as Iron.' A motto," he continued, "I am sure you will agree is well suited to the earls Tiern-Cope down to the present day."

The door swung inward on its hinges and they filed inside. "We now enter the oldest portion of Castle Pennhyll. Take especial care as you walk. Watch the shadows, for you may see not the first earl but the fourth earl, the Black Earl, he was called, as we draw nearer his former chamber. Ladies, keep your shawls at hand, for I've heard the chill air signifies the presence of the unhappy dead." This brought a shriek from Diana. Price's somber expression deepened. He would, Olivia thought, have made a fine actor.

"Terrifying, isn't he?" Fitzalan said. "No, please, Miss Willow," he said when she tried to return his coat.

"Thank you, but I insist." She slipped free of the garment and held it out.

"Very well."

From the corner of her eye, she saw Tiern-Cope watching the viscount. She found it impossible to act naturally around Fitzalan and even less so around Lord Tiern-Cope.

"The day of my arrival at Pennhyll," Fitzalan said, "three different servants made a particular point of warning me the fourth earl yet walked the castle halls. I think they must have taken lessons from Price." He paused. "Your cousin is watching you again." Her feeling of unease increased, for indeed, Hew stared at her, eyes narrowed. "I do believe he's jealous."

"Of what, my Lord?"

"Me."

"Who wouldn't be?" She laughed. "With the wealth and position that is yours, you are to be envied, indeed."

He gave her a dazzling smile. "If you mean my position next to you, you're quite right."

"Ridiculous." But she burst out laughing despite not meaning to. They'd reached a set of stone stairs, and Price waited for them to assemble before leading them upward. Fitzalan moved closer, speaking in a low voice.

"I would not for the world have you uncomfortable, Miss Willow. But I confess he's made me wildly jealous."

The others started up the stairs. She stopped at the first step and faced him. Fitzalan kept his distance, for which she was grateful. "You have no cause for jealousy. Nor does my cousin."

"Don't marry him." He grabbed her hands and went down on one knee. "Miss Willow. Olivia. I must speak."

"Pray do not."

"Whatever Sebastian told you about me, he was wrong." Fitzalan tightened his fingers around her hands. "He wasn't once, but my feelings are not what they were. I admire you and respect you. You're a lovely, lovely woman, and I am out of my mind with love for you. Olivia, I want to marry you. The honor would be mine, I assure you. I will cherish you to the end of my days."

"For pity's sake, stand up."

"Olivia. I adore you. I want you to be my wife."

"Stand up."

He did, thrusting his hands deep into his pockets. "I love you."

"That's nonsense."

He stepped toward her, too close, slipping an arm around her waist. She retreated. Her stomach pitched. "All I ask is that you not reject me out of hand."

She laughed because the scene was so horribly accurate. Exactly what Tiern-Cope had warned. "Someone once told me never to trade a present liberty for a promise."

"Sebastian told you that, didn't he?"

"He was right."

Some of the light went out of his eyes. "If I even try to kiss you, you'll think he was, and that I'm trying to seduce you."

"Aren't you?"

"It's only natural I'd want to kiss the woman I love. The woman I intend to make my wife."

"Shall we go? Before we're missed."

"Olivia, I love you."

"I am not much amused."

"For once, I don't mean to amuse you. I am free to marry where I choose. There is no impediment. No reason in the world why I cannot marry you and no reason for you to marry your cousin. Not when my heart is yours." He took her arm. "I won't badger you, but I promise you, you'll make me the happiest man in the world soon."

Olivia looked pointedly ahead of them. "Shall we?"

"The fourth earl," Price was saying when she and Fitzalan rejoined the others, "whom some call the Black Earl, died before his time, found dead in a pool of blood that to this day stains the floor of the lord's chamber. Neither soap nor lye can remove that mark of unholy death."

They were, she realized, not just in the north tower, but heading toward the stairs to her room.

Tiern-Cope turned his head toward them, catching Olivia in the act of tucking a curl into place at the back of her head. Fitzalan stood close behind her, and the earl's cold gaze flicked from her to Fitzalan. She felt a rush of heat because she knew what he thought had just happened.

Single-file, they ascended the stairs and exited on the floor below her room. They halted midway to the parlor. The air felt cooler, and she shivered again. With two long strides and a flourish of his hands, Price threw open the parlor door. "Behold, my Lords, ladies and gentlemen. The scene of the Black Earl's murder most foul."

"I thought you said this was the earl's chamber," said Diana, who was the first to enter after Price himself.

"Not the present earl's chamber, of course," Price said. He walked farther in, turning to the guests. "The family now resides in a more modern wing. Five hundred years ago this was the earl's chamber. You must imagine not this gilt-edged desk but an oaken table, thick and solid enough to withstand use by a warrior knight of the realm. No delicate sofa or book-lined shelves, but an enormous black wardrobe and a carved chest. There a stand for a knight's sword. Imagine, if you will, silk hangings surrounding the bed. Rushes cover the floor and firelight flickers over the walls. The air, despite the fire, chills. Imagine not this exquisite marble mantel straight from the finest quarries in all of Italy, but the stone hearth beneath. Captain Egremont, perhaps you will be kind enough to stand just here. Facing the fireplace, just off the carpet, as if back from a melee." Egremont shrugged and moved into place.

As one of the last in, Olivia stood farthest from the fireplace. No one paid her the slightest attention, not even Fitzalan who, at the moment, stood next to his sister and Mr. Cage. Not Hew either, for that matter.

"Listen for the sound of treacherous footsteps," Price said standing behind Captain Egremont. "The door makes no sound, for the hinges have been well oiled against this night's dark deed. A soft padding behind the Black Earl who stands unaware the sanctuary of his rooms has been breached. He contemplates his day, thinking perhaps of his lady wife, or planning a campaign for the next." Egremont put a booted foot on the grate. Suddenly, Price bent and grasped the edge of the carpet. "Imagine murder." With a practiced motion, he threw back the carpet, baring the stone floor to Egremont's right. An irregular stain marred the floor. Diana threw herself against Tiern-Cope's chest. He patted her shoulder, then put her into the care of Mr. Cage. He backed away to let others examine the floor.

While awaiting her turn to look, her eye was caught by something glittering in the darkened angle where the wall met the floor. Intrigued, Olivia stooped and peered into the corner. She stretched out an arm. Her fingers closed on something small and cool to the touch. The object felt like a bit of sharp-edged ice. Her blood ran cold when she saw what it was; the urge to throw it back to its shadowy corner made her fingers twitch. She stared at the letter engraved on the surface, then closed her hand around it.

Dr. Fansher leaned toward Olivia. "Have you found something, lass?" His eyebrows shot upward when she opened her fingers. "What is it?"

Behind them the others crowded around the stained floor, oblivious. She knew what she held and even, it seemed, how it came to rest in the corner. Not a dream. Gracious, she and the earl— Oh, heavens.

"A cufflink." Dr. Fansher took it from her. "A for Alexander. Captain Alexander?" He bowed. "My Lord, is this yours?"

Tiern-Cope took the cufflink. The center of Olivia's palm tingled when the earl's gaze lifted from the bit of metal and landed squarely on her. "Where did you find it, Ned?"

"Didn't. Miss Willow did." He cleared his throat. "Ah, I want a closer look at the floor, and I can see Captain Egremont is wanting a word with me. Do excuse me, Captain. Miss Willow."

Tiern-Cope pocketed the bit of metal when Fansher took his leave. "Did we?" he said.

"Onward," Price said. "If the ladies dare—"

On cue, Diana said, "Where?"

"The dungeons, Miss. Where the Black Earl once imprisoned his own dear Lady wife."

People shifted position, moving toward the door. Fitzalan joined Tiern-Cope and tucked Olivia's arm under his, obstructing Hew's attempt to join Olivia. "Hullo there, Mr. Willow. Chilling sight, wasn't it? Come along, Miss Willow. You, my dear Captain, most shamefully neglect my sister. Shall we, Olivia?"

The dungeons extended the length and width of the north tower, but were reached via stairs from the

Great Hall. Bare stone steps descended to blackness.
Price, lamp held high, led the way. At the bottom, he
distributed oil lamps to several of the gentlemen.
Within the circle of light, the corridor was comfort-
ably bright but ahead lay impenetrable darkness.
"Stay close to the gentlemen, ladies." Price laughed.
"If we lose you in here, the only way we'll find you
again is by the gleam of your bones in the darkness."

Olivia wished her cloak was warmer as Price ush-
ered them down several steps into a chamber that
angled back into solid darkness. Cell doors opened
to enclosures no larger than a carriage. The smell of
decay and damp and of things left to rot made the air
heavy. Several of the ladies pressed handkerchiefs to
their noses. Walls glistened with blackish-green mold.
Frost and ice clung to the stone. Manacles hung from
the walls, a gruesome reminder of the former use of
Pennhyll's dungeons. Olivia could not help thinking
the lanterns did not entirely relieve the dark. Blackness waited to reclaim its own. A shiver crawled up
her spine at the thought of being trapped here, closed
in by a brute of an earl.

Price took them down another flight of stairs to a
cell no less cold and dank than the others, but smaller
yet. He pushed on the black metal door, opening it
wide. "We stand at the extreme rear of the castle in
Pennhyll's most infamous cell. *La Morte Froide*," he
said. " 'The Cold Death.' Where the Black Earl imprisoned his countess. Come in. Come in. No more
than five at a time."

Olivia was in the last group to enter to cell. Price
pointed to an opening high up the wall. "That aper-
ture admits air. And snow or rain or water. And—
other things. Disagreeable things. No fewer than six

gutters converge there and empty into this cell. A prisoner held here during a winter storm might well drown, if the cold did not kill him first."

"But could he not escape?" Hew asked. "The hole seems rather generous. Could not a prisoner climb out that passage?"

"Indeed, sir." Price nudged a manacle hanging beneath the opening. The metal scraped against the stone. "He could if the guard forgot to secure him. But, I assure you, no one at Pennhyll was ever so forgetful. And if one was, the prisoner who managed to navigate the tunnel would likely fall to his death on the rocks below, for beyond this wall lies a sheer drop down the mountain."

Upon their exit, Olivia was at the back of the group because a jagged bit of metal from the manacles snagged the hem of her gown. She tugged. This was her only dress. If this one were damaged, quite literally, she had nothing else to wear. She tugged again, fingers searching the snarl of fabric in the hope of avoiding a tear that couldn't be easily mended. Metal sliced her fingertip. The cell door screeched on its hinges. She cried out, and jerked her skirt. The muslin ripped free. Olivia turned in time to see a flash of bright fabric disappear into darkness.

"Wait." She dashed for the door but slipped on the slime-coated floor. Her arms flailed, and she teetered disastrously close to falling flat. The time it took to regain her footing cost her. The door closed with a resounding *clang* and trapped her in a world without light. In the blackness, she felt for the door. There wasn't any handle on the inside. She hooked her fingers in the gap between the door and the stone wall, but it was jammed too tightly to open. With a fist, she pounded on door, bruising the side of her clenched hand on one of the metal cross struts. "There's someone here. Open the door!"

Thunder boomed, drowning out her voice. The heavens opened. Five minutes later, water and melting sleet poured through the grate and cascaded to the floor. The stench overpowered her. Frantic, she thumped on the door again. She could hear nothing through the walls. A sense of unreality took hold, deepened by the darkness.

Couldn't this be a dream, too? Just as she'd imagined the earl back there in the library kissing her or the Black Earl leading her to Tiern-Cope's private quarters, mightn't she now be imagining herself trapped in this cell? The cold felt bitterly real. Her eyes adjusted to the black. She could see the walls now, dank with mold. A glimmer of gray came from the opening in the far wall. Runoff converged at the hole in a collision of water and granite. She leaned against the door and waited. Forever, it seemed. Her shawl did not protect her from the cold. She shivered. The water seemed to be coming down faster now.

Before long, water lapped over her feet, covering her boots. The stench choked her. She waded toward the duct, one arm extended until she felt the wall. Her skin crawled at the contact. Two feet above the tips of her extended arms, she could see a shimmer of light. Water cascaded onto her with force that whipped away her shawl. With leverage from one foot on the iron-fitting that secured the manacles to the wall, she stretched and jammed her fingers into a seam in the wall. Her shoulders and ribs protested, but she hauled herself upward. She held her breath against the onrush as by dint of sheer desperation, she clawed her way into the tunnel.

She shimmied forward. The wetter her clothes got, the harder it was to move. The tunnel angled upward. Every so often, she had to push herself up to release dammed up water, letting it rush beneath her. She focused on the light. The opening narrowed, and for a panicky moment she could not move in any direction. Water splashed into her face. Her feet scrabbled, sliding off the walls, but at last the toe of her boot caught a seam in the stone. She exhaled every last bit of air in her lungs, pushed with all her strength and slid forward. One hand extended outside. She inched her way forward until, like a snake, she slithered out. Shards of rock bruised her feet and the wind blew so fiercely that if she hadn't flung her arms around a boulder protruding from the foundation she'd have been blown off the mountain. A gust caught her hair and sent her cap whirling into the sky.

Chapter Twenty-six

Sebastian closed the cell door, giving it a push so that with a sigh of putrid air, iron fittings ground against stone. He shook off a shiver of unease. At his side, Diana shivered, too. Lord, that door sounded like death. What must hapless prisoners have felt to be on the other side when they heard that sound? Thunder roared, a tremendous clap to be heard from so deep within Pennhyll. Diana cringed.

"*Après moi, le deluge,*" Sebastian murmured.

"Oh, do hurry," said Diana, motioning in Price's direction. "I do not like this at all. I want to go."

Price cleared his throat. "Perhaps some tea to settle ruffled nerves? Before the ladies make their preparations for tonight's festivities."

"Tea." Diana tugged on Sebastian's sleeve. "Already I feel warmer, don't you, my Lord?"

"Yes."

"If everyone is with us now. This way, please." Price lifted his light. Thunder boomed and with it, as if propelled by the storm, a gust of arctic air.

Fansher's lamp went out.

Diana gasped and most of the young ladies cried out. Sebastian took Diana's hand. Another gust of cold air raced through the corridor. Price's lamp winked out, then Mr. Cage's.

Hew shouted and dropped his lantern. It crashed to the floor, flared and went out. "Something touched me."

"Did you hear that?" said Miss Cage.

"I didn't hear anything," James said. In the darkness now lit only by Sebastian's lantern, his face gleamed. "Unless"—he waggled his eyebrows—"you meant that blood-curdling howl."

Diana made a face. "You're beastly, James."

"I thought I heard someone calling for help," said Miss Cage.

"I heard something, too," said Hew.

"The wind," Sebastian said.

"A spirit," said James. "Some poor soul lost here in centuries past and who wishes to communicate with the living."

Fansher picked up Hew's lantern. "Broken." The

273

glass on two sides had shattered and the oil reservoir cracked.

"Perhaps," James said, "the Black Earl himself."

A rat skittered just at the edge of the light. Miss Cage shrieked and Diana, catching a glimpse of the beast, let out a scream of her own. One of the other girls sobbed.

"Hold up your lantern, Captain," Egremont said. "It's dark enough here as it is." Sebastian complied, and the circle of flickering light widened.

James rubbed his palms together. "Perhaps I'm right about the spirits, Diana. If I'd been clapped in here for upsetting the first Lord Tiern-Cope, I'd still be calling for help however long I'd been dead."

Price turned to Diana. Light flickered on his cheeks. "A ghostly call from centuries past, Miss. For there's no denying many a blue-painted barbarian felt the cold chill of iron here. Their unfortunate souls linger still."

"You see?" James said.

"Oh, do let's go."

One of the girls in the back still sobbed. Sebastian gave Price his lamp. "You know the way, best hold this."

"My Lord." He took the lantern, but the granite passage was so dark the single flame hardly penetrated the blackness head. "Have we everyone with us?"

"Who can tell?" Hew said.

"Whoever's not here," said James, "speak now or forever hold your peace."

"Oh, let's be gone from here." Diana stamped a foot. Something skittered again, two high-pitched squeaks rose from the blackness. When they reached the stairs leading to the upper floors, Diana clutched Sebastian's arm. "What was that?"

"I heard something, too," one of the men said.

"Thunder," said Hew. "The storm's broken."

In the gloom and dankness they all heard a low wail, thin and distant. *"Helppppp."*

Diana shrieked.

"Help me, laird," a voice said. "For it's dying I am, mon." A shape lurched from the darkness. "Helppp."

The figure staggered and knocked over a pile of rusty pikes with a sound like a roar. Several of the ladies screamed. Diana would have fled for the stairs had not Sebastian had an arm around her.

James lumbered into the light, grinning. "Boo."

"James," Diana cried. "You are horrible. Horrible."

"I thought you wanted to commune with the spirits, Diana."

"Don't be a beast, James."

He was unrepentant. "Oh, come now, Diana. Admit it. It was an excellent jest."

Diana walked to her brother and hit him right between the middle buttons of his waistcoat. "You're awful, James, and I hate you."

"Ahem." Price held up his lantern. "Tea in the red salon?"

When Sebastian reached his room, the Black Earl stood by his bed. Sebastian turned away, fingering the cufflink in his pocket. He didn't need the Black Earl's help in debauching Olivia anymore, he had apparently at last managed that well enough all on his own. He threw himself onto a chair, full of his memory of his hands on Olivia. Cold air sent a prickle along the backs of his arms. He opened his eyes and saw the Black Earl again. In one hand, he gripped a sword of unearthly silver, but held downward so that the point of the weapon touched the floor. He wept as if his heart were broken. *"Aidez-la."* Help her.

Sebastian heard nothing but the roar of those words tearing through his soul. *Help her.*

The Black Earl, weeping still, turned to the stone wall. A rent marred his crimson tunic, the edges jagged and blackened, and then he, too, vanished and left behind him nothing but an aching, unfillable emptiness.

Help her.

In the fireplace, the heat found a flaw in several of the coals and sent hissing, popping flares upward. He shivered, for the room felt cold. He heard the jingle of metal, the ring of a sword replaced in its scabbard. Foreboding weighed him down, pressed upon him so that he felt he could not breathe for the certainty of disaster looming.

Help her.

The last time he remembered seeing Olivia was in the dungeon. In that atrocious cell that stank of death and decay. Before the lamps went out. Standing, he remembered, at the rear of the cell into which Price had led them. She'd have been the last one out. He remembered the scraping pull of the cell door closing. Certainty gnawed at his gut. He'd closed her in there. He knew it. Just like his ancestor the Black Earl, he'd locked a woman in that God-awful cell. His blood ran cold as he recalled Diana's conviction that she'd heard someone calling for help. And no one actually confirmed everyone had come out.

"Help her."

Sebastian turned, knowing what he would see at the same time he wondered what sort of madman conjured ghosts of long-dead ancestors and conversed with them about women gone missing. "She'll be in her room," he said. "Changing like the others."

The Black Earl faced the window. "Help her."

Sebastian walked to the window, shuddering when he passed through the Black Earl. He looked out. The storm boiled in the sky. "There's nothing—" To his right, he saw a flash of white. Movement. A woman clinging to the ledge between the castle and the steep drop to the cairn below. Olivia. Wind whipped her hair and gown. "I'll wring her bloody neck."

In his sitting room he ran down a servant carrying an armful of linens. Sprawled on the floor, she tugged at her cap.

"What's the quickest way to the outside? The back of the castle?"

She pointed to the outline of a door in the wall. Without thinking, he strode to the door, his fingers finding the release mechanism. A staircase spiraled down, his feet took him wherever it led, spinning downward. He came out near the rear of Pennhyll, into a fierce wind that battered him as hard as any gale. Sleet pelted him as he worked his way around the tower. The rear of the north tower faced nothing but the sky and a drop down the mountain. He crouched, peering along the jumble of rock and flurries of snow, searching for the safest route. Any route at all. He took a cautious step in the shifting mass of loose shale and flint, keeping low to make himself a smaller target for the wind.

Olivia continued to pick her way along rock and crumbled brick, treacherous footing. Wind whipped her hair and gown. Her head bowed as she concentrated on the patch of rock in front of her. She slipped twice before he thought he was close enough that the wind wouldn't carry away his voice. He called out. "Olivia."

Her head jerked up.

"Stay where you are." His words flew into the wind. Lifting his voice, he shouted. "I'll come to you."

She sank down, arms around a bulge of rock that formed the foundation of Pennhyll. Six feet more. His skin crawled. The sky exploded in a flash of lightning. He threw himself toward her, reaching for her outstretched hand. His fingers closed around her wrist, but he lost his footing in the shifting flint and slid below the ledge. Olivia shouted and threw out a hand. Instinctively, he reached. Their fingers caught. She slipped and shot past him, riding loose rocks. He squeezed her hands, slid farther down but caught himself. They teetered, and she flung herself at another boulder. An avalanche of shale and flint rolled and skittered down the mountainside. Sebastian threw himself over Olivia, his arms around their heads, protecting them both.

When the rocks stopped flying, he embraced his relief as tightly as he embraced her. Ignoring the sleet pelting them, he grasped her head between his hands. "Out for a stroll, Miss Willow?" he said.

"Lovely evening, my Lord. So good of you to come along."

Another flash of lightning lit the sky. He felt his stomach drop. Nothing below them but a fall to certain death. "Bloody, sodding little fool."

He threw up a hand, grabbed the ledge and, together, they ascended the hill. When they reached firm ground, Sebastian swung Olivia into his arms and leaned against the castle wall. She shivered, and he held her more tightly yet. Lord, she felt small and vulnerable. "Thank God," he said into her hair.

Taking care where he stepped because the sleet had changed to snow and turned the ground icy, he headed for the tower door. The squelch of his boots and the whisk of his breeches echoed in the stairwell. It was dark as pitch. He turned sideways to get up the stairs, and she helped matters by pressing herself tight against him. She felt like ice.

"I ought to wring your silly little neck," he said to the dark.

"Why?" She was soaked to the skin, and she smelled like a privy.

"You could have killed yourself." He was so used to having control of his emotions that he didn't recognize his reaction for what it was. "What were you thinking, climbing out that hole?" He adjusted her in his arms again. "It's a damn good thing you're so small." He could feel her body, the shape of her backside against his belly and his forearm.

"Thank you."

"For what?"

"Coming after me."

"I'm the one who closed you in."

She hesitated. "On purpose?"

"No, I didn't close you in on purpose." His emotions grew larger than life, and he could no more sort out the panic from the relief than he could speak in tongues. "It's bloody storming out there."

"Yes."

They exited into the sitting room connected to his bedchamber. He kicked the door closed. Olivia blinked and wiped her eyes. Water plastered her hair to her head and ran in rivulets down her face. The gown was black with mud. Her nose was red, her skin pale and waxy, her lips blue. She dragged more water-logged hair off her forehead. Her teeth chattered. Even when she clenched her jaw, it didn't stop nor did the shivers.

McNaught heard the noise for he came at a run. His eyes went round as his belly. "She needs a hot bath, McNaught. Is mine ready?"

"My Lord." He took a step back.

"Then see to it, McNaught."

He shifted Olivia in his arms and to keep her balance and his, she clutched his neck. "Whatever possessed you to attempt such a foolhardy and dangerous stunt as that? Hell, Olivia. You stink."

"I know."

He carried her into his dressing room. Steam rose off his bathwater, but the cold hit him the minute he walked in. Colors flashed behind his eyes, and he felt pressure in his head. The light shifted, the fireplace coals hissed and popped. His eyes sought the shadows. There, in far corner, a man. Holding a broadsword. Well, he wasn't going to pay any attention.

Olivia shivered. Slowly, he set her down. The sense of belonging nearly bowled him over. Not him, but her. She belonged here. They belonged here. Together. Their clothes dripped on the carpet while he knelt at the fireplace, ignoring the Black Earl standing in the corner. He dumped the contents of the scuttle onto the fire. Brushing off his hands, he glanced at her. "It'll be warmer soon. Come stand near the fire a while. Jesus, you look a fright."

"Thank you," she muttered. But she did as he directed. In the corner, the Black Earl hadn't moved. "You're soaked to the skin."

He stripped off his coat and stood looking for someplace where it wouldn't do any damage. There wasn't any place except the marble floor around the tub. "It's bloody freezing in here. Where the hell is that draft coming from?" Abruptly, he turned. "You're wet," he said in a soft, low voice. He went to her, ostensibly to stand near the fire, but really just to be close to her. He rested his hands on her shoulders. Where the devil was McNaught? Anyone? If they stayed alone much longer, he would end by dishonoring them both. "And I would not have you fall ill."

They jumped when someone knocked.

"Enter," he said, torn between relief and disappointment.

The door opened, and a serving girl came in. Her eyes lit on him. She dropped into a deep curtsey. "My Lord."

"Who the hell are you?"

"Edith," Olivia said. She sounded relieved. "Her name is Edith."

"Is that so?"

Edith bowed her head lower yet. "My Lord."

"Well, Edith. I take it, despite my not having seen you before— No." He snapped his fingers. "I have seen you. I ran you down. Just before I went after Olivia. I presume McNaught told you to come here."

"Aye, sir."

Sebastian looked at Olivia. Something tugged at him. "She needs to get out of those wet clothes, immediately. You're shivering still, Olivia. Move closer to the fire."

"Any closer and I'll be standing in it."

"Edith," he said. "Immediately does not mean later. It means now. Do as I say, young woman." He swung his attention back to Olivia. "What did I tell you about those wet clothes?"

"My Lord," Olivia said, clenching her jaw to keep her teeth from chattering.

"Delightful as is the sight of your gown clinging to your body, I cannot help but be aware it is not healthy for you."

"Nor for you."

"Well then?"

His dressing room door opened, and all three of them whirled. "McNaught."

The valet glanced at the two women and then at Sebastian. "I have taken the liberty, my Lord, of calling for another bath. In your sitting room." He emphasized *sitting room*, so as to be sure, Sebastian imagined, the women respected the privacy of his bath.

Olivia said, "Off with you, Sebastian."

He bowed. "I expect you ready for dancing in less than an hour."

She grabbed two handfuls of her gown. "I was going to wear this."

"That," he said, "is easily remedied." He glanced at Edith. "Keep an eye on her. Call me immediately if anything happens."

"Aye, my Lord."

McNaught followed him into the sitting room. Disapproval rolled off him. Footmen had already brought a tub and were filling it with steaming water. He stripped his outer clothes and peeled off his shirt and linens. While he waited for the rest of the water, he submitted without complaint to a thoroughly awful potion administered by a silent McNaught. He stepped into the bath and while he soaped himself he wondered if Olivia was naked. He didn't need much imagination at all to conjure her in her bath. Skin damp and slick, her hair curling around her face.

"Bugger it," he said, leaning forward so that water sloshed out of the tub. He couldn't keep his mind off Olivia even when she wasn't here. Once he was dry and wrapped in his robe, he let McNaught shave him despite being worried that his valet was affronted enough to be careless with the razor. He dressed as impatiently as he'd bathed, fidgeting while McNaught tied his cravat. "Do you think she's decent yet?"

"I cannot make a knot if you will not stand still, my Lord."

"Devil take you. I haven't ravished her."

His valet blew air into his cheeks. "This is a complicated fold that requires you to stand without moving."

"Better?"

"Yes, my Lord. A moment longer. There."

"She needs something to wear." Snatching up his gloves, he strode into his bedroom and knocked on his dressing room door.

Chapter Twenty-seven

8:02 P.M.

Olivia slipped into the scented water. "Heaven. Positively heaven."

"Aye, it's lovely, my Lady." Edith soaped a cloth and Olivia, with wicked decadence, allowed the servant to wash her back. She reveled in the warm water, and relished the scent of verbena. Edith washed her hair, too, with fingers surprisingly strong for a girl her age.

"Verbena," Olivia said with a sigh. "I adore verbena."

"Aye, my Lady."

"I'll just soak awhile, Edith, if you don't mind. I don't think I've ever been so tired in all my life."

"Call when you're done, my Lady."

Eyes closed, Olivia leaned against the side of the tub. Wouldn't it be lovely to think nothing of having a servant to look after her every need? A draft raised goose pimples on her shoulders, which surprised her because the water remained quite warm, and she knew from the warmth of the air that the fire hadn't gone out. She sank deeper into the tub. Was Tiern-Cope in his bath right now? Water lapping at his thighs. The draft persisted. "Edith? Has the fire gone out?"

"I'll see to it, Mistress." Edith's voice sounded faint, as if she were far away.

Olivia had the oddest sensation that the world had shifted. Her head felt full. She rubbed her temples, but the feeling only increased. Beads of water slid down the metal sides of the tub, eventually joining the bathwater. Condensation fogged the cheval mirror. The wardrobe door was open, revealing shirts neatly stacked on a shelf.

Air swirled over her shoulders leaving a wake of chilled skin. To her left something stirred in the shadows. She blinked. The swordsman stood by the fire, as clear and solid as day. Her heart thundered in her ears so loud he must surely hear. She started to sit up, then remembered her naked state. Water sloshed in the tub. "I beg your pardon."

He inclined his head. Steam from the water swirled, but Olivia saw his dark hair. He was tall and wore a tunic worked with red and gold. A leather strap crossed from right shoulder to left waist and held the scabbard fastened across his back. A jeweled belt circled his waist. His eyes matched the blue of the sky. The way he stood struck her as familiar. She closed her eyes. He was still there when she opened them again. "I am not mad," she said. "Is that you? Edith?"

Even with the distance between them and the mist swirling in the air, she saw his blue eyes, the arrogant set to his shoulders that came of years of wealth and breeding. His grin sent a flare of alarm up her spine. He took a step toward her, and for one dreadful moment, she was convinced he was as real as she was. He tipped his head and spread his arms wide, as if to prove himself harmless. "Go away." She wasn't afraid of him precisely. She was afraid of being mad. "Please, just go away."

He shook his head.

"I am not mad," she whispered.

He shook his head again. "I wish you were real." With a sigh—whether of resignation or something else, she did not know—she sat forward in the tub and set a wave of water in motion. She had the oddest sensation of moving not just through space but through time. Her head felt heavy, as if the very air were thickening, slowing her down, and she had to pull herself through the wake of her forward motion. Then, like the snapping of wire stretched beyond its length, the heaviness vanished.

Water lapped against the end of the tub, rolling

back and forth like tiny waves. She rose and stepped out of the tub. The steam had cleared so she could see her reflection in the cheval glass. Edith's arm stretched into the mirror view, snatching a towel from a bench. Behind her and behind Edith, stood Tiern-Cope. Sebastian. He wore evening dress and held a package of awkward shape. Dun breeches, gold waistcoat, blue tail coat and shoes with gold buckles. His cravat had a rather bold knot for him. Like her, his attention was fixed on the mirror. Edith unfurled a towel, holding it up to hide her. Too late, of course. Her stomach fell straight to the bottom of the earth.

"My Lord." Olivia raised her arms so that Edith could wrap the towel around her.

"Olivia."

"You look handsome."

He walked to the table while Edith toweled her off. She heard the clatter of porcelain, the wetness of liquid poured. "Here." He wheeled around, cup and saucer in hand. "Sit near the fire so your hair will dry."

She took the cup and breathed in the steam. "I didn't know you knew how to make tea." Edith brought a chair to the hearth and Olivia, wrapped in her towel, sat.

"I'm not useless." His package lay on the desk, a bulky shape. The tea warmed her hands and when she sipped, cradling the cup, she sighed with pleasure. Fresh, strong tea. Not leaves saved from a second or third brewing. "Oolong," he told her. "Sweet enough for you?"

"Perfect."

"Good." He took a step toward her. With the tip of his finger, he traced the line of her jaw. She felt his soul reach for hers, and she wanted to wrap herself in the feeling as if it were a blanket. He coiled one of her damp curls around his finger. "Edith, I've brought her something to wear." With his free hand, he pointed at the desk. "See to her, won't you? She has a ball tonight."

"My Lord."

Sebastian sat on the chair Olivia left, legs stretched out and crossed at the ankles. Muscle shaped the back of his thighs in a way Olivia thought she'd never tire of seeing. With Edith's help, she dressed quickly. He'd forgotten nothing, not stockings, chemise, petticoats, stays, slippers, garters, or gloves. Even the reticule and a fan that matched the gown. Olivia ran her hands down the black velvet skirt and fingered the gold cord that trimmed the neckline. "It nearly broke my heart to sell this. I cut it down from one of Mama's. Took me weeks to make it. Thank you for getting it back."

"It suits you." He studied her. "Do something with her hair, Edith. Something to show off these lovely curls."

"Yes, your Lordship." Edith placed two ivory combs in her hair, bringing the mass of curls away from her face. She pinned the rest into a fall of copper at the back of her head.

"There are women, Olivia, who would kill to have your curls."

She smiled. "Sometimes I think I'd kill to give them away."

"There's one last thing you need," he said.

"What's that?"

He took a string of gold beads from his pocket. They settled around her neck, surprisingly warm. His fingers brushed the corner of her mouth. "You'll do," he said. "You'll do."

Chapter Twenty-eight

9:13 P.M.

Everyone turned when Sebastian came into the Great Hall with Olivia on his arm. Egremont and Ned stood next to each other at one side of the hall. Sebastian knew from the expressions of his two closest friends they approved. Ned's smile split his face. Egremont nodded. Olivia tightened her fingers on his arm at the silence occasioned by their entrance. He watched James look long and hard at them and knew he'd been right to believe James would fall. Nor was James the only man to notice her. Hew, who thought he was going to marry the woman, stared as intently as James. His eyes flashed, but not with admiration of his cousin.

James approached them. "A vision," he said, bowing to Olivia. "You are without a doubt the loveliest woman I have seen in all my life." Sebastian did not release his grip on Olivia's arm. They descended the remaining steps.

A side door opened, admitting the musicians. They took seats and began a warm-up. A man raised his fiddle and began a lament. Next came the rolling beat of a tympan, then pipes and last, the strum of a harp. Sebastian's chest felt tight, and he ached inside, but not from physical pain. The music echoed his feelings. He did not like the way James and Hew looked at Olivia. As for the rest of the young men, they were

THE SPARE

dandies or else stout yeomen more at home with their sheep and border collies than dancing at Pennhyll Castle. Not a one worthy of Olivia.

At his side, she tugged on his hand. "Let go."

He released her, gave her three steps' lead and followed her farther into the Great Hall. Jesus. Had he actually stood in his dressing room, watching her step dripping from the tub? Jesus. Yes. He'd sprawled on a chair and watched a servant help her dress, too. And Olivia never objected. The maid never objected. Not even McNaught came rushing in to protest. Every damn person in the castle must be completely insane.

Applause and laughter rang out when they came to a halt in the center of the room because the crowd permitted no further access. Diana giggled, holding on to Mr. Cage's arm. Sebastian bowed to Diana and held out his hand. She took it. "My Lord." She curtseyed, as fresh and pink as the rose-petal silk of her ballgown. He disliked pink.

Another roar rose up, hoots of laughter. "Kiss her, my Lord," said several of the gentlemen. James, smirking, pointed upward and Sebastian glanced up. A sprig of mistletoe hung a foot above his head, suspended from a line thrown over one of the arms of the chandelier overhead.

"Can't go against custom."

"How now, my Lord."

"Kiss her."

Sebastian shrugged and drew Diana toward him. Laughter bubbled up again; giggles from the ladies, chuckles from the men. When she rested her gloved palms on his shoulder, he thought that at least he would not have to crane his neck to reach her lips. Diana raised her chin, her eyelashes fluttering down.

289

He felt nothing, not a shred of anticipation or pleasure. Diana, the woman whom he was supposed to make his life's companion, might as well have been his sister for all the desire he felt.

"Come now, my Lord," one of the men said.

He kissed her. A brief kiss that brushed her lips. Not even the faintest stirring of passion. He was empty inside. He reached up and plucked one of the three remaining berries from the sprig. The grandest ass since the dawn of time.

Miss Cage tittered behind her fan. "My Lord," she said, looking around with exaggerated concern. "Miss Willow walked beneath the mistletoe with you. You'll have to kiss her, too." He looked at Olivia and found her watching him. He didn't dare. God only knows what would happen if he took Olivia in his arms. What if he came to his senses to find he'd an audience to his ravishment of her? To his great relief, James came to his rescue by grabbing Olivia's hand and waist and whirling her in a circle. She held the skirt of her gown, wrist arching just so, the tassel of her ebony fan dangling.

"Why, Miss Willow," said James, bringing their tight circle to a halt. He looked up. "Here we are under the mistletoe." Despite his laughter, he appeared deadly serious about kissing Olivia, and it was all Sebastian could do not to plant him a facer for the presumption. James put an arm around her waist, drew her much too close, and gave a smile that sent alarm bells ringing in his head.

Olivia put her hands on James's shoulders and on tiptoe, gave him a peck on the lips worthy of one's maiden aunt.

"Aren't you going to kiss me?" James asked, hands raised in a questioning manner.

"I have," Olivia said, pushing him away. She laughed with the others, but her cheeks flushed with color. "Take your berry, my Lord."

James reached up and plucked a berry. "I'll be revenged upon you for that poor excuse for a kiss, just you see." He turned to Sebastian. "My dear Captain, Miss Cage is right. You must claim your kiss from Miss Willow."

Another round of cheering, stomping and clapping rose up. Sebastian mouthed the words "sodding bugger" at James who took Olivia's hand and pulled her forward. By habit, his glance swept down. Oh, indeed. The black gown draped her figure in a way that drew attention to the curve of her hips, caressing the slope from her hip to backside. With her pale skin and copper hair so much in contrast with the ebony velvet, she was as lovely as any woman he'd seen in all his life. Refusal was impossible. He swore again. If he didn't kiss her, he would call attention to what otherwise everyone would quickly forget. If he didn't kiss her, she'd be humiliated, and she didn't deserve such a public set down. He steeled himself, made a quick inventory of his state and found no trace of oddness, no suggestion that the circumstances were anything but completely ridiculous and utterly safe. No shifting shadows or half-glimpsed men.

"Get on with it," someone cried.

He had to lean down, and, he supposed, she to stretch up. His hand touched her back, steadying her. The scent of verbena hung in the air. He drew her nearer. Heat enveloped him. His body clenched from being close to her.

"My dear Captain," he heard James say. "Pretend you like her, why don't you? Just this once. It won't kill you. And I won't take offense at your kissing her, either."

Sebastian still held her, quite aware of his hand pressed to the small of her back. She smelled good. He wanted to kiss her. He wanted her mouth under his with an ache that went clear to the bone. There wasn't anything he wanted more than to possess her mouth. He didn't dare. God only knows what might happen. Olivia stretched up and kissed his cheek.

Shouts of protest came up and laughter, too.

"She's not your sister, my Lord."

"Foul, sir."

"Not well done."

"Kiss her properly, I say."

"That's not a kiss," Egremont said. He clapped Ned on the shoulder. Ned grinned.

"I have kissed her." He reached up and plucked the last berry from the mistletoe. The music stopped. At a quick signal from James, the orchestra struck up a country dance. Bold planning from the ladies to dispense with the minuet.

Diana gave him a look when he walked with her to the spot where they would begin their dance. "My Lord," she said, adding a quick glance over her shoulder to where Hew and James stood with Olivia. "That wasn't kind of you. Perhaps James should not have urged you to kiss her when you dislike her so, but, honestly, I wouldn't have minded if you had." She smiled. "Much."

He looked at Diana. Nothing. He felt nothing. How had his life come to such a pass that he should consider marriage to a girl who did not remotely suit him?

"You hurt her feelings," she said.

"Whose feelings?"

She rolled her eyes. "Miss Willow's," she said with a meaningful glace to the side of the room. The dance began. "You must make it up to her. She did not deserve such a slight."

"As you wish, Miss Royce."

Olivia, Sebastian noticed while he danced, stood in the line between James and her cousin, James none pleased that her head was bent toward Hew. Black velvet set off her pallor and made her hair gleam like copper fire. When he found himself craning his neck to keep an eye on Olivia and with whom she was presently dancing, he forced himself to look at Diana. She tipped her head, showing her cheek and a graceful stretch of throat. Diana danced wonderfully, exactly what one expected of a future countess. Someone else's countess.

The course of the dancing meant a pattern with Olivia, but when he expected to meet her in the pattern, another young lady had taken her place. He wanted to dance with Olivia, not another simpering girl. At the end of the dance, Ned joined Sebastian at the side of the room. "Miss Willow is certainly looking fine tonight."

"Yes."

"She's a nymph in that gown," Ned said. "Pretty enough to be taken for a Scottish lass. Wonder where she got it?" He rocked back on his heels. "You should have kissed her."

"I can manage my social obligations without your interference."

Ned gave him a look without any of his usual dry humor. "Are you in love with her?"

293

"Miss Royce?"

"Since you mention her."

"We will not suit."

"What about Olivia? Will the two of you suit?"

"Jesus."

"I'm serious, Captain. My Lord. Whatever you think, she did not deserve to be humiliated before all the people with whom she must live."

"I haven't humiliated her."

"You did." Ned blew out a breath. "The mistletoe was Miss Royce's idea, Sebastian. Meant in fun. You had no call to refuse to kiss Miss Willow. It was ungentlemanly of you. Apologize to her." At Sebastian's look, he said, "Make it right. Or she'll never live it down."

Sebastian found Olivia in an alcove formed by what had, in centuries gone by, been the passageway to the buttery. She sat on a green-velvet bench, fanning herself. With her unaware of his presence, he devoured her. Ned was right. The gown suited her. She ought to have trunks full of such gowns. Dozens and dozens of silks, velvets and satins in deep, rich hues. As if she sensed his thoughts, her head turned and their eyes met, connecting like a key put to a lock. She smiled. He bowed and held out his hand. "Dance with me, Olivia."

She shook her head and winced. "My head is pounding. Awfully."

"We'll talk a while, then." She made room for him on the bench, and he sat. "I've been ordered to make you an apology," he said, extending one leg in front of him.

"What for?"

"For not kissing you."

He crossed his arms over his chest, winced, and uncrossed them. "Will you accept an apology from me?"

Her grin was infectious. "I am a toad swallower of great skill and experience. No apology is necessary."

"James is right about my manners."

"Sailor and all." She opened her fan. "Yes, I understand."

"Rest assured, I have now been educated on the finer points of acceptable behavior with ladies."

Her mouth twitched. "Have you?"

Sebastian tried very hard not to smile in return. "If I insulted you or distressed you, I am, of course, desolate."

"Does it hurt a great deal?" she asked. His eyebrows lifted, and she chuckled. "Your wound, my Lord. Your wound. Not your apology."

The corners of his mouth curled. He hoped she never stopped smiling. "At the moment," he said, "the apology hurts more."

Her mouth twitched again and then she gave up and smiled full on. He could not help but laugh with her. What else could they do when the day's events so far outstripped propriety? She did laugh, and he knew she was thinking about being in his room. The image of her stepping from the bath stuck in his head.

"It's been a very odd day," she said. "I've felt odd all day. My head feels stuffed full." She straightened and lifted a hand to the spot where a killer's bullet had left a scar. "Hew wants to marry me. I told him to talk to you." Tears filled her eyes, a fact of which she appeared entirely unaware. A blink sent them rolling down her cheeks. He found his handkerchief and handed it to her. With a nod of thanks, she wadded it in her fist. "I don't want to marry him. I'll be miserable if I do. But what am I to do, Sebastian? I haven't anything left. No money, no place to live. Mama is so ill, and Mrs. Leveret's nephew is going to teach at the school instead of me."

"Hush, love. All will be well."

"How can it be when Hew turns my stomach?" She leaned against him again, lifting her face to his, eyes full of misery. He gathered her into the crook of his arm. "Whenever I am with Hew, I feel like I'm living in one of my nightmares. Frightened without knowing why, and I can't trust anyone but you."

He put his arms around her, pulling her against him, and her hands came up and clutched his shoulders. He felt that odd and familiar sense of sliding into another life. "Olivia."

"I don't want to be frightened anymore." Her fingers curled in his shirt front. "Please." With her face buried against his chest, her voice was muffled.

He kissed the top of her head. "Look at me." What he saw in her eyes when she did made him pause. "Olivia. How badly does your head hurt?"

"Like someone's going at me with an axe. I can hardly see for the pain. I shall go mad if it doesn't stop."

"Shall I call Ned?"

"Not yet."

"Olivia. Did my brother ever give you reason to fear him?"

She was pale, but when he said that, she turned the color of chalk. "Andrew would never hurt me." Her attention flicked past her shoulder, toward the top of the stairs. He turned, expecting to see the Black Earl. But it was James walking toward them. He re-

leased Olivia but did not put any more distance between them.

"Miss Willow," James called, eyes shifting between
them. "Has he apologized? I told him I'd never speak
to him again if he did not."

She rose and shook out her skirts. "Yes, Lord Fitzalan, he has." But her voice shook.

"Prettily, I trust?" James came into the alcove.

"Lord Tiern-Cope is yours to command, my Lord."

Sebastian laughed. He stood and bent to her ear.
"No one commands me, Olivia. Not James, not his
sister. No one, that is, but you. Pray do not forget it."
He straightened. "She's going to dance with me,
James, to prove she has no hard feelings."

"I don't—"

He grabbed her hand. "That's an order," he said.
He gripped her hand. Five minutes dancing, ten
minutes alone to plead his case.

"You'll have to dance with her later, Sebastian. It's
time."

"For what?" Sebastian said.

James rolled his eyes and lifted his hands, fingers
wiggling. "To summon the Black Earl."

Diana appeared at the top of the stairs, making
frantic gestures. "Come along. Oh, do hurry. Everyone's waiting."

Not until they reached the darkened parlor and
Diana had them arranged in a circle with hands linked
did Sebastian realize that from the alcove to the parlor
he'd never let go of Olivia's hand. Diana stood on one
side of him, Olivia on the other. Hew Willow stood
between Miss Cage and Diana. At a signal from Diana,
a footman put out the last light. The room plunged
into darkness.

"Oh, spirit of Pennhyll," Diana intoned.

In the darkness, he felt Olivia's fingers against his palm. He smelled verbena. He gave her hand a squeeze. The light was less black now that his eyes had adjusted. He could make out faces and bodies. Hew Willow among them.

"Earl of Tiern-Cope." Diana lifted her chin to the ceiling. "We summon you to us tonight, the anniversary of your passing to the spirit world. Give us a sign of your presence."

In the silence, someone choked off a laugh. Someone else cleared his throat.

"We must have absolute silence. Lord Tiern-Cope, who walks the halls of his ancestral home. We summon you. Give us a sign."

Sebastian felt pressure increasing behind his eyes and in his ears. Olivia's fingers tightened around his. She swayed, her shoulder brushed his upper arm.

"Tiern-Cope. You are summoned."

Thump.

Not a near sound. The noise came from outside the circle.

Thump.

"Remain calm," Diana said. "I do not sense evil."

Thump!

The light shifted, a draft whistled through the room. Several people gasped. Olivia crushed Sebastian's fingers when a shape emerged from the wall opposite them. Draped in white and uttering a wailing, low-pitched moan, the figure moved toward the circle, dragging a length of chain behind it.

"The Black Earl," Hew said, right on cue.

With arms raised, the figure moved toward Sebastian. At his side, Olivia bumped his shoulder again.

The spirit pointed at Sebastian, moaning in agony and shaking the chain. Sebastian had every intention of letting the trick play out, but matters took a farcical turn. The "ghost" took a step, tripped over his sheeting, got his feet tangled in the chain and landed on the floor with an undignified thud.

"Dash it," said the ghost.

One of the footmen turned up his lantern, then another. Black Earl indeed. James pulled the sheet off his head and after untangling his feet from the chain and the sheet, stood, grinning amid the clamor and exclamation. Sebastian wished James were closer, because he dearly wanted to give him a black eye. Behind him, an opening gaped in the wall, and James, still in the throes of delight over his joke, pointed. "Came in through that door. Willow told me where it was, and with a bit of luck and some help from Price, we found it. Just in time, too."

Sebastian felt Olivia's hand slip from his. He left off listening to James crow over his joke and looked at her. The black dress highlighted her natural pallor but her color wasn't right. She stared at the doorway as if watching the gathering of Satan's hordes. He took her elbow and bent to her ear. "We need to settle this once and for all," he said in a low voice. "In privacy."

Her head whipped around.

"I'll wait in my office for you." He released her. "Give me half an hour."

Chapter Twenty-nine

11:03 P.M.

Olivia touched the door to Tiern-Cope's office, but hesitated before making herself known. For this one moment, just one moment more, her life was the same as ever. And after she went in? Nothing would be the same, she believed that to her core. What if he wasn't even there? With a deep breath, she tapped on the gilt panel.

"Enter."

She went in, smoothing her velvet skirt. "My Lord."

Tiern-Cope faced the window, hands clasped behind his back. A spark of awareness shot through her and made her stop rather than continue in. His broad shoulders were a familiar sight now, which surprised her. She'd not realized how used she'd become to him.

He turned. "Olivia."

She didn't move, and neither did he.

"Thank you for coming," he said. "I wasn't sure you would."

"I wasn't sure you'd be here."

"You're beautiful in that gown."

A hush settled over the room, and Olivia filled it by closing the door. Her fingers trembled. "Thank you."

"Sit."

She did. "My Lord."

"Can you not call me Sebastian?"

Her heart tripped. "I don't think so."

"He's not here. The Black Earl."

"I know."

"So, for the moment, we are safe from that madness."

"I am always safe with you. No matter what happens, no matter what, I am safe with you and not with anyone else."

He inhaled. "How long have you been seeing the Black Earl?"

"A few days now." She bit her lower lip. "You?"

"Since I came to Pennhyll." He walked to the fireplace. She turned sideways on her chair, but all he did was stare at the fire, hands clasped and pressed against the small of his back. The fingers of one hand clenched and unclenched. He turned. "What of me? How long have I been in your head?"

"Before the Black Earl, I think. Only I didn't know they weren't just dreams."

"More and more intimate." His mouth thinned. "I confess to once or twice in my life imagining making love to a woman I admire. God knows you're a pretty woman, but I don't just imagine being with you. When I make love to you, you're not thoughts and images in my head, you're in my arms, real and warm. I can taste you and breathe in the scent of you, feel your skin against mine. We've never made love, but I've been inside you. Jesus, Olivia, you know I have."

She nodded.

"Hell, for all we know it's possible I've made a child in you." His eyes pinned her. "Did anything like that happen between you and Andrew?"

"No."

"You sound certain."

"I am."

"You never saw the Black Earl until I was at Penn-hyll?"

"Never."

"Andrew never came to you in—as I have. As we have together?"

"No. I never thought of him that way."

"You do me, though."

She nodded.

Tiern-Cope regarded her for what seemed an eternity. "Very well," he said at last.

"My Lord?"

"Your cousin has relayed to me your wishes in the matter of your marriage."

"Yes." She clasped her hands on her lap, interlacing her fingers. Her heart turned into a lump of clay.

"Do you want to marry him?"

"Yes."

He tilted his head. "May I ask why, when tonight you told me you feel sick at the thought of him?"

Her throat threatened to close up. "Mama and I cannot stay here forever and not past your marriage."

"That does not answer the question I asked."

"I haven't any choice. You know that."

He went to the fireplace, grabbed a poker and stirred the embers then threw the poker back into the stand by the grate. "It's my doing. Every bit of it. I'm the reason you weren't hired for the school. I believed you were inches from James's bed, and I told Mrs. Leveret I could not recommend you. I told you James was not sincere in his attentions even though I suspected his feelings had changed. I closed you in that cell tonight and nearly got you killed in the process."

He walked to his desk and put his hand on a sheet of parchment. "This is a deed, Olivia. The estate was yours, free and clear, but your uncle, with my father's complicity, mortgaged it for twice what it was worth. I have signed over the deed to you. It's now truly yours. As it should have been. You have three tenants. I expect you and your mother can live well enough on the rents." He drew in a breath. "The issue of your marriage settlement is, therefore, somewhat more complicated than you believed when you spoke to your cousin, as there is now property to consider. That is," he said, "if you still wish to marry him."

She stared at the document in her hand.

"Perhaps, Olivia, you ought to consider other options."

"Such as?"

"James. There are marriage contracts on their way to me."

"Do you think I should?"

His eyes settled on her and after a bit, he said, "Egremont and I leave for Falmouth on Saturday."

"So soon?" Just four days away. Oh, God. In four days, he would be gone from her life. Four days. That must mean he would marry Diana immediately. "And your wedding, sir? Can it be arranged so quickly?"

"I think so."

She forced her mouth to curve. "Please accept my congratulations, my Lord."

"Thank you, but felicitations are, perhaps, premature. I have not yet settled matters with my intended."

"Oh."

"I have cried off to James."

"About me?"

"Do not be obtuse. I mean Diana. Diana is a lovely

303

girl, but I have no affection or desire for her and she about as much for me. She would marry me out of duty to her brother, and for no other reason. If we married, her heart would slowly grow still less fond. And mine as well. I must marry, that is certain, but I do not want a flighty wife, no tender slip of a girl raised only for the ballroom. I want a wife of good sense, who knows something of the world and who will deal well with my absence for the duration of the war." He went still, but his eyes fixed on her. "In short, I want you, Olivia. Will you marry me?"

All the emotion ever to exist in the world lodged in her throat. She swallowed a lump the size of Pennhyll and tried to speak. All that came out was a croak.

His gaze remained on her. "I have not time for anything but honesty and plain speaking. You are constantly in my thoughts, at the center of my most intimate desires."

"I am irreverent. Outspoken and at times undignified."

"As ill-befits your age and station in life. Yes, I agree that's so. But that changes nothing."

"Marriage, my Lord, is for a lifetime."

His mouth twitched. "Marry in haste, repent at leisure?"

"Have you considered that?"

"That fact has not been far from my mind. I have no romance in me. No fine words. No high sentiment. I am as incapable of sweeping a woman off her feet as thoroughly as I lack the polish expected of my present situation. Believe me, Miss Willow, I have considered my feelings at great length and am quite content with them. Use that logical brain of yours. Not only am I a more eligible husband than your cousin, you have less reason to dislike me. Do you love James?"

"No."

"In that case, it would be illogical for you to refuse me."

"You must be the most perverse man in creation."

"We are well matched."

"What of Andrew? And Guenevere?"

"There is that." He shrugged. "If you remember, well and good. If you do not, I am prepared for that as well." He put a hand on the deed. "Olivia. Among the reasons I gave you this property is that I did not want you to feel compelled to marry by reason of your circumstances. Provided you are not a spendthrift, you need never worry for the future. Marry or not," he said in a low voice, "as your heart tells you."

He walked toward her and didn't stop until he stood inches from her. "I should do this properly," he said. He went down on one knee and reached for her hand. "Olivia, will you marry me?"

She touched his mouth, laying a finger across his lips. "Oh, my. Are you sure of this?"

"Yes."

"Then, yes. Yes." Her heart swelled, and when she tried to speak she almost couldn't make any more words come. "I love you so desperately."

He bowed his head, then rose, still holding her hand, and hauled her to her feet. One arm curled around her waist and like that, her chest pressed against him. "I am pleased and honored," he said softly. "This is right. You know it is." His other hand touched her cheek and curved around the back of her head. "Pennhyll wants you. The Black Earl wants you. I want you. And I will not dishonor you by offering you anything less than my name. I don't give a damn how many times I've made love to you in my head, I want you in life, undisputably and without the Black Earl standing around. When next we make love, Olivia, you will be my wife, and James must find a way to overcome his disappointment."

Time stopped when he lowered his head. Her skin flushed hot and then cold and then hot again as his lips brushed hers and lingered. A short while later, he drew back. "I think," he said with no change in expression, "that *deplorable lack of restraint* should be removed from the list of your faults." And then he looked over her shoulder and said, "Right on time."

Olivia looked back, too. Mr. Verney stood in the open doorway, Bible in one hand. Captain Egremont and Ned Fansher were right behind him.

Chapter Thirty

January 22, 12:01 A.M.

Sebastian stood unnoticed in the doorway and watched Olivia pace. Fifteen steps from the fireplace to the foot of his bed. She was his. At last. For the first time in more than a year, the world felt right. Hell. For the first time in his adult life. He'd done a splendid thing, marrying her. Tonight, at long, long last, he wouldn't doubt the reality. He would unfasten her hair and thread his fingers through those curls. His mouth would cover hers in fact instead of in thought. Tonight, he would hold her as tenderly and lovingly as any man ever held a woman.

He kept his hands on the sides of his thighs, thinking of how he would uncover her and how he would ask her to use her mouth on him. All manner of shocking requests entered his head, but in the main he wanted to lay her down on the bed right now, flat on her back and come into her as a man was meant to come into his wife.

One lamp burned in the room so that she walked in soft and furious darkness. Any minute she would see him, turn those gold-as-honey eyes on him, and he would be unable to do anything but fall on her in a mad, rutting lust when he ought instead to maintain a comfortable and distant aloofness. Jesus. He needed control over himself. Her bare feet trod the silk carpet, her thick braid swinging with the rhythm of each step. Her arm swung forward, and the ring he'd put on her finger flashed in the lamplight. He reached behind him for the door and gave it a push. Metal parts slid past each other with a sharp click as the fittings engaged.

She whirled. "My Lord."

"Olivia." He stepped away from the door between his sitting room and his bedchamber. There hadn't been time to prepare the adjoining room that had once been Guenevere's, so their wedding bed was his. He'd practically pushed McNaught out the door in his haste to join his bride. Jesus. He'd made Olivia his countess. His. Even in the dimness, her eyes shone like gold. He walked to the center of the room. She looked him over, pausing at the V made by the two halves of his robe. Good, he thought. Let her think what that meant, his bare skin showing. "My apologies for keeping you waiting," he said, pleased he managed not to sound as impatient as he felt.

Her hair caught the light and flared like molten fire. Tonight, at long last, he would have his hands full of glorious copper curls. He would know exactly how they felt against his fingers. With some effort, he looked at her face instead of her bosom. Her eyes threatened to swallow him whole. A man could lose himself in her eyes. "This is just an awful mistake," she said.

"No, it isn't."

"I feel like jumping out of my skin or screaming or maybe just dissolving into a shapeless heap."

"Restrain yourself, if you will." He smiled. "For now."

"This must be a dream. It must be."

"I don't see the Black Earl anywhere, do you?"

"Then it's a dream. An ordinary dream. Tell me it is. That I'll wake up any moment now."

"Not until sometime tomorrow morning. Late. If I have anything to say about it. Think, Olivia, of how you feel. You know this is real. The Black Earl isn't here because we've done what he wants. We're alone. At last, by God." He tilted his head. "Now, what am I to make of that panicked look?"

She bit her lower lip.

"Olivia?"

"I'm afraid."

His hope of a relatively uneventful wedding night evaporated in the face of what he knew was more than the usual bride's trepidation. "Of me or of the unknown?"

"Both."

"Do you think I will hurt you? I won't." But he knew he might. What he did tonight would affect them both. The thought of what his brother had done to her that day at Pennhyll made his chest tight with anxiety. What if she'd married Verney or James or, God forbid, her sodding cousin Hew Willow or even someone else entirely, with her not knowing what had happened to her? Believing, even, that she was a virgin? Men put such store in a bride's innocence. At least he would not commit that crime against her. He didn't want her to know. Not ever. That secret he meant to take to his grave.

"It's that not. Not precisely, anyway."

"What then?"

"This happened too fast. Neither one of us was thinking." Her words came out on top of each other, like a waterfall onto rocks. "What happened to my dull life?" Her eyes looked suspiciously bright. "What possessed me to say I would marry you?"

"Whatever did possess you, Olivia, you accepted, and you spoke your vows before witnesses. Now, tell me why you are afraid when you must know I would never hurt you."

"You don't like me. You never have. Not from the moment we met. You were insufferably rude to me. Then those— Those dreams began. Things happened and we neither of us understand how or why."

He shrugged. "Put that notion out of your head, please, that I don't like you." He walked toward her.

"You want me to remember. I know you do, but what if I can't? What if I never do?"

"For tonight, my dear, put that worry out of your head as well. I will be satisfied with you whether you remember or not. You must believe that." He took another step toward her, but she retreated with each step he took. He wanted to murder the man who'd hurt her. The fact that it was his own brother made the anger deeper, a betrayal that he could never, ever forgive. "Have you forgotten the other reason I married you?"

She shook her head. At last, she could retreat no farther unless she meant to step into the fire. He put his hands on either side of her head and looked into her face. The heat of sexual desire uncurled in his belly like embers rising into flame. "I adore you, Olivia."

"Why?"

"From the first moment I first saw you, I wanted you. And I adore your red hair."

"That makes no sense. No one adores red hair, least of all you."

"But there it is."

She grasped both his wrists. "What if I disappoint you?"

"That is not possible." He slid his hands to her shoulders, pulling her toward him so she pressed against him. His fingers caressed, soothing, following the curve of her spine. "What pains I've been at to tell you all I dislike about you. God knows the list is a long one."

"There, you see?"

"If I ever took you to task for your joy, Olivia, it was because I lack the capacity myself." He brought her tight against him with just the pressure of his hand in the small of her back. "I have for too long believed the world a cheerless place. Then I met you and could not fathom you. If anyone deserves to see all that is dark and bitter in life, it's you. And you don't." He spread his fingers, angling them downward so that the tips touched the upper curve of her backside. "You're a mirror of my soul, Olivia, exactly my opposite. Can you wonder that I dislike you so when you cannot help but reflect everything lacking in me? You burn with life, Olivia, and I would at least bask in your warmth before I spend eternity burning in Hell. You cannot disappoint me. It's I who will disappoint you."

"No."

He stepped back. "Enough talk. You're too clever by half, Olivia. If I let you, you'd talk all night until you'd convinced yourself the moon will rise in place of the sun and that I would rather have Diana than you. Come now, I want to see you with your hair down. Do as I say." Sebastian watched her bring her braid over her shoulder and slip the ribbon off the end. Her fingers trembled. "Allow me," he said. "Turn around." She did, facing the fire while he unplaited her hair. "A stream of copper."

"Exactly like a new pot."

He shook out twisting curls that reached to the middle of her back. Hands on her shoulders, he turned her to him, threading his fingers through her hair. "The first time I saw you," he said, "I thought you a pretty woman. Oh, it's true, Olivia, never believe it isn't. And since that day, you don't know the times I've imagined you with your hair like this, a creature of faerie, a nymph." He laughed. "Or maybe you do know." He slid his hands free of her hair. He had all the time in the world, but he felt every moment's delay. "I want to see you, Olivia. All of you."

Her cheeks turned as red as her hair.

"Very well." He reached for the tie around his waist and unfastened the knot. The silk fell away from his body. With a shrug of his shoulders, he let the fabric slide off. "Look at me."

"Oh. Oh, my."

"You see, I have imperfections. All of us do."

"No. You don't."

"I have an ugly scar." He touched his ribs.

"You're beautiful."

"Good of you to say so." His mouth twitched. "My body, such as it is, is yours, Olivia. When we are alone, its purpose is to give you pleasure. I expect you to take it." She flushed. "I see I must teach you something of that. So be it." He reached for the fastenings of her nightrobe. "Ladies wear far too many clothes."

"I thought so until now."

"Particularly on their wedding nights." She turned bright red, and Sebastian laughed. "Olivia. You are a constant delight." He watched her face while he gathered her chemise in his hands. "This, too, must go." He pulled upward until she had no choice but to lift her arms. His breath left him, utterly abandoned him. All this time he'd thought her a bit slender for his taste, and she was, but Lord, what lovely, sinful skin. All in proportion to her size, long legs, her bosom curving as if made for a man to cradle. Her belly not so flat as he would have supposed, considering how slender she was, but her waist was indeed so narrow he could circle her with his two hands.

"My God, just look at you." He took her chin between thumb and forefinger. "Open your eyes."

Her eyes closed tighter yet. "Don't," she whispered. "Don't look at me."

"Have I married a disobedient wife? Open your eyes. That's an order."

She fixed on his face with a blandness that made him want to weep. "As you say, too short, too small, too pale, too red."

On the instant, his eyes met hers. "At the moment," he said, "you are too noisy. And that is all I wish to say on the subject of your many shortcomings."

"That doesn't leave us much in the way of conversation, does it?"

He tipped his chin toward the ceiling. Sod it. This was his fault. "I don't know exactly how to proceed. I can't get it out of my head that we've done this before. But we haven't. And he isn't here. . . ." He was once again overtaken by the sight of her nudity and her vulnerability to him because of it. Jesus, women were exquisite things, and the one he'd married was most exquisite of all. "Mm, no," he said when she moved her hair. "Leave it behind your shoulders. Do you remember the day I escorted you to Far Caister? When you were carrying away bread from my kitchens that you later had the effrontery to serve me as if it had just come from your larder?"

She nodded, which he knew from the flash of movement in his peripheral vision, for he was devouring her figure, studying the shape of her chest and the way her ribs melted away to her waist.

"I imagined then you must have long legs, and I was right. If I was wrong in any particular, it was about your bosom, which I find admirable indeed. You're the most delicate thing I've ever seen. You ravish me. I told you once you make me feel a brute, and now I'm glad that you do. You're the only woman with the mettle to accept me as I am. I'll show you absolutely no mercy in that quarter." Her eyes flew to his, and he gave her his coldest, most chilling stare. "If you give in to your fear now, Olivia, you won't be able to stand against me in anything, and I might as well be married to Diana. Show me some backbone."

313

He smiled just the slightest bit. "I trust I've made myself plain."

She nodded.

"Excellent. Because I have not the time nor the inclination to coddle any woman, particularly not my wife." He put his arms around her. His thoughts kept slipping off to his dreams of her, how she'd already satisfied him a dozen times over. Now, it would be real.

She stepped forward, sliding her hands to his shoulders. He groaned when she went on tiptoe to reach his mouth. He buried his fingers in her hair and brought her head toward his, curls sweeping over the backs of his hands and down his forearms. His dreams crashed over him, how he'd already held her, taken her mouth, his overwhelming longing to sate himself with her again and again. Their lips met, brushed, and then his mouth opened over hers. He didn't bring her along slowly or start out mildly. He ravished her mouth the way she ravished his senses. He could no more hold back his passion than he could stop an incoming tide. He caught her in his arms and sat on the bed with her across his lap.

The kiss slowed. He savored every moment, exploring her, touching and seeking. Her arms tightened around his neck, and he took advantage by sliding his hand down her side, following the outside curve of her waist, hip and thigh. Her skin warmed beneath his fingers. He wanted to learn every inch of her by touch alone, to memorize her just from kissing like this, slow and deep. He opened his eyes and saw a fan of copper curls around her forehead, more spilling over her shoulder and across her chest. He threaded his fingers in flame and pulled back, turning his head away from hers to study her body. He put one hand on her thigh, enjoying the contrast between color and texture.

"You sat in my office with your stiff back and your gloved hands clasped on your lap." He spread his fingers over her outside knee, pulling her leg away from the other. "These lovely thighs pressed together. Your prim mouth and eyes that deceived." His fingers touched the curls between her legs. "A modest gown covering this body, stockings and garters clinging to these legs. Corset, petticoats. Everything polite and proper and so respectable."

"You didn't believe it."

"But you looked it. You can't begin to image how badly I wanted to ruin you. A lovely, respectable, innocent young lady." He pressed his palm over her. "Fix that image in your head, Olivia, because later, after you've lost yourself in me, you'll know just how far I've taken you."

"Sebastian."

He moved his head back to meet her eyes. "I think, for now, I would prefer that you call me my Lord. There can be no question then of what's real and what may not be." His index finger slipped between the curls and then inside her. Tight and damp. "Besides, I have an inclination tonight to have some mastery over you, so, for now, it's my Lord." He slid his finger along her. "Say it. Not 'Sebastian,' but *my Lord*."

"My Lord."

"Did you ever guess what was on my mind when I looked at you? I'd be sitting at supper watching you eat and, Jesus, I wanted your mouth on me. Yes, there." He laughed. "There's fire inside you, Olivia, and I mean to touch the very center of it."

With her still in his arms, he lay back, turning as he did so that she ended on her back, both of them crossways to the length of the bed. His battle plan was simple enough to be foolproof. Distract her such that when he came into her, she knew nothing but pleasure. Every advantage lay on his side, knowledge, experience and tactics. She knew nothing of men, their bodies and needs. She was unsure and already rattled by the nature of his demands on her. He meant to continue.

He slid down, feathering kisses along her throat, breathing in verbena and the essence of Olivia. In all his life, he'd never felt more alive, more aware of the moment. Considering how much time had passed since he last made love, he felt in control of his passions. He had, in the course of his life, indulged in sexual relations to satisfy the urges of his body but, in the main, he'd not been one to love indiscriminately. He'd found he did not care much for intimacy with women for whom he felt nothing. And on the open sea, women of any sort were few and far between.

His hand stroked the curve of her breast, a shape and size in keeping with her body, enough to comfortably fit his palm. Not insubstantial, considering the size of his hand. He slid a palm over her, feeling the peak of her nipple against his fingers. Her body arched. With a sigh of pure contentment, he opened his eyes. Coils of copper hair shone against the emerald coverlet. With his free hand, he gathered a handful, closing his fingers around the mass of curls. "You're so very beautiful, Olivia."

"My Lord." A whisper caught on desire.

He parted the fingers that cupped her breast and

lowered his head. She gasped when his mouth closed around her. He felt one of her legs bend, pressing against his side, and he let go of her hair to caress as much of her leg as he could reach. He slid farther down her body, caressing and kissing her belly. He blew across her navel. Her skin prickled in response, and he was pleased as well to hear her moan. His fingers slid between her legs, and he smiled, a slow, knowing smile just for himself because he knew the pleasure he would bring her. When his mouth settled there, just there, her body tensed, but he refused to ease up until the moment he believed she would have her release. He moved until he was looking at her face, very nearly in exactly the right position.

The campaign was won, passion and the frustration of pleasure denied clouded her eyes. He held himself over her, settling himself between her legs. He was a brute, twice her weight and every nerve in his out-sized body screamed at him to hold nothing back. "God in heaven, Olivia, you are too dainty for me. I am afraid I'll hurt you without meaning it."

But even as he spoke, his hand curled around her thigh, pulling up and easing them both into better position. He adjusted himself, found her entrance and discovered she was small inside, too. She tensed, and he had to push harder than he expected, considering she was as ready as any woman could get. Whether he was larger than other men he had no real notion. What he did know was that she was small, and he was not. "Relax, love. I have you."

She eased a little. Heat and wet surrounded the part of his sex that was inside her, and it wasn't enough. He wanted all of him inside that warm, slick place. Each millimeter of penetration brought him that much closer to losing himself. How could a man think tactics under such exquisite torment? He felt his foreskin sliding down, exposing him to her body. "Oh, Jesus," he said.

She made a noise in the back of her throat. He opened his eyes and met eyes wide and anxious. In fact, he could not just push through to her core. She wasn't perfectly placed, for one thing, and for another, if he surged into her as he wanted to do, he would hurt her. He withdrew a bit, something his body told him was beyond stupid.

"Olivia. Olivia, lift your knees. You must meet me." She did.

His pelvis rocked forward and at last, she understood the point of the maneuver because her hips tipped, and he came all the way in. Their eyes met, but he was beyond speech, mindless with sensation. That sweet spot right at the base of his spine tightened, his throat closed off any words. Her palms, which had been just touching his biceps, slapped the mattress. She got a breath of air, a feat beyond him, and her hips raised up again.

Absolutely nothing existed but him. Nothing but an arc of pleasure that took him over. He teetered there, dying, and thank God she didn't know what the hell she was doing because it would have been all over for him right then. But she didn't. She didn't move and that gave his incipient orgasm time to subside. In a manner of speaking, he was in a worse way now than just a moment ago, because he knew when he was there again, the peak would be higher, he would fall as hard as a man could fall and still live.

Right now, however, he had himself in hand, as it were. Enough himself that he could recall other parts of his body. And hers. "Now," he said, "would be an appropriate moment for you to tell me I am too big, too powerful, too manly for your bridal state." He moved in her, rolling onto his side and drawing her uppermost leg up over his waist. His hips came hard against her, his chest pressed to hers, his head near her ear. One hand cupped the back of her head, tangling in her hair. "Compliment my husbandly prowess, Olivia, and say not a word of your failure to please me."

His hips came forward again, hand wrapped around her thigh bringing her close. She threw back her head but his fingers in her hair kept her near. Her breath came hard, timed to his thrusts. "My Lord."

He rolled once more and lay on his back, keeping himself in her. Her hair hung down, a riot of corkscrew curls that partially hid her face from him. She knew just enough now to give herself time to adjust. With shallow breaths and fingertips curled around the top of his shoulders, her body eased around him. His entire being coiled around the new sensations of having her atop him, her thighs outside of his hips, of feeling himself farther inside than he'd have believed possible. His hands gripped her, thumbs just at her pelvis, fingers and palms meeting around her back. "Are you all right?"

She nodded, lifting her eyes so that they looked at each other, and he willingly drowned in the golden depths. Slowly, she straightened, a motion that opened her farther. He kept his hands around her, and after a bit, her fingers curled around his forearms and her pelvis rocked forward, taking him with her. "You're inside me," she whispered, looking down so that all he could see was the crescent spray of eyelashes on her cheekbones. "All of you. I feel as if you're too big for me, but you aren't hurting me."

"I think," he said, "because you are deep inside." Her hips moved with more confidence. "Jesus, you feel good." His hands tightened around her hips, pushing her down but slowing their motion. Their eyes met and he saw how very close she was, only they hadn't done even the quarter of what he wanted for her. Worse, he was perilously close himself.

He rolled them over again, keeping himself inside and moved into her, as far as he could get. She gasped, arching against him, lifting herself, opening herself. He felt her tighten around him. Somehow, despite his thinking only about himself, he got it just right, a pause at the right moment, a deep push inside to exactly the right depth. She came apart.

Her eyes flew open, and she grasped his head, looking into his face while she shuddered beneath him. "I love you," she said, straining upward. "Sebastian, I love you. I've always loved you. Since before we met."

"I know," he whispered. The confession made him want to shout with triumph.

When she was past the peak, he drew her arms over her head and held her tight while he reached for his own rhythm, harder and faster than perhaps she was ready for, only she was. Each time he went in, his belly slid on hers, over a layer of sweat, his and hers. He let go of her hands, but they stayed above her head, clutching the bedpost to keep herself in place for him.

He shouted when he felt the first shiver, a wave that shook him as hard as anything in his life. Better than his dreams. Better than anything he'd felt in all his years. There came a moment right before his seed came that he thought he couldn't reach his own pleasure, that he would be at this unendurable pitch of intensity until it killed him. But he did come, and it didn't kill him, though it felt a close thing. He collapsed, the whole of his weight on her. Sweat dripped from him. He was wrung out and more alive than he'd ever felt in all his life.

She pushed against his shoulders. He pried open his eyes and to his astonishment, her eyes were panicked. He must outweigh her by a hundred pounds at least; he must be crushing her, lying on her like that. He lifted himself onto his elbows, easing his torso off her. Huge, silent tears slid down her cheeks. He slid out of her, and when he tried to take her into his arms, she turned away. "Olivia?"

"Don't."

"What is it?"

"I remember." Her shoulders heaved. "I remember everything."

He pulled her into the curve of his body and said, "Forgive me."

Chapter Thirty-one

2:06 A.M.

Sebastian waited until the worst of her sobs subsided, then hauled himself to his knees. Immediately, she sat up, clutching her drawn-up legs, head bent, in retreat from him and the world. He sat behind her, legs on either side of her hips, her back to his front, but not touching her. He gathered her hair into his hands, lifting the copper weight off her back to arrange it over one shoulder. She rocked, forehead bowed to the tops of her knees. He didn't know whether to touch her or leave her be. His hands lay useless at his sides.

"Tell me, Olivia."

She moved her head a bit so that her voice sounded clearer. "A vicar can't marry someone like me. He felt just awfully about it, I could tell."

"Nonsense."

"Now you've married me, and there's nothing to be done about it. There's no way to fix it or make it better." The devastation in her voice shook him to his core. What if she'd remembered without him, without even the meager protection of his name? Without anyone to hold her.

He wanted to throttle his brother, he truly did. He pulled her sideways, despite her attempt to resist, resting her back against his good arm. As soon as he had her cradled in his embrace, she wriggled free, scooting back on her knees and raising the sheet to cover her. "Look at me, Olivia," he said. When she did, he said, "I wish to God you'd never remembered."

"How can you say that?"

"Because of what happened to you. I cannot bear the thought of you—" A shiver of foreboding ran up his spine at the despair in her eyes. What if she didn't want him anymore? What if her restored memory meant she was lost to him? "It doesn't change anything between us." He exhaled. "I knew. Olivia, I've known for some time what happened to you. I'm not like Verney who didn't want you afterward."

"How could you know when I didn't?"

"Dr. Richards examined you twice that day. Once, after the assault and again after Andrew and Guenevere were killed. If Andrew were alive, I'd thrash him for what he did. I don't know how he could have done something so despicable."

"No." She lifted a hand to her head, tracing the scar along her temple. Her hair spilled over her shoulders, curling wildly around her temples. "Not Andrew."

Sebastian's heart stopped. "Dr. Richards told me it was."

"No. It wasn't him."

"If it wasn't Andrew, who was it?"

"Hew. It was Hew."

He rolled off the bed and shot to his feet. He wanted to run, to stay still, to collapse all at the same time. The world pressed on him, crushing him with the weight of his own stupidity. "I should have guessed." He threw a hand in the air. "I should have guessed."

"He hurt me."

"And I want to murder him for it."

"He shot Andrew and Guenevere."

"Right now, I don't give a damn about them, Olivia. I'll throttle the bastard for laying a hand on you." His belly twisted into a knot. "What an imbecile I am." He felt sick. Sick to his heart. He grabbed his robe from the floor and thrust his arms through the sleeves. "I told you to marry the man who tried to murder you. Stay here, Olivia. You're not to go anywhere." He strode to the bed and glared at her. "Do you understand me?"

"Yes."

"That's an order. I'm not to be disobeyed."

"Yes."

"I'll throw you in the dungeon myself, if you do." He threw on his clothes, shirt, breeches, and coat and boots and went downstairs. The party continued. Music and laughter. Did no one realize the momentous events of the evening? He slowed, reining in his emotions during the descent to the Great Hall. Eventually, he found Hew in a room set aside for men who wanted to smoke. The air was thick with tobacco. Mr. Cage was there, leaning against the mantel, and several other of his neighbors. The stuffed head of an antlered buck hung on one wall, a rack of hunting guns on another. On the mantel, a box inlaid with mother-of-pearl displayed a set of dueling pistols. Sebastian well-remembered a blistering lecture from his father, received on the occasion of being discovered holding one of the pistols without permission or supervision.

"Gentlemen," he said. He had just enough control over himself that his voice sounded cold and flat.

"My Lord." The men bowed respectfully.

Hew was stretched on a sofa by the fire, smoking a cigar. He rose, holding a drink in his other hand. His affable smile appeared, though Sebastian was certain he was drunk. "Lord Tiern-Cope."

"I need a word alone with Mr. Willow. If you gentlemen would be so kind."

When they were alone, Hew ran his hands through his hair, leaving it standing up at the back. "Drink? There's port decanted."

"Thank you." He glanced around and imagined Hew with Olivia. Unspeakable. He curled his fingers into fists.

Hew ground out his cigar in an ashtray by the sofa. "Port it is, my Lord." He went to the table and poured two glasses. He extended one to Sebastian. "Here you are." He bent his knees. "One cannot help but think, my Lord, that everything I have ought to be Olivia's. And will be soon. Thirteen years later." He raised his glass. "Everything. Even the bloody port in my cellar was her father's." Drink in hand, he pointed to the dueling pistols. "Except the guns. All the guns at my home belong to me. Her father didn't hunt."

"Indeed."

"If this is about Lord Fitzalan and my cousin, I tell you I won't permit it. She's already agreed to marry me."

"I am not here about Fitzalan and Olivia."

"Then this must be about my dear cousin's request that you broker our marriage settlement." He laughed. "Shouldn't take long. She hasn't a thing to bring to the marriage."

Here stood the man who'd murdered his brother and his sister-in-law, and all he could think of was Olivia. He wanted to strangle the man with his bare hands for what he'd done. "Congratulate me, Willow. I am now a married man."

"Indeed?" He lifted his port in salute. "Felicitations, my Lord. I am sure the former Miss Royce is deliriously happy."

"I did not marry Miss Royce."

"Really?"

"I married your cousin."

"You can't be serious." He tipped back his glass, swallowing half the contents in one gulp.

"I am."

"I'll sue her for breach of promise. And you for the interference in my expectations."

"Be my guest."

"On the other hand, perhaps I'll wait. Once you've consummated the union, you may want to annul the marriage."

"There won't be any annulment."

Hew laughed. "Then she tricked you, my Lord. I assure you, she's no innocent."

"My wife is safe from you now."

Hew blanched. "Safe from me?" His eyebrows drew together. "Whatever do you mean?" But his confusion rang false, and they both knew it. He sat down hard, staring at his hands. He gulped the rest of his port.

"Safe, Hew Willow, as my brother and his wife were not."

He stared at his trembling fingers. "She's recovered her memory."

"There wasn't any duel."

Hew took a long breath and collapsed on the chair like a man without bones to hold him straight. "No, of course not."

"You killed my brother and his wife, and you tried to kill Olivia."

"I'm glad you know. It's a relief in a way." He shook his head, chewing on his lower lip. "I haven't been able to tell a soul. Sometimes I can almost convince myself none of it happened. God knows I wish it hadn't. Ever since that day, it's been eating at me." He stared at his hands, now palm up on his lap. "I'm rotten inside. I lie in bed at night, and I feel the rot. I dream about it, you know. Imagine that it didn't really happen that way. I see it all in my head, only instead, I leave. Sometimes I miss and other times someone comes in and stops it, and my life goes on as it was meant to."

"What did happen?"

"Everything went wrong. Right from the start." He sighed heavily. "I suppose you found Mr. Melchior."

"Yes."

"Then you know about my father. Stubborn old fool. Every penny of their fortune. By the time I found out, it was too late. Nothing left. Then, after your father died, your brother came to live at Pennhyll, and he took quite an interest in her." He raised his hands. "Not in that way. At least not so I could tell. He was pleasant enough about it when he confronted me. Didn't threaten. Just said he expected Olivia and her mother to be made whole. That, of course, was not possible."

"How did they die?"

"I never meant to kill anyone." He took a drink, but his hand trembled so badly he only just managed to get the last drops. He rose, scrubbing one hand through his hair. "God it's a relief to tell somebody. More port, my Lord? No?" He refilled his glass and lifted it to the light. "Hands are shaking." He faced Sebastian. "People have affairs everyday. Though I never did until I met Guenevere. Saving myself for my bride, don't you know. But she was such a lovely woman, so unhappy, and we fell into the habit of talking about London and how she wanted to live there and how her husband neglected her. One day I took her in my arms, just to stop her sobbing, make her feel better and once I had her in my arms . . . Well. She was so lovely." He hung his head. "I adored her."

"Go on."

"Then, one day, we were in the library. Olivia and your brother walked in on us. If I didn't know better, I'd think Guenevere planned it that way. She was certain he was carrying on with some other woman. God, but she was jealous. Beautiful woman, but jealous of her husband and jealous of me, too.

"I'm not making excuses." He shrugged. "Tiern-Cope, your brother, I mean, meant to divorce Guenevere and seek damages against me. Thanks to Guenevere, proof wasn't at issue. He had the crim con and Olivia as a witness to back up what he'd seen with his own eyes. He'd have gotten his divorce and ruined me in the bargain. Well, I thought, if I married Olivia, he wouldn't dare ruin me, would he? She'd be worse off than ever if she was my wife, and he ruined me. That was the very last thing he wanted. Trouble was Olivia and the vicar were all but engaged. So, I decided I'd get us caught but good so we'd have to be married." He laughed. "Your brother would have done anything to protect her from scandal, even if that meant her marrying me. I'm not so bad a catch, you know. Lots of girls set their caps at me. It would have worked. It really would have."

Sebastian put down his glass and walked to the window. He got there and turned. "Mr. Willow, I am the magistrate—"

"Oh, I know that.

"Then you should also know I mean to see you hang."

"I'll put my affairs in order then." Hew took another drink. "Had it all worked out for the next day. For your brother's festivities at Pennhyll. I got Olivia alone and—" He lifted his hands again. "And—didn't matter who caught us, as long as we were caught. Only no one came. I—just lost my head, I suppose. I never thought I'd have to go through with it, but she's a pretty woman, and I'm a red-blooded man. Lovely, really, even with that hair. Besides, I meant to marry her. God, it just all went wrong, and I— She shouldn't have gone anywhere alone, you know. In a way, it's her own fault. If she hadn't fought so hard. The door was open, for God's sake, but no one came." He shuddered. "She screamed and even though I wanted her to scream, I couldn't bear the noise and, well, things . . . got to a point where I wanted to finish. So I made her be quiet. But then she fell. I thought sure her head was cracked open. She didn't move. I thought I'd killed her or that she was dying, and I ran. Back to the party." He made a sort of helpless gesture. "Not long after that, I saw Dr. Richards arrive."

"Poor devil."

"Yes. We soon heard there'd been an accident, and that Olivia had been injured. I was glad she wasn't dead. I'm not a monster. I didn't want her dead. I thought I could still manage the situation. Even better, actually. How could something like that be kept quiet? Tell your brother I'd heard what happened and offer to marry her if he'd keep my involvement with Guenevere quiet." He clapped his hands on either side of his head. "A few hours went by. The party was in full flow, dozens of people wandering about. No one remarked on me leaving. I found them in one of the parlors, all three, Guenevere, Andrew and Olivia. Olivia wanted to go home, but Andrew wouldn't let her. Would have been foolish, her going anywhere. She was white as a sheet. Her head dressed, her arm splinted.

"The problem was, Olivia took one look at me, and Andrew, I'm afraid, guessed right away. Wouldn't listen to a word I had to say. I had a gun with me—I didn't mean to use it, but I thought—I'm not sure what I thought. I suppose I thought I might have to use it to make them see reason. But I never meant to shoot anyone. I could see my life unraveling just like that, and I hadn't done anything so awful. I was mad, of course, not in my right mind at all. I know that now. Olivia jumped in the way, thought she could save him, I suppose. It all happened so quickly, and like that, they were all three of them dead, or so I thought." He shrugged. "I could hear the servants calling out. I left. Went through that door I showed your friend Fitzalan, and then out the library way."

"You left them for dead." A draft swept through the room, and whatever wind had sprung up found its way down the flue because the fire flared, sending a swirl of ashes and embers above the height of the screen before it settled back to a softer glow.

"I thought I'd killed them all. I rarely miss, even under duress, and I saw the bullet hit her. Marksman's instinct, I suppose." He shuddered, unaware of the tears spilling down his cheeks. "Killing women. A nasty business. Not at all like a duel. I never wanted to kill anyone like that. I've consigned my immortal soul to Hell when all I wanted to do was marry Olivia so I wouldn't lose everything when your bother got through with me. I fled the country, for God's sake, and nobody came after me." He swiped the back of a hand across his eyes.

"Why did you come back?"

"After a while, I decided they must all be dead, and no one knew it was me. So I came back. You can't imagine what went through my head when I saw the two of you in Far Caister that day. Have you any idea how much you resemble your brother? I thought you were Andrew."

"How do you live with yourself?"

His eyes held a desperate appeal. "You've killed men. How do you live with yourself? Knowing you've committed the blackest sin of them all?"

"Maybe you don't."

He gave a shrill laugh. "Do the dead haunt you?" He raised red-rimmed eyes to Sebastian. "I think we're both going to Hell."

"Perhaps so."

"I'm going mad, you know. Ever since I came back, he's been haunting me. Your brother. Every time I close my eyes I see his face." He drew in a shuddering breath and pointed at Sebastian. "I can see him right now. There, behind you."

Sebastian rose. "There's no one here but us."

"Yes, there is. He came in with you. Can't you hear him? He's calling my name."

"Let me summon your servant."

Willow stood, staring past Sebastian's shoulder with eyes the size of sixpence. "He's talking to me." His voice was a low, coarse whisper. Then he laughed, a sound that sent the hairs on the back of Sebastian's neck standing upright. "Don't you hear him? He's right you know. I only have to pull the trigger one more time."

Chapter Thirty-two

4:07 A.M.

Sebastian stood outside staring at the lighted windows of Pennhyll. Hew Willow's suicide put a quick end to the party. Most of the guests had gone once the word got out, taking advantage of the break in the weather to go home. By now, he imagined, only Ned and Egremont remained. James and Diana, too, of course, though they were leaving at first light. He walked to the right of Pennhyll's gated entrance with its doors permanently open, portcullis forever raised. The rooms on the north side were darkened. Lights shown in a few upper floors in the servant's wing, and one in a parlor a floor down. Olivia's tower was darkened, of course. Soft light shone from his window. Strange he'd never noticed before just how close their rooms were. One story and a hundred yards at most. He shoved his hands deeper into his coat pockets. The storm had long since blown itself out. New snow covered the ground, drifts piled high along the walls. Despite the chill, his head didn't feel any clearer.

Somehow, he thought, as he stared at the castle, Pennhyll had become home. His wife was there. His future. He crossed the courtyard, the sound of his boots on the snow-covered cobbles a comforting sound. Olivia was his now. His wife, and the future mother of his children, though the thought of facing her after what had happened with Hew this evening filled him with a dreadful anticipation. He'd made a lifetime commitment to her, and he hoped to hell she felt the same. He was not a God-fearing man, or hadn't been in some time, but he found the vow he'd made meant something.

He reached an outcropping of the granite that formed the foundation of the most ancient towers of Pennhyll. If he picked his way around the side, he'd be at the back entrance, not far from where he and Olivia had nearly plunged down the mountain. He put a hand on the rock to steady his footing, and he could swear he felt something, some flow of energy pass from the granite to him. Olivia was right. Pennhyll had changed him. He wasn't the man he'd been when he came here.

Today, he'd begun as an unmarried man and ended a married one and few changes were more life altering than that. He had his commission and more, command of a fleet. The sort of responsibility and challenge he'd dreamed of, had lived for. Now that he had it, his heart lay like a boulder in his chest. Cold. Lifeless. What if something happened to him while he was away from everything he loved? He might die, and she'd never know how he grateful he was for the gift of her heart and her passion. Here he thought he had yet another momentous decision to make, and he didn't at all. He was home at long last, and he didn't want to leave.

"You've been a low and scurvy craven," he muttered. He drew his coat closer. The moon dipped behind the clouds and blurred the distant details of wood and bramble. He turned the corner that would take him to the door and found he'd walked into a wall of gray. His outstretched hand disappeared into the mist.

In the blink of an eye, darkness and fog reduced visibility to less than the length of his outstretched hand. The moon reappeared, scattering light in all directions. He looked behind him and saw the indistinct shape of the granite outcrop he'd passed. He took a step forward, then another. Mist swirled around him. He could taste and smell the thick fog with every breath. Now, if he looked over his shoulder, he couldn't even see the rock. Pennhyll, he knew, stood to his left. Too much to the right, and he'd plunge down the hillside.

He heard something. A whisper? The faint sound of metal moving against metal. He waited. Another moment later and the fog swirled, but low to the ground. Pandelion emerged from the mist, and he bent to pat the hound's head. The dog whined and nudged him. "Have you brought him with you?" he asked. The dog barked once and turned its muzzle toward its tail. The mist swirled again and for a moment, he was convinced he'd seen someone. He slowly walked. Ahead of him, the fog shifted. The sound of metal moving rang gently as Pandelion dropped back. He stared at the shape materializing before him. Pandelion whined and then trotted to the very limit of Sebastian's sight. The hound sat, staring forward into the fog and he joined the dog, peering ahead, trying to pierce both dark and mist. "Are you there?"

The reply, if any there was, could have been nothing more than the wind that sometimes howled over the ramparts of Pennhyll. He'd reached the door to the tower. The moon illuminated a man wearing a tunic emblazoned with the sigil of the earls of Tiern-Cope. His eyes were blue beneath dark and unruly hair. The hilt of a broadsword poked over his shoulder. Fresh from his haunting of Hew Willow? "Are you going to tell me what the bloody hell to do about Olivia?" he asked.

The man shook his head and took a step toward him and then another and another. A blaze of cold shot through him, a jolt that shook him with the force of a blow. His head snapped back, and then the sensation was gone. He shook his head, but for the space of two breaths he felt dizzied by the sensation of someone else looking out his eyes. Then, the separation was gone. His head swam and he thrust out an arm to keep his balance. Pandelion nudged his hand.

By the time he opened the tower door, he knew what to do. The stairwell was pitch black, but the hound knew where it was going. Had he ever climbed these narrow twisting stairs? He had, with Olivia cradled in his arms. He touched the wall and other memories crowded behind his recollection of Olivia. Impressions from a different time, from different men. Andrew, too, had walked the stairs. He felt his brother, his father, and all the earls Tiern-Cope.

He stopped at a wooden door even though the stairs continued upward. He opened it easily, and found he was, indeed, in his suite of rooms. Not the bedroom, but the anteroom he used as a private office. The door to his bed chamber was ajar. He slipped off his coat but did not go to Olivia because he had one thing yet to do. Pandelion padded in.

When he returned, he went straight to his bedroom. She was dressed in her black velvet, sitting on a chair by the fire. Pandelion had come in and was being petted by Olivia.

"Olivia," he said.

"My Lord."

"*Sebastian*," he said.

"You got what you wanted."

He faced her, keeping his hands behind his back. "What are you talking about?"

"My head. You got what is in my head."

"I did at that."

Her eyes flicked over him and then settled on the floor to the right of where he stood. "What now?"

"We make a life together."

"Do you think we can?"

"Yes." He rocked back on his heels.

"Is Hew dead?"

"Yes."

"Did you kill him?"

He grimaced. "I wanted to see him hang for what he did. But he . . . took matters into his own hands. There was nothing I could do. Price was there, and I was telling him to fetch me two footmen to watch over him." For a moment, the wall between them seemed as high and vast as the towers of Pennhyll. "No. Olivia, no, don't cry. Please do not cry. I cannot abide women who cry." He brought his hands from behind his back. Feeling ridiculous and annoyed that he'd spoiled his grand gesture, he stared at the disordered bouquet of roses and orange blossoms he'd gathered from the conservatory. "Price will have my head for this."

When he looked at her, her eyes fixed on the roses.

"They're for you," he said. What a clod he was. A bumbling display worthy of the likes of Mickey Twilling. "Bugger it," he muttered when a thorn jabbed his thumb. He walked to the washstand and plunked the flowers into the ewer. He faced her. "They're for you,

Olivia, and I wish I had words to go with them."

She walked past him to the washstand and bent her head over the ewer. "They smell heavenly."

"Olivia." He reached for her, pulled her close, burying his fingers in her hair, well aware that though she stood close, she was quiescent in his arms. "Olivia." Her hair smelled of verbena. He took a deep breath and the world wasn't big enough for his feelings and he didn't give a tinker's curse how big they were. They came out because they had no place else to go but to the woman in his arms. "I love you," he said. "I love you."

Slowly, very slowly, her body relaxed against his. "I love you, too." Her arms crept around his shoulders and then his neck. "When do you leave?" she whispered. "How long do we have?"

He broke their embrace in order to fetch Egremont's packet. He tapped the parchment before handing the papers to her. "I have many duties. To my title, my King and to you. Until today it seemed they diverged and there was no resolution to satisfy them all."

"You must go," she said. "If it's command of a single ship or of a fleet makes no difference, you must go. You cannot do anything else."

"I don't want to go."

"It might be weeks before you sail. I could come with you as far as Falmouth."

"I should like that." He touched her shoulder. "But read these first." He watched her open the packet. "Read."

She unfolded the pages and held them flat. There were several sheets inside, and after a bit she stopped reading. "Command of a fleet. I knew it. I knew it! Your brother would be so proud."

"He would be."

"I'm proud of you. A fleet."

"If I want it."

"Of course you do."

He could not help smiling. "There's more," he said.

She returned to the papers and gasped when she reached the page covered with seals and ribbons. "Oh, my. You've been raised to the peerage. A Viscount. An hereditary peerage. An estate and an income. Twenty thousand a year. You must have been brave indeed to merit this. Well, I know you were. You're the bravest man I know."

"The petition," he said while she scanned the letters patent, "was made before Andrew died. There's another letter in here hinting at raising me further in the peerage than Viscount, but I expect they'll think that unnecessary now."

"I don't see why."

"Keep reading, Olivia."

He knew the moment she found the letter because she drew in an outraged breath, God love her. "A position in the Admiralty." She scowled at the papers. "Give up command of a fleet? Never. This you cannot possibly accept."

"Why not?" He wanted to laugh, because for him there wasn't any question of leaving Pennhyll, and that been true for quite some time. Her outrage on his behalf pleased him.

Letters clutched in one hand and the rest of the packet in the other, she stared at him. "I won't let you. Unthinkable. You have the command of a fleet. It's everything you've wanted. What your brother

338

knew you would have. What you've wanted all these years."

"I don't want it anymore."

"Of course you do."

"I've been a sailor twelve years, Olivia. Oh, you're right, I've loved the sea. I let the Navy consume me until I really did believe my blood was salt water in His Majesty's service. But since I came to Pennhyll, I've felt something missing. Missing in me. I thought if I went back to the ocean everything would be the way it used to be, but I was wrong, and the minute I saw those papers, I knew in my heart I was done with the sea." He let his voice drop. "I am done. Twelve years is enough, Olivia."

"You want to go back. You know you do."

"You were what was missing, Olivia, not the sea." He took the packet from her, letting the papers scatter to the floor as he hauled her to her feet. "If the sea were my heart and soul, I would go back, Admiralty or no. You can't begin to know my relief when I realized I could serve my King in another way. If you believe nothing else, believe this; I want a life here with you. I want Pennhyll and I want you, and I want a family."

"An heir and a spare?"

Laughing, he pulled her into his arms. "That's right. An heir and a spare. Besides," he whispered over the top of her head, "the bloody dead Black Earl told me he'd never stop haunting me if I left."

Neither one of them felt the draft or heard the embers pop in the fireplace. The next day in Far Caister anyone up at dawn swore he or she saw the Black Earl pacing the ramparts, but by evening, there wasn't even one tale of disaster or misfortune to be boasted of in the Crown's Ease.

LORD RUIN
CAROLYN JEWEL

The Duke of Cynssyr doesn't believe in love. But a night of passion leaves him a changed man—a man tied to a bespectacled spinster. Anne Sinclair drives him wild with desire, and her quick wit challenges his mind. Ruined for any other, the notorious rake must court his wife. To win her confidence, nothing less than his love will do.

Anne Sinclair swore to protect her sister from the infamous Lord Ruin. Forced to give the rogue her hand in marriage, she vows never to relinquish her heart. But Ruan worships her body and values her intelligence, making Anne long to succumb to the ultimate temptation: falling for her husband.

The Temptation
CLAUDIA DAIN

In England of 1156, a gently bred lady is taught to obey, first her father, next her bridegroom. But ever since Eve it has been in every woman to defy any lord. And Elsbeth of Sunnandune is determined to trade the submission of the marriage bed for the serenity of the convent. Yet never did she suppose the difficulty of her task, for the husband given her is a golden knight of godly beauty and grace. His every word and look is a seduction, his every caress cause for capitulation. In this war of wills, she discovers, blood, honor, even the thrill of victory, can take on new meaning, and no matter how much time a wife spends on her knees in prayer, every path can lead into temptation.

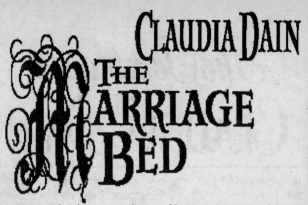

ATTENTION
BOOK LOVERS!

Can't get enough of your favorite **ROMANCE**?

Call **1-800-481-9191** to:

＊ order books,

＊ receive a **FREE** catalog,

＊ join our book clubs to **SAVE 20%!**

Open Mon.-Fri. 10 AM-9 PM EST

Visit **www.dorchesterpub.com**
for special offers and inside
information on the authors you love.

We accept Visa, MasterCard or Discover®.
LEISURE BOOKS ♥ LOVE SPELL